THE WORST PUCKING DEAL

B. LYBAEK

FOLLOW

B. Cybaek

ACKNOWLEDGMENTS

Nikita, without you, this story would never have been completed. I love you girl, and I'm beyond grateful for all your help, encouragement, and just for you!

Erin, without you, The Worst Pucking Deal would never have been struck.

Poppy, you've completely blown me away with your words of wisdom and loving critique.

Emma—my BAH; thank you for yet another amazing picture, and for being an amazing part of my life.

Cady—Thank you so much for another amazing cover, your inputs, and for everything you do.

To my amazing alphas and betas; thank you so much for all your help.

CONTENT WARNING

The Worst Pucking Deal is a dark hockey standalone that features overlap to other series, but it's unnecessary to read them to dive into this one.

   Please note; while I've done my best to list all the triggers and warnings me and my team have picked up on, everyone views content differently. **Please read responsibly and remember, your mental health always comes first.**

   Blood play | Death of parent | Domestic abuse/violence (not by MC) | Forced fake dating | Forced marriage | Forced proximity | Knife play | Marriage of convenience | Physical & mental abuse | Rape (off page, not by MC) | SA (the FMC was a minor by US laws, but not Italian.) | Trauma | Violence/murder (off page)

DEDICATION

To my cousin, who went through hell.
You didn't let your trauma define you.
You clawed your way back to the surface.
You refused to be a victim and instead stood tall.
You showed everyone what real strength looks like, and I'm beyond inspired and proud to be your family.

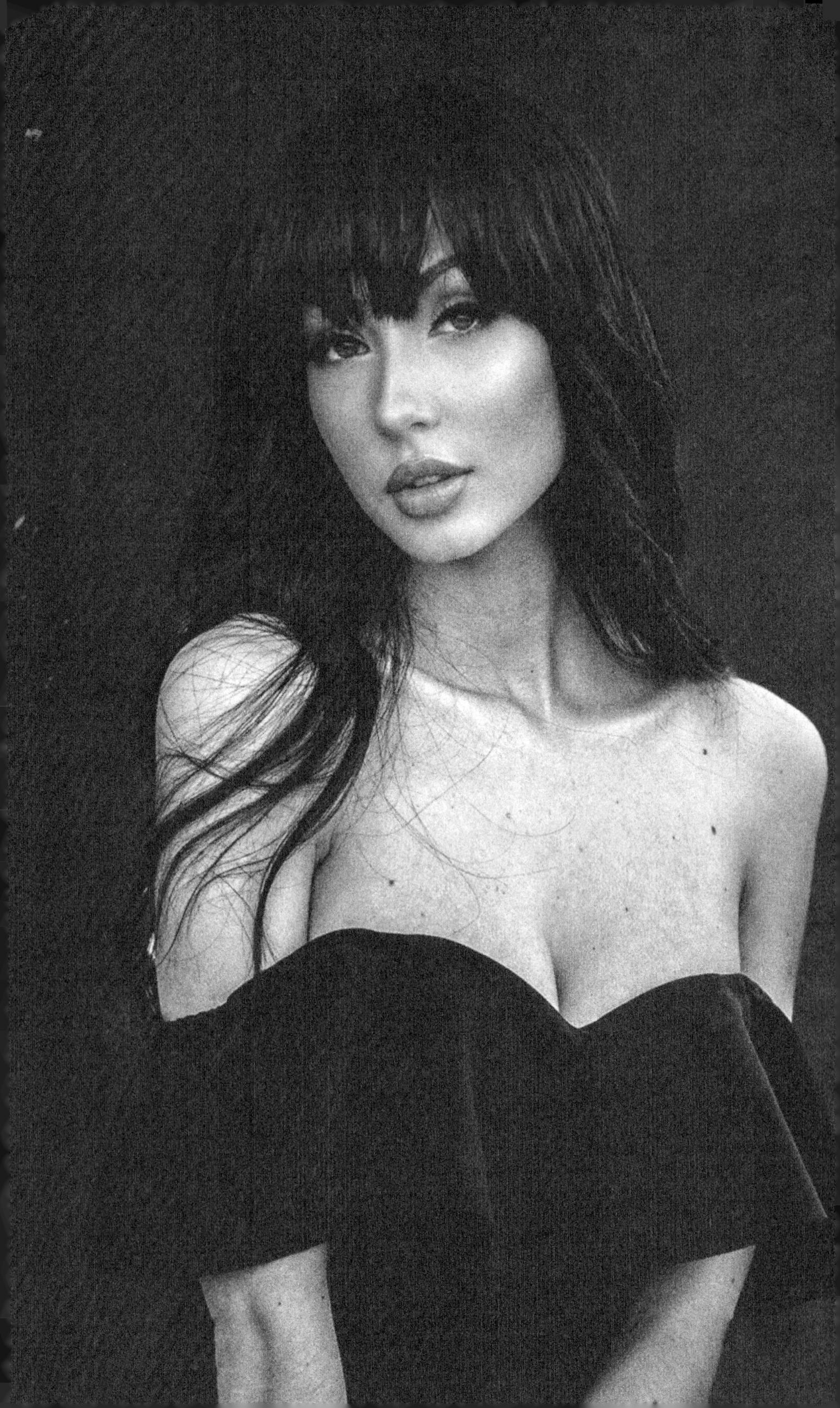

CHAPTER 1

Lucia

"Ahhh, I needed that," my best friend and roommate, Gail, declares. She brings the bottle of red wine to her lips and takes another large swig. "And that. Fuck, Luce. You won't believe how insane today's been." She dramatically sweeps her free hand through her light brown hair and scrunches up her face.

I arch an eyebrow, amused by her theatrics. "What did the little brats do to make you this thirsty?" I ask, hinting at the kids she teaches.

Gail huffs. "Hey now. You know I love them..." She trails off, waiting for me to react, and I dutifully nod. "But man. The twins drove me crazy. All day they've tested my limits. One of them even..." She trails off and twirls a brown lock of hair around her finger. "...put a painted hand on my ass."

I burst out laughing at the admission that a little boy got to second base with her. "Well damn. The twins have game," I cackle. When she pouts, I cluck at her. "Come on,

Gail. Don't be like that. Just the other day, you told me that no one has touched you in two months. Now you can't say that anymore."

Her facial expression twists into pure horror. "What the fuck's the matter with you, Luce? This isn't funny."

Refusing to let her drag me down, I shrug. "It's a little funny."

"You think joking about… that with a kid is funny?"

I roll my eyes. "Obviously not. That's sick, Gail. I think the fact you're so bent out of shape and have lost the ability to see the funny in the situation calls for immediate intervention. So spill it. Why are you so stressed?"

She stretches her legs, kicking the empty Chinese containers away and clutching the wine bottle tighter. "The district is cutting back and has fired three teachers already this week," she admits. I nod while she shares her fear of being the next one to go. "I know I complain a lot, but I love my job, Luce. The kids are incredible, and it's… well, it's hard to explain."

"Hey now, none of that. We have a pact, Gail. On Fridays, we complain about the world while getting shit-faced. And on Saturday we—"

She laughs. "I know, I know. It's just hard not knowing where I stand. But enough about me, how was your week? I feel like I haven't seen you at all."

That's the sucky thing about my job as an account executive for the Minneapolis Sabertooths PR team. Where my hours are crazy, Gail's are normal. Sometimes we can go days without seeing each other. If we didn't live together, it would be close to impossible to spend time with each other, which is why we've continued to share an apartment even though we both have successful jobs and could afford our own places.

"It's been okay," I say, snatching the bottle from Gail instead of reaching for mine. "Jo's been acting weird."

"Weird how?"

I take a moment, searching for the words to best describe it. "She's kept me out of a few meetings." Though it annoyed me when it happened, I'm grateful now. Because if my boss hadn't removed me from tonight's meeting, I might not have been home yet.

Gail's eyes widen. "That's new, isn't it? Last week, you told me how she looped you in on everything. Oh, my God!" She clasps her hand across her mouth, looking at me with concern in her blue eyes. "You don't think you're getting fired, do you?"

I bark out a laugh. "Why are you seeing firings everywhere? You know there can be other reasons, right? Like maybe whatever Jo's focused on isn't part of my job description. Or maybe it mainly revolves around the players whose social media accounts I don't run. Or maybe, just maybe, she's using one of the other account executives to give me a goddamn breather."

"I suppose..." she trails off.

"Gail." I say her name softly. "The Sabertooths have their first game in just four days. Everything is fucking crazy right now. So read nothing into it."

I'm not saying it to calm her down, but because it's true. With only four days left until we have our away game in Anaheim means it's all hands on deck. So I'm not worried about Jo not keeping me in the loop. Especially not when I have more than enough to juggle already. But this is what we do. I bring reason to Gail's brain that sees red flags and warnings everywhere. No, that's not quite right. She's extremely level-headed six days of the week, but Friday is the day she lets go and lets her thoughts and insecurities fly free.

"You're probably right," she mumbles as she tries to get up from the living room floor we're camping out on. "We need more wine."

I burst out laughing as she clumsily gets to her feet, only falling twice. "Yes we do," I agree. "You're almost walking in a straight line, so we need a lot more."

While Gail goes to the bathroom and to get more wine from the kitchen, I reach for my phone. It's tucked away under one of the couch cushions so it doesn't interrupt our tradition. But now that Gail isn't here to stop me, I don't have enough self-control to ignore the device.

I huff with annoyance when I notice a text, and for a split second I consider ignoring it since I'm ninety-nine percent sure it's from my boss. It wouldn't be the first weekend I've lost before it could properly begin because the Sabertooths forward, Sawyer Perry, hockey God and playboy extraordinaire, can't behave.

The text isn't from Jo.

Remus: Long time no see, Lucia. Are you ready to come home yet?

Fuck.

My blood runs cold, and my palms become so clammy I can barely hold on to my phone.

Fuck. Fuck. Fuck.

While I'm busy panicking, another text pops in.

Remus: You know I can see you've read my message. I want to see you, so make yourself available next Friday.

I bite down on my bottom lip as I stare at the texts in horror. I knew my time was running out, so I should have expected for my cousin to contact me sooner rather than later. But fuck. I've kind of been in denial, my brain holding on to the fact that I have one month left of my freedom. If I'm honest, a miniscule part of me even considered that Remus might have decided not to hold me to the deal I made with my uncle. Obviously, that's not the case.

Me: When?

My hands are so slippery with sweat I almost dropped my phone three times while writing those four letters.

Remus: Lunch works for me. I can't wait to see you again, Lucia.

Instead of returning the sentiment that I don't feel at all, I stay on topic.

Me: Where? You're not expecting me to fly to Rome for lunch, right?

Remus: I'll come to you. Minneapolis, Minnesota, is where you share an apartment with your friend Abigail Wilson, correct?

Oh, fuck me. Trust my cousin to take this small interaction as an opportunity to remind me that he knows everything about my life.

Me: Just text me the details and I'll see you then!

I know I should be nicer, maybe even groveling. But I can't make myself type out anything but the barest of words. I'm not ready. I don't want to meet with him, and I most definitely don't want to leave the place I consider home and move back to Rome.

"Why so serious?" Gail asks when she comes back into the living room, clutching a bottle of wine in each hand.

I gulp and reach for one of them, not hesitating before I put it to my lips and greedily down half the bottle. "Just some family stuff," I mutter, not wanting to get into it.

Gail sits down on the floor next to me, pulling me to her side. "You never talk about your family, Luce. And from the look on your face, I'm guessing it's not happy news?"

Unable to answer, I shake my head. My throat feels clogged, like I'm about to cry. But what I feel isn't sadness, it's pure unadulterated fear of being forced out of the cozy life I've built for myself far, far away from Rome.

I let Gail hold me until my heart no longer gallops in my chest, and breathing becomes easier. "My cousin is coming to visit next week," I say, my voice monotone. "He wants... no, demands we meet for lunch."

When I look up at her, her brows are sitting high on her forehead, and her eyes are as wide as saucers. "He's *demanding* you have lunch with him?" she asks incredulously. "Can't you just tell him to fuck off or something?"

I laugh bitterly. "No one tells Remus to fuck off," I reply. I know I should keep my mouth shut, but the unexpected text has completely obliterated the walls I've mentally erected around anything to do with my family, and now that they're down, I can't seem to stop talking. "Remus is the... for lack of a better word, he's the head of our family. If he wants me home, there's really nothing I can do about it."

No one says no to the Mafia and lives to tell the tale.

"So you're leaving?" Gail asks, her voice hoarse and her eyes glistening with unshed tears.

"No!" I shout, startling both of us.

"But you just said—"

I wave her off. "I'll find a way, Gail. I made the deal with my uncle before he died and every deal has a loophole. There are ways around it."

"But what about—"

Again, I interrupt her. "I'll figure it out." Then I force a smile I don't really feel. "I promise you I'm not going anywhere. You're stuck with me, Abigail."

She blows out a breath. "You better not be fucking with me, Lucia."

I want to promise her that everything will be okay. Fuck, I want to believe that myself. And I need to get into that headspace, if for no other reason than because Gail can never know the truth about my family.

Gail and I spend another few hours drinking and talking, but it's not the same. I can feel her nervous and concerned glances when she thinks I'm not looking, and I know she feels how tense I am. In the end, I give up and get up from the floor. "I'm going to get some sleep," I say, forcing a yawn. "How about we go for brunch tomorrow? My treat."

"Yeah," Gail easily agrees. "Sweet dreams, Luce."

After getting ready to turn in, I get naked and into bed. Normally, I end my evening with an orgasm or two courtesy of my pink vibrator. But tonight I don't even reach for it. I'm not in the mood, and I doubt I'd be able to switch my brain off long enough to enjoy anything.

Fuck.

I knew this day would come, so it pisses me off that I'm so unsettled—scared, even. It's not me I'm scared for, though. Not exactly. No, I know I'll be okay. Remus won't kill me unless he feels he has no choice, or if I betray him by running or trying to hide. If I do that, he'd have no problem tearing through my meager list of loved ones, killing them off one-by-one until he finds me.

Fuck.

Maybe going home to Rome wouldn't be the worst thing. I have family, and surely I could look up some old friends. The cost would be my happiness, and very possibly my sanity. But... no. Fuck no. I'm not giving up. There are ways out, my uncle said I could stay if I got married. I really should have spent more time dating, maybe then I'd have a steady boyfriend—someone I could marry and learn to love.

It's only now, in the darkness, that I realize I've gone about my freedom in the wrong way. I've let myself become complacent, weak, and not thought about the deadline I was given almost ten years ago. This is all my fault, and blaming Remus isn't the answer.

Think, Lucia, fucking think.

Ugh, coming up with any ideas while my brain's turned to mush from the wine and surprise text is impossible. Or maybe it's just because I know how much I've fucked up. I can't change the past, but hopefully I can rectify the mistake I made tonight. I should never have said anything to Gail, and I need her to think I was just having a melodramatic, drunken meltdown. I know my bestie, though. She's not one to let things go. She knows me too well. But maybe if I manage to act all cool and aloof for the next week… maybe then she'll let it go.

It's not a perfect plan, but for now, it's all I've got.

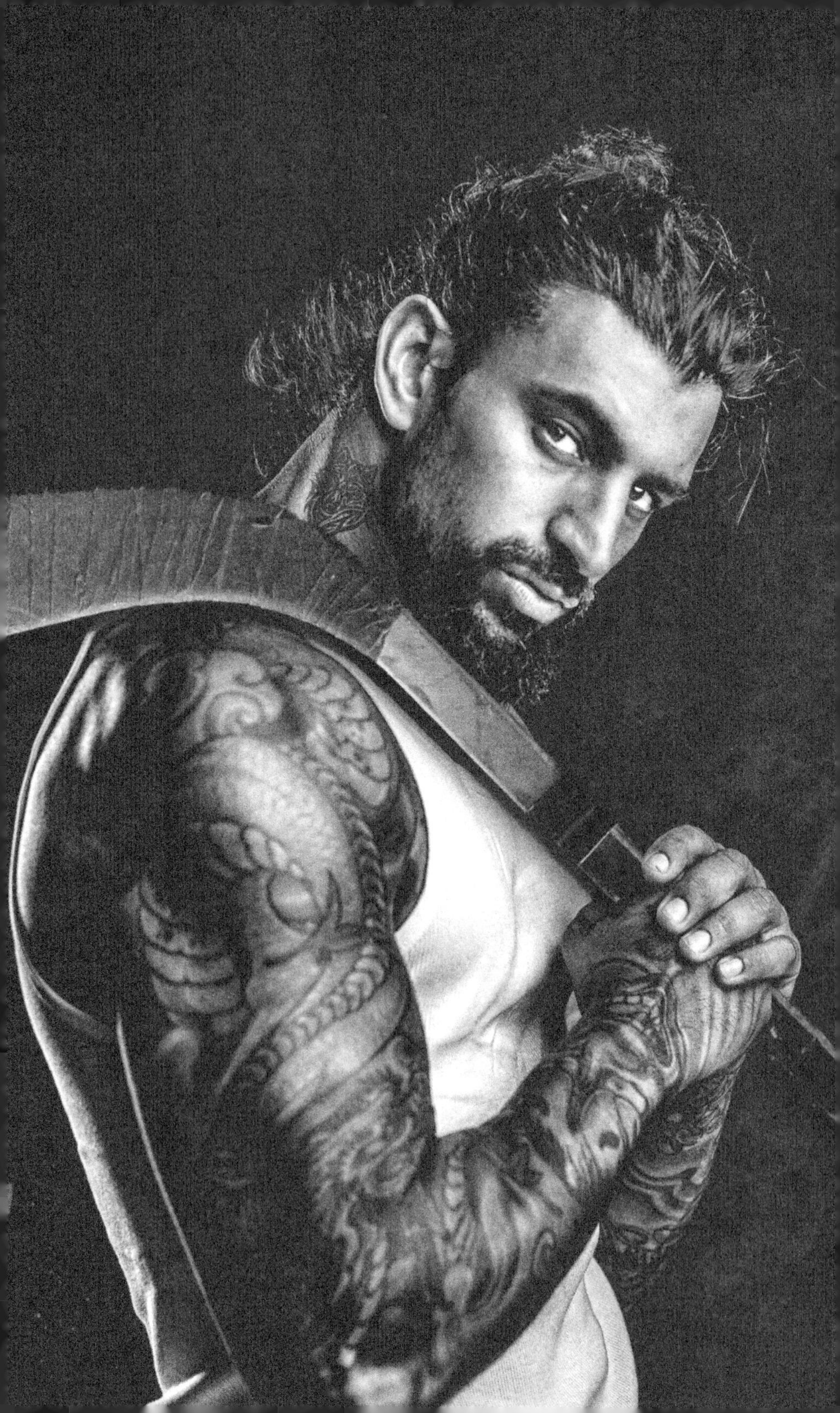

CHAPTER 2

Sawyer

"That's what I'm talking about," I roar, grinning widely at my teammates. We bump chests, slap each other on the back, and cheer uproariously. It's Tuesday, and the season is now in full swing, and we won our away game in Anaheim.

The locker room is filled with cheers as we shower and get dressed in our suits. Even our grumpy looking coach is smiling, if you can call it that. Personally, I just think his frown is less intense.

"You did good," he praises as I loop my belt through the hoops on my suit pants.

"Is that coach speak for 'we kicked ass'?" one of my teammates sniggers.

Coach snorts. "Don't get cocky, boy. This was only the first game of the season, and I'm still not holding the damn Stanley Cup in my hands." He looks around at all of us. "You did good. And if anyone asks, I'm not embarrassed to say I'm your coach."

I suppress a smirk. The old bastard is stingy with his praise, but it works. It makes everyone work harder and better. Reaching for my dark gray suit jacket, I shrug it on and button it. While I shove my shit into my bag and focus on my hair, Coach goes on about the media circus waiting outside.

"I want everyone on their best behavior when you leave this room. You're winners, boys. But you're gracious winners. No bashing the Anaheim team. Got it?" He glares at one of the assistant coaches when he chokes back a laugh. "I'm serious. We have an image to maintain. Don't you dare fucking ruin it by being cocky shits."

We all nod to show him we've heard what he said. "Yes, Coach," we answer in unison, just the way he likes it.

Once I've tied my long hair into a bun and combed my beard so it doesn't stick out all over the place, I hoist my bag over my shoulder, ready to get the fuck out of here and back to Minneapolis. My phone buzzes in my pocket, but when I see who's calling, I hit the ignore button. I don't have it in me to talk to my bitch of a mom right now.

"I wish we were staying," the assistant coach next to me whines. "The women here are so much better than the ones back home."

Shaking my head, I walk by him. "It's not about the quality of the woman," I say with a wink. "It's about the man."

He looks up from his phone long enough to follow me out of the locker room, and we're quickly flanked by our PR team that traveled here with us. "Easy for you to say. You have panties dropping left, right, and fucking center."

"Jealous much?" Soren, our goalie, guffaws as he joins us. "Sex is like pizza, my man. Even if it's bad, it's still good."

I don't know what's worse... the fact that a grown ass man is complaining about the quality of pussy his job gives him, or my buddy comparing sex to food. It might be a tie. I tune them out as we walk out of there. Since I'm not gonna get my dick wet, I don't care about the fact that we're flying back home tonight.

My last public stunt cost me an endorsement deal, and to say that our GM is unhappy that I fucked someone in public and ended up causing yet another scandal is an understatement. All he's done so far is issue some fines and threats, but I know he's at the end of his tether. Which is why I'm on a self-imposed hiatus from PBP; Puck Bunny Pussy.

Shame, though, I'm going to miss the easy tail. Plus the added bonus of no strings attached. Since I don't do relationships, it's been the perfect way to get my dick wet.

All thoughts of not getting laid tonight disappear when Coach bellows from behind us. "Hang on a moment." We all stop walking, giving him and Jo from PR time to move to the front. "Jo has some things to say before you go out there." He points at the door behind him.

As head of the Sabertooths PR team, Jo doesn't normally travel with us. She usually sends her worker bees. But she's always there for the first game of the season. "Congratulations on the win, Sabertooths." Most of the guys whoop and shout excitedly. "Get ready to smile at the cameras. Oh, and don't forget to congratulate the home team on their efforts," she says. "And don't react, no matter what they say or ask." As she adds the last part, she looks straight at me, much to the amusement of my teammates who break out in laughter. Jerks.

She makes a call, and after confirming we're good to go, she opens the door. Since the weather in Anaheim is a lot warmer than back home in Minneapolis, I haven't bothered with anything but my suit jacket. The second we walk through the doors, we're assaulted by questions and lights flashing in our faces.

"You did amazing tonight, Soren. Do you have a new regime since you blocked every attempted goal?"

"Sawyer... over here, Sawyer." I turn my head toward the voice. "Are you staying the night to sample the local women?" Rather than answering, I smile and shake my head.

We push our way through the throng of reporters and photographers, and despite this not being my first time, it's hard not to react when they shout my name. But I do my best to keep my gaze down and ignore the questions that grow more and more taunting.

"What happened to that woman sneaking out of your hotel room last month, Sawyer?"

"Did you know there are speculations that you're overcompensating for being gay?"

Jesus, fuck. They're reaching, and it's beyond pathetic. I'm not gay, but if I were, I'd like to think I'd act the same way. I sigh as we reach the bus that's taking us to the airport. Fans and puck bunnies have gathered around it. Damn, some of those women are pushing my self-control to the limit. So while my teammates stop and talk, I push my way toward the bus.

"Excuse me." I turn at the voice, noticing mini Jo, or Lucia as she's called, pushing her way to the front.

I stop walking and gesture for her to walk in front of me. "Be my guest," I smirk, not bothering to hide that I'm checking her out. My eyes stay glued to the top of her tits that look like they're barely kept in place by the bra that's teasing through her button-up shirt. And as she passes me, I drop my gaze to her ass as it sways enticingly in her tight pants.

I've seen Lucia around the arena and on our trips more times than I can count, yet I don't think we've ever spoken much. She's one of the people working directly on my social media accounts, that much I know. But beyond being nice to look at, that's it.

She gives me a tight smile that doesn't reach her eyes. "Thank you, Sawyer."

Giving her a curt nod, I file into the back of the bus, waiting for everyone else to take their seats. I know this part sucks for those with partners. Our GM and Coach have a very strict policy barring partners from traveling with us.

So when we leave right after a game, they don't get to see them until we're back home. Sucks to be them.

The drive to the airport goes smoothly. We're all pretty high on the win, so there are lots of cheers, and talk about the game. "It was like you were flying. Fucking flying, man," Mickey, our left defender, says as he sits next to me.

Grinning, I slap him on the shoulder. "Right back at ya."

"Don't make his ego bigger than it already is," Soren groans, throwing himself into the seat in front of us. "Tell him he did shit."

"Which one of us?" Mickey asks with a sly smile.

I laugh. "Don't get jealous just because no one ever gives you a compliment, Soren."

Scoffing, he flips me off.

I've known the two of them since before we joined the Sabertooths. Soren was the first to join, then Mickey, and I was the last one. While the Sabertooths is the only NHL team Soren's played for, both Mickey and I have played for others. Before signing here in Minneapolis, I played in Boston. But that's the past, and now that we've played on the same team, I can honestly say I never want to be against either of them again.

On the ice, Mickey is the person you want next to you, and Soren's the one you want guarding the goal. Not that I'd ever tell them that, their egos don't need to get bigger. They're two of my closest friends on and off the team, and that's all that matters.

The driver takes us to the private landing strip where two different Sabertooths jets are waiting. Our GM doesn't want the players and other staff flying together. I'm not really sure why that's a thing, but I guess it has something to do with the PR team working while we just want to celebrate and relax.

As soon as we're on board the private jet, I lean against the window and give in to some much needed sleep. I don't notice the chatter going on around me or the drinks being supplied. I'm blissfully unaware of anything until we land in Minneapolis.

We're once again met by reporters, but now that we're on our home turf, they're less confrontational with their questions. They're congratulating us on the win and wanting to know if we think we have what it takes to go all the way this year.

"I can smell the Cup," Coach says in his gruff voice. "It belongs to us this year." Some locals that have gathered to show their support whoop in excitement.

Jo and her mini me, aka Lucia, stand with Coach, nodding their heads like this is all part of their plan. For all I fucking know, it might be. "We like our chances this year," Jo says.

"How long do we have to stay here?" Mickey whispers.

I shrug. "Until we're done." That's the best answer I have.

Jo carries on, talking about the team more than the game. She's telling them all about the charity stuff we're doing this year, competitions for the fans, and things like that. I've heard it all before, we all have, so I barely pay attention.

"And if you want to follow the players, we're—" Jo lets out a startling cry as she stumbles forward. I frown as Coach moves forward to catch her before she falls. "I'm sorry about that," Jo says, smiling sheepishly at the camera while looking around. Probably to find the reason she almost fell down. There's none as far as I can see.

Lucia still stands there, but she isn't looking at the cameras or Jo. I don't know what she's seeing, but it's something that's causing her to frown. I nudge Mickey and incline my head in the direction Lucia's still looking.

"This really isn't the fucking time to check her out," Mickey deadpans.

I open my mouth, about to tell him that's not what I'm doing. But before I can make a sound, an agitated man forces his way toward us. Lucia takes a step back, but it isn't enough to avoid him as he barrels forward, shoving her out of the way. An unwarranted surge of protectiveness runs through me, making me wish I'd pulled her out of the way.

"What the fuck?" I ask. I'm barely aware I'm moving until I find myself next to Coach.

"Where's the goddamn security?" he barks, looking like an angry bull.

It's all happening so fast, and I'm so fucking confused by what's going on that I don't register the man's shouting my name until Mickey clamps his hand around my arm. "Don't react," he warns, pulling me backward.

"Sawyer, you fucking piece of shit!" the man roars. "Show yourself, fucker."

I have no fucking idea who this guy is, and I don't particularly care right now. I'm too preoccupied wondering where the fuck our security team is. It's not like we really need them as most of us are bigger than them, but unlike those guys, we're not armed or allowed to strike back.

"Calm down, son," Coach says, trying to calm the angry man down.

The guy, who's looking like an unhinged mad man, pushes Coach out of the way. "How could you fucking do it? Only a coward sleeps with another man's wife." When he finds me in the crowd, he points an accusing finger in my direction.

"What the fuck?" I growl, immediately angered by the fucking accusation.

"Get out of here," Mickey urges, pulling at my arm.

I don't budge. I cross my arms over my chest and stare the man down. "Who the hell are you?" I ask, trying like hell not to give in to my temper. I might be many things, but I'm not a fucking cheater or home-wrecker, and it pisses me off to hear him call me that.

"You fucking slept with my wife," the guy shouts, spittle flying from his mouth. "She told me everything, so there's no point in denying it."

As I open my mouth to tell him to fuck off, the sounds of more commotion reach my ear. A woman that I've seen before runs toward the guy. "I told you it was only a one time thing," she cries as she attempts to take his hand.

The guy shrugs her off, barely paying her any attention. Instead, he narrows his eyes on me. "You recognize her." It's not a question, so I don't give him an answer. Yeah, I fucking recognize her. It was only a month ago I was balls deep in her, but she didn't wear a wedding band.

I don't need to look around to know that everyone's attention is on us. The tension in the air is growing and twisting, becoming its own entity, feeding off the hostility. Fuck me, there's no point in denying what the guy already knows. Especially not since his wife was spotted leaving my hotel room the next morning.

Knowing that I have to play this cool with cameras on us, I say, "I didn't know she was married." Is that the right thing to say? I'm not sure there's such a thing, given the circumstances. All I can do is hope it doesn't escalate.

Without warning, the guy lunges at me. "You fucking disgusting coward," he roars. Before I can move out of the way, he punches me square in the jaw. His hand comes back again, but I manage to push him away from me. "You ruined my marriage. Why did you have to go after my wife?"

I'm distantly aware that Jo's calling for security while Mickey and Coach are trying to hold me back. If the guy was just some deranged fucker, I might have let them. I can't when he's publicly accusing me of doing the one thing I've sworn I'd never do. "You don't know what the fuck you're talking about," I shout.

When the guy tries to punch me again, I see red. I duck before slamming my fist into his face. With one hand, I grab a hold of his shirt and throw him on the ground. I lose count of how many hits I get in before I'm pulled off the guy, and it's only then I notice the blood smeared across his face and my fist.

"I. Did. Not. Fucking. Know," I seethe, barely out of breath and still high on my anger.

"Calm the fuck down."

"I didn't know," I repeat, less angry this time.

"Get him out of here," Coach barks, and Mickey is quick to grab me.

"Let's go," my buddy says, pushing me away from the crowd.

We don't get far before we're stopped by the police.

"Sawyer Perry..."

"Fuck off. He was defending himself," Mickey growls.

"... You're under arrest."

I feel like I'm walking through a fucking dream as I'm placed in handcuffs while the cops read me my rights. All I hear is the blood rushing to my ears and the wild pumping of my heart.

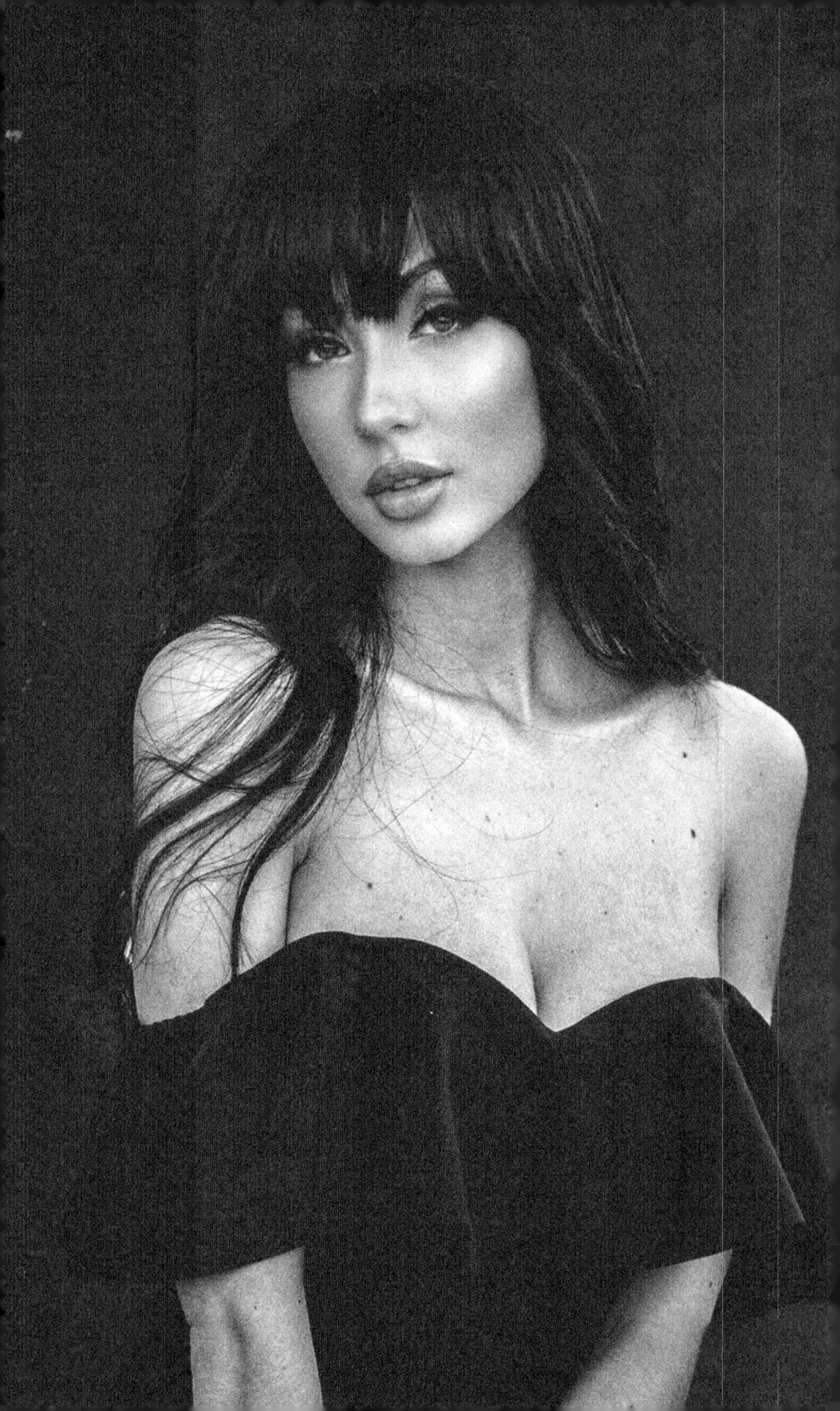

CHAPTER 3

Lucia

Remus: I can't wait to see you in two days, Lucia.

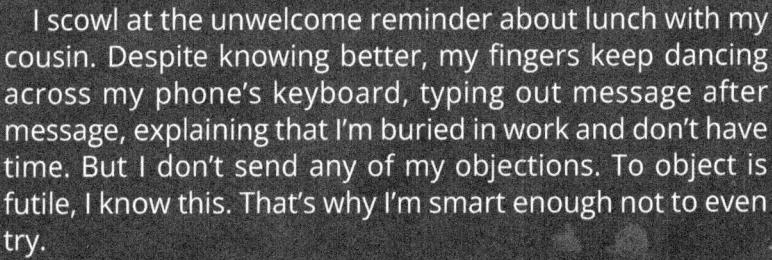

I scowl at the unwelcome reminder about lunch with my cousin. Despite knowing better, my fingers keep dancing across my phone's keyboard, typing out message after message, explaining that I'm buried in work and don't have time. But I don't send any of my objections. To object is futile, I know this. That's why I'm smart enough not to even try.

Not only has he sent me reminders via text, he also randomly changed the background picture on my work laptop to a lone wolf, sent me a scarf with wolf paws, and a box of what looked like tufts of fur. Talk about over-fucking-doing it.

After checking the time, I start gathering my things and shutting down for a quick break. It's much earlier than I usually have my dinner, but I'm starving and need to clear my head.

"There you are." I gasp out in surprise as Jo walks up to my desk. She twirls a finger through her blonde hair as she eyes my laptop that's already shut. "Are you leaving already?"

I'm not sure how to answer her. I mean, yes, obviously I'm leaving. But she's never paid much attention to when we're leaving the office as long as we do our job. "Just to get something to eat," I clarify. "I already finished—"

She holds up her perfectly manicured hand. "Normally, it would be fine, Lucia. But I came by to tell you that the meeting tomorrow evening, the one you asked Nick to take instead of you, has been changed to in an hour and Tom wants you there."

I'm surprised to hear the GM wants me there specifically. "Why?"

Shrugging, she runs a finger across my desk. "Tom changed his mind," she replies, which isn't really answering why he wants me there. But I'll overlook that. This isn't like our GM. Normally, he's a stickler for keeping appointments, and only changes things like this if he has to.

"Okay," I say, unsure what else I can respond with.

"Well, I won't keep you," Jo says, pulling at her tailored suit jacket. "I only came by to let you know so you can be prepared."

I swallow down the urge to snort. Prepared? I'm not sure how prepared I can be in less than an hour. "Thank you," I say, schooling my expression. "Oh, is there any news on Sawyer?" I ask.

Having the first game commemorated by a scorned husband showing up and causing a scene is beyond messed up. But to make matters worse, with Sawyer's arrest yesterday, we don't know much. Or, at least I don't. I have a feeling that Jo knows more than she lets on since the

Sabertooths' legal team has been working constantly to get him out.

"Tom will give us all an update during the meeting," she answers. Leaning closer, she lowers her voice. "Since you work on his account, you should know that the legal team and Tom are still working on getting him out. Plus, Tom's had to smooth the waters of the entire NHL, as well as our sponsors."

I let out a sigh. "How bad is it, Jo?"

"From a legal perspective, I don't know. From ours, it could be worse." I arch an eyebrow, but Jo just smiles. "As much as it sucks that the entire thing was broadcasted live, it was also Sawyer's saving grace. Everyone knows he was provoked, attacked. There can be no doubt about that. Though, knowing it doesn't excuse his overreaction…"

"But it explains it," I supply when she trails off.

"Exactly," she beams. "And if we focus on the charities, we might be able to turn it around."

I get the feeling there's something she's very deliberately not telling me, but I already know that it won't help to ask more questions. Jo isn't head of PR for nothing. She knows exactly what to divulge and what she needs to keep to herself to get the outcome she wants. It's part of why I like her and respect her so much. She never asks for something she wouldn't do herself, and she's very dedicated to the people on her team.

She only hangs around for a few more minutes. But it's enough to give me a few hints about what the meeting with the GM will be like. He doesn't want here and now solutions; he wants a long-term plan and for us to find a way to rehabilitate Sawyer Perry's image.

"Oh, it's almost time," Jo exclaims after checking her phone. "Do you mind grabbing me a coffee and brownie from the cafe?"

I look at the time. "I don't think I can make it there and back on time," I object weakly. Although it's in the building, it's not on the same floor. And there's usually always a long line in the cafe at this time. Everyone working late needs their next coffee fix at the same time.

Jo smiles widely. "For that coffee and those brownies, it's worth being a little late."

"Okay," I agree. Then I grab my coat and bag and leave the office. My mouth is already watering by the thought of biting into one of those brownies. Jo's right, they're worth being a little late.

Luckily, there's no line at the elevators on my way down or up, and after promising never to do it again, the guys in line at the cafe allowed me to move in front of them when I explained I couldn't be late for my meeting with Tom. I guess it helps that most know what's going on, and the severity of the situation.

As I ride the elevator, I check my appearance in the shiny walls, happy that I don't look as flustered as I feel. Being part of Jo's team means always looking our best, something she takes very seriously. Superficial as it might be, I get it. We're selling the image of the Sabertooths and the players, which means we have to look our best.

Once the doors open, I rush out and along the corridor to the room. I reach the door at the same time as Jo and our GM do, which technically means I'm on time. But the disapproving look in Jo's eyes tells me she considers me late, which is rich since she sent me on the coffee and brownie errand.

"Hi," I chirp, holding out her cup and the small container with the brownie.

She takes the items from my outstretched hand. "Nice to see you're on time," Jo sniffs, making it sound like I'm prone to being late. Newsflash, this is the first time I'm not showing up at least half an hour before I'm supposed to be somewhere.

"Hi there. Lucia, right?" the GM, also known as Tom Redding, asks while holding out his hand.

Meeting his blue eyes, I shake his hand while nodding. "Yes sir. I'm Lucia Carter."

Even wearing killer stilettos, I'm used to feeling small around the players. And with Tom, it's no different. He's at least six-two and in good shape. Though he's older, which is evident by his salt and pepper hair, he takes good care of himself. But above all of that, he smiles more than most, so it's never intimidating to be near him.

He scans the room behind me. "I like your work on our team's social media accounts," he says, surprising me. "You've made it more relatable and I hear that fans are interacting more." He beams at me.

Well damn, I never thought the GM looked that close at what we do. I mean, I obviously know Jo and the other executives scrutinize everything, but it never occurred to me that the GM is personally looking at it as well. "Umm, thanks?" I want to slap myself when it comes out as a question rather than an appreciative statement.

"Right, yes," Jo says, still staring daggers at me. "Lucia is one of our best PR account executives. She has an eye for detail and is very good at researching the trends."

I am fucking fuming. She's making it sound like I'm just copying shit rather than spending an ungodly amount of hours doing research before finding ways to tweak the trends to fit the Minneapolis Sabertooths.

"Keep up the good work," Tom says, smiling encouragingly. "Now, let's get this meeting started."

Walking into the room, I try to remain poised and not let on that I feel Jo's heated eyes burrowing into my back. Really, what's her problem? I don't want to sound all full of myself, but I thought she liked me. I do a good job and work my ass off without ever asking for credit. Hell, I've never even asked for a raise or a vacation day. Just like I've never called in sick.

"Are you okay?" Nick, one of the senior executives, asks. "It's not like you to be late."

I suppress the need to roll my eyes. "I wasn't late," I whisper. "And yes. I'm good." Today is clearly not my day at all, and I don't like how everyone seems to notice it. Just as I don't like how sourly I come across when Nick has done nothing to earn my attitude.

Luckily, I'm spared from more small talk when Jo slides into the seat next to me, and our GM stands at the end of the table. "Good evening everyone. I'm glad you could all be here on such short notice," Tom says. I've never interacted much with the man, which makes me all the more curious as to why he wanted me here. Usually, he gives his orders to Jo, who then briefs us on what we need to know to do our jobs. "I'm not going to sugarcoat the shitstorm we're facing or pretend it isn't all due to one player."

While he gives us a quick rundown of what he expects from today's meeting, I pull my laptop out of my backpack and start typing notes.

"Sawyer Perry is our strongest player. I don't have to remind you about his record-breaking goals from last season," Tom says, looking at all of us. "But I'm not blind to the PR nightmare that follows him, or the hard work you've suffered because of him. And that's why I thought it was time we all talked together. Because whatever we've done up to now is clearly not enough."

I bite the inside of my cheek, debating whether or not I should speak up. If Tom wasn't here, I'd never hesitate. But he is, and I'm not sure if it's a good idea to draw more attention to myself. Then again, he's clearly asking for help, and this is part of my job.

"Maybe it would help to talk to Sawyer," I suggest, my mouth working of its own volition and completely ignoring my brain that's begging for it to stop drawing attention to us... me.

"To what end?" Tom asks, sounding curious.

"Can I speak freely?" I ask, looking up in time to see the GM nod encouragingly at me. "So far, most of his scandals have been about... indulgence." My cheeks heat at the thinly veiled reference to sex. I'm far from a shy virgin or prudish. In fact, I make sure my vagina is happy and satisfied, but that doesn't mean it isn't awkward to discuss in a professional meeting. "But yesterday, he publicly beat the guy who accused him of sleeping with his wife."

Another woman nods eagerly. "It seemed like the guy got under his skin."

Despite Sawyer's image as the bad boy of the Minneapolis Sabertooths, there's no denying the incident from last night was different altogether. It wasn't about him being drunk and belligerent, or being caught with his hand up some puck bunny's skirt.

Not only was I there, watching it as it happened, but from the clip I've watched over and over, it's clear the scorned husband appeared out of nowhere. And he's the one who confronted Sawyer, even threw the first punch. The forward wasn't the one to start the fight, but he damn well made sure he ended it.

"Our legal team is assuring me that Sawyer will be out tonight," Tom says. "And then they want him for most of the day tomorrow. But if you think it'll help to talk to him, I can ask him to come by after lunch. What do you think, Jo?"

Jo nods thoughtfully. "It can't hurt. But if we're working with him, I would feel better if we have some suggestions on how to repair his image at the ready."

"Excellent," Tom says. Then he pulls out the chair at the end of the table and sits down. "I want to hear everyone's ideas. We need a way to keep his image squeaky clean for the rest of the season. Most of our sponsors are married and don't want to be associated with a man in his thirties acting like an out-of-control teenager."

Some of the women trade looks that make it clear they don't see Sawyer's behavior as a problem. I guess that's what happens when you have the luxury of thinking with your vagina instead of your brain. I'm not going to deny his wow factor and hotness, which he has plenty of. But where most of the women in the PR department find that enough to overlook his flaws, I've been more focused on his flaws. Probably because I'm the one who has to deal with them and smooth things over on his socials every time.

In another life, yeah, I'd totally join them in their swooning. Sawyer is the epitome of a hockey God, and he has the intense eyes, chiseled jaw, and abs that just beg to be licked to prove it. But in this life, I find him nothing but a sad cliche. I come from a family that's big on rules, hierarchy, and discipline. So seeing an adult acting like the rules of his contract are beneath him, like he's taking pleasure in breaking as many as possible, is... odd. Since he's not a teenage boy—as Tom put it—but a grown man at thirty-two, it's incredibly sad.

The hours fly by and it's almost 10pm when Nick says, "It sounds like we keep coming back to the same problem, and if you ask me, there's a simple solution."

"Which is?" Tom asks, rolling his hand in the air to indicate Nick should explain his thought.

"We need him to have a steady partner—"

One of the women sniggers, "Sawyer isn't exactly steady relationship material." She doesn't say what we all know; he's the kind to fuck you and leave you, not hang around for cuddles and breakfast in the morning.

Unbothered by the interruption, Nick goes on. "It doesn't have to be real. But it will improve his image and hopefully make him more relatable and likable to the investors. It would also limit all the damage control we constantly have to do on his social media accounts."

When Nick stops talking, the room's so quiet you'd be able to hear a pin fall onto the carpet. It's as though we're all holding our breath, waiting for Jo and Tom to weigh in and either shut down the suggestion, or run with it. I'm not sure which would be better. Yes, constantly having to monitor Sawyer is ridiculous, but at the same time, I don't relish the idea of having to interview candidates to be his fake girlfriend.

Tom looks down at his phone, silencing it when it vibrates again. "Is it doable?" he asks, turning to look directly at Jo.

"Yes, but—"

He shakes his head when his phone begins to vibrate again. "Jesus," he mutters as he furiously types out something. "I have to go. Sawyer's been let out, and the lawyers need me. We can discuss logistics later or tomorrow. But is it possible? Can it be done?"

"I suppose so," Jo says, straightening in her chair. "But where would we even start to look?"

The GM's eyes crinkle as he smiles. "Within your team, of course. In this room are some of the people who scrutinize him the most. You're all constantly watching his every move and spinning every word he says into gold. Plus, if it comes from within, we can claim it was kept secret to avoid a conflict of interest within the Sabertooths' family." He stands abruptly and claps his hands together. "I like it. Make it happen. I want three candidates in my email before you go home."

As soon as Tom leaves, Jo takes the seat at the end of the table, and I use the opportunity to create some space between myself and Nick. He's a nice guy and with his sharp suit, shaggy sandy hair, and dimpled smile, he's very good looking. It's not exactly a hardship to sit next to him. But he's also let his interest be known at every single opportunity—most of which he'd make sure to create—and that makes it awkward to sit that close.

"Okay, I want names," Jo says, moving over to the whiteboard and holding a pen between her fingers, ready to write.

"Can we suggest ourselves?" one of the women asks, unable to keep her snigger out of her tone.

Jo rolls her eyes. "You can suggest whoever the fuck you want. But this is work, not pleasure. Whoever Tom ends up picking needs to be able to keep Sawyer on a short leash, and be ready to deal with puck bunnies, and the media. Also," she quirks her eyebrow. "It obviously has to be someone who's single."

I dutifully take notes of the requirements and pull up our employee list so I can see who's immediately ruled out on the grounds of being married or in a known relationship. I also don't think anyone with kids is suitable. And then there's the fact that it needs to be a woman, and ironically, our department is mostly made up of men.

"How about Ellen?" Nick suggests, looking over at the woman who earlier said that Sawyer isn't relationship material.

Before she can answer, I ask, "Ellen, are you still looking after your sister?" When she nods, I shake my head. "It needs to be someone without commitments. If we're selling this, the person needs to be able to attend the away games, and hang on his arm at all the events he has to attend."

"Absolutely right," Jo agrees. "We also need someone who hasn't dated anyone on the team. The last thing we need is for the media to spin this into some kind of love triangle and make people think there's jealousy within the ranks."

I'm so engrossed in cross checking and pulling potential names that I don't notice a hush falling over the room until Nick discreetly kicks me under the table. "What?" I hiss, turning to glare at him. He tilts his head toward Jo, who's looking expectantly at me. "Oh."

She points between me and Nick. "The two of you seem to have a good grasp on what's expected, so I don't see a reason to keep the entire team here all night." Making a show of looking at the gold watch on her wrist, she sighs. "Let's break, and then you two can continue. The rest of you, back to work or go home if you're done."

As much as I don't want to do this, I don't have a reason to decline, so I nod. "Sure thing."

Nick also agrees, and like me, he looks anything but keen. At least, it was his idea.

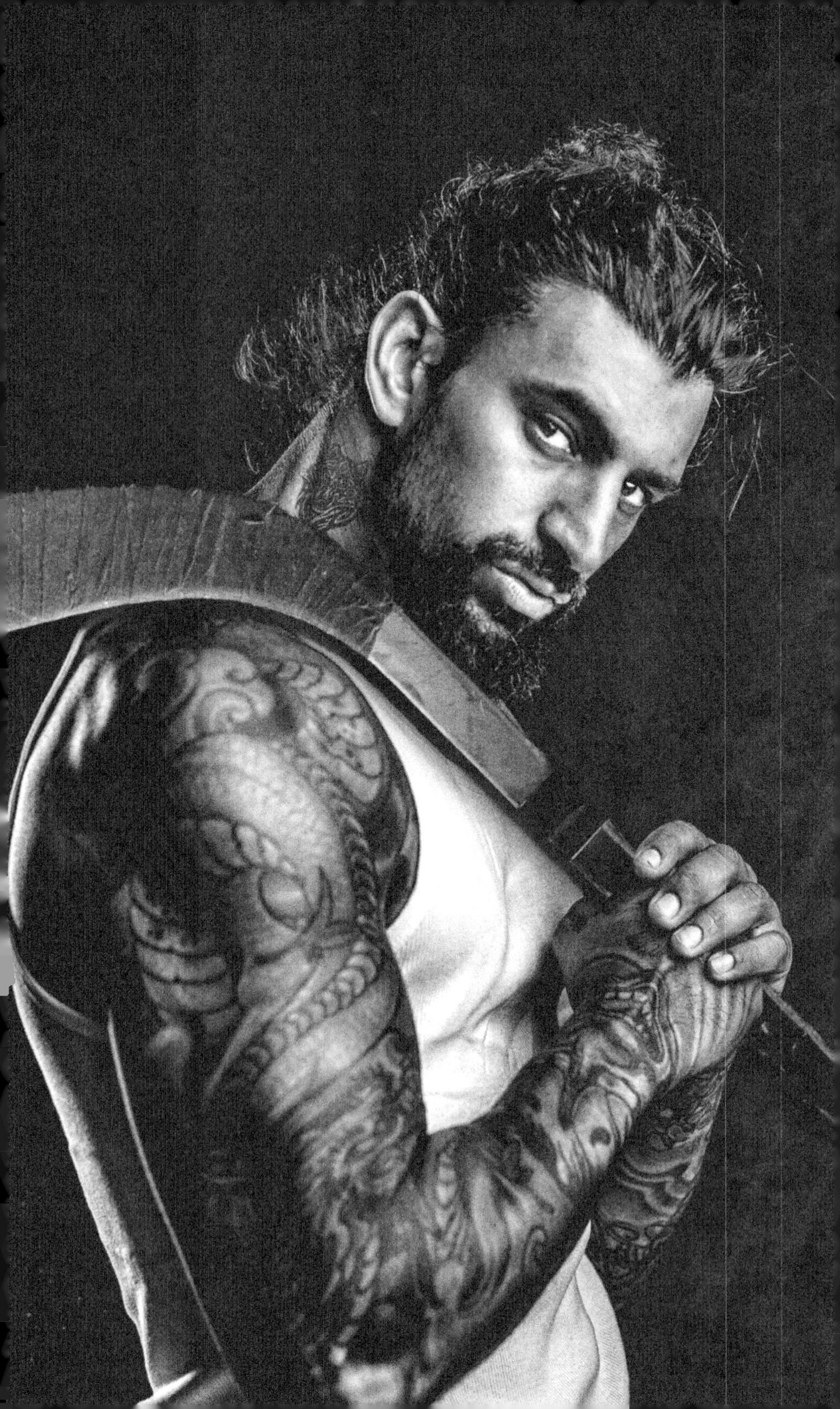

CHAPTER

4

Sawyer

After being released from jail last night, I'm not in the mood for any more bullshit. I just want to get back on the ice. Yet, here I am, sitting in Tom's office while he tells me about his latest plan for me. Maggie, my agent, clears her throat and nudges her head toward Tom, who's still talking. Shit, yes, I need to pay attention.

"... so we think if we pair a fake girlfriend with some extra charity stuff, it'll help turn things around," Tom says.

"You've got to be fucking kidding me," I seethe. Is it possible I didn't hear the orders from my GM correctly? Yes, I must have misheard him because there's no fucking way he'd force me to...

"Don't give me that attitude," Tom replies calmly. The GM folds his arms across his chest. "Your behavior is now jeopardizing the entire fucking team, Sawyer. You've spent a night in jail. We've already tried fines and threats, but it's clearly not working. So if you don't want me to bench you for the rest of the season, you'll agree to this and keep up the charade until the season ends."

I run a hand down my face, doing my damndest to calm the fuck down. This is bullshit. "It was not my fucking fault," I growl. Just like the other times I've said it; at the police station, to the lawyers, and to Tom, it falls on deaf ears. No one fucking cares. "The guy came at me. He broke through the fucking line of people and attacked me."

At the time, it all happened so quickly I didn't quite grasp how it happened. Now I know the guy snuck around back and mixed in with the reporters. That's how he got so close.

"You're right," Tom agrees solemnly. "You didn't start it, Sawyer. And I'm sorry it happened. But you didn't have to fucking beat him."

"So you just wanted me to act like his punching bag?"

Tom sighs. "Of course not. If you'd just pushed him away, we wouldn't be having this discussion. Even if you'd only punched him once or twice, I'd be on your side. But that's not what happened. You let your temper control you, and everyone saw it live."

I get what he's saying, and yeah, he's right to some extent. But fuck me. The guy accused me of the one thing I'd never knowingly do. And now my GM wants to fucking shackle me to a fake girlfriend just to restore my reputation. "Do I even get a choice in who I'll be fake dating?" I grind out through clenched teeth. Fuck me, there's a sentence I never thought I'd have to say.

Tom grins. "No. The PR team has sent over three candidates that I'll personally look into before making my decision."

I force my fists at my side to unclench. "Just spit it out already," I demand, wanting Tom to disclose everything instead of this half-truth bullshit I very much feel like he's giving me. "What's this really about?"

The thing is, I know I'm not a good person and I'm okay with that. Sure, I like to fuck my way through the puck bunnies, but since I always leave them satisfied, I've never had any complaints. So what's the fucking problem? Yeah, I could do with being more discreet, I'll agree to that. But that doesn't warrant a fake fucking girlfriend just because I punched that dick last night. He had it coming. Accusing me of ruining his marriage was too fucking far.

While I might be okay with bending the rules and morals of the world, there are certain things that are black and white. I don't fuck anyone who isn't single. Even though I've never been in a relationship, I know in my bones that I'd never cheat. Just the thought of being accused of ruining that guy's marriage has me vibrating with anger again.

Fuck.

I'm not a bleeding heart hiding insecurities from being cheated on in the past. But I saw what it did to my dad when my mom cheated on him time and time again. In the end, he couldn't cope and ran away like a coward. Leaving his dignity and me, his only son, behind. I still remember his last words to me.

"Don't do it, son. Don't ever let a bitch tie you to her because you'll regret it for the rest of your life."

Words I fucking live by.

I don't need to be in a relationship to know it's not for me. I won't ever allow myself to become that weak, so dependent on another person. Which is also why I don't date.

"Sawyer." It's not until Maggie, my treacherous agent, speaks I realize I'm now standing. "Don't give me that look," she warns, using her business tone.

"What?" I ask, incredulous. "Aren't you supposed to be on my fucking side?"

She shrugs and crosses one leg over the other, not bothering to stand. "I am on your side, Sawyer. I happen to think this is a good move. You've already lost two endorsements. Is it really worth risking the last ones over your pride?" Smiling widely, she continues. "Besides, this is the best offer. Some of the sponsors claimed they wouldn't be happy unless you got married. But Tom talked them down. This is a lot less drastic and by far the better deal."

Oh, for fuck's sake. This is about so much more than pride. How about the fact I'm a grown man who makes both my agent and GM ungodly amounts of money? That should fucking count for something.

"Why?" I ask, probably focusing on the wrong thing. "He dropped the charges, and I've agreed to go to anger management sessions. You've already gotten your pound of flesh."

Tom sighs, and it's one of those soul-deep sounds that makes it clear I better fucking listen. "Sit down." Sensing that now isn't the time to fight back, I do as he says, waiting while he does the same. "Normally, I wouldn't tell you what I'm about to share. But given how hard you're fighting this, you don't give me much choice."

He looks over at Maggie. Since I daren't take my eyes off the GM, I don't turn to see if she moves, though I feel her lean closer. "Go ahead," she says, making it abundantly fucking clear she already knows what I don't.

"Some of our sponsors are threatening to walk," Tom starts. I open my mouth to tell him just how little that matters to me, but he silences me with a glare. "I can only imagine your opinion is something like a lack of concern, which is your prerogative, one that I don't share. The Sabertooths are a family, Sawyer. One that your immature and selfish actions are threatening to tear apart. I can't have that. If you refuse to follow the recommendation from the PR team, I will bench you and trade you the first opportunity I get. Do you know what that would mean?"

I grit my teeth, determined not to make the situation worse by suggesting where the fucking sponsors can go. The Sabertooths are my family, too, and Minneapolis is my home. I'm not willing to lose it all. "I didn't fucking start it. It wasn't me tracking his ass down and throwing accusations just because he can't keep his wife satisfied. But I get it," I say. Then I swallow, my pride going down with an audible sound. "Look, I'm sorry, Tom. I'll do whatever you want me to do." I don't add that I'm not happy about it since I'm pretty sure my face says that all on its own.

"What's the length of this deal?" Maggie asks, though I'm pretty sure Tom already mentioned that.

"The rest of the season," the GM says without missing a beat. "And I want her to attend events with you. You also need to go on dates together. I don't want this blowing up in our faces, which means the public has to believe it."

I pull at the tie that suddenly feels too tight around my throat. Fucking monkey suit. If it wasn't because I've been forced to spend the day with the lawyers and now Tom, I'd be down in the rink, smelling the ice and skating across it with my teammates. Instead, I'm in a fucking suit listening to people calling my behavior erratic, out of control, and other shit. They aren't wrong, but it's not until Tom just threatened my career and my home that I've really taken it to heart.

"I can do that," I say, knowing it's pointless to fight it.

"We should at least know who the candidates are," Maggie says. When I shake my head, she argues, "Sawyer, you need to make sure it's someone you want to spend time with."

And this is exactly why it doesn't matter. "No, I don't," I retort. "This isn't about who they are as a person. It's a job." Standing up, I hold my hand out to Tom. "I'll fake date whoever you want me to, and I'll make it believable. But when the season is over, you better have a good reason for the breakup, one that doesn't make me the asshole."

He gets to his feet and takes my outstretched hand, clasping it harder than needed. "You have my word, Sawyer. I don't enjoy doing this to you, but you've left me no choice. Keep up your end of the bargain, and I'll make sure the breakup favors you."

Even though I know what's coming next, I'm still dumbstruck by the sheer amount of papers he wants me to sign. But I do it. I sign my name on almost every dotted line he puts in front of me. The one that makes me pause and peer up at my GM is the NDA warning me not to disclose the agreement to anyone.

"I'm not signing that," I say brusquely.

"Sawyer," Tom sighs. "The entire point is to make it seem legit. How can we do that if you can share the information with anyone you want to?"

Though I get his point, I shake my head. "I'm not signing that," I repeat. "What if I need help from one of my teammates? As you've just spent the afternoon pointing out, I'm not used to relationships. And if you want it to seem like we've been hiding our relationship from the public, not all my teammates can be surprised."

"He makes a good point," Maggie says. "Amend the NDA, Tom. He can tell Mickey and Soren. But that's it." When the GM opens his mouth to argue, she forges on. "If they don't know, what's going to stop them from making it seem weird? Unknowingly discredit the entire thing?"

"Fine," Tom huffs, relenting after a few moments. Then he calls someone and tells them to make the necessary corrections to the NDA and bring him the updated contract.

We don't talk while waiting for the legal wiz to join us. I don't know what the fuck's going through Tom's or Maggie's heads, but I'm wondering how the fuck I tell this to the guys. It's not exactly a normal conversation to have.

A knock sounds at the door, and Tom goes to open it, taking the printed paper from the poor guy who just had to haul ass to get here in barely any time at all.

Handing me the paper, Tom says, "Have a read through. I trust this is fine?"

I read over the paper, which now includes the names of my two closest friends. "Perfect," I say, signing the NDA without any more interruptions. When I'm finally done, I'm so fucking ready to get out of here.

"Good. I'll email a copy to Mickey and Soren. Don't tell them anything until I let you know it's okay." Tom's tone is stern, like I thought he was kidding.

"Sure thing."

"Enjoy your last few days of freedom," Maggie says, walking toward the door to the meeting room. "But not too much." The last part is called over her shoulder as she leaves. The way she sways her hips has to be for Tom's benefit because she knows better than to do it for me.

Fuck me. This is going to be one long ass season.

"Go home, Sawyer," Tom says, not unkindly. "Take the rest of the day and tomorrow. I'll let the coach know you'll be back on Saturday."

Shaking my head, I say, "I'll be here tomorrow."

He shrugs. "As you wish. But make sure your head is straight."

With nothing else to do or say, I make my way down to the locker rooms and wait for my teammates to enter when their training is over. I spend the time looking around the room, taking in details I've never noticed before. Like, how the hampers for dirty towels are always in the same place, and seemingly always empty. There's no smudge on any of the mirrors or fingerprints on the shiny taps.

As I walk around, I run my finger across the top locker, mildly surprised the pad comes off clean. Damn, Tom really keeps this place top notch. I can't say I'm surprised because that's the kind of person he is. He demands one-hundred and ten percent from everyone around him while never giving less than a thousand himself.

If I'm being completely honest with myself, I feel ashamed that my shit has gotten so out of control. I know Tom looks at every single player like part of his family, and it gnaws at me to know I've let him down. Maybe what he's proposing—demanding—isn't the worst thing. It might do me good to put some distance between myself and the puck bunnies.

I snort to myself and sit down on the bench. Fuck, me and my right hand are going to be glued together for the next six months and… however many days left until the season ends in April. Guess it's time to consider buying lube in bulk or something.

While I'm mentally preparing myself for months of jacking off, like when I was a teenager, my team files into the locker room. Their gruff voices and friendly banter pull me from my thoughts.

"Sawyer, man." Soren, our starting goalie, comes over and slaps me on the back. "Where the fuck have you been? You missed one helluva practice," he says.

I appreciate that he isn't mentioning that we all know I've been in jail. Then again, since I got out last night, I suppose it's a valid question. "Dealing with the lawyers," I say. While the guys begin removing their gear, I contemplate how much I should say while we're still here. "And making a deal with Tom." Our GM isn't the only one who considers the team his family. It's how we all feel. These men are my brothers, and we don't keep secrets from each other. Well, at least I can share with Soren and Mickey.

"How bad was it?" Mickey asks with a grimace.

I shrug. "Bad enough that I need to get out of here."

Soren stops moving and turns back to me. "Just tell me this, man. Are you willingly walking out of the doors? Or is this your way of..." He trails off, but I don't need him to complete the sentence. This is what they all want to know, and hell, if I were in their shoes, I don't think I could stop myself from asking.

"Don't worry," I say, forcing a grin. "You'll still have my ass to look at when I skate away from your ugly faces."

Now that's out of the way, the guys ease up and want to make plans for what we're doing tonight. Normally, I'm pretty strict with myself during the hockey season, but fuck it. Talking about all of this in the gym or rink isn't enough. I need a fucking beer.

"Let's go out for a steak or something," I suggest. The last thing I want is to go back to my apartment and be alone with my thoughts. Besides, Tom said these were my last few days of freedom... or maybe it was Maggie who said it. Fuck, it doesn't matter who spoke the words, they were both there, and no one contradicted the statement.

"Why the fuck not?" Soren says, before getting naked and sauntering over to the shower.

The other three, Henry, Danny, and Peter, quickly excuse themselves. Luckily for me, they already have plans with their girlfriends—or in Henry's case, wife. Fuck, this is what my life is going to be, isn't it? Saying no to stuff with the guys because I have to spend my free time parading a woman around. And if we're not out, I'll have to stay home, pretend we have a quiet, romantic night in.

For fuck's sake.

As soon as Soren and Mickey are ready, we take off, leaving mine and Soren's cars at the arena instead of driving three different vehicles.

"Wanna tell me why I have an NDA from Tom in my inbox?" Soren asks, turning to look at me in the back seat.

"Because he needs you to keep that big mouth of yours shut," I reply, forcing a grin, making Mickey chuckle. "There's one for you as well."

"Of course there is," he retorts, looking at me through the rearview mirror. "I guess it's about whatever deal you two made?"

I look away and shrug. "Could be."

"It's all standard shit," Soren says. "Nothing to be alarmed about, Mickey boy."

Mickey pulls over to the side of the road, reaches for his phone and taps away on the screen. Less than five minutes later, they both confirm they've signed the NDA and returned it, which is confirmed by a text from Tom that I get almost instantaneously.

Tom Redding: Mickey and Soren have signed the NDA. You can tell them.

I don't bother replying to the text since there's nothing to say. Instead, I ask Mickey to hurry the fuck up. "Are you sure you don't want to go home and change first?" Mickey asks for the third time.

I shake my head. "Nah, man. If I have to behave like a trained monkey, I might as well dress like one."

Soren chuckles, but is wise enough not to comment further. "So, where are we going to eat? If you want to go to an actual restaurant I should probably change," he says, gesturing at his overwashed jeans.

"Why?" I ask from the back seat. "We're fucking royalty in this town. They'll let you in anywhere, even if you are naked."

With how big hockey is here, I feel pretty certain my statement is true. More often than not, we receive invites to different clubs and restaurants, basically begging us to show our faces. Not that finer dining is our scene, not unless it's one of the sponsor or team events we can't get out of.

"So the usual haunt?" Mickey asks, looking at me in the rearview mirror.

"Yeah, let's go to O'Jackie's."

Though it's early on a Thursday, the multi-roomed Irish pub will be almost full. That's the way it always is. The place is nice, and it's our go to whenever we want to go out without being seen or having to deal with fans. Fuck, that sounds bad. But sometimes we just want to eat food and hang out without having to worry about the public.

Parking around the back, we use the back entrance like we usually do. As soon as we're through the doors, we're greeted by Jackie herself. "My guys," she greets us in that warm way of hers. She looks behind us, her eyes narrowing when she realizes three are missing. "Where are the others? Did you scare them off by making them dress all formal?" She gives me an accusatory glare.

Used to Jackie's antics, I chuckle. "You wound me with your accusations." I waggle my eyebrows at the woman that's easily twice my age. "I only dressed up for your benefit, so you'll finally realize I'm your favorite."

She playfully punches me in the stomach. "Behave yourself, Sawyer. You know your charms don't work on me. Besides, I could never be with a man who has longer hair than me, and a beard that hides his face." Turning to Soren, she asks, "How the hell do you guys put up with him?"

Mickey grins. "You know us, Jackie. We're always up for some charity work."

The matron wraps her arms around Soren and Mickey, leading us toward one of the quieter and private rooms. I'm not sure she ever lets anyone but us in here, and the thought is humbling. This woman is tough as nails and with a heart of gold.

As soon as we're seated, she removes the wine and hard liquor card from the table. "I ain't serving you anything stronger than beer tonight. And you can only have two each. If you want more, you'll have to go somewhere else."

"Jackie," Mickey laughs.

She holds up her hand. "No way, no how, boy. I've seen the news. I know why that one is wearing a suit and why you're here hiding in my backroom." Then she turns to me. "Tell me something."

"What?" I ask.

"Did he deserve the beating?"

Before I can answer, Soren growls, "He deserved that, and so much more."

Jackie nods, pleased with the answer. "In that case, you can have three beers. But that's it. Now, do you want to pretend to peruse the menu, or should I just go ahead and whip up my famous steaks for you?"

I laugh and wink at her. "We want your steaks, Jackie. Please."

With the menus in hand, she leaves, all the while mumbling something about us being the bane of her existence and that we were put in her path as a test from God. Jackie's one of a kind. She's odd, but apart from my teammates, she's the realest person I know.

When I first met her a couple of years ago, she was quick to tell me what's what, demanding that I don't cost us the season after I'd fumbled a goal in the previous game. She's never been one to sugarcoat things, so you always know where you stand with her. But she's also protective, and has more than once, personally, thrown paparazzi out on their asses when they've followed us here.

"Okay," Mickey says, leaning closer to me. "Now that we're here, tell us exactly what went down with the lawyers and Tom."

I don't answer until Jackie has brought us our first beer, and I vow to myself this is the only one I'm having tonight. "The lawyers got the guy to drop the case after I agreed to attend anger management sessions." I roll my eyes, still not happy I have to do that. I don't have anger issues, only asshole issues.

"Is that it?" Soren prompts, knowing it isn't.

I take a large swig of my beer, loving the taste of Jackie's own brew. "Nah. I also had to agree to fake date someone for the season. Apparently, I'm damaging the family brand and sponsors are threatening to walk if I don't change."

"What the fuck?" Mickey growls, agitatedly running his hand through his white, messy waves. It feels good to have someone else be annoyed on my behalf. "That shit can't be legal."

I shrug because I don't know whether it's legal or not. "Doesn't matter since I agreed to it."

Soren's lips pull upward in a twisted smile. "So Mr. Fuck-Her-And-Leave is suddenly going to have a relationship."

"Fake relationship." I feel the need to clarify.

"Well, hell. This season suddenly got more interesting." Mickey tips his head in Soren's direction. "Should we take bets on how long it lasts before our boy here fucks it up?"

"I feel like giving him one week is generous. Ten days." Turning to me, Soren clarifies. "I added the extra three because we're friends."

"Fuck you, man." There's zero heat in my tone. Their banter is exactly what I need. "I'll ace this fake relationship shit. How hard can it be, anyway? If Henry, Peter, and Danny can do it, so can I."

"Have you thought about asking them for advice?" Mickey suggests. "Because whatever they're doing seems to be working, and you're not exactly…"

I bark out a laugh. "Seriously, I can fake it like the best of them. I only have to pretend I care in public. It's not like I need to get to know her for real."

"Are you sure about that?" Soren scratches his chin as he looks at me. "You know how personal the reporters like to get. They're going to ask you shit like where you met, what her favorite flower is, and all sorts of shit. You need to know the answers to that."

Well… fuck.

How hadn't I considered that? I don't want to get to know whoever the GM picks for me. I just want to pose in public, smile, and wind my arm around her. I don't care if she's a dog or cat person. If she prefers… well, any-fucking-thing.

"Maybe you can get by without knowing all that shit," Mickey suggests, reading my slumped shoulders perfectly. "I mean, you're still you. So, can't you spin it so you're still a commitment-phobe in public or something? Chicks love being the one to change a guy, so if you tell people—"

"How exactly will that improve his image?" Soren challenges. "People need to see the change to believe it. I don't think there are any shortcuts here."

I fucking hate that he's right. "I can do it."

"Are you sure?" Mickey asks.

"No," I answer honestly. "I fucking know I can't. But what choice do I have?"

"Wow," Soren says, reaching for his beer. "So, is that why we're here? Do we need to find you a—"

I bark out a laugh. "You really think they'd leave that decision up to me? Tom is going to pick someone from the PR department to be my doting girlfriend." My phone vibrates in my pocket, and I pull it out to see a text from Tom.

> **Tom Redding: There's no point in waiting until Monday. I've picked Lucia Carter to be your publicity girlfriend.**

I make a face and show the text to the other two. "Guess it's official," Soren says with a shrug.

"Could be a lot worse," Mickey adds. "Lucia is fucking hot."

"Like that matters," I say. "But yes, she is." There's no point in denying it when we've all checked her out at one point or another.

Lucia's like one of those items you see on a shopping channel. She's flawless, poised, and beautiful—the whole package. But with no chinks in her armor, she's too damn perfect, which is something I don't trust. She always wears the right thing, says the right thing, and just... there's no personality to be detected whatsoever.

"Maybe you'll finally find out what she's really like," Soren offers, like he heard my thoughts.

"Doesn't matter," I say dryly. "We have a role to play, that's all. As long as we do it convincingly, I don't need anything else from her."

"Exactly how convincing do you need to be?" Mickey asks. "Like, do you need to get engaged? What about marriage?"

I bark out a laugh. "Yeah, that's not fucking happening."

Soren tilts his head to the side, his green eyes sparkling with amusement. "Maybe save that for your Hail Mary if you need it."

Shaking my head, I ignore them. I'm not getting fucking married, ever.

When we're done eating, we pay, leaving a generous tip for Jackie. Then we sneak out the back, and Mickey drives us back to the arena so Soren and I can get our own cars.

"Are you going to be at practice tomorrow?" Mickey asks as I'm about to slam the door after getting out.

"Probably not," I admit. "Tom told me not to come back until Saturday."

"Alright," Soren says, grasping my shoulder. "I'll keep Mickey boy busy tomorrow then."

I walk to my car and drive home, only to discover that every time I try to summon a mental image of a puck bunny to fit around my cock, it's Lucia's face that pops up.

Fuck!

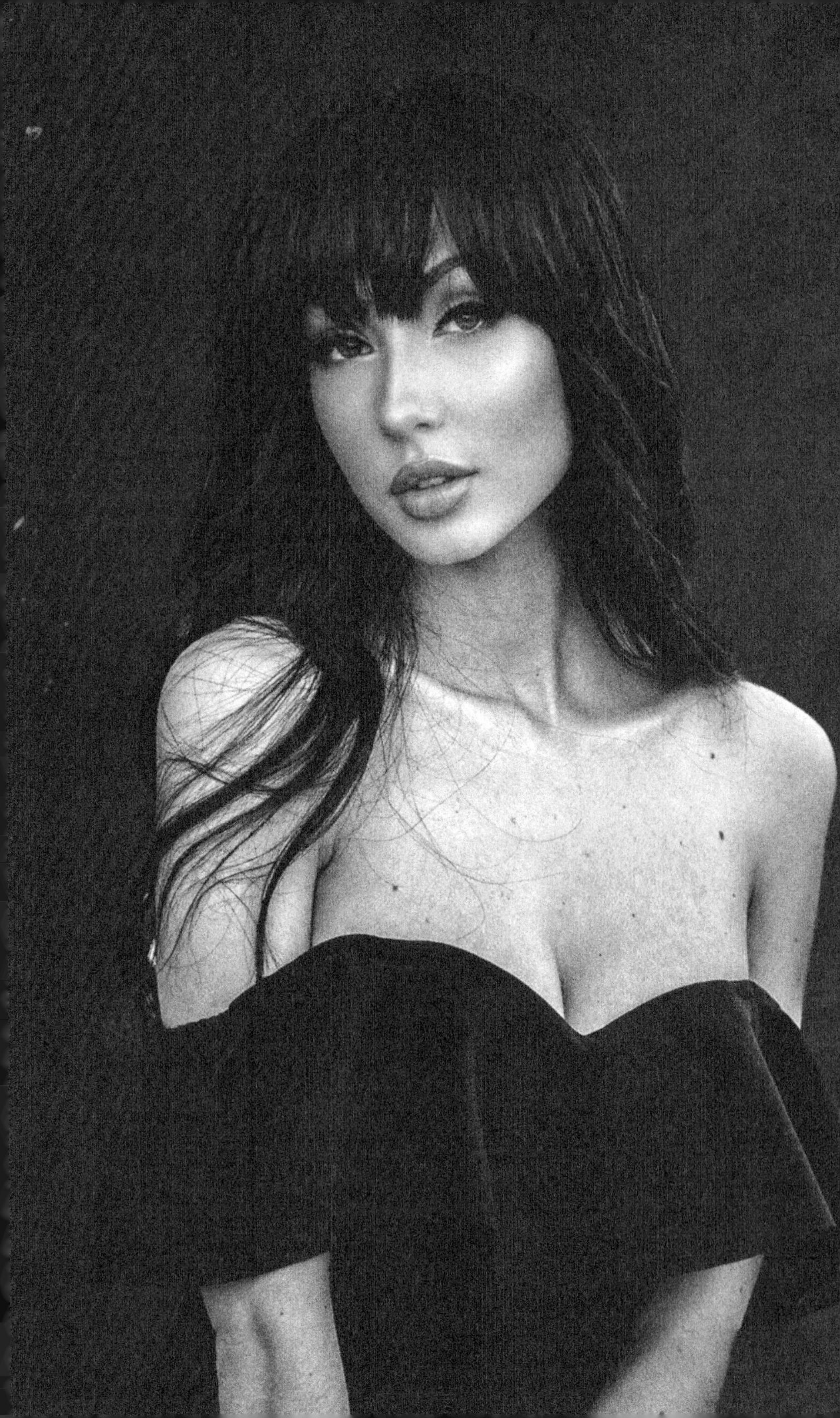

CHAPTER 5

Lucia

It's Friday morning, and I don't think I've slept at all. No matter how much I've tried, I can't stop thinking about what it will be like to see Remus today. I hate not knowing what he expects from me. Gail already knows I'm off work today to see him, and I can feel her looking at me as I sit at our kitchen table while she's running around, getting ready for her day.

"Stop looking at me," I huff into my bowl of cereal.

"But you're so pretty when you scowl at your breakfast." Her sing-song voice is calming, and her words make me laugh. "Don't even think about canceling tonight. I won't let you. And who knows, it might be fun to see your cousin for lunch—"

"It won't be," I grumble, once again regretting I told her about Remus visiting.

Gail rolls her eyes at me and sighs. "Well then, I guess you'll have a miserable ol' time. No matter. Do your duty to the family or whatever. And then tonight..." She pauses theatrically and waggles her eyebrows. "...We go out and party instead of staying in. You and me, babe, and a helluva lot of tequila." With those words, she discards her bowl into the sink and turns back to look at me.

"Easy for you to say," I mutter. Then I let go of my spoon and give up on the drenched corn flakes that look anything but appetizing.

She rolls her eyes at me. "Well, can't say I'm going to miss this version of you, Luce. So try to ditch it tonight, kay?"

"Okay," I agree.

"Once more with feeling."

I laugh at Gail's over the top antics, which are clearly orchestrated to lighten my mood. "I promise I'll be... more fun tonight."

"That's the spirit." She shoots me a smile before pouring the rest of the coffee into her travel cup. "How are things going with Sawyer, by the way? He's out now, right?"

I scrunch up my nose. "Yeah, he's out," I confirm. While I love Gail and trust her implicitly, we both know there are things I don't tell her. As far as she's aware, it's only the finer details of my job I don't share, and I'd like to keep it that way. After all these years, I don't want her to know how dishonest I've been in our friendship. "We had a meeting the other night. The GM wanted us to come up with a strategy to make Sawyer more..." I swirl my hand in the air as I try to come up with a suitable word.

"Likable? Tame?" Gail asks, curious.

None of those words sounds right, but they're not wrong. "I guess," I say with a grimace. "Tom wants Sawyer to enter a fake relationship to make him seem more..." Pausing, I blow out some air. "Likable."

Gail nods slowly, her eyebrows scrunching together in that way that tells me she's concerned. "Well, you knew the shit with Sawyer would hit the fan after he punched that guy bloody. So now I have to ask, is your mood really about your cousin visiting?"

Fuck. I thought I'd done so well at acting annoyed rather than concerned, scared. Ugh, I really don't want to make up more lies, but I also can't have her knowing just how much I dread Remus being here.

When Gail clears her throat, I realize I haven't answered her. Not that I'm going to, not in the way she wants. "Don't worry about it," I say, trying to sound convincing. I don't want her to know that I might not be here for our tequila date tonight. If I'm called back to Rome, I'll have no option but to obey the orders from the Mafia Don ruling my family.

"You'll be okay with your cousin, right? Or do you need me to fake an emergency?" she asks, making it clear I'm doing a shit job at making it seem like nothing is wrong.

As tempting as that is, I shake my head. "It'll be fine. I'm just tired. Too many long nights this week is making me dramatic," I say, needing to convince her that it's not all bad. Dammit, everything would be so much easier if I'd kept my mouth shut the night I got the first text from Remus. Jesus, has it really only been a week? It feels much longer.

"If you say so," Gail says, and I let out a sigh of relief that she isn't pushing the issue further.

I watch her as she goes to pick up her shoulder bag and coat while mumbling something about hating arts and crafts day as she leaves. Can't say I envy her spending her days with the kids she teaches, but sometimes I am jealous that she's always out of her workplace no later than 4pm.

A quick glance at the microwave clock tells me I have to hurry if I want to meet Remus on time, which I do. It's not in my best interest to be late. My family is too disciplined to allow lateness, and Remus would read too much into it. He might even consider it a weakness, and I can't afford that.

I sprint to the bathroom, indulging in a long shower, where I make sure to perfect every part of my body. Back in my room, I rummage through my closet until I find a suitcase I've hidden behind my shoes, and other things. I drag it onto my bed and carefully remove the clothing inside. I haven't worn it since my uncle set me free, and I'd naively hoped I'd never have to.

During the years, I've made sure to clean it at least once a month so it's fresh. Why? It's a good fucking question. But I guess it's because I knew that if the head of my family ever called upon me, I'd have no choice but to wear it.

Zipping up the dress I'm expected to wear, I'm relieved to see it still fits. Although it's more snug than it was almost ten years ago, the zipper glides up the side easily enough, so I count that as a win. Ugh, I hate having to wear this, but the tradition is important. And I can't afford any blunders.

While looking in my mirror, I adjust the halter neck and the belt so the white she-wolf's head isn't crooked. The skirt reaches me mid-thigh, making it shorter than I like for a family meeting. But then again, this isn't really a family gathering. We may share blood, but it's still the head of the family calling upon one of his subordinates. Me.

After towel-drying my long red hair, I braid a few random locks across my scalp. Then I brush it all back, leaving my shoulders free. I tilt my head to the side, narrowing my eyes as I try to imagine what I'll look like to Remus. The only thing I'm not happy about is my bangs. They're too long, but my busy work schedule hasn't allowed any time off to make an appointment with my hairdresser. If only my cousin had given me more notice. Then again, maybe it's better that he didn't. This way there's less time for me to stress and get lost in my head about it.

My makeup is the last thing I do, and I keep it in nude and light nuances. While I apply my mascara, I keep having to tell myself to breathe. My head is swimming with thoughts, and my heart is thundering in my chest. My breathing flits between being labored or… well, I hold it.

"Calm the fuck down," I hiss at my reflection. "Don't let him see your nerves."

After that pep-talk, I reach for the charm bracelet with wolves dangling from it. It was delivered yesterday, so I assume Remus wants me to wear it. Then I sit down on the bed and put my black pumps on, meanwhile reciting facts about my family.

Bravery, loyalty, respect, and authority.
Discipline shows strength.
A wolf never attacks alone, it knows it's stronger in a pack.
Senatus Populusque Romanus.

Fuck... okay... I can do this.

Before I can change my mind, I quickly gather my things and rush out of the apartment I share with Gail and into my beaten down Honda Civic. It's not as luxurious as the cars I used to have access to before I bargained my way to freedom, but it's *mine*. I bought it from a shady-looking guy who probably scammed me, and, too blinded by the prospect of my first big purchase, I happily let him. Though I could afford a newer or better car now, I'm too emotionally attached to the deathtrap.

During the drive, I again try my best to think up things to tell Remus. Or rather, reasons he needs to let me stay and continue my life. I like the life I've built for myself. It's not much, but I like it this way because everything I have is mine, untainted by my sordid family. But I already know he didn't make his way all the way from Rome to Minneapolis, Minnesota, to grant me my freedom.

Reaching the restaurant, I'm met by a valet that greets me with the words, "Senatus Populusque Romanus" before bowing deeply. I don't know why I didn't expect that Remus had bought and infiltrated the restaurant with his men, but I should have. Because of-fucking-course he has made himself a foothold in my world.

As I walk into the upscale restaurant where my cousin wants to meet me, I feel at least one presence at my back, silently moving closer. "Lucia Russo." Spinning around, I come face-to-face with a handful of guards, and I immediately recognize one of them. I open my mouth to say hi, but close it again when he discreetly shakes his head and averts his gaze. Right. We don't greet the guards. Shit, maybe I should have spent more time actually practicing for Remus instead of constantly pushing it out of my mind.

The guards lead me through the restaurant, shielding me from the people eating there. During the walk, I unbutton my black coat and throw it over my arm. It does nothing to cool me down. I still feel like I'm overheating as sweat trickles down my spine. My fucking cousin. Why couldn't we just meet at a burger van or... I struggle to come up with other ideas because it's not like they matter. We're here, and I have a part to play.

When we finally come to a stop, the guard next to me knocks once on the door, which is opened from the inside by yet another member of my cousin's entourage. I hesitate for a moment, doing my best to ignore my brain that's screaming at me to get out of here, to flee. I guess this is a byproduct of being away from the fold for so long I no longer feel safe in the presence of my family.

After handing my coat to the guard, I turn around, ready to face my cousin. "Ahh, Lucia," he croons, stepping out of the shadows where I already knew he was standing.

Remus looks exactly like he did the last time I saw him, at my uncle's, his dad's, funeral. His dark eyes are intense, his hair slicked back, and there's a five o'clock shadow covering the hard lines of his jaw. Of course, he's dressed impeccably in a suit that probably cost more than everything on the menu combined. He oozes power, it radiates off him in a way that's almost suffocating.

I've known him all his life, which to me means that when you take away all the pomp and circumstance, he's still the same little boy I babysat in what feels like a different lifetime. If I'm being completely honest with myself, none of that shit is true. It's just what I have to tell myself to remain undaunted by his mere presence.

"Remus," I say, bowing deeply while placing my hand on the family saying and crest that's burned into my skin. I hate having to do it, but since he's now the Don of the Russo Mafia and our family, I can't completely ignore tradition. No matter how much I want to, it's too deeply ingrained in me. "It's good to see you."

To my surprise, he throws his head back and lets out a booming laugh. "Fuck off," he hiccups through his laughter. "Seriously, Luce. I'm glad you're not an actress because I would have to do some serious bribing to get you a job." While I debate whether to be offended by the insult or happy my cousin is still himself, he pulls me in for a tight hug that I eagerly return.

The embrace we share feels almost symbolic. With a sigh, I pull back. "Aren't you going to wine and dine me?" I ask, pointedly, looking at the table.

He chuckles. "How could I forget that the way to your heart is through your stomach? Sure, let's eat before we get down to why I'm here." The reminder that this isn't merely a family reunion isn't a welcome one.

One of the guards pulls my seat out for me, and I daintily sit down, even allowing him to push the chair in under me. I haven't missed this. Not one bit. "Why don't you just tell me why I'm here?" I ask, reaching for the water the guard poured before becoming one with the wall. "You know I don't like waiting around."

Remus raises an eyebrow. "I've missed you, Luce. We all have." I grit my teeth, stopping myself from making a snarky comment about how I haven't missed them. It wouldn't go down well. Besides, it's a lie. I have missed *some* of them, actually. Just not enough to go back to a place that was never more than a gilded cage. "Tell me about your life here," he insists, breaking the silence that spread between us when I didn't return the sentiment.

"There's not much to tell," I say, blowing my bangs out of my eyes. "You already know everything, Remus. We both know it, so why pretend differently?"

Annoyance makes his smile disappear. "Reports only give me the facts. It doesn't tell me what it's like for you. So why don't you humor me?" Even though he phrases it like a question, I know it's not a request, it's a demand.

"What is it you want to know? I graduated, I found a job, and I make my own money. I haven't touched the family funds since I graduated. My job is..." Trailing off, I try to decide on the best way to describe how much I love my job. "It's challenging and unpredictable. No two days are the same, and I love that about it."

Remus snorts. "How ironic that you, of all people, have found a job that's all about being dishonest and unethical. Isn't that part of why you wanted to leave the family? Because you found us controlling and immoral?"

"That's not it at all," I volley. Feeling indignant, he's making it sound like it's a shady business. "People are people. They aren't perfect, but I help people get what they want."

"Explain." The demand is sharp, his tone making it clear the niceties are over.

It takes everything in me not to react to the shift in his attitude, but I refuse to let him see how affected—scared—I am. "What I'm doing isn't really for the players, Remus. I help shape their image and manage their social media accounts so the fans get what they want, what they expect. Some of them live for a reply, a like, or a share from their icon. What I do is for the fans. They believe in the players. Some even feel a connection to them, and I help strengthen that by giving them what it is they're looking for."

I know Remus wants to grill me further, and probably call me out for being such a dreamer—that's what his dad called me when he agreed to let me move away. But luckily two servers join us, delivering the food and topping up our drinks. They don't speak at all, barely even look at us.

During my years away, I've learned I suffer from a self-diagnosed disease that makes it damn near impossible to keep my mouth shut even when I know I should. So avoiding saying something I shouldn't, I quickly dig into the food. On my plate is a green salad masterfully placed to look all fancy. The potato slices form a heart around the chicken breast, which is covered in bacon with cream cheese in the middle. My mouth salivates, and it feels like it's taking forever to slice into the tender meat.

"Mhmm," I moan as the herbs and spices the chicken has been marinated in wrap around my tongue. "That's delicious." Using my fork, I push the greens to the side because with how good this is, I need to prioritize. I'm not a salad eater on my best of days, and I'm definitely not one to choose it over meat and carbs.

I make it through three bites before Remus puts his cutlery down. "You need to come home, Luce. People are questioning why you're still allowed to roam around free." I nod to show him I'm listening, but I don't stop eating. "Your deal with my dad was for ten years, which is coming up next month on your twenty-eighth birthday. Have you made preparations to leave yet?"

The food suddenly tastes like ash on my tongue, and I reach for my water to help it down. When I feel like I can breathe again, I say, "Romulus made it clear I could earn my freedom if—"

Remus makes an impatient sound. "I know what my dad said. The agreement is that you would be free if you got married. But Luce, you're not even dating. So don't insult me by giving me some elaborate lie about getting married."

"How would you know?" I volley.

He lets out a mirthless laugh. "Because if you truly were about to get married, you would have asked me for a divorce."

My blood runs cold at his words. "A divorce?" I croak. "But I thought..." Trailing off, I try to recall my uncle's exact words. He set me free from my marriage, but... did he ever say divorce? Shit, I can't remember.

"I see you're finally getting it," Remus says. "Giving you ten years of freedom isn't the same as granting you a divorce. Your marriage might only be a technicality, but it still exists on paper, Luce."

Scoffing, I ask, "Don't tell me Fabian has spent ten years being a faithful husband missing his wife."

"Of course not," Remus snorts. "Your time away gave you both a temporary separation—"

"But then why—"

"Stop fucking interrupting me," he roars, slamming his fist down on the table. The cutlery and glasses shake on the table at the impact, and it's making the hairs on my neck rise as a sliver of cold runs down my spine. "Once your time is up, you revert to your marital status."

Giving up on the food, I push the plate away and fold my arms over my chest to hide my trembling hands. "Whatever's going on or not going on in my life is none of your business, Remus. At least not for the next month," I say, getting us back to the beginning since I don't know how to feel about this, any of it.

This can't be fucking happening. Married... hell fucking no. I'll slit my own throat before I ever return to my husband's side.

Remus rakes a hand through his hair and down his neck. The movement and the heaviness in his eyes make him look much older than the twenty-two years he is, and I can't help feeling bad for him. It's not my cousin I'm fighting. I mean, it is, but it isn't. It's the fact he wants to control me I have an issue with. But I also know that isn't who he is, it's just who he had to become when his dad died and he took over.

"Is this really how you want to do this?" he asks, giving me a look I can't decipher.

Rather than answering him, I repeat my previous statement. "I have one more month of freedom. What I do with it is up to me." Maybe I'm wrong, but I could have sworn I see begrudging respect in the way he's looking at me. I hope I'm reading him correctly, because if not... nope, can't think about that. I have to stand my ground.

Remus picks his knife and fork back up and resumes eating. He chews slowly, like he's thinking too hard to focus on his food. Since I don't have that problem, I dive back into the chicken. Like my cousin, I chew slower than normal. But it's not because my head is full of important thoughts. Or maybe that's the exact reason, I can no longer tell as my thoughts run rampant.

I probably should think of ways to get out of my deal. Make suggestions or cut another deal, but I know it wouldn't help. The only reason he isn't hauling my ass back to Rome at this very moment is because he's honoring the deal I made with his dad.

"You know," I say as soon as I'm done eating and the servers have cleared the table. "I don't hate all the family, Remus. You know I love you. Some of my life in Rome was good, but the bad parts overshadowed that."

Remus opens his mouth to answer, but before he can say anything, the servers come back with dessert and coffee. Once they're gone, my cousin arches an eyebrow and casually leans back in his chair while swirling his wine. "Why are you telling me this?"

Eyeing the elaborate dessert in front of me, I pick up my spoon. It's a chocolate bowl filled with fresh fruit and what looks like sorbet. Wasting no time, I eagerly dive in. All the flavors explode on my tongue immediately, and damn, it's good.

"Luce," Remus says. His tone makes it sound like a warning, but when I look at him he's smiling.

Oh, right. He asked me why I was telling him I don't hate the entire family. It's a good question, but the answer isn't. The reason I'm telling him is that I want him to know I'm not coming home. Not now, not ever. "Because you're wrong. Because you're not all-knowing."

"Meaning?"

I force my shoulders to relax and a smile to splay across my lips. "I need a divorce, because I'm getting married."

Much to my dismay, he starts laughing. This time it isn't good-naturedly and infectious. It's cruel and calculated. "Is that so? Then tell me this, Luce. Where's your engagement ring?"

Fueled by anger at his reaction and fear of having to return to Rome, I hiss, "It's on a part of my body that you'll never see."

Remus chuckles, and it pisses me off that he's seeing through my lies so easily. "For your sake, I hope you're being honest."

"Remus—" I begin, but he interrupts me.

"There's no point in lying to me, Lucia. I know you're not dating. I know your job and your friend Abigail are your entire life—"

My breath hitches as a surge of panic flows through me. "Keep her out of it," I demand.

He carries on, completely ignoring what I just said. "And that's fine. You don't need to make up elaborate stories. Your deal doesn't hinge on a relationship already existing. So let me give you a friendly piece of advice—"

"You're not my friend," I grumble, unable to stop myself.

Shrugging, Remus amends, "Then consider it unfriendly advice. But if you want to stay here, you have to get a ring on your finger. And you have to find a husband that can stand before the Senate in the Vatican City. Your *current* husband will demand the involvement of the Senate, and you know I can't stop him from evoking them."

I gape at Remus, unsure of whether or not I'm reading him correctly. Gulping, I play the words on repeat in my head. It sounds like he just told me how to win my freedom. Is... is Remus on my side? "Why are you telling me that?" I ask, needing to know if I'm understanding him correctly.

Remus shrugs again, the motion warring with the intense look in his eyes. "We all have a role to play, Lucia. And when... *if* you come home, the Senate wants you back with Fabian."

"But you're the head of the family," I argue. "Can't you just let me go?"

Ignoring my question, he shoots me a toothy smile. "You can make it happen, Luce. If it helps, the only one I'm worried about is the poor guy you set your eyes on. You're too conniving for anyone to know what's happening if you really put your mind to it."

"Remus," I hiss, not amused by the way he's describing me. When he narrows his eyes, I shake my head and instead repeat the question. "Why can't you just let me go? You could pretend you didn't find me or something."

He sighs audibly. "You know that's not how it works. Nothing worth having is given for free, Lucia. So if you really want your freedom, you have to make it happen."

The Senate... I don't know much about it, only what I've heard whispered. If the rumors are to be believed, the Senate is made up of the heads of the most important members of our family, and they do their shady dealings amongst the ancient bones in the Vatican City. At least, that's what I heard as a kid. I don't know how much is real. Hell, up until now, I didn't even know they actually existed. So I suppose the part about them only answering to our Don, Remus, is true. But from the way he's talking, it doesn't sound like he can control them.

"Does the Senate have to approve my new husband?" I ask softly.

"Not necessarily," Remus says. "The only stipulation my dad wrote was that you had to be married. He didn't specify that anyone had to approve the man you marry. But they do have to approve that you've satisfied the terms of the deal."

"What?"

Remus rolls his eyes like I'm being dense, which irks me so much I have to swallow down the retort I want to throw at him. "They have to agree you've successfully fulfilled your duty, and that they're satisfied with the result. Call it approval or blessing, either way, it's the same."

"So they do have to approve," I grumble, feeling like he's talking in a circle.

He shrugs. "Not of your husband. You can marry whomever you want, Luce. But they do have to be okay with it."

I nod, unable to speak. My head is too busy trying to form an idea or a plan to do something. Knowing that Remus doesn't care what I do and isn't personally going to stand in my way should make it easier for me. Yet, it feels even harder now that I know he isn't the only one keeping an eye on me. Okay, technically, I don't know if the Senate is watching me, but I feel like they are if they're asking him to bring me home.

"How long do I have to be married?" I ask. Remus arches an eyebrow and gives me an unimpressed look. "I mean, what if my new husband dies or wants a divorce? What's the timeframe for my marriage, Remus?"

He cups his chin and runs his thumb thoughtfully up and down his cheek. "I'd say at least a year," he answers thoughtfully. "But I'd also caution you that exactly three hundred and sixty-five days would look odd if that's when your husband mysteriously dies or divorces you."

I should be repulsed that Remus obviously doesn't care if I kill my husband, not as long as it doesn't look suspicious. Yet all I can think about is when it won't look off anymore. Is that at the thirteen month mark? Fourteen? Who can really tell.

"What happens if I run?" I ask, immediately slapping my hand over my mouth. That wasn't even a real question. Just an errant thought my stupid brain decided to give voice.

"Don't test me, and you won't have to find out," Remus answers darkly without missing a beat. "Oh, and before I forget, Fabian wanted me to give you a present." Snapping his fingers, Remus waits for his guard to step closer, holding a small box in his hand.

"What is it?" I ask, physically flinching as he pushes the box toward me.

"Open it and find out."

I vehemently shake my head. "No, I'm good."

"Open it, Lucia," he growls, making it clear I don't have a choice.

Sighing, I remove the lid with shaky fingers, and to my horror, nested inside the box is my wedding band. "Nope!" I whisper-yell in horror. "Take it back or throw it away. I don't want it."

I look around the table, and at the candlesticks that are almost burned all the way down, making the room darker. I don't know what time it is or how long I've been here. All I know is that I want to get as far away as possible. Even though I haven't been excused, I stand on trembling legs, gather my things, and leave. Only slightly surprised none of the guards or Remus stop me.

"One month, Lucia," my cousin calls after me.

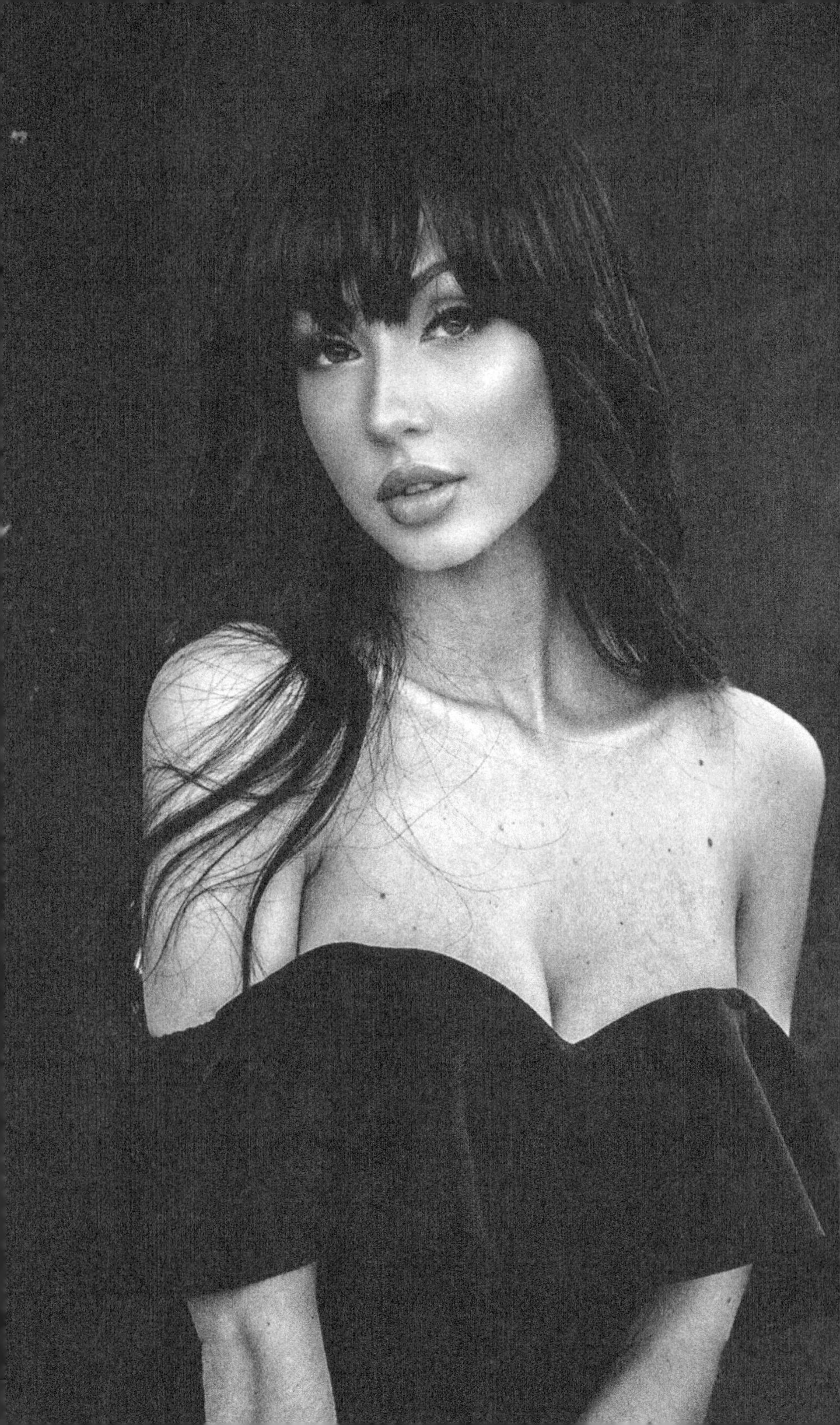

CHAPTER 6

Lucia

The deadline reverberates and plays on an endless loop in my head. One month... one month... one month...

Knowing that Fabian and the Senate are involved, I can't just hire someone to be my fake husband. I need to get married for real. Since that's what it takes to win my freedom, I'll do it in a heartbeat. I don't even have any scruples about condemning someone in the eyes of the Russo Mafia.

I've never claimed to be a good person, and I'm sure as hell not going to start lying to myself about it now. I'm selfish, entitled, and stubborn. Not exactly endearing or attractive qualities, but that's neither here nor there right now.

As soon as I'm in my car and have put a few miles between myself and Remus, I pull my phone out of my pocket and text Gail.

Me: Soooo... tequila? I really fucking need it.

Gail: You got it, girl. @O'Jackie's?

Me: Where else? Be there in half an hour.

Gail: *kiss emoji*

I park across the street from the Irish pub Gail found last year. I can hear the music all the way over here, and there are drunk people hanging out around the doors. A part of me envies them for their alcohol fused state of mind, and the fact that they have no inhibitions. At least the one peeing while facing the street doesn't. He doesn't care about the people pointing and glaring, and that's what I want. Not to pee in the street, but to reach that level of uncaring.

Entering the pub, I'm immediately hit with the smell of beer—or pints—sweat, and perfume. The latter is so potent, I can taste it on my tongue when I spot Gail at the bar and call her name. She doesn't hear me above the loud music, so I push through the throng of people to get to her.

"Hey buttercup," she squeals. Spinning on the bar stool, she pulls me in for a hug. "I ordered some shots for us, but since it took you so long to get here—"

"They're all gone," I say, finishing her sentence with a smile. "I'll get us more."

I know my bestie, and the time it took me to get here isn't why the small glasses are empty. She loves tequila and letting loose on the weekends. So even if I'd materialized one minute after texting her, there's a good chance she still would've emptied them.

"I looove your dress," she coos, dragging out the word like it has way more than two vowels. "It's funky."

Looking down at myself, I run a hand down the skirt. "It's…" Not knowing how to explain it, I stop talking. To me it looks close enough to a normal dress. The seams give the effect of it being wrapped around my body rather than zipped close at the side, which is the current trend in some of the fashion houses.

"No, seriously," Gail gushes. "It's fucking awesome. Where the hell did you buy it? It looks like a designer dress."

Oh… so maybe I was right in my assessment of the dress. "It's just something my uncle gave me, so it seemed fitting to wear it today," I say, hoping that's enough of an explanation.

Gail doesn't ask anymore questions, instead she puts all her attention into trying to grab the bartender's attention. "Helloooo," she shouts, waving her empty shot glass around in the air. When he waves her off and points at the people he's serving, she turns around with a pout. "Well, this is going to take forever… oh wait." She grabs my arm and points at an empty table.

"Go get it," I laugh.

Wasting no time, Gail runs to the table, pushing two other women out of her way when they try to claim the table as theirs. This is so her; nice teacher by day, determined drunk on the weekends.

As the bartender places a line of shot glasses on the counter, I snatch the first two he fills and ask for a refill. I need the liquid courage so much I do a third one, ignoring his arched eyebrow and playful smile.

"Thirsty?" he asks, and I nod while forcing a smile I don't feel.

After paying for more shots and drinks than what's good for either of us, I gesture at the table Gail's guarding and ask the bartender to help me get the drinks over there. After looking me up and down, he licks his lips and agrees.

Reaching Gail, I place two Cosmopolitans I'm carrying on the table. She frowns, but it's immediately turned upside down when she spots the tray the bartender carries. "Ohhh," she coos and claps. "Are all those for us?"

I tip the bartender and thank him before sitting down. Then I reach for another two shots, downing them before answering Gail. "I don't know how many you're seeing," I say, wincing as the alcohol burns down my throat, warming my stomach. "But yes. Fucking cheers." Without pausing, I take another two.

There we go. Now I'm no longer feeling anxious, and I can finally breathe.

"Wow," Gail grins. "Guess the lunch with your cousin didn't go well?"

I grimace. "Actually, it wasn't bad. It was... as expected." When Gail's eyes soften and she takes my hand, I shake my head. "Don't."

"Don't what?" she asks with a puzzled expression on her face.

"Whatever that look is, don't. I don't want to talk about my fucked up family."

I watch as Gail takes two shots, emptying the small glasses in record time. "So what do you want to talk about, cupcake? The financial views? World hunger?" She winks. "Or maybe you want to tell me why you keep looking at the bartender?"

"Am not," I deny half-heartedly even though there's no point. I was definitely checking him out, but not for the reasons she thinks. "I'm looking for a potential husband," I admit.

Gail snorts so hard I'm almost concerned for her. "Sure, sure."

I take a moment to consider whether telling her is a good idea or not. The thing is, I already know it isn't, but I also know I have to. I can't just suddenly show up with a husband in tow and no explanation, and since I'm determined to buy my freedom with a wedding band, there's no way around it. This definitely calls for more alcohol.

"I'm not joking," I say after emptying my first Cosmopolitan. Gail doesn't know what the hell she's missing by declaring vodka her enemy. "I need to get married before my cousin forces me back to Rome in a month. And that can't happen. Because if I go back, I'll be forced back together with my husband."

Gail rears back, looking like I just slapped her. "Rome? Husband? Luce, what the fuck?" she whispers, horrified. Fuck, did I really just say that out loud? "I thought you were single and from fucking Kansas."

I avert my gaze, embarrassed I just blurted it out like that. Though I never meant to tell her where I'm really from, if I did, she deserved to be told in a better way. Then again, how the hell do you dress up the fact you've lied to your best friend for years?

Clearing my throat, I lamely say, "Yeah, well. I'm not." If it wasn't for the alcohol coursing through my veins, I would never have slipped up. Fuck, I feel terrible. But there are too many lies for me to allow *one* to ruin the evening. "I made a deal with my uncle one year before I came to America. And that year was spent teaching me to blend in as an American," I explain.

"What?"

Maybe it wasn't as much of an explanation as I thought. I wince at the shocked look on Gail's face. Reaching for the liquid courage on the table, I do another shot. "Okay, here goes," I mumble. "I made a deal with my uncle to get away from my psycho husband, and part of the deal to come here was to get rid of my accent, understand the culture, and all those things."

"But why?"

I shrug. "I never asked, but I assume it was to avoid drawing attention to myself."

Gail makes a frustrated sound. "Are you intentionally being a bitch right now?"

Shame makes it hard to look at her. "No. I'm trying to explain—"

"Well, you're not doing a good job," she shouts. "What the actual hell, Luce?"

I quickly look around, wanting to make sure we aren't drawing attention to ourselves. Of course, we're not. In the crowded and loud pub, we're just another two women talking at a table.

"Why did you lie to me?" Gail continues, sounding like she's on the verge of crying.

"Because I had to," I answer, regret lacing my words. "I didn't want to. There have been so many times where I wanted to tell you the truth, but I couldn't, Gail. If you knew... no. I just couldn't."

She hasn't removed her hand from mine, still squeezing it as she scrutinizes me. I wish I knew what she's seeing on my face. Am I like a stranger to her now?

"So when you went to your uncle's funeral, you went to—"

"Rome," I clarify.

Gail huffs. "At least that explains the tan you came back with. Did you see your husband?"

I wince at the mention of Fabian. "Only from a distance. We haven't talked in almost ten years and that's how I want to keep it."

We both fall silent. I imagine Gail's thoughts are running like crazy, and I... well, I don't fucking know what to say. This is one big clusterfuck. Sure, it's of my own making, but that doesn't mean I have the answers.

"Ten years," Gail mumbles, narrowing her eyes like she's trying to do complex math. "How old were you when you got married, Luce?"

I swallow and look everywhere but at my best friend. "I don't want to talk about it." My tone is as small as I feel. "Not tonight. Please."

Although she nods, I can see Gail is hurt by my continued refusal to talk to her about it. "Fine," she finally agrees.

"I wanted to tell you," I admit. "There have been so many times where I almost blurted it out. But I couldn't, Gail. And I need you to understand I never liked lying to you." My words are rushed, spurred on by the soul-deep need for her to hear me—believe me.

Gail lets go of my hand and helps herself to a shot. "I'm so fucking glad I'm drunk right now," she says, wiping her hand across her lips. "I don't think I'd still be here if I was sober. So let's get it all out in the open now, Luce. What's really going on? Why's your cousin here? What does it all mean? And why are you really telling me now?"

I lean back in the chair, pondering which question to start with. "Okay, so you want complete honesty?"

She nods. "I do. Don't hold anything back."

Exhaling slowly, I meet her gaze. "Remember a few years ago when it seemed like there was a lot of shit going on all over the world at the same time? You said it seemed weird that there were royal weddings, huge celebrity scandals, and the Pope showed himself in public areas of the Vatican—"

"Yeah, I remember. We were texting about it while you were visiting your family in Kan... well, I guess Rome." Gail tilts her head to the side. "Wait, where are you going with this?"

Leaning closer to her, I lower my voice. "It was set up by my family. Something big was happening. That was when two of my cousins were chosen to be the next in line to run our family."

"No fucking way. You're joking. This can't be..."

"Can't be what?" I ask when she stops talking. "Listen, this isn't something we can ever speak about again. You're not even supposed to know, Gail. So you might as well get all your questions out now."

I hate that I can't give her the time to digest the news properly. She deserves time to ask for a timeout, even mull it over for days, weeks, or months if she needs to. But there's no way. Not just because of my own deadline, but because she has to let it go after tonight. We can't ever talk about this again for her safety. I'm a fucking terrible friend.

"This is so fucked up," she murmurs. I'm not sure if she's talking to me or making an observation, so I don't say anything. Gail takes a deep, shuddering breath. "Why are you telling me now, Luce?"

She's still calling me Luce, which I take as a good sign. "Honestly, I didn't mean to," I admit, determined to remain honest. "But my cousin's visit fucked with my head, and—"

"And the alcohol isn't helping," Gail says, finishing my sentence. "Okay, so let me make sure I have this straight. You come from some kind of fucked up Mafia-like family who basically runs the world. You have secrets that'll take us years to uncover and discuss, and now you need to get married to keep your freedom from said Mafia family and your husband. Is that about the gist of it?"

I can't help it. I burst out laughing at the simple way she's managed to sum it all up. "That's it," I hiccup. Laughing when you don't feel an inch of happiness is weird. It's wrong, it's illogical, but it's all I can do not to succumb to the darker emotions swirling inside me. "That's it," I confirm again with a sharp nod. Shit, I shouldn't have done that. My vision is slowly becoming blurry, and my words slurred as the alcohol takes root.

"But... like... how are you planning on marrying when you're already married?"

I asked Remus the same thing, so I repeat what he told me. "My cousin is the only one allowed to perform the ceremony. So he'll prepare some papers ahead of time, granting me the divorce just before I get re-married."

"Okay. Well, I want to make three things very clear. The first is that I'm so fucking pissed at you. The second is that I need time to sort through the messed up knowledge bomb you just dropped on me." I flinch at the harsh tone Gail's using.

"What's the third?" I ask, scared to hear the answer.

Without warning, Gail gets up and moves to my side of the table. She pulls me in for a hug. "I love you, Luce. You're my sister from another mister, and no amount of secret identity shit is going to ruin that. So I'm going to help you find a fucking husband. Because if you leave, you can't make it up to me."

I hug her back, practically clinging to her as tears stream down my face. "I love you, too, Gail. And I'm so sorry."

"I know," she says, tightening her hold on me. "But you're still going to make it up to me for the rest of our lives. And the next time I want the last egg roll, you'll give it to me without a fight." She might be making light of the situation by joking, but the tremor in her voice gives her away.

"Deal," I say, my voice cracking. "You can have all the egg rolls you want. On me."

Once we've both collected ourselves, Gail returns to her seat. "So when you say husband, you're not using some Italian slang I'm not familiar with, right?"

Though I know I shouldn't, I reach for the second Cosmopolitan and bring the black straw to my lips. God, this really is the stuff dreams are made of. "Not even a little," I say.

"Right," Gail muses. "So you want to convince your all-powerful Mafia family that you're in love? And all this is despite never dating anyone for more than a good dicking, and—"

I cut her off by waving my hand in front of her. "I don't need love or sex. Just a husband," I clarify. "But I told my cousin I'm engaged. Even if I wanted to, I can't go back on that now." This is stupid. Remus knows I was lying. I need to let this go and stick to mentally berating myself for such a stupid lie.

Gail's lips twitch and a wry smile spreads across her face. "Cool, cool. So how do you want to approach this? You could always have a one-night-stand and 'forget' the condom. Trap the guy the ol' fashioned way." I make a derisive sound while rolling my eyes. "Or we can troll the hospital's amnesia ward to find someone handsome and single."

"Really?" I say, dryly. "Those are your best ideas?"

"No," she shoots back. "Those are my fucking desperate ideas. What the fuck, Luce. It's not like you're giving me a lot to work with."

I'm just about to tell her I'm all too aware of how fucked up my situation is when a commotion near the bar steals my focus. "What the?" I ask, perplexed, when I see Sawyer Perry approaching the bar alone.

Gail turns in her chair, following my gaze. "Hey, isn't that Sawyer?" she asks without looking back at me. "Speaking of, have you found his fake girlfriend yet?"

I sit straighter, immediately scanning the area to see if there's a need for me to make myself known to Sawyer. He looks relaxed, but not drunk or like he's done something he shouldn't. I can't help but notice the way his washed-out jeans hug his ass, and his dark shirt that looks like it's working overtime to keep his torso contained. His shoulder length, curly hair is in a bun, and his beard is neatly groomed, emphasizing his chiseled jaw. There really is no denying he's beyond ruggedly handsome. He's sex on a pair of very long and heavily muscled legs.

"Hello... earth to Luce," Gail says, snapping her fingers in my face.

"What?" I ask, only half paying attention as I keep my eyes peeled on the player.

"I asked if there was an update on Sawyer."

"Umm..." I shake my head to clear my thoughts. "I don't know. I wasn't at work today," I say, wondering how she could have forgotten.

Gail smiles shyly. "I know that. But Luce, if there was an update, wouldn't someone have made sure you knew?"

"I guess."

"Sooo... if there isn't an update, couldn't you... you know..."

It takes me a moment to catch on to what she's saying, or rather, hinting at, since she's being annoyingly vague.

"He only needs to fake date someone for the season," I rush out. "I need someone for life. Well, not exactly. Just long enough to be considered a marriage." This is why I didn't want my name in the mix when Nick and I made the list of potential candidates to fake date Sawyer. I was adamant we kept my name away from the pool. But now... if I could... it's not marriage, but it would be a relationship, and a steady one at that. Fuck, I really shouldn't have turned down Nick's idea of adding myself to the mix.

"But marriage would be good for him as well, wouldn't it?" Gail continues. "Nothing says stability like being a loving and caring husband." There's no finesse, only urgency in her tone as she explains.

"Umm... say what?" I look at my friend with a puzzled expression on my face. "You want me to convince Mr. Anti-Relationship to get married?"

She shrugs. "Do you have any other options?"

"Plenty," I shoot back.

Gail tuts. "Be real, Luce. You're both in a desperate situation. So why not join forces since it'll clearly benefit the both of you?"

Though I want to argue it's a bad idea, I can't. Yes, it *is* a bad idea, but it's also the only idea. No matter how I look at it, the best way to go about this is to do it with someone that gains something from it as well. It would ensure we both stick to our part of the deal, and for Sawyer, it would *look* good.

Gail pushes another shot toward me. "Well, go get him, buttercup," she says. Then she takes one for herself, and we clink the glasses together before downing the alcohol that now tastes like ash and regret.

The way I wobble has nothing to do with nerves, and everything to do with the copious amounts of alcohol I've consumed since getting here. Fuck, I almost think I'm... nope, strike that. I'm most definitely seeing double. I tell myself it's for the best, because when the alcohol goes in, reason goes out. And I don't need a sound mind in order to proposition Sawyer Perry.

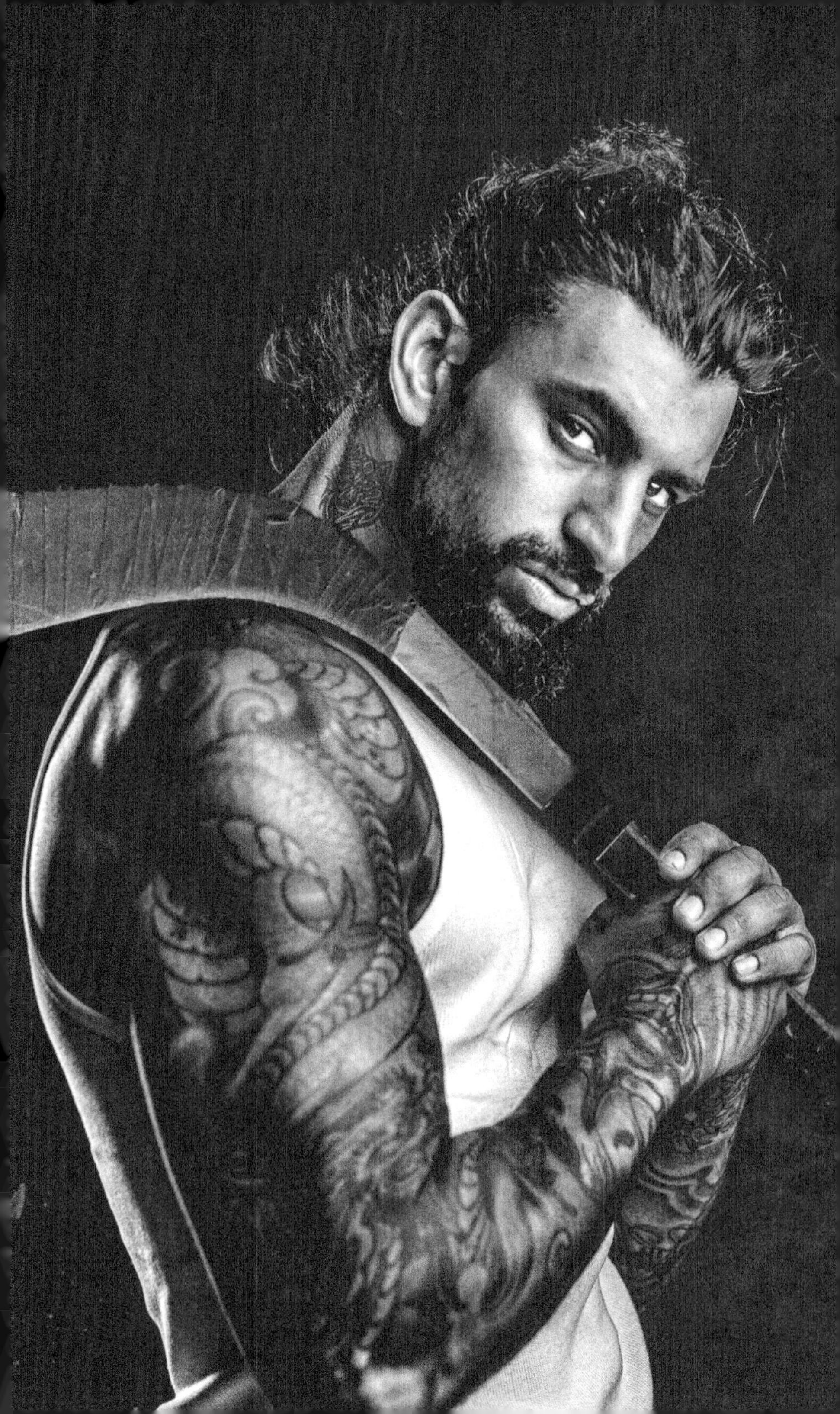

CHAPTER

7

Sawyer

It's been a long fucking day. I'm not used to going entire days without practice and weight training with the guys. Sure, I worked out in my home gym, but that's not the same. So by now, I'm going a little stir crazy. Thank fuck it's Friday. Tomorrow I can return to the rink, and it can't come soon enough. Tom said I could return yesterday if I wanted, but after my dinner with Soren and Mickey, I agreed it might be better to wait until tomorrow.

Fuck, I was so desperate for something to do that I even answered my mom's call. The irony of me talking to the woman who's directly responsible for making cheating such a hardcore trigger for me isn't lost on me. One hour of agony while listening to her tells me how selfish I am for not calling enough, visiting enough, and that I don't show an interest in her new family. Cry me a fucking river.

Just because she eventually married one of the guys whose dick was more important than our family doesn't mean I have to be part of it. Especially not on Thanksgiving.

When I couldn't take her whining anymore, I reminded her that I gave my half-brother a trust fund that basically covers his college tuition for his fifth birthday, and the house they all live in was also a present from me. You'd think that would earn me a thank you, right? Wrong. Apparently, that just shows how little I care.

She isn't wrong; I don't care. Those were obligation gifts and nothing else. A thank you would still be nice. But that's not how my mom operates. She used the guilt as an excuse to try to make me come for Thanksgiving next month. Although I don't see that fucking happening, I ended up promising I'd think about it. I suppose I'm keeping my promise since I am in fact thinking about it right now—contemplating when I should text her to let her know I'm not coming.

It's obviously too soon to do it right now. Maybe the week of or a few days before. I pull my phone out and make a calendar reminder for Monday the twentieth of November, so I don't forget to cancel. There, familial obligations are sorted.

My idea of celebrating Thanksgiving is with some fancy bourbon and a puck bunny or two. Sheesh, this year I'll probably have to at least pretend to be with Lucia. Or maybe I can convince Tom it's enough to bring her to the annual Sabertooths event.

Tom usually does a big family thing the weekend before for all the players, coaches, and our families. Mickey and I are usually the only ones who show up alone, but with everyone else there, it doesn't feel odd. We're one big family and everyone shares. Hell, Soren's Nana insists we all call her that. She's an awesome woman with a penchant for cheating in cards.

"Why the long face, lad?" Jackie asks as she comes into the backroom I'm occupying by myself. "And don't tell me it was the food. I'm an outstanding cook." Her eyes light up as she eyes my empty plate.

"There was nothing wrong with the food," I say, forcing a smile.

"Then it has to be the company."

I bark out a laugh at the accuracy and bluntness of her remark. "That's one way to put it." She isn't wrong since I'm sitting alone and it's my fucking choices and thoughts that are dragging me down.

Jackie starts placing my plate and cutlery on the tray, taking her time. "Maybe you should go out there and be around other people, lad," she suggests. "It would do you some good, you know."

"Maybe," I allow.

"Ain't no maybe about it, lad. Do as Jackie says."

I shake my head and get up. "Thanks for the food, Jackie," I say before placing a kiss on her cheek. "It was delicious, as always."

She scoffs and mumbles, "Like I need you to tell me what I already know. My food is outstanding." But the softness in her eyes and smile tugging at the corner of her lips show just how much she likes her food being praised.

I throw some bills on the table, grossly overpaying for my meal. Then I walk out of the private room before she can give me a lecture about not wanting the tip. It's the same song and dance every time.

There are only a few people sitting at the bar, neither of which pay me any attention as I sit down at the end. After getting a beer from the bartender who did a double-take as he saw me, I study the surrounding people. The pub grows louder and becomes more crowded by the minute. People are shouting, swaying to the music, and just having a great time.

I'm about to head home when I see Lucia walk up to the bar, only a few feet from where I'm sitting. I quickly turn my head in the other direction, not wanting her to see me. The dark window I'm facing shows me her reflection, and I grit my teeth as she hugs who I assume to be a friend. I clench the bottle tighter, pissed that she's enjoying herself when I'm not allowed to.

As her friend drunkenly darts off, I continue to watch Lucia while she waits to be served. She looks as perfect as always, but there's something in the depth of her eyes. An uneasiness, or maybe it's desperation? Ah, fuck it. I don't know her well enough to guess. For all I know, she's unhappy because she chipped a nail or some shit like that.

When she leaves with more alcohol than I ever thought someone of her size could drink, I chuckle. Looks like Miss Perfect might be worth watching for an hour or so. I might get my first glance at who Lucia is without her guard up.

My luck of not getting noticed lasts for a couple of hours, all of which I spend discreetly eyeing Lucia and her friend. Now that I think about it, I think I've seen her before at some of our games. But when a woman bumps into me and spills her drink on my arm, I forget to keep my head down and she lets out a shriek. "Oh my God, you're Sawyer Perry."

I smile indulgently. "Sorry, did my arm get in the way?"

She laughs nervously. "No, that was all me. I was... I mean... holy shit. You're Sawyer Perry."

By now, her loud shrieks have gathered the attention of the surrounding people, and they start closing in. "It is you," a guy says. "I thought it was, but I wasn't sure. Look, man, what happened to you was bullshit."

"Yeah, you should have punched the dude harder," another adds.

"Did you really sleep with his wife?" the girl who spilled her drink on me asks, flicking her long, blonde hair over her shoulder.

"What does it matter?" the first guy says. "You should never blame the third party, since they didn't make any vows."

The conversation about me continues to flow around me. No one is looking for me to say anything. They just carry on discussing my life like it's the juiciest gossip, and maybe it is.

"Let me buy you another beer as an apology," the blonde croons, running her hand up my wet sleeve until she's running her fingers across my jaw.

I shake my head. "That's not necessary. In fact, I was just about to leave—"

"Aww, do you really have to go right now?" she purrs, batting her lashes so much it looks like she's suffering through a fucking seizure. Jesus. "And here I thought things were about to get interesting."

I force a laugh. "Well, in that case, I'm sorry to disappoint you..." I trail off when she stands straighter and moves so close I feel her tit rub against my arm. My dick doesn't even twitch.

"What do you want?" she asks, her tone no longer playful. It's fucking colder than ice as she looks at someone or something over my shoulder.

As I turn, I come face-to-face with none other than my soon to be fake girlfriend, according to Tom. "Get your hands off him," she seethes, meeting the blonde's icy stare with one of her own. "Sawyer isn't yours to touch."

What the actual fuck? Our fake as fuck relationship doesn't begin until Monday, so she has no right to stir up unnecessary drama. "Watch yourself," I growl.

The blonde laughs and tosses her long strands over her bare shoulder. "He isn't yours, either. So why don't you scurry along and let the pretty people talk?"

Lucia doesn't seem fazed at all as she combs her fingers through her deep red hair and plasters herself to my other side. "You're wrong about that," she says matter-of-factly. "Sawyer's mine. So get your filthy paws off him."

The blonde takes a few steps back, then she thinks better of it and looks at me. "Is that true?"

Fuck Lucia Carter. Fuck Tom Redding. Fuck the fucking deal I already hate. Just... fuck it all. It's not like I can say no and then publicly claim her as my girlfriend on Monday.

Judging by the canary-like smile on Lucia's plump lips, she's all too aware of the wall she's backed me up against. And that shit pisses me off.

Despite wanting to push her away, I throw my arm around Lucia's shoulder and pull her closer. "Yeah. This is Lucia." I swallow. "My girlfriend."

The blonde rears back, looking like I called her a dirty name. "Oh." That's all she says. Then she tilts her head to the side. "I guess congratulations are in order." With those words, she turns on her heel and walks away.

I give her a tight smile and watch her walk off. Now that Lucia's here, the crowd around me backs off, giving us some space. I place my lips against Lucia's ear and whisper, "What the fuck do you think you're doing?"

She shivers, looking up at me through hazy eyes. "I need you to pick me." She says it like it's a normal fucking request or response. "I know Tom is the one making the official decision, but I *need* it to be me."

I arch an eyebrow. "What do you mean, it *has* to be you?" I ask brusquely. As she sways on her heels and narrows her eyes like she's having a hard time focusing, I realize that she's beyond fucking drunk, but is she drunk enough to forget Tom already picked her? That makes no sense.

Lucia licks her lips. "I'm not fucking stuttering, Sawyer. We both know Tom's giving you a fake girlfriend, and I'm saying I need that to be me."

Oh, for fuck's sake. This chick is batshit crazy. "I'm not discussing it here," I bark. I turn to look at the table she was sitting at with her friend, but it's empty now. "Come on." Still with my arm around her, I drag her out of the pub.

"Where are we going?" she slurs, nearly stumbling for the fifth time.

As much as I want to just take off, I can't leave her here alone. She's too drunk for her own good, and I just publicly claimed her. So at the very least, I have to make sure she gets home safely. "Taking you home," I answer curtly. She doesn't protest when I help her into the passenger seat in my car, or when I secure the seat belt.

"I like my home," she breathes. "It's nice and I don't want to lose it."

Slamming the door closed, I walk around and get into the driver's seat. It can't take more than a few minutes at most before I have the car started, but Lucia's fast asleep. I nudge her. "Hey," I say. "Wake up. I need your address."

She sits up straighter, looking at me from beneath her long, dark eyelashes. "I live at home." She frowns, like my question is strange. "That's where I live." Her words are so slurred there's a good chance she said something else, but I'm pretty sure none of her words included an address.

"Oh, yeah?" I ask. "Where is that?"

"Where's what? Oh, can we get a taco? I like tacos. And cheese. And..." Her head thuds against the window and her snores start up again.

Fuck me. What am I supposed to do with her now? I can't just fucking leave her here. And I can't call Tom for her address. With a growl, I pull out of the parking spot and head home. She can sleep it off in one of my guest rooms, and then I can grill her tomorrow.

Carrying a sleeping, drunk woman into my home isn't something I've ever done before, and I'm not happy about doing it now. Especially not when I know the entire building is covered with security cameras. Maybe I should try to get them to erase the footage so it doesn't look like... who cares? I'm sick of fucking caring.

After getting us inside, I carry Lucia to my guest room and place her so she's lying on her side. She doesn't stir once; not when I remove her shoes, or when I throw the cover over her. Maybe a better person would wake her up and offer her a shirt to sleep in. But that's not me. I don't care about her comfort.

That's what I keep telling myself as I leave her and head toward my bedroom and get ready for bed. As I lie down, images of her choking in her sleep spring to mind. With a curse, I get back out of bed and go to join her in the guest room. I'm only wearing my boxer briefs, but it's all I need because I do care about *my* comfort.

I groan, winding my fingers into the hair of the puck bunny, swallowing my cock. Her mouth is fucking incredible. "Fu-uuck."

"That's it," she mumbles around my length. "Let me make this easy for you."

Throwing my arm across my eyes, I let her suck me. It feels fucking good. Who did I bring home last night? Wait a second... I went to Jackie's, where I only had one beer. I didn't hook up with anyone and definitely didn't bring anyone home with me... "Lucia!"

Pulling on her hair until her mouth pops off my dick. "Why did you stop me?" she whines.

I reach for the light on the nightstand and switch it on. Lucia's on all fours between my legs, her head tilted awkwardly to the side due to the way I'm pulling on her hair. "What the fuck do you think you're doing?" I seethe.

"Showing you how good it'll be if you pick me," she purrs. "I won't deny you anything, Sawyer."

I groan again, but this time it isn't from pleasure. What fucking game is she playing? "And you thought sucking me off in my sleep was the perfect way to audition?"

She quirks an eyebrow. "Are you saying you aren't enjoying it?"

Laughing darkly, I sit up so I can look down on her. "I'll be asking the questions." She gulps. "What made you think I wanted you to suck my cock? That it was okay for you to do it while I was sleeping?" It's not like I wasn't enjoying it. My dream was hot as fuck, and what man doesn't like waking up by getting their dick serviced?

Instead of looking contrite or embarrassed, Lucia rolls her eyes. "Everyone likes getting blown, Sawyer. And you didn't get your reputation by being chaste."

Smiling coldly, I tighten my hand in her hair. "Doesn't mean I want you touching me."

She whimpers in pain. "Your cock seems to like me."

"It's been a while," I admit. "Anyone could get me off right now. Doesn't make you special." The barb doesn't faze her. Letting go of her hair, I point at my still hard cock. "Get down on the floor and finish what you started."

While Lucia willingly crawls off the bed and onto the floor, I scoot to the end of the bed and spread my legs wide so she can sit between them. She's still wearing her tight dress, her hair is in disarray, and some of her makeup is smudged around her eyes. The imperfections make her look sexy as hell.

"Does this mean you'll convince Tom to pick me?" she asks, her voice small like she hates asking.

"Why should I?" I ask, slightly amused we're both overlooking the fact that Tom already picked her, and I confirmed our relationship status to the blonde who could have posted it online for all we know. Or maybe Lucia doesn't remember. God, I hope that's the case. I fucking hope she's begging for something she doesn't know she already has.

Lucia leans closer and licks her lips. "It doesn't matter why. All that matters is that I need it. So name your price."

I snort. "Are you fucking for real?"

"I am," she confirms. "But I don't expect you to choose me as a favor. I'm willing to pay for it."

For fuck's sake, she's making it sound like it's my choice. "So I ask again, why should I?" When she doesn't answer, I decide to press her further. "If you want me to pick you, you need to sweeten the deal. Convince me."

"What do you want?" she asks, throwing her arms up in the air. "Just name your price."

Hmm, she's fucking desperate, and I'm just horny enough that I need to see how far she's willing to go. "Finish sucking me off," I smirk. "If you give good head, I'll recommend that Tom pick you. If not, well, then you're shit out of luck."

To my surprise, she doesn't even blink as she nods. "You want regular blowjobs to be part of the deal? Anything else?"

I smirk down at her. "Why don't you tell me what's off limits?" I run a finger through the precum gathered on my slit and wipe it across her lips. "And if you mention anything I want, there's no deal."

Lucia looks up at me while licking her lips. Fuck if the desperate look in her eyes and pink tongue wetting her lips isn't making me even harder. "Let's get one thing straight, Sawyer. I don't have any fucking limits. I *need* this. So if you want sex to be part of the deal, I'm okay with that." She pauses, swallowing. "Now that I think about it, it's probably for the best. Our relationship needs to seem one thousand percent real, which means you can't discreetly fuck someone else."

Well, color me fucking surprised. Something's driving Lucia, something or someone who is worse than being stuck and used in a fake relationship. I'm officially harder and more intrigued than I've ever been. A dark need I haven't felt in a long time stirs inside me. Her words are breathing life into it, and for a second I consider putting words to it to see how far she's willing to go.

"So, if I want you to make me come daily?" I ask, arching my eyebrow.

Rather than shying away from the challenge, Lucia cups my cock. "Then I'll make you come once a day."

Hmm, could I ask her to give me what I crave? "And if I want to fuck you once a day?"

She tightens her grip on my cock. "Then I'll let you fuck me. Make no mistake, Sawyer. I'm not backing down. So make a list if you want to, and I'll make sure to fulfill every single fucking item on it. But in return, you're going to be my boyfriend for thirteen months."

I let out a surprised laugh, all thoughts about my dark kinks forgotten. "No way. Tom said it was only for this season."

She rolls her eyes and starts to move her hand up and down my shaft. "Come on," she purrs. "I know you're smarter than this, Sawyer. Everyone will see through it if it's only for the duration of the season. But for longer... it'll look more real."

A groan bubbles up my throat as she increases her pace. Fuck me, this woman is trouble. "You have a point." And she does. When you decide to live in an elaborate lie, it looks better if it seems random. A year and one month means it's a random as fuck date rather than one that's benchmarked by a big event. "Is that your only demand?" I rasp, doing my best to remain alert despite the way she's working my cock.

"As long as it looks real and you don't cheat on me, I'll do whatever you want." Her expression is all business, which is turning me on even more. These aren't the actions of a meek girl, this is a determined woman, and I'm going to take full advantage of it.

"Hmm," I hum, pretending to think about it. I move my hand, slowly sliding it up her back until I wrap it around her neck, and then I add pressure. "You say all the right things which tells me you actually want this. What are you hiding, Lucia?"

"Nothing that concerns you," she volleys, tightening her hold on my cock. "I've told you everything you need to know."

There we go; the devil is in the details, and Lucia Carter apparently has loose lips when there's alcohol in her system. She might as well have said there's a lot she doesn't want to tell me. From my previous interactions with her, I know she's usually composed, and I've never once heard her slip up like that.

"So let me get this straight," I rasp, letting my suspicions go for now. "You're basically offering me anything I want, your body included, to be my fake girlfriend?"

"Yes," she breathes, still stroking my cock.

"Prove it," I challenge. "Open your mouth."

I'm not surprised when her lips part, forming an O. I move my hand from her neck to her chin, holding her still. Then I lean forward while gathering some spit and slowly let it drip from my mouth into hers. To her credit, Lucia doesn't flinch or try to move away. She kneels there, taking it without complaining. Maybe she doesn't think I see the spark of anger flashing in her eyes, but I do. And it's fucking glorious.

"Good girl," I praise, squeezing her chin. "Suck me off, and I promise I'll talk to Tom about picking you."

"I want your word," Lucia demands. It comes out slightly muffled, since I'm still holding her chin.

"You got it," I smirk. "If you can make me come in three minutes or less, I'll call Tom as soon as you've swallowed my jizz."

Rather than challenging me, Lucia looks up at me while her lips almost graze the tip. "I only need two minutes." When I arch a brow, she shrugs. "Go ahead and time me. See how long it'll take until I've swallowed it all."

Because I'm a curious asshole, I reach for my phone and pull it out from under the pillow. I start the timer. "Let's see how skilled that mouth of yours really is," I rasp. I want to say more, but I lose the ability to think of ways to taunt her when she licks along my shaft. Reaching the head, she swirls her tongue around my slit, making it impossible to keep my groan in, and she smiles in response.

"Thirty seconds gone," I rasp.

Lucia guides my cock into her mouth. She wraps her lips around the tip, swirling her tongue around it as she gently cups my balls, rolling them in her hand. I try my hardest to keep my groans inside, not wanting her to know just how fucking amazing her mouth feels.

Without warning, she eagerly sucks me all the way to the back, and when I hit her throat, she doesn't pause. She picks up the pace, using her mouth to fuck me while digging her long nails into my ass cheeks.

"Fuck," I groan, moving my hand to the back of her neck.

Lucia continues to bob her head, bringing me closer to the edge with every fucking movement. I close my eyes and tangle my fingers in her red locks, pulling her closer until I'm completely inside her hot little mouth.

I growl as she sucks, swirls, and jerks me off at the same time. Oh, fuck me, it's incredible. Lucia moves faster, and it only takes a few moments before my balls tighten as pleasure shoots up my spine.

"Fuck. Fuck. Fuck." I groan the word over and over as I shoot my cum deep in her throat. "So fucking good."

I don't move until I'm spent, my cock softening in her mouth. Before pulling out, I check the phone clutched in my hand. "One minute and fifty-seven seconds," I chuckle, feeling impressed. Lucia remains on her knees while shuffling backward, and I watch her as I stand up. "Did you swallow?" I ask.

She opens her mouth wide and sticks her tongue out, showing me she did. "I said I would," she says, not at all sounding bothered by what happened.

Well, that's about to change. "Good. I'll call Tom now." Even though it's the middle of the night, I stay true to my word. I scroll through my contacts until I find him. Then I tap the phone icon and put the call on speaker.

"What?" Tom barks. "Don't tell me you're backing out."

My smirk grows as I lock eyes with Lucia. "Not at all," I confirm. "I just called to say I'm glad you picked Lucia Carter. I think she's an excellent choice." At my words, she gasps softly, and her eyes harden as she gracefully gets up from the floor.

"Glad to hear it," Tom says sarcastically. "Now, if there's nothing else, I'm going back to sleep."

The moment Tom hangs up, Lucia slaps me across the cheek. "Tom had already picked?" she asks, anger dripping from her tone.

"He did," I confirm.

"You fucking bastard," she hisses. "I would have done anything you asked. There was literally no need to lie to me."

When she lifts her hand again, I slap it away. Then I advance on her, using my chest to force her against the wall. "You think you can manipulate me, Lucia? You're the one who lied. Tom sent that message days ago, and I don't fucking believe he didn't inform you as well."

"But I never put myself up as a candidate," she says, her tone calmer. "Why would he pick me?"

With a shrug, I wrap my hand around her throat. "You don't actually expect me to believe your bullshit, do you? Get it through your head, Lucia. No one manipulates me. Ever."

Rather than backing down, she straightens her spine. "What about our deal?"

I laugh darkly. "Oh, I always keep my promises. Thirteen months, Lucia. And unlimited access to your body. This will be fun."

She sends me a scathing look. "You fucking better. I don't appreciate being lied to," she hisses, causing me to smirk.

"I didn't lie," I grin. "I called Tom just as promised."

Arching a brow, she asks, "Why exactly am I here?"

I'm not sure why that wasn't her first question, or why she prioritized sucking me off before getting answers. Not that I'm complaining since it turned out with me coming in her mouth. "You don't remember falling asleep in my car?" She shakes her head. "Hmm, okay. Well, you were at O'Jackie's with a friend and when you saw me, you came up to me and chased some blonde away—"

"Oh," she gasps, looking around while sucking her bottom lip between her teeth. "I remember now. You said you were going to take me home."

"I did," I agree. "But you fell asleep before you could give me your address, so here we are."

She nods, seemingly accepting the way things played out. Since she isn't questioning why we're in the same bed, I see no need to fill in her blanks. "I guess I should get going," she laughs nervously.

"No," I say, and her head snaps up. Her mouth opens, ready to argue, but I continue before she can say anything. "You can't leave my place in the middle of the night. You're my girlfriend, remember? We have pretenses to keep up. So you'll stay until I have practice, and I'll drop you off on the way."

She nods and looks down at her body. "I need a shower," she states. "And then I need to borrow some clothes. I can't leave in the same outfit I arrived in. Not if I spent my night at..." she makes air quotes with her fingers. "...my boyfriend's."

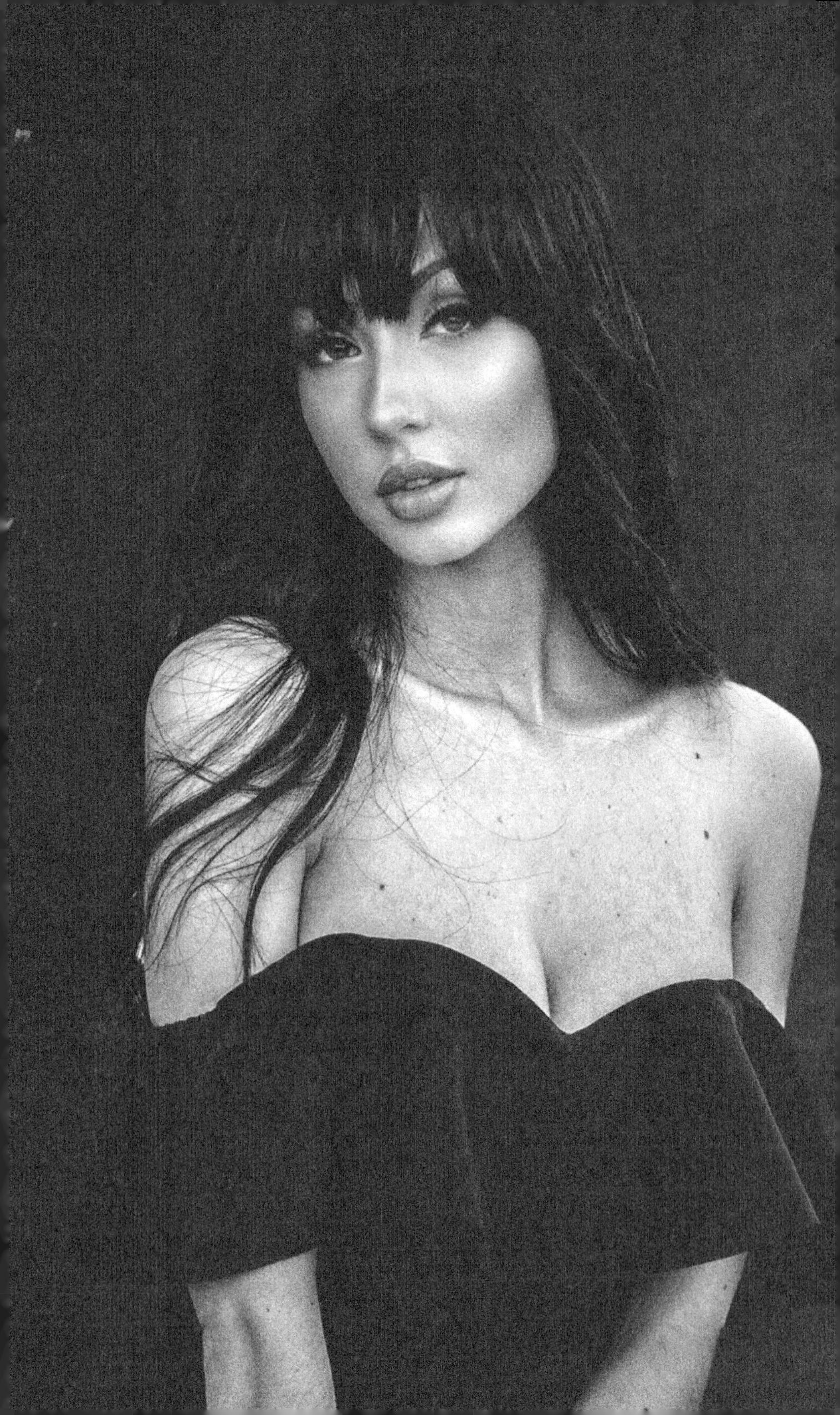

CHAPTER 8

Lucia

My head is pounding, and my throat feels like I've crossed the Sahara without having even the smallest sip of water for days. Seriously, my mouth is so dry my tongue sticks to the roof. This hangover of all hangovers might just kill me.

"Must you do that?" I hiss, staring pointedly at Sawyer's fingers as he drums them against the steering wheel.

"Do what?" he asks, amused.

I groan and squint my eyes. "Make that noise." How much did Gail and I drink last night? I don't think I've ever been this hungover before.

Yesterday is a blur of activities and broken memories. I remember meeting with Remus, what he said about the Senate and marriage. I even remember meeting Gail at O'Jackie's and seeing Sawyer. But it's more like I'm watching an old movie where some of the reel has been damaged, not giving me the complete picture.

I need much more sleep than the few hours I got at Sawyer's place. When I woke up and saw him next to me, I didn't even question it. The only thing I could think about was that it needed to be me, and that I'd do anything to make myself a better choice. So, yeah, I took his cock in my mouth. God, I wish I could blame the alcohol or an aneurysm. But the shameful truth is that I was just that desperate.

The drive isn't all that long. Yet it feels like an eternity as I suffer through the sun and sounds of traffic. When we're finally here, I thank him for the ride and get out of the car. I blink in confusion as Sawyer gets out as well. "What are you doing?" I ask, perplexed.

"Walking you in, of course," he states. Then he places his hand on the small of my back and walks so close our bodies brush against each other with each step. Warmth spreads where his hand is touching me, causing me to shiver.

I hate how good he looks and smells, like a fucking ad for healthy and clean living. Whereas I feel like death warmed over. It's not fair, and it's enough to make me rethink my stance on alcohol consumption.

The apartment I share with Gail is only on the second floor, so instead of using the shady looking and sounding elevator, we take the stairs. I walk up first, with Sawyer closely behind me. He keeps his hand on my back for the first set, but by the time we climb the last few stairs, it's fallen to my ass.

"This is me," I say, my back to the door as I fish my keys out of my coat pocket. Sawyer told me I didn't have my handbag or coat with me when he saw me last night, so we swung by O'Jackie's before he dropped me off. Apparently, he's tight with the owner, a grumpy-looking woman who looked like she had a lot to say to me, yet didn't even say hi. "Thanks for the ride. And umm... for getting me my things."

When a door opens below us, Sawyer moves closer. He grips my hips and shoves me against the wall. "Thank you

for the blowjob," he whispers against my ear. "I can't wait to repeat that."
His nearness overwhelms me, causing my breath to hitch. What can I say? Oh, it's fine. No worries. Thank you for letting me suck you dry... none of that sounds right. "Don't mention it."
His answering smirk is infuriatingly knowing. "I'll come pick you up after practice. Be ready for me," he rasps.
"What? Why?"
"Isn't that what couples do?" he asks, putting some distance between us. "Spend the weekend together."
"Yeah, but—"
He shakes his head. "No buts, Lucia. You wanted this. Now that you have it, you need to live up to your end of the deal."
His words penetrate my hazy brain, which is good, because I was on the verge of doing something stupid like turning my head and kissing him. "Fine," I sniff. "I'll see you later." With those words, I turn to unlock the door. "What the hell?" I gasp, shocked at what I see. There's white spray paint on our door, in the shape of a wolf's head. The way some of the paint has bled down the wood makes it look ominous.
"Did you do that?" Sawyer asks from behind me. "If you did, I wouldn't quit your day job just yet."
"N-no... it wasn't me," I say, running my hand over the dried paint. Fucking Remus and his not-so-subtle reminders.
I feel Sawyer's eyes burn into my back, but I refuse to turn around. I'm too tired, too hungover to deal with him right now. "See you later," he finally says, and I unlock the door and walk into my apartment, leaving him standing outside as I close the door without inviting him inside.
I lean against the door, not moving until I hear him descend the stairs. And only when he's gone does it feel like I can breathe freely again. I don't allow myself time to think about what I did, or how being picked to be Sawyer's fake

girlfriend is only step one. I have too far to go and can't lose sight of the big picture.

As I walk into my room, I find a note on the bed.

> Hi Luce,
>
> I'm so sorry to do this. But I can't... it's all too fucking much, you know? I need a few days to clear my head.
>
> So I'm going to my brother's.
>
> Please don't try to contact me.
>
> Love you, girl.
>
> Gail <3

Tears gather in my eyes as I read the note over and over, not letting the small piece of paper go until it's practically soaked from my tears. Gail. I should have gone home with her last night. I should have made sure she was okay with everything I told her.

Sighing, I wipe my eyes with the back of my hand. I can't lose my best friend, but I also can't risk losing my freedom. Right now, it feels like I'll push one away by pursuing the other, and I don't like that gnawing feeling in my gut.

After a quick shower, I get dressed in a pair of jeans and a white cashmere sweater. I throw my hair up in a messy bun and pull on a pair of ugly-as-sin but oh-so-comfortable socks I got from Gail for Christmas. Then I pull out my phone and look at it. Well, there's no time like the present.

Despite Gail asking me not to contact her, I call her. The first three times it rings out, but on attempt four and five I'm sent straight to voicemail.

"Damn it, Gail," I growl at her voicemail. "You knew I'd try to contact you. I have to know you're okay, and... and that you forgive me. So I don't know, send me a smoke signal or something to let me know you're okay. Please?"

Hanging up, I write the same in a text and send it to her. It immediately shows as read, but no answer or typing dots ever appear. I guess that's fair. Her reading it shows me she's okay, right?

Shaking my head, I tell myself to get over it. I need to move on with my plan. If I don't, I can kiss my freedom goodbye, and then it really won't matter if Gail's upset now. If I'm forced back to Rome, I have to make my parting gift a hate-filled one. As in, I'll have to make sure she hates me. I can't risk her getting the attention of my Mafia family because she's trying to find me. That would open her up to being used as a pawn, which I'll never allow to happen.

A knock sounds on the door, interrupting my mental pity party. When I open it, I recognize one of Remus' guards. He bows slightly. "Remus asked me to bring you this," he says, thrusting a black folder toward me.

"What is it?" I ask, taking it from his hand.

"I wouldn't know," he says dismissively. "I was ordered to deliver it to you, not to read it. Have a good day."

"Wait," I call after him. "Tell Remus he owes me a new door."

The guard looks from me to the door and back again. "Why?" he asks, sounding genuinely curious. "Our Don isn't in the habit of destroying property."

"Whatever, I'll tell him myself."

I'm tempted to flip him the bird as he walks down the stairs with his back to me, but I refrain and walk back inside the apartment. As soon as the door is closed and locked, I open the folder.

"Huh?" I murmur, looking down at the marriage license for Lucia Carter and Sawyer Perry.

I'm stunned speechless, barely able to form a thought. Logically, I know this means my cousin is keeping a close eye on me and what's going on. But I can't let myself dwell on that. This is... a gift. It's his way of helping me indirectly, which I'm grateful for. I remove the paper from the folder and neatly fold it before stuffing it into my purse. Okay, so maybe painting my door was a ploy to make it look like he isn't helping me? I guess that's possible.

Hunger gnaws at my stomach, a reminder that I can't even remember the last time I ate. Was it with Remus yesterday? If so, food is long overdue. With a sigh, I head to the kitchen to scavenge for something edible.

As I rummage through the cabinets, my phone buzzes in my pocket. Glancing at the screen, I see Jo's name flashing. Even though it's Saturday, it's not exactly abnormal for her to contact me if there's anything she needs to update me on.

"Hey, Jo," I answer, curiosity mingling with the tiredness in my voice.

"Lucia, where have you been? I've been trying to reach you since yesterday." Jo's tone is sharp, cutting through the air like a knife. "Have you received my emails?"

I furrow my brows, confusion swirling in my mind. "I had the day off yesterday. But hang on, let me check." Putting her on speaker, I check my inbox on both my private and work emails, but there's nothing from her. "There are no new emails from you, Jo. Is everything okay?"

There's a moment of silence on the other end before Jo speaks again, her voice tinged with frustration. "We need to talk. Can you come to the arena and meet me at Tom's office? It's urgent."

My mind races with possibilities. What could be so urgent that Jo needs me? "Sure, I can be there," I agree, trying to keep the worry out of my voice.

As I end the call, I can't shake the feeling of unease that settles in the pit of my stomach. What could this meeting be about? Since Tom's already picked me, it's not like I did anything wrong by spending the night at Sawyer's.

I look down at myself and decide to quickly swap my jeans for a pair of black pants. After changing, I grab my coat and bag and head out the door.

The arena is quiet as I make my way to Tom's office, my footsteps echoing in the empty corridors. When I enter, I find Jo and Tom waiting for me—she's scowling, and he's smiling. Jesus, what the hell is this about?

"Lucia, thank you for coming," Tom says, gesturing for me to take a seat.

I nod, my head throbbing from the remnants of last night's indulgence. "Of course. What's going on?"

Tom exchanges a glance with Jo before speaking. "I wanted to talk to you yesterday, but since you had the day off I was going to wait until Monday. But then pictures started circling of you and Sawyer. You were seen together late last night and this morning."

When I look at Jo, she shakes her head subtly. I have no idea if that means I've messed up, or that she doesn't know where Tom's going either.

"Okay," I say slowly, like I'm tasting the word. "Umm, Sawyer told me that you had picked me, and—"

"Ah!" Tom exclaims, slapping his hands together. "So he finally embraced it and decided to step up. I'm happy to hear that, Lucia."

That's not exactly what I meant to say, but now that I see Tom's reaction, I'm glad I let him interrupt me. This looks better with him thinking Sawyer's the one who took charge and started the charade. Hell, it's a much better spin than me sucking him off as my—how did he put it?—audition. Dick.

"We asked you to come in here so we can go over the contractual side of the arrangement," Jo says, eyeing the mountain of papers in front of her. I gulp, not too proud to admit it's intimidating. "Obviously, there's going to be an NDA, and—"

Tom interrupts her with a wave of his hand. "And we'll suspend your regular duties as well as give you a raise. Your sole focus for the remainder of the season will be to improve Sawyer's image as his girlfriend. Anything else will be assigned to someone else."

"Right," I mumble. I should have expected that. "Okay, where do I sign?" I force a smile.

Jo pushes the first mountain of papers toward me, and I lean forward in the chair so I can read it through. It all looks very standard. I'm not allowed to mention or discuss the agreement with anyone. I half expect it to be the rules of Fight Club, but this contract is sadly not that simple.

"Wait," I say. "It says here that Mickey and Soren are aware of the situation."

Tom nods. "Yes. Sawyer made an excellent case that you might need the credibility of others pretending they already knew."

I debate telling him that Gail knows, but then I decide against it. There's no point. I bite down on my bottom lip and continue reading. So far there's nothing alarming there. I'm allowed a clothing budget to buy clothes for events I'm required to attend as Sawyer's girlfriend. Including, but not limited to; sponsor events, interviews, charity events, etc.

Picking up the pen Tom discreetly nudged in my direction, I sign my name with a flourish.

As I continue reading, I come across the addendum regarding the length of this. "There's an issue," I say, pointing at the end date, which is two days after the season ends.

"Oh?" Jo asks, looking at where I'm pointing. "We can't make it the exact end date of the season, Lucia. That would look odd."

I nod. "Sawyer is aware of that. He suggested thirteen months."

"Sawyer did?" Tom asks. His eyebrows sit high on his forehead, making his surprised expression almost comical.

"Yes. He told me all about it last night." The lie falls easily from my lips. "He worried that even a little after the season ending would look off. He also said that such a short commitment might make the investors think he can't commit longer. So he suggested thirteen months."

"Well, I'll be damned," Tom says, running his hand through his hair. "It seems he's really all in. Of course. I'm happy to take his suggestion if you are."

"I am," I confirm.

"And you're sure this was Sawyer's idea?" Jo asks suspiciously.

Of course, it wasn't his idea, but there's no way I'll tell them that. If I'm somehow going to make a marriage out of this, it's important I make Sawyer seem like he's on board, so taking the next step won't seem so... random. "Absolutely."

She narrows her eyes on me, showing me she doesn't believe me for a second. Well, too fucking bad. It's not her I need to fool. And considering the way she treated me when we had the meeting with the GM only days ago, I'm not too happy with her right now.

"Alright. The guys are almost done, so I'll text Sawyer and have him come to my office. Then the two of you can discuss how best to run this show." Tom picks his phone up from the table and taps away on it. "Done."

"Okay," I say, unsure of what else there is to say.

"I guess I'll leave you to it," Jo says. Walking over to the door, she pauses after opening it. "Come see me on Monday, Lucia. I have a few things regarding your accounts I need clarified before I can hand them over to someone else."

Sawyer

Tom Redding: Come to my office ASAP!

I sigh and grab my leather jacket, shrugging it on. "The big chief wants to see me, so I'll see you two later."

"Sure thing," Soren says. "Keep us updated on what's going on."

Mickey slaps me on the back. "What Soren said."

Even though it's the weekend, there are people buzzing around everywhere. I have no clue what half of them do, actually; I think it's only the cleaners I've spoken to before. But I still smile and wave when I make eye contact with some of them on my way to Tom's office.

"Come in," Tom calls when I knock on his door.

Stepping inside, I stiffen when I immediately spot Lucia sitting on the leather couch, looking too comfortable for my liking. She's gathered her red hair in a braid that falls across one shoulder, and she's dressed in a pair of black pants and a white sweater that hugs her curves perfectly. I narrow my eyes, but instead of having the good sense to look away, she lifts her chin. Her eyes sparkle with the same determination I saw last night, and it's all it takes for my dick to twitch.

"Good. Good. We're all here," Tom says, steepling his fingers together.

"What's this?" I ask, tipping my head in Lucia's direction, refusing to acknowledge her with words.

Tom sighs. "I take it you haven't checked social media today," he huffs.

I shake my head. "No." This isn't new since they all know I barely ever go on there.

"Well, imagine my surprise when Jo called me this morning, disturbing my family breakfast, with news about the two of you making your relationship official last night."

"We… what?"

He waves me off. "She told me that there was a video that's gone viral where you dismissed another woman and declared Lucia yours."

Fuck. My. Life.

"So I called Lucia and asked her to come in so we can discuss how to move forward, since you're both ready to play your roles now instead of waiting until Monday."

I glare daggers at Lucia, who just smirks at me. With the self-satisfied look on her face, it wouldn't surprise me if she's the one who leaked the video. But she wasn't recording, was she? Not that it matters. Her job is literally to spin straws into gold, so I'm not putting anything past her.

"That's not exactly what happened—"

Lucia interrupts me. "Don't be so humble, Sawyer." I… fucking what? "I told Tom how you were so eager to repair the damage that you didn't see a need to wait."

Tom's eyes dart between us. "She did," he confirms. "And I have to admit, it was a pleasant surprise to know you're ready to be a team player. I was especially pleased to hear you want to extend the relationship instead of ending it promptly after the season ends."

"Glad it makes you happy," I grumble, folding my arms across my chest.

"I'm sorry I was the one to tell him," Lucia says, smiling too widely for my liking. "But I had to tell him about your idea and initiative when he wanted me to sign the contract."

Tom nods. "And on that note, I have an amended version of yours, Sawyer. If you go ahead and sign it now, we're good to go."

"Right." What the fuck is Lucia's game? The words she's saying sound good, but the wry twist of her lips makes it clear she's working on her own agenda. I'm not going to let her make a fucking fool out of me. If she wants to make me look good in front of the GM, I'll let her. But I'm still going to find out what the hell she's getting out of this. "I'll sign them now."

The GM hands me some papers, and I don't even bother reading before scribbling out my signature on the amended passages that are already highlighted.

"You know," Tom says, gaining my attention. "With this recent development, there's no reason Lucia shouldn't join you for your interview on Thursday."

"Wait a damn second," I growl. "That interview is about the team and not my personal life."

Tom's eyebrows shoot up on his forehead. "Your personal life is causing an issue for the team. You made the two bleed together, Sawyer. This could help smooth the waters."

I resist the urge to shout at Lucia, who's clearly orchestrated this. Maybe I shouldn't let it bother me, but I'm practically vibrating with anger, and the smug look in her eyes isn't helping. "Anything else?" I grind out.

"That's all," Tom confirms. "So I'll see the both of you then. Make sure you spend some time together between then and now."

Lucia stands, and my eyes are drawn to her thighs as she smoothes the fabric there. "Of course," she sing-songs. "Sawyer already told me we're going for dinner tonight. We'll make sure to be seen."

"Oh, one more thing," Tom adds. "I don't have to tell you how important it is that you look like a couple. So that means you have to get your stories straight for the interview."

"Absolutely," Lucia replies. "Jo has already emailed me a list of things we need to work on before the interview." She points at her phone where I assume the email is open.

Tom gives us a sharp nod. "See that you follow her recommendations. You don't have to know everything about each other, but you need the damn basics, or this will unravel before it can begin."

"Like what?" I ask, needing to know what he expects from me.

"When did you start dating? How did you manage to sneak around? And why did you keep it a secret? Where was your first date? Things like that. The devil is in the details," Tom replies.

A groan slips free and I quickly try to cover it up as a cough, but I'm not sure I completely succeed. "Right," I agree. "So we're done now?"

"We are—"

Lucia interrupts Tom. "If I may make a suggestion…" When Tom nods, she continues. "The original idea was to spin the story to make it seem like our relationship was kept a secret because of our jobs. So what better way to show the world we have your blessing than posting a selfie?"

"I don't think that's a good idea," I grumble.

"Why not?" Lucia volleys, her tone taking on a sharp edge, making it clear she isn't happy with my interference. Well, too fucking bad for her.

I summon a smirk despite knowing I don't have a good reason for saying no. "Because that shit would look stupid on my socials. If anything—"

"Sawyer," Tom grumbles.

I ignore him and carry on. "It should be on the Sabertooths' socials and not mine."

"You have a point," Tom says, thoughtfully scratching his chin. "Yeah, I like the idea of that. Okay, let's do it and then Lucia can send the picture for Jo to handle."

I wonder if Tom notices that Lucia straightens her spine and closes her eyes like she needs to collect herself. But when she says, "Sounds good," there's no trace of annoyance in her tone. She's good, I'll give her that. Unfortunately for her, I'm better, and I'm already noticing some of her tells.

We move to the Sabertooths banner in Tom's office and stand in front of it, Lucia between me and Tom. Then we take the picture, one where we're all smiling, and my arm is around Lucia's middle while she's leaning against me. In other words, it's as fake as our relationship.

While Lucia sends the picture to Jo, Tom pulls me to the side. "I know this isn't ideal for you, and I want you to know I'm sorry it's come to this, Sawyer." His tone rings with sincerity, as does the solemn look on his face. "But I was glad when Lucia told me that you're the one who pushed her to embrace it straight away. It tells me you're taking your career and place here seriously."

I should accept the fact Lucia did me a solid by painting a different picture than what really happened last night. I'm not going to. I can't when I know she has ulterior motives that mean I have to watch her carefully. But I still know I should.

"Why did you pick her?" I ask Tom, needing to know if she was being honest about not putting her name on the list.

"She didn't want it," he answers. "If I'm being honest, she's impressed me for a long time, and the meeting was no different. But when she didn't use the opportunity to suggest herself, I knew she'd be the right person."

I can't decide if I'm surprised or not that Lucia was telling the truth. Either way, I don't feel bad for questioning her. She's too... perfect. And I don't mean her spankable ass, plump lips, or tits that just beg to be fucked... right, thoughts about her body aside, she's still too damn perfect.

In my experience, the cleaner your image, the more you're hiding.

So the question is, what's Lucia Carter hiding?

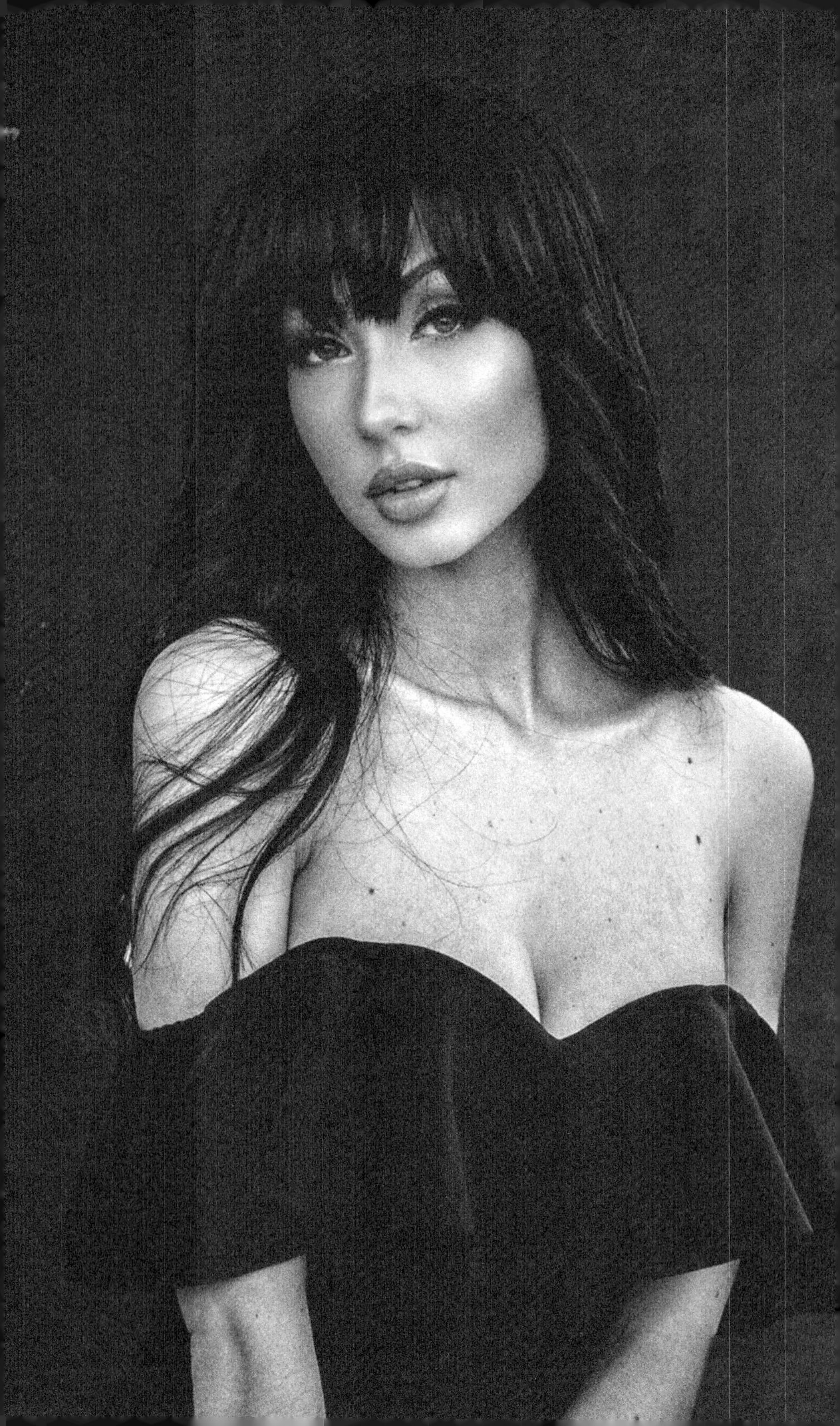

CHAPTER 9

Lucia

The memory of last night's dinner with Sawyer weighs heavily on my mind as I sit at home, curled up on the couch, lost in my thoughts. After leaving the arena together, Sawyer had suggested we go out for dinner again, and I had reluctantly agreed, knowing it was time. It's been three days since our meeting in Tom's office, so we had to do something other than post couple-selfies from the arena on our socials. Now, as I replay the excruciating conversation in my head, I can't help but cringe.

The restaurant Sawyer had chosen was elegant and dimly lit, with soft music playing in the background. As we settled into our seats, there was a palpable tension between us, neither of us quite sure how to break the ice.

"So... Lucia," Sawyer had started, his voice bored as he fiddled with the menu. "How's your day been?"

I had forced a smile, trying to ignore the butterflies fluttering in my stomach. "It's been... fine. How about yours?"

Sawyer had shrugged, avoiding my gaze. "Yeah, it's been okay. Just the usual stuff, you know?"

My heart sank at his lackluster response, the weight of our fabricated relationship suddenly feeling heavier than I'd prepared myself for. "Right, yeah. The usual stuff," I had echoed, my voice barely above a whisper. I kept looking around, feeling like we were being watched. But no one seemed to pay us much attention.

As the waiter approached, we both tensed, the awkwardness between us growing with each passing moment. We ordered our meals in strained tones, neither of us daring to meet the other's eyes.

Throughout the dinner, the conversation was stilted and forced, filled with empty pleasantries and awkward pauses. We smiled like polite, deranged strangers, pretending to be a couple, when in reality, we were nothing more than two people trapped in an uncomfortable charade.

I could feel Sawyer's displeasure with me brewing beneath the surface, his frustration palpable even in the silence between us. But neither of us addressed it, both of us determined to act our part, no matter how strained it may feel.

As I sit alone in my living room, the memory of that dinner weighs heavily on my mind. If one evening was that excruciating, how will I manage to keep up this ruse for thirteen months? The thought sends a shiver down my spine, but I push it aside, reminding myself that the freedom I crave is worth this facade. I can endure thirteen months for a lifetime of happiness.

I glance down at my phone; more specifically, the list of points Jo emailed me yesterday, feeling a knot tighten in my stomach as I read through the instructions. First, she wants us to document our first date—where it was, what we did, and all the other details that make it sound like a fairy tale romance. I suppress a sigh, knowing that recounting that disastrous dinner with Sawyer will be anything but romantic.

Then there's the request to find three things I like about him. Three things. As if that's some easy feat. I run my fingers through my hair, frustration building within me. Apart from his looks—which I begrudgingly admit are attractive—I can't think of a single thing I genuinely like about him. He's arrogant, self-absorbed, and completely oblivious to anyone else's feelings. How am I supposed to find anything redeeming in that?

I close my eyes, trying to calm the rising tide of irritation. This whole situation feels like a cruel joke—a never-ending cycle of pretending and then pretending some more. But I can't afford to let my emotions get the better of me. Not when so much is at stake.

With a resigned sigh, I force myself to focus on the task at hand. If I want to maintain my freedom from my family, I have to play this game. And if that means finding three things I like about Sawyer Perry, then so be it. It's not like I have a choice in the matter.

But as I realize what I have to do, I can't help but wonder if this whole charade is worth it. If sacrificing my integrity and pretending to like someone I can't stand is the price I have to pay for my freedom, then what does that say about me?

I shake my head, banishing the doubts and uncertainties from my mind. There's no point dwelling on what-ifs and maybes. All I can do is focus on the present and do whatever it takes to survive in this twisted game of make-believe. And if that means throwing myself completely into this, then I'll make it happen—no matter how impossible it may seem. And that all starts with an uncomfortable phone call.

Taking a deep breath, I steel myself for the inevitable as I hit Sawyer in my saved contacts. After a few rings, he answers, his voice crisp and businesslike.

"What's up?" Sawyer's voice carries a hint of annoyance, as if he's already tired of my call.

"Hey, Sawyer," I reply, trying to keep my tone neutral. "I was thinking that maybe we should spend some time together. You know, get to know each other better. For the interview and all that." I add the last part as a reminder of what we're expected to do.

There's a pause on the other end of the line, and I can practically feel Sawyer's reluctance through the phone. "I don't know. I've got a lot on my plate right now. Can't this wait?"

I grit my teeth, frustration bubbling up inside me. "No, it can't fucking wait," I hiss, my composure slipping momentarily. "We both know that last night was a fiasco. If we continue like that, it's not going to help either of us."

"That sounds like a *you* problem," he drawls, and I swear I can hear the smirk in his voice.

Inhaling sharply, I pinch the bridge of my nose. "Because you don't care if you're not playing for the Sabertooths next year?" His answering growl is all the confirmation I need to know I'm getting to him. "That's what I thought."

"Are you threatening me? Because that would be very fucking stupid of you. I'm not the only one with something to lose, Lucia. I might not know what you're getting out of this yet, but trust me when I say I'll find out."

I'm not scared of Sawyer finding out my secret. My family is hiding in plain sight. We're everywhere, and most politicians are either part of my family or owned by them. So, no, I don't think Sawyer is going to stumble over the truth. Besides, it's nothing to him. He needs a girlfriend and I need a husband. We're both using each other and if that isn't just fucking perfect, I don't know what is.

"Do your worst," I say, forcing my tone to sound like I'm bored. "But in the meantime, we have a deal, Sawyer. You get my body and I get your time. If that isn't enough of an incentive, then think about what I did for you with Tom."

"What do you mean?"

I laugh. "With almost no effort, I made you look good in front of your GM. How hard do you think it would be for me to undo that?"

Sawyer lets out a low growl, his tone dripping with anger. "Fine, Lucia. I'll make some time for us to hang out. But don't expect me to drop everything for you."

I resist the urge to roll my eyes. "Of course not, Sawyer. In fact, I barely have any expectations. So, you know, you can only surprise me." Without giving him the chance to retort, I hang up.

That man infuriates me way more than he has the right to. I didn't think this would be easy, but fuck. I didn't think it would be this hard. Shouldn't Sawyer want to save his career? It's almost like he's given up and resigned himself to whatever fate Tom has in store for him if he doesn't get his shit together. While that shouldn't bother me, it does. Our fates are intertwined and Sawyer might be okay with not getting what he wants, but I'm not.

Getting up from the couch, I march into my room. Before I can talk myself out of what I'm about to do, I strip naked. Then I stand in front of my full body mirror, strategically turning to the side to hide the mark on my hip, and raise my phone. I position it just right, capturing my entire body. My free hand cups my boob as I take the picture, which I immediately send.

Not two minutes pass before I get a text from Sawyer.

Sawyer: More!

I let out a frustrated breath. One word, really? That's all I get. No, I can't let this be about me. "Don't lose sight of the bigger picture, Lucia," I remind myself.

Lying down on my bed, I reach for my vibrator in the bedside drawer. Then I make myself comfortable, spread my legs wide and pull them up. Taking a selfie in this position isn't as effortless as it looks, and there's no pleasure to be gained from the way I'm holding the vibrator against my pussy. But I manage, and just as quickly as before, I shoot the picture off to him.

When my phone vibrates in my hand, I expect it to be another text, but it's not. Sawyer's calling me.

"What do you want?" I say as a way of greeting.

"To get off, and you're going to help me," he rasps, getting straight to the point. "Turn your camera on. I want to see you play with yourself."

I pause for a moment. "Are you going to turn yours on as well?"

He chuckles darkly. "Not a chance in hell, Lucia. You see, unlike you, I'm actually important. Do you think I'm going to give you more ammunition against me?"

Though it feels like the words are meant to hurt me, they make me smile. Because the fact Sawyer doesn't trust me also shows he knows I'm not a mindless puck bunny. Which means he should be careful with what he gives me. "Fair enough," I say, unable to hide the smile in my tone.

I put Sawyer on speaker and prop my phone up against a pillow before activating my camera. It's not a perfect shot; it's mostly my tits and cunt… come to think about it, that makes it rather perfect.

Sawyer groans as I lie back down and spread my legs like before. I switch the vibrator on, using it to circle my clit. Fuck, it feels so fucking good. It doesn't take long before I'm wet, ready to fuck myself with the toy.

"I want to hear you," he rasps.

Closing my eyes, I let myself get lost in the moment. I move the vibrator between my pussy lips, teasing my hole before pushing it into me. "Fuck," I moan.

"How does it feel?" he asks, his tone filled with gravel.

"Like more." I push the toy farther into me. "It feels like more."

I hear the sound of something being squirted, like a lotion or maybe lube, and it's followed by the sounds of him jacking off. "Take all of it," he groans. "I want to see your cunt swallow that big toy."

"Hang on," I pant. The toy I've chosen isn't one of those you can just ram all the way in. It needs to be eased inside me, give my inner walls time to stretch around it. I moan out loud as the burn from the stretch washes over me. "Almost there."

"You're such a dirty slut," he rasps. "Letting me watch you play with that pretty cunt. Are you thinking about my cock?"

"No," I lie. I don't want him to know that I am, in fact, thinking of his huge, throbbing cock. Fuck, I never knew a dick could be pretty. But Sawyer proved me wrong. "I'm thinking about my ex." Where the hell did those words come from?

Sawyer lets out a growl. "Your ex?"

"Mhmm, yes," I moan, fucking myself slowly. "A big dick doesn't matter if you don't know how to use it. He was so generous. Not only with his cock, but he also knew exactly how to use it. And don't even get me started on his tongue. And... fuck... his fingers." I don't have an ex like that. The closest is an old fuck-buddy who wasn't nearly as skilled as I'm making it sound.

For a moment, everything goes quiet on Sawyer's end. Even his breathing has disappeared. "What are you trying to do?" he asks, sounding incredulous. "Do you really think you can make me jealous?"

The laugh bubbling up my throat turns into a drawn-out moan as I push the vibrator so far inside me it grazes my G-spot, making it hard to focus. "Jealous?" I scoff. "I don't want you to be jealous. I don't even want you, Sawyer. But I still need to fantasize about something to get myself off."

What's the saying, when confronted with something you don't want to answer, lie, and then lie some more. The part about not wanting him to be jealous is true enough... kinda. It *has* to be. I don't care enough about him for that... I think. I just don't want him to know I'm imagining what it would be like to have his dick fill my drenched pussy. Have him stretch and pound it until I'm crying out for a mercy he'd never give me. A girl can dream.

"Keep fucking yourself," Sawyer demands. His breathing is heavier and the sound of skin against skin is a lot louder now.

I move my free hand to my boob, kneading the heavy flesh while doing as he says. My pussy is so drenched it's leaking out, and the wet sounds are hard to ignore. My legs tense as I find myself on the edge. I only need a little bit more to fall over.

"That's it, Lucia. Let me watch you fuck yourself." Though I don't want to, I whimper. The lust in his voice is so damn potent, and it washes over me, making me desperate for more. "Show me how wet your toy is."

"But I'm so close…"

"Show me," he repeats, his tone husky and dark. "Don't make me repeat myself."

I obediently pull the vibrator out and hold it up so he can see the glistening toy. Jesus, it's almost dripping. "Can I put it back in my pussy?" I ask, already feeling the loss deep inside me.

He groans, sounding like he's barely holding himself together. "Go ahead. But I want to watch you lick it clean when you're done."

Not needing to be told twice, I slide it back inside me, moaning as my pussy swallows it inch by inch. "Fuck," I cry out. The vibrations take me right to the precipice, and it only takes a few more pumps before I'm free-falling over the edge. "God. I… fuck…"

I squeeze my eyes shut, basking in the after tingles as they course through my veins. Damn, I never thought phone sex could be that hot. But that orgasm I just had, epic. There's no other way to describe it.

When my breathing slows down, I ease the vibrator out, wincing as my muscles protest. I'm definitely going to be sore tomorrow. "You better be watching," I purr as I move the toy closer to my mouth and open up.

At first, I swirl my tongue around the tip, much like I did when sucking off Sawyer. I lick the length before returning to the rounded top and suck it into my mouth. Sawyer's breathing deepens, making me wish I could see him. Are his eyes squeezed shut? His jaw clenched? Or is he barely into it? No, he's definitely liking our little game. Otherwise, he would have hung up long ago.

"Fuck." The deep and raspy tenor of his voice makes my cunt clench almost painfully. "I wonder what you taste like," he muses out loud. "One day I'll find out for myself."

A not-so-happy memory from many years ago sneaks into my mind. Fabian wanted to reward me for being the perfect hostess during dinner with his friends. So he went down on me, intending to 'Taste my dirty hole.'

I tried to tell him not to, but he wouldn't listen. When he saw the white string from my tampon, he flew into a blind rage. Accusing me of trying to trick him. He was furious, and he... he... fuck. No. I'll not go down that particular lane in my memories. This one will just open up to the others, and it's best they all stay forgotten.

"I've got to go," I croak out, emotions clogging my throat.

"What?" Ignoring Sawyer's incredulous bark, I roll to my side and reach for my phone. In my haste to end the call, I accidentally angle the camera toward my face. Fuck. I look... as wrong as I feel. "Lucia?"

"I'm sorry. I can't talk right now, Sawyer. I'll have to owe you or something."

His angry expression falters, making room for something I don't ever want to see. Pity. "Do you need me to... umm—"

"I don't need anything. Bye." Then I end the call and pull my legs up under me.

Fuck.

Fuck.

I thought I'd successfully banished those memories for good. I can't afford to have them stir now, preferably not ever.

When I move again, I feel like I haven't slept at all, though the darkness falling in through my bedroom windows makes it clear hours have passed since I ended my call with Sawyer. It takes me a moment to realize what's disturbed my comatose state; my phone. Picking it up, I see five missed calls from Sawyer and a text from Remus. Ignoring the former, I open my messages app.

Remus: I see you're in a relationship now, Lucia. What an interesting development.

My stomach churns, and I leap off the bed and into the bathroom. Managing to get my head into the toilet bowl just in time for my stomach to expel everything I have in me. I dry-heave as snot, tears, and half-digested food fall from me in a steady stream. I shouldn't have opened the text when I'm feeling like this. I should have left it, waited until I'd pulled myself together again.

At the thought of Remus keeping track of me, I retch again, but there's nothing left to throw up except for disgusting bile. "Fuck!" I scream, punching the toilet bowl like it's personally offended me. "Fuck. Fuck. Fuck."

I stay on the floor until tears are no longer distorting my vision and I can breathe without shuddering. Then I get up, and on autopilot I shower, brush my teeth, clean my face, and braid my hair. There, my reflection tells me I look good as new. Well, almost… but nothing a good night's sleep won't fix.

Locking eyes with my reflection, I vow to do better. I haven't had a panic attack or any memories of those years in so long, I often forget they actually happened and aren't just a cruel nightmare. That's my mistake, one I can't afford to repeat.

As I think back on what happened, I know exactly what triggered me. It was Sawyer asking how I taste, which was a normal question given our activities. Okay, so I need to… fuck, I don't know what I can do. Time isn't on my side, so I just have to keep on keeping on. Preferably without falling to pieces.

Returning to my bedroom, I pick my phone up from the bed and type a reply out to Remus.

> **Me: That's hardly a congratulations.**

> **Remus: I'm not sure there's anything to congratulate you on just yet.**

> **Me: There will be soon!**

> **Remus: I can't wait for the wedding invitation.**

> **Me: I appreciate your latest gift, but please stop sending me wolf related presents. Stop destroying my things. And don't mess with my shit at work again. Just stop.**

> **Remus: Funny. That almost sounds like you're accusing me of something. But that can't be true, right, Lucia?**

Even through texts, I can feel the chill emanating from him. I want to thank my cousin for the marriage certificate, but I don't. I have no way of knowing who has access to his phone, and since he sent one of his trusted men to deliver the paper without a heads up, I have to assume there was a reason for that.

Besides, if I want to be on my own, I have to deal with this alone. I can't ask for my freedom one minute, and then the next, ask for help. That's not how this works.

When my phone rings again, I don't bother looking at the caller before switching the damn thing off. I don't have the patience to deal with anyone right now. After shutting the blinds in my bedroom, I undress and get into bed. Refusing to switch my phone on, I set my old-fashioned alarm clock, a present from Gail. She gave it to me seven or so years ago. It was a gag gift, but I can't for the life of me remember the joke anymore.

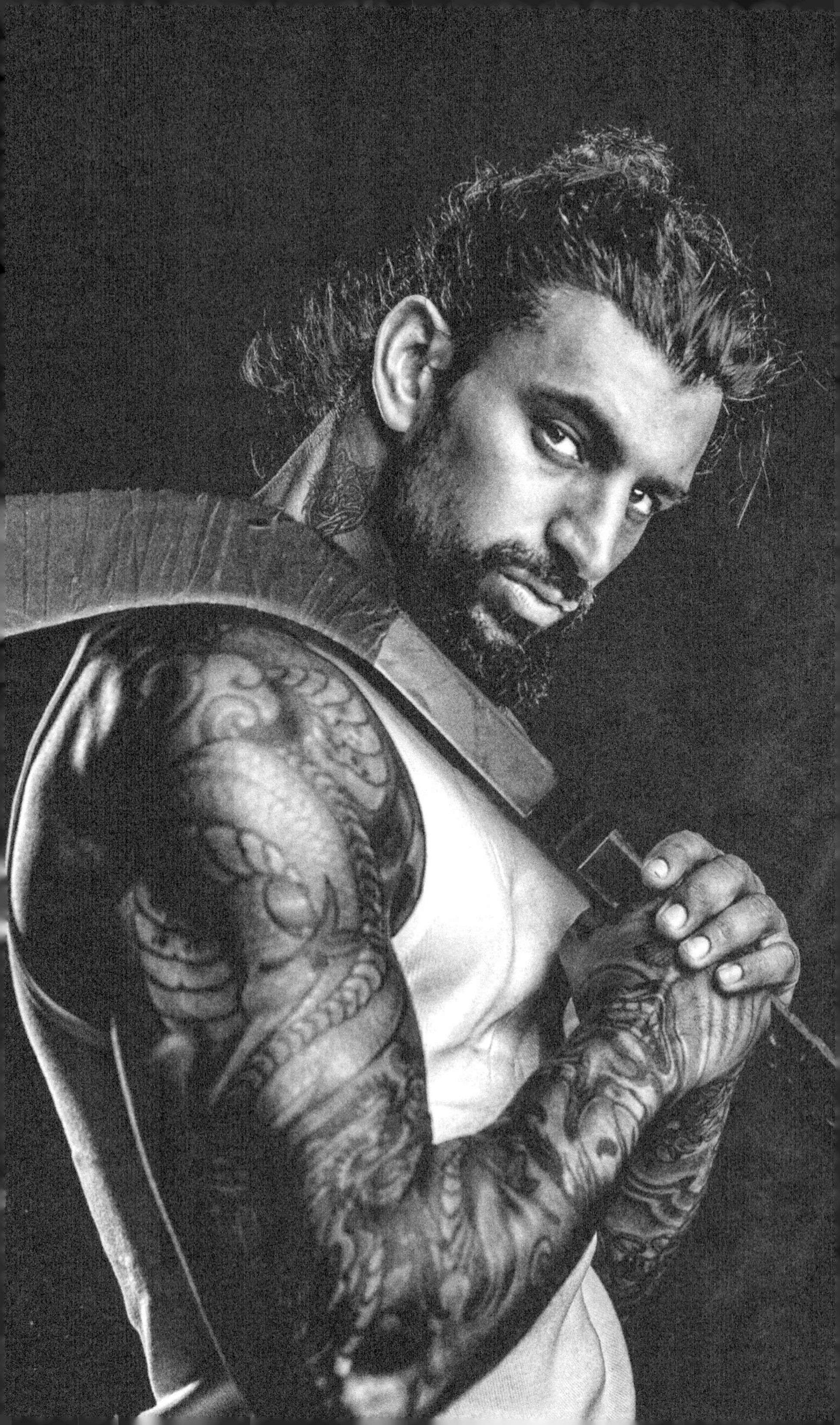

CHAPTER 10

Sawyer

I'm the first one on the ice the next morning, and I take full advantage of the quiet. The rink always seems bigger when I'm alone. It reminds me of when I was a kid. Back then, it felt like I was flying, like I was invincible, when I skated the length of the ice.

But of course my whore of a mom ruined that pretty fucking quickly. After dropping me off, she'd hide somewhere nearby with one of her many affairs. At first, I didn't know exactly what she was doing. I just knew it was wrong. But when you hear your mom moan and beg for cock, you don't remain oblivious for long.

Shaking my head, I push those thoughts away, and instead focus on turning faster, angling my stick one way, feigning another turn that never comes. I know unpredictability on the ice is my greatest advantage, and I'm not about to let bitter childhood memories take that away.

I pick up speed, skating the length of the rink when I sense movement out of the corner of my eye. But all I see when I turn my head is a perfect ass and red hair disappearing through the door. There's no mistaking who it belongs to, and I'm not sure I like knowing Lucia is around. I've never thought much about her presence before. She's always just been one of many people buzzing around the arena. But now... I fucking hate that I'm noticing her. Fuck, I even hate the way I discreetly look for her when she isn't nearby.

Something happened with her yesterday, and at the most inconvenient fucking time as well. I was just about to bust a nut when she... I don't fucking know. Froze up? No, the look on her face was pure, unadulterated panic. But what the fuck could make her act like that? All I did was ask how she tasted. Hmm, maybe she's not as sexually open as she wants me to think.

I let out an annoyed breath when my dick stirs to life. "This isn't the fucking time to wake up," I mumble to myself.

"Dude, are you really talking to yourself right now?" Soren's amused voice rings out as he comes onto the ice.

"What can I say? Sometimes I need to talk to someone intelligent." I shrug and shoot him a shit-eating grin.

He chuckles. "Whatever you need to tell yourself to feel better." He looks around, wanting to make sure we're still alone. We are. "So..."

"So what?" I shoot back, already knowing what he's fishing for.

He rolls his eyes. "You and Lucia. Don't we get an update? Because it seems you've been busy since Friday."

I should be happy it looks that way because that's exactly what we want it to seem like. "We made a deal," I smirk.

"What kind of deal?" Mickey asks, as he joins us.

This is why I've dodged their calls and made sure not to be alone with them for the past few days. It's one thing to live the charade, another to talk about it. It sounds stupid when I say it all out loud, and believe me, I've tried.

"Dude." Soren interrupts my thoughts. "What's the deal?" That's a good fucking question, and I'm still not entirely sure. Sighing, I decide to start at the beginning. "She made it seem like she didn't know Tom had already picked her. She wanted to convince me to make her case with our GM."

Soren whistles and tilts his head to the side. "Really? So why did she chase off the blonde if she didn't know?"

I shrug. "Fuck if I know. But I promised her I would talk to Tom if she blew me."

"You fucking didn't?" Mickey sounds equal parts surprised and impressed.

Nodding, I confirm, "I did. And I did call him after—"

"What are you three standing around gossiping like little girls for? Get fucking moving." Coach's voice rings out, sharp and impatient. "I want every one of you on the ice with your stick in your hand within the next ten seconds. Anyone who isn't ready shouldn't be on the fucking team. Go." As soon as he blows his whistle, people start moving.

Fuck me, I hadn't noticed that we're no longer alone. Luckily, no one else was close enough to hear our conversation, which is a fucking relief. I still should have paid enough attention to notice everyone has arrived.

Practice is fucking brutal, but in the best way possible. It's forcing my mind to stay on the puck, and not wonder why the hell Lucia is here this early. What is she doing? Was she serious about letting me use her body? Those are all things I'm definitely not considering.

Coach blows his whistle. "That's what I'm talking about. You recovered nicely today, but next time, show up with this goddamn energy from the beginning instead of wasting my time. Now get the fuck off my ice. You're dismissed." He blows his whistle again, looking mighty satisfied with himself. Which is to say he isn't scowling. The man only has two expressions; a big scowl and a smaller scowl. That's it.

We all file into the locker room and hit the showers. While we're getting dressed, Soren asks, "Are you bringing Lucia to the event this weekend?"

I curse under my breath, hating the reminder that I have to wear my suit again while parading around and shaking the hands of sponsors. "I guess," I reply. Looking around, I notice the other teammates aren't close enough to overhear our conversation. "Tom mentioned it earlier. But we have an interview tomorrow, so I guess it'll look weird if she isn't there with me this weekend."

"Speaking of," Mickey says. "What deal did you make with her?"

I swallow harshly. "She wanted more time than just the season." They open their mouths, probably to assault me with more questions. "She made a compelling argument, so when she made me come in less than two minutes, I agreed to recommend her to Tom and to extend the arrangement to thirteen months."

"What the fuck?" Mickey asks, incredulous. "Are you telling me she played you with a blowjob?"

"It was one hell of a blowjob," I clarify. "Mind blowing, really."

Soren grins. "Must be if you agreed to almost double the time together with her."

Running my hand through my wet hair, I gather it into a bun and wrap my elastic band around it. "Here's the thing. I only agreed because I wanted to see how far she was willing to go at first. But the more I think about it, the better it sounds."

"She is hot," Mickey agrees like that's all it takes.

I shake my head and punch his shoulder. "That's not why. She was right in saying that marking our imminent breakup by a memorable date like the season ending seems sus as fuck."

The guys exchange glances that make it clear they think I'm losing my damn mind, and maybe I am. Because the logic makes sense to me, and it gives me even more wiggle room once the season is over. I can spend that time hooking better endorsements, and...

"So basically you're going to be celibate for over a year?" Mickey asks, shuddering like it's the worst possible thing that could happen.

"Not exactly," I smirk. Taking my time, I pull my hoodie on and tie my boots before answering them. "She offered up her body and promised me free access if I gave her the extra time."

Should I feel bad for talking about her this way? Probably. Am I feeling bad? Fuck no. Lucia is a grown-ass-woman and she ran her own negotiation. Yet, even as I think that I do feel a twinge of guilt. Especially after her panic whatever-the-hell that was.

"No fucking way," Mickey gasps. "Well damn. I'd sign away thirteen months of my life to fuck her."

Soren laughs. "I'm not so sure. Lucia's nice looking and all, but she's so fucking cold I wouldn't be surprised if her pussy gave me frostbite."

I throw my head back and laugh. "Unlike you, you big coward, I'm not scared of her pussy." As much as I hate admitting it, I am intrigued by her. Whatever happened last night it wasn't her working an angle, it was real. And now that I've seen a glimpse of what's going on beneath her polished exterior, I want to know more.

Before either of them can retort, my phone vibrates with an incoming text.

Lucia: We only have one more day to get ready for the interview.

Me: I know.

Lucia: So what's your big plan?

Me: Are you still at the arena?

Lucia: Just about to leave.

Me: Meet me at my car in ten.

Holding up my phone, I look at my friends, speaking louder than I need to. But I want to make sure everyone hears me. "Gotta go. The little missus wants me."

Mickey grins. "Pussy whipped already."

"Don't pout, Mickey boy. One day, a woman will want your pickle as well," I say with a wink.

"Have fun," Soren calls at my retreating back. "And don't forget to rubber up. No one wants mini 'yous' running around."

I flip them off as I leave, heading out to meet with Lucia. It doesn't matter that I don't want to, I can't postpone it much longer. We do need to have our stories straight with how we met, which I assume will be easy. The first date is tougher since no one will have seen us together.

The cool air hits me as I step out of the arena and make my way toward my car. As I approach, I notice Lucia already waiting there, her posture rigid, and her expression guarded. She's dressed in one of her signature office skirts, a blouse, her long coat hanging open. Her hair is pulled into a tight ponytail, and she's wearing more makeup than usual. There's an air of coldness around her, like she's putting on an act.

As I take in the frostiness exuding from her, I decide not to ask about last night's abrupt end to our call. It's not like it would make a difference, anyway. Instead, I bark, "Get in," motioning to the passenger seat.

Without a word, Lucia obeys, her movements stiff as she settles into the car. As I start the engine and pull out of the parking lot, I glance at her, noticing the tension in her posture and the distant look in her eyes.

"Want to go to your place?" I offer, trying to extend an olive branch.

Lucia's response is blunt and distant. "No."

I feel a growl building in my chest, frustration bubbling to the surface. "Fine," I snap, irritated by her refusal. "Where then?"

She doesn't answer, and the silence stretches between us like a chasm. I grip the steering wheel tightly, feeling the tension thickening in the air. It's clear she's playing games, but for the life of me, I can't figure out why. And here I was at least somewhat worried about her. Yeah, fuck that shit.

"Where then?" I repeat, my tone sharp with annoyance.

"Somewhere neutral," Lucia finally responds, her voice clipped.

I grit my teeth, trying to contain my frustration. "Like where?"

"The cafe downtown," she says, her voice devoid of emotion.

Shaking my head, I bark, "I'm not fucking discussing this in public. Pick a place, Lucia. Your place or mine. Those are the options." She can't be stupid enough to think attracting attention is a good idea when we're literally going to make up lies.

Lucia's expression tightens, but she doesn't protest. "Fine. Your place then."

I catch the hint of discomfort in her voice, but I'm not in the mood to deal with her shit right now. We need to get this done, and I offered to go to her place.

We arrive at my apartment building, and I lead Lucia up to my place in silence. The tension between us is thick, and I can practically feel her reluctance with each step we take. It's almost amusing. The feisty woman who seduced me with a blowjob just the other night is nowhere to be found. I've changed my mind because that's not amusing, it's disappointing.

As we enter my apartment, I gesture for her to take a seat while I grab us some drinks. Lucia sits stiffly on the couch, her arms folded tightly across her chest. I hand her a glass of water, and she takes it with a nod of thanks, but her eyes remain guarded.

I clear my throat, breaking the awkward silence. "So, let's get down to it. We need to work out the details of our story for tomorrow's interview."

Lucia nods, her gaze focused on her drink. "Right."

I take a seat opposite her, eyeing her expectantly. She's the fucking PR wiz, so she should be the one to come up with something. "Got more for me than one-word answers?" I ask, annoyed she isn't participating more.

She exhales slowly. "How about we say we bonded last season during some away games? You know, spending time together on the road, getting to know each other better."

I nod slowly. "That could work. But that was last year, and this is now."

Lucia rolls her eyes. "I know that," she snaps. It feels like a win that she's finally showing some real emotion instead of that robotic shit. "It still had to begin somewhere, and that's as good a place to start as any."

Instead of answering her, I wave my hand in the air, silently telling her to go on.

"Since I was working on your account and was at a few ad shoots with you, we can say we went out for dinner after one of the shoots—"

"Where?" I interject.

"At O'Jackie's," she volleys, making me shake my head.

"Jackie won't lie for us. So that would be too easy to unravel."

Lucia puts the glass down, hard. "What do you suggest then, Sawyer? Tell me your brilliant plan."

I flash her my teeth in a smile. "Easy. You invited me home, and I said yes, which fits my image. And after dinner we—"

"No," she holds her hand up. "We didn't sleep together."

"Of course we did," I say. "No one is going to believe we didn't."

A smile grazes her lips. "And no one is going to believe you treated me like one of your puck bunnies. There has to be something setting me apart from your never-ending parade of willing pussy."

Okay, so she's got me there. It does need to be different. "Fine," I relent. "So we dated privately. Why are we taking it public now?" She looks down at her fingers, and I only now notice they're trembling. A part of me wants to ask if she's okay, but I don't. I don't do that shit, and it's not why we're here. So I ignore it while waiting for her reply.

"Because," she says, blowing her bangs away from her eyes. "We're moving in together."

I choke on my water. "Come again?" I cough.

She shrugs. "There's no other logical explanation. It's not like we were caught in public, so we don't have that excuse."

"Weren't we?" I ask, arching my eyebrow. "We could say we were caught at O'Jackie's."

She shakes her head. "That doesn't count. Technically we outed ourselves." She lets out a deep breath. "Back to what I was saying. If we were about to move in together, it would make sense we tell the world before they spot the moving vans outside your apartment."

This... she's had this planned all fucking day. That's why she's been acting off. Fuck me, it's probably why she hung up last night and then ignored my calls. She wanted to be in my head, and she succeeded because I've thought about her more than I care to admit.

Well then, Lucia. I hope you're up for the fucking game you've started.

"Strip." My voice is sharp like a whip, making her jump. "Now."

"W-what?"

I shake my head. "I didn't say fucking stutter, did I? I said strip."

Getting up from the couch, with trembling fingers, she unzips her skirt and pulls it down her shapely legs. Her glare is frosty, but she doesn't look away as she unbuttons her blouse and unclasps her bra. Her gaze doesn't even waver as she kicks her shoes off before rolling her pantyhose down, stepping out of them. "Enjoying the show?" she asks with a flat tone as she hooks her thumbs into her thong and gets rid of that as well.

"Not particularly," I answer honestly. She's way too uncomfortable for it to be sexy. It's an act of defiance, one she's carrying out to show me she isn't backing down. "But it seems fair I have something worth looking at while we discuss this. So be a good girl for me and sit back down with your legs spread so I can see your cunt."

Her lips curl in distaste, but she still does as I say. Hmm, it's not as satisfying as I thought it would be. "Happy now?" she hisses.

"Never been happier," I lie, running my hand through my beard. I devour her body with my eyes. Her tits are an extraordinary fucking masterpiece. My gaze travels lower, reaching her... "What's that?" I growl, moving so I'm crouched in front of her before I realize I've moved.

As I reach out, Lucia's breath hitches, but I don't stop. I trail a finger over the scars on her inner thighs. I count eight on each leg. "A reminder," she mumbles.

"A reminder of what?" I ask. While the sight and feel of her marred skin should horrify me, all I feel is angry that someone else has marked her before I had the chance.

Is it possible Lucia craves the same thing I do? No, her reaction isn't that of someone who suffered through it willingly. The scars don't seem recent, but the way they've healed gives the impression they're violent. How the hell didn't I notice those last night?

"None of your damn business," she hisses. She's back to looking distant, like she doesn't have a care in the world.

That she can look so aloof and bored while I'm this close to her exposed cunt and touching scars that penetrate deeper than her skin just cements the fact I can't trust her.

"Fine," I agree, matching her tone. "You can move in here. But I have one rule."

"Which is?"

"You don't wear clothes in my apartment."

"Never?"

I sneer. "Not unless I've given you permission." She presses her lips together and folds her arms over her chest. "Do we have a deal or not?" I ask.

Tilting her head to the side, she looks at me through green eyes that flash with so much anger it's amusing. "Fine," she says. "But I want something in return."

I expected this much. "What?"

"Do you promise?" she asks, hopefully.

Laughing, I let go of her thighs and stand back up, towering over her. "Not until I hear your terms."

"Never ask me about my scars again. Not any of them." Her tone makes it clear she isn't kidding around.

Though I'm even more intrigued now that I know she finds it more uncomfortable to talk about her scars than be naked, I say, "Deal."

The marred flesh is like a fucking beacon, making it impossible to look away from it. So many questions swirl around in my head. And, to my surprise, pure rage at whoever did this to her. It's one thing to force her to be naked, another to scar her so badly she's clearly still suffering from whatever happened to her.

I know I shouldn't care, but I do. I really fucking do, and I don't like that some jerk put their hands on my bunny.

Motherfucker!

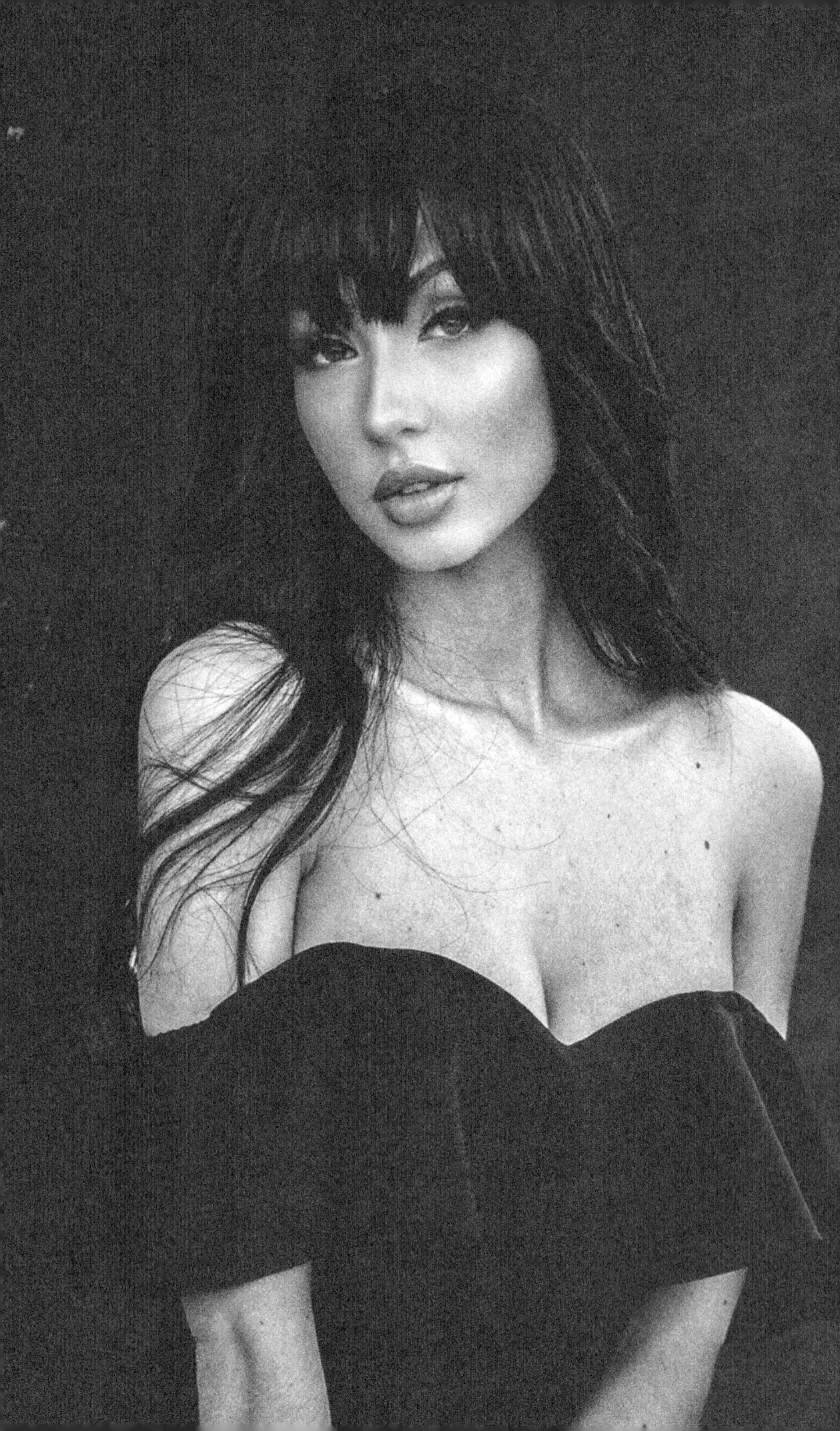

CHAPTER 11

Lucia

I glance at myself in the mirror one last time, adjusting the sleek, form-fitting black blazer I'm wearing. Beneath it, I wear nothing but a lacy black bra. Paired with tailored black pants that hug my curves and strappy heels that elongate my legs. My long red hair cascades down my back, and I've kept my makeup light.

As I step out of my apartment, I find Sawyer waiting by the limousine. He's wearing a tailored suit that makes his impressive body look incredible, his beard is neatly groomed, and his long hair is gathered on top of his head. His jaw is set in a determined line, his eyes focused ahead. But as he sees me approaching, his demeanor softens, and a small smile plays on his lips. Stepping forward, he leans in to press a gentle kiss on my cheek before offering me his hand to help me inside the car.

He's so smooth I almost believe the lie we're concocting. At least until I remember his demand last night. I have no problem being naked if that's what he wants, that's not what kept me awake last night. It's the way he studied my scars. Like he saw more than just the remnants on my skin, and I don't like that.

During the drive to the studio, neither of us speaks. The weight of our impending interview hangs heavy in the air, and I can feel my nerves beginning to fray at the edges. But I push aside the doubt, forcing myself to stay composed.

As we pull up to the studio, the paparazzi descend upon us like a swarm of locusts, shouting questions from every angle.

"Sawyer, is it true that you and Lucia are dating?"

"Lucia, how does it feel to be dating one of the hottest hockey players in the league?"

"Are you two planning to get married soon?"

"Lucia, can you give us any details about your relationship with Sawyer?"

"Are you guys planning on starting a family?"

"Sawyer, do you have any comments on the rumors about your relationship with Lucia being a PR stunt?"

"Oh my God, is that an engagement ring you're wearing, Lucia?"

I keep my head down, pretending I didn't notice the last question. It's not an engagement ring, obviously. But it is a diamond on my left ring finger. With any luck, people will draw their own conclusions. I know it's desperate and somewhat foolish, but right now, I don't have anything else. Nothing else I can do to move my plan along.

I feel Sawyer's hand slip into mine, his touch offering a small but comforting anchor amidst the chaos. Together, we navigate through the throng of reporters. I thought I was prepared for this, but as I struggle not to acknowledge or answer any of the questions, I get a new appreciation for what it's like for the players. These reporters are relentless, and no question is too personal or off-limits.

Finally, we make it inside the building, where we are greeted by the station manager. His smile is warm but tinged with a hint of anticipation. "Welcome, Sawyer and Lucia," he says, extending a hand to each of us. "We're thrilled to have you here for the interview. Follow me, please. We have a waiting area set up for you before you go on stage."

We're led to a cozy lounge area where he tells us to wait until the host couple calls for us. Sawyer takes a seat on one of the plush sofas, and I join him. Though my immediate reaction is to sit with distance between us, I sit so close our arms touch.

With every minute we're waiting, my nerves grow stronger. "Relax," Sawyer breathes, taking my hand and squeezing it. "You'll be fine. And if you run out of things to say, talk about my stats."

I look up at him from beneath my lashes, unsure of what to say. This is a lot harder than I thought it would be, and the interview hasn't even started yet. So, yeah, I'm grateful for Sawyer's small act of kindness. "Thank you," I murmur.

After what feels like an eternity, the station manager returns with a nod. "They're ready for you now. Just follow me, and I'll take you to the stage." We rise from our seats, exchanging a final glance before following the station manager out of the lounge and toward the stage.

As we step onto the stage, the bright lights of the studio blind me momentarily, and I can feel the electric energy of the live audience wash over me. The roar of the crowd fills the air, a cacophony of cheers and applause that reverberates through the room.

Sawyer's arm is wrapped securely around my waist, his touch offering a steady anchor for me to lean on, and I feel a wave of gratitude wash over me as I lean into him, the weight of the moment almost too much to bear. My heart is racing, and despite the cool air of the studio, I can feel sweat trickling down the back of my neck.

But Sawyer's presence beside me is a reassuring constant, his strength bolstering me as we make our way across the stage. With each step, I can feel myself sagging against him, needing his support to keep moving forward.

The host couple smiles warmly at us, but the thunderous applause of the audience drowns out whatever they were trying to say. I force myself to straighten up, to plaster a smile on my face and project an air of confidence, even as my nerves threaten to overwhelm me.

Reaching the area the host couple is waiting in, they pull us in for hugs and cheek kisses. "Sawyer, Lucia, it's wonderful to have you here with us tonight," the female host, Cammy, says, her voice filled with warmth. "We're excited to hear all about your relationship."

As soon as we begin, I notice the easy rapport between the hosts, Cammy and Cam. Their chemistry is palpable, and it's clear that they're not just professional partners but also a couple in real life. The set of the show, aptly named "The Cams Know," exudes an aura of intimacy, with cozy seating arrangements and soft lighting that adds to the atmosphere.

"So, Sawyer and Lucia," Cammy begins with a playful grin, "rumors have been swirling about your relationship ever since you two became a known item. Care to shed some light on any of the juicy gossip?"

Sawyer chuckles, his arm tightening around me. "Well, you know how it is with the paparazzi," he replies, his tone light. "They love to speculate about everything."

I nod in agreement, trying to keep the smile on my face despite the butterflies in my stomach. "Exactly. But the truth is, our relationship is just like any other. We're two people who care about each other and enjoy spending time together."

Cam leans forward, his expression curious. "But what about the rumors that your relationship is just for show? That it's all a publicity stunt?"

I feel a surge of frustration at the question, but I force myself to remain composed. "Those rumors couldn't be further from the truth," I say firmly, meeting Cam's gaze head-on. "Our relationship is genuine, and while there may be outside pressures and expectations, at the end of the day, we're in this together."

Cammy nods in understanding, her expression sympathetic. "It must be tough to deal with all the scrutiny and speculation," she says, her tone empathetic. "But it seems like you two are handling it all with grace and dignity."

Sawyer gives me a reassuring squeeze, and I smile gratefully at him. "We're doing our best," he says, his voice sincere.

"Well, sweet as that all sounds, we all want to know how an NHL star comes to date one of the Sabertooths' PR account executives."

I swallow thickly before answering. "I'm afraid it's not that interesting, really. We started bonding last year during some away games—"

"You mean while he still slept with one... what are they called... puck bunny after the other?"

Forcing a giggle, I rest my head on Sawyer's shoulder. "We all have a past, Cam. The good thing about Sawyer is that there are no surprises."

"Aww," Cammy coos, placing her hand on her heart. "That's so sweet. So would you say you're okay with knowing your boyfriend has a bit of an edgy reputation?"

I press my lips together and lean forward. "I'm not sure I would say I'm okay with it. But you know what it's like. Woman to woman, it's not fun. But I will say this, the fact that he's so honest and upfront about it made it easier to deal with."

"Wow," Cam adds. "Sounds like you got lucky there, Sawyer."

"Lucia's an incredible woman," he says, running his hand down my back. "I'm lucky I've found her."

The hosts make more comments and gush about how cute we look as we sit here on the couch. I take that moment to scratch my cheek with my left hand, flaunting the diamond I'm wearing. "Wait, what's that on your hand? Are you two… engaged?" Cammy asks, shock palpable in her voice.

I wink at her. "Of course not."

Sawyer looks at my hand like it's mortally offended him. "No," he simply says.

Both hosts look at us with doubt written all over their faces. "Well, okay then," Cam says, clearing his throat.

Then they play some kind of video montage on the screen behind us, it's flicking through pictures of us from last year. Luckily, we are walking alongside each other in some of them, which I guess could look like we're talking? I don't know.

"Now pause it," Cam exclaims. The video stops on a picture of Sawyer holding the door for me and Jo. His gaze is very clearly on my ass. "If that's not a man checking out a prime piece of ass, I don't know what to call it."

The men in the audience all let out raucous laughs, and the women sigh in contentment. I look at Sawyer and run my hand down his cheek. "Guess we weren't being as discreet as we hoped," I laugh.

As the interview progresses, Cammy and Cam announce that they'll be taking questions from the audience. A wave of anticipation ripples through the crowd as eager hands shoot up, vying for the chance to interact with us.

Cammy selects a woman from the audience, who stands up eagerly, her eyes fixed on Sawyer. "Hi, Sawyer and Lucia," she begins, her voice tinged with excitement. "I just wanted to say that you two make such a cute couple. But I have to ask, is Sawyer definitely off the market? Because if not, I'd be more than happy to marry him!"

The audience erupts into laughter at her boldness, and I feel a surge of amusement despite the awkwardness of the situation. Sawyer flashes a charming smile, his arm tightening around me as he responds. "Well, I appreciate the offer," he says, his tone light. "But I'm afraid I'm happily taken. Lucia and I are in a committed relationship, and I wouldn't have it any other way."

A smile tugs at the woman's lips as she nods in understanding. "Well, I had to try!" she says with a laugh, before taking her seat amidst the applause of the audience.

As the audience settles down from the previous question, Cam scans the sea of eager faces and selects a man in the back. "You there, what's your question?"

"Yes, hi. My question is for Lucia."

My heart leaps to my throat.

That voice... no. It can't be. But even as I'm thinking that, I feel a chill down my spine. My body remembers him better than I ever wanted to. Fabian. I can't believe he's here, that he's found me. Panic sets in as I discreetly try to get a good look. I can't, though. Without writhing like a circus contortionist, which definitely wouldn't be discreet, I can't see him.

I don't need to see him to imagine his cruel smile, it's forever etched into my memory. I begin to fidget, my grip on Sawyer's hand tightening so much that my nails dig into his skin. Sawyer immediately notices my unease and squeezes my hand reassuringly, but other than that he doesn't give anything away.

"And what's your name?" Cam asks the man, completely oblivious to my rising panic. "Do you maybe want to remove your hat so we can see your face?"

"John," he lies. "And no. I prefer to be anonymous. I just wanted to say that I'm impressed with how Lucia embraces Sawyer's past. It's commendable that you two are being so honest with each other."

My heart pounds in my chest, my mind racing as I try to keep up with the sudden turn of events.

"So, my question is for Lucia," Fabian, or John as he claims his name is, continues, his voice dripping with arrogance and insincerity. "Have you been just as honest about your past, Lucia?"

His words send another shiver down my spine, and I feel a lump forming in my throat. I search for the right words as I struggle to maintain my composure. I know I can't blow the interview, but the fear of Fabian unraveling everything threatens to consume me.

I try to gather my thoughts, but Fabian's presence overwhelms me. Memories of our tumultuous past flood my mind, each one more haunting than the last. He's always been a master manipulator, capable of twisting the truth to suit his own agenda. I can't let him derail everything I've worked so hard for, but the fear of what he might reveal gnaws at me.

Glancing at Sawyer, I'm hoping for some semblance of reassurance. "I have no reason not to believe Lucia's been completely honest with me," he answers easily, leaning in like he's about to kiss my cheek. "What the fuck's going on, Lucia? Who's he?" The words are barely a whisper.

"I..." I begin, my voice faltering as I struggle to find the words. I can't tell anyone about Fabian. Not now, not ever. I can barely form a coherent thought, let alone string a sentence together. For a moment, my vision swims, making me feel like the onslaught of emotions is going to pull me under.

Luckily, I'm spared from having to answer when Sawyer stands up, taking the opportunity to divert attention away from Fabian's question. "Actually," he interjects, his voice projecting confidence, "Lucia and I have some exciting news to share with everyone."

The audience's attention shifts, curiosity piqued as they turn their focus toward Sawyer.

"We've decided to take the next step in our relationship," he continues, his gaze locking with mine. "We're moving in together."

A wave of murmurs ripples through the audience, followed by a round of applause and cheers. I feel a surge of gratitude toward Sawyer for his quick thinking, grateful that he's managed to steer the conversation away from dangerous territory.

"Oh my God," Cammy squeals. "Is that why the two of you made your relationship public?"

"I told you there was a reason for their timing," Cam interjects, lovingly poking his partner and co-host.

As the applause dies down, Cammy and Cam wrap up the interview, thanking us for joining them on "The Cams Know."

With one last smile for the audience, we rise from our seats and make our way off the stage, the weight of Fabian's question still lingering in the air. I might have dodged the proverbial bullet on stage, but I have no doubt Sawyer and Jo are going to dig deeper.

Proving how right I was, we barely make it into the limo waiting for us before there's a text from Jo.

> **Jo: What the fuck, Lucia? My office tomorrow!!!**

> **Me: What time?**

> **Jo: 9am or kiss your job goodbye. This is a disaster, Lucia.**

Another text comes in, and this time our phones ping at the same time.

> **Tom: When I said to come up with a reasonable explanation, I never thought you'd take it to this level. But as long as you're both comfortable with it, I support it.**

The look Sawyer sends my way is so dark it makes chills run down my spine. Fuck, I'm in trouble. Just as I'm about to tell the limo driver to take me home, Sawyer exhales angrily and leans forward, asking the limo driver to take us to his place. I want to tell him no, explain that I want to go home. Still too shocked about Fabian's appearance, I can't make my mouth speak the words, so I just sit there, feeling like I'm awaiting my execution.

Sawyer's so fucking angry his hands are shaking. Seriously, he looks like he wants to punch something. I can only imagine the questions swirling around in his head, I'm sure some of them match my own. I want to know how Fabian found me, and how he knew to show up for the interview.

"Sawyer," I hear myself say, and he rounds on me.

"No!" he bellows. "I don't want to fucking hear it. Do you have any idea what just happened?"

I take a step back, biting down on my bottom lip. "Is this about the engagement? I swear I never thought… it's just a piece of jewelry."

Sawyer scoffs. "I find that fucking hard to believe. But no, this isn't about the engagement. They were going to say that eventually, anyway."

"Oh."

"Yeah, oh," he says mockingly.

"If this is about that man, he—"

He interrupts me with a growl. "That man? Is that what we're going to call him? Who is he?"

I look down at my feet. "He's nobody."

Before I can react, he lunges at me, his hand wrapping around my throat. He pushes me backward until my back hits the wall, and I let out a soft gasp. "Wanna try that again?" he asks, his voice dangerously low. "If he was truly nobody, why did he scare you so much?"

"He didn't scare me," I reply, lifting my chin defiantly. "Just surprised me. That's all."

"Do. Not. Fucking. Lie. To. Me," he shouts. "Who is he, Lucia?"

"Let go of me."

"Who is he?"

Deciding to change tactics before the situation gets out of hand, I lick my lips, meeting his gaze head-on. "You're keeping me from complying with your rules."

"I'm... what?"

I wrap my fingers around his wrist and pull, surprising both of us with my sudden boldness. "You told me to always be naked," I purr as I unbutton my blazer and toss it to the floor. "But I can't do that when you're manhandling me, can I?"

Surprise is visible in his features, and I take full advantage of it. I feel his eyes on me as I undress, and a part of me revels in the attention. Once I'm completely naked, I let my hand rest on my hip, covering the burn mark only my family and husband have seen.

"Remove your hand," he says, his tone demanding.

"No," I hiss. "Your demand was for me to get naked. You said nothing about where I could place my hands. And since I'm not using them to cover up, I think I'll continue to stand like this."

I see the surprise in his eyes, and I know I've caught him off guard. It's empowering, and I refuse to back down now.

"This just got a helluva lot more interesting," he says, his voice filled with a hint of intrigue.

I raise an eyebrow, challenging him to say more. But he remains silent for so long I think I've won this round.

"Fine," he finally says, shrugging. "But you threw your body into the deal. And I can't fuck you when you stand like that."

I almost laugh at his bluntness. "You want to fuck me?"

"Why not?" he replies with indifference. "It's not like you're going to bore me to sleep by telling me who John is. So might as well fuck you before I go to bed."

I'm taken aback by his cruel words, and if I'm completely honest, I'm hurt. Dammit, I shouldn't be hurt. This is Sawyer, a means to my end. He's not someone who I should allow to have this power over me. Since I refuse to let him see the effect his words have on me, and I definitely won't allow myself to *really* feel said effect, I play it off with a shrug.

"Fine," I say, throwing my hands up in the air. "Where do you want to fuck me? On the floor? In your bed? Against the wall?"

His smirk tells me that I just acted how he wanted me to, and I fucking hate that he played me. Without a word, Sawyer crooks his finger in a 'come here' motion, and I follow him into the spare bedroom where I blew him after waking up there.

"Lie down on your back and spread your legs," he says. His tone is monotone, like we're discussing the weather or something inconsequential and boring. A shiver of anticipation runs down my spine as I do what he says. Sawyer follows me, lying on his side next to me while using his hand to hold his head up.

"So, Lucia Carter," he rasps, placing his hand on my upper thigh. "You're not originally from Minneapolis or Minnesota, are you?"

"No," I answer, cursing inwardly when my voice wavers. "I'm from—"

"Before you answer, I want you to understand something. Something that's non-negotiable."

I let out a shaky breath. "What's that?"

He lets go of my thigh and pulls at the elastic band, holding his hair up, letting it out of his signature man-bun before answering. "I don't want you to lie to me. If there's something you don't want to answer, be honest and say that. I know your social media accounts claim you're from Kansas, but we both know that's a lie."

The way he looks at me is alarming, and I don't like where this is going. Every instinct in my body screams at me to put some distance between us, but I refuse to bow down. "You're right," I say, earnestly.

Sawyer moves his hand to my lower stomach, the tips of his fingers ghosting across my skin as he nods, seemingly satisfied with my answer. "Why lie about where you're from?"

Resisting the urge to roll my eyes at the stupid question, I quip, "Because I don't want people to know where I'm from." He chuckles wryly and slides his hand between my legs, cupping my naked sex. I shudder and my nipples immediately stand at attention. "What are you—"

He shushes me before I can finish talking. "I'll be asking the questions tonight," he replies. "Tell me, Lucia, how old are you?"

Sawyer runs a finger through my folds, and I hate that I'm wet for him. "Twenty-seven," I moan as he finds my clit and slowly rolls it in circles.

"What do your parents do?" he asks, almost giving me whiplash from the change in our conversation.

"I don't want to talk about my parents while you're touching me," I say incredulously. When he removes his finger, my hips lift from the bed, chasing his hand.

"Looks like you don't really want me to stop," he observes. "Want me to continue?"

I throw my arm over my eyes. "Yes," I admit in a small voice.

"Then remove your fucking arm and answer the question."

"I don't know what my mom does with her time, and my dad is dead." His finger immediately returns, picking right back up. My reward for answering.

"Any brothers or sisters?"

"I… I…" Fuck, words are hard when he's expertly playing with my needy nub. "Too many to count. I come from an enormous family. Just the immediate family alone is more than thirty people."

He tilts his head to the side, giving me an appreciative look. "I believe you so far."

Then he moves his hand so two fingers are prodding against my opening. "Please," I moan, ashamed of how needy I sound. Then I remember what he just said. "Is this a test?" I ask, genuinely curious about what he's hoping to achieve with these questions.

Sawyer slides his fingers inside my cunt, curling them when they're all the way inside me. I moan and arch my back. "You're so pretty when you're consumed by what I can do to your body," he rasps.

Then he shifts so he can kiss and lick his way down my neck and all the way to my chest. He leaves a wet trail of saliva behind that he blows on, making me shiver. I moan as he sucks my nipple into his hot mouth, grazing the sensitive skin with his teeth.

"Not a test," he answers around my nipple in his mouth. He lets go with a pop and elaborates. "Your evasive answer about your parents means you aren't close with your mom. Neither am I, by the way. And knowing you have a big family should mean you're comfortable in a crowd. Which you were tonight, at least until John showed up."

Well fuck, he's noticing a lot more than I've given him credit for, and I'm not sure how to feel about that. But I lose the ability to think straight when he pumps his fingers harder into me. Without thinking, I move my hand to the back of his head, holding him against my chest. My breath hitching as he lazily licks my areola.

The intimacy of the position hits me hard, and I immediately let go, pushing him back so there's more distance between us. Needing to remember this is nothing more than a transaction, I pick the conversation back up with a question of my own. "Why do you need to know those things about me?" He's looking straight at my exposed sex, and for some reason that's turning me on and making my voice breathier. "Wouldn't it be better to ask me... I don't know. More specific questions?"

"And why would I do that?" He finally looks up, staring at me through dark, fiery orbs. "Anyone can look into you and learn what your first pet was, or how old you were when you got your first period."

That's probably true enough, except my past is hidden by the Don of my family. Then again, with Fabian turning up tonight, maybe I've taken that for granted. Shit, now that my husband's found me, I'm in an even bigger hurry than I thought.

Sawyer pulls his fingers out of me and lifts the hand to his lips. "You never answered me the other day, Lucia. So I guess I have to find out for myself."

I ignore the dark reminder as I watch Sawyer lick his fingers clean, which is as obscene as it is hot. His eyes flutter closed, and he groans as the taste of my pussy hits his taste buds. Fuck, the sight is making me even wetter and I'm seriously contemplating begging him to fuck me. Sex is part of our deal, so I don't imagine he'd need much persuasion.

Before I can form the words, he gets off the bed and rids himself of his clothes until he's standing in only his boxer briefs. Without looking away, he crawls onto the bed and settles himself between my spread legs. My breath hitches as excitement spreads through my body.

As if reading my thoughts, he rasps. "I'm not going to fuck you tonight. But I promise to make you come."

"O-okay," I stutter, his words barely registering. I wrap my legs around his waist, trying to push him closer as he grinds his boxer-covered hardness against my pussy. "Sawyer."

Rutting into me like an animal, he leans down so our chests are pressed together, resting his weight on his forearms on either side of my head so he's not crushing me. The coarse hair on his chest feels amazing against my sensitive nipples, and I moan unashamedly loud at the contact. Paired with the movements of his hips, my pleasure soars higher, taking me closer to the peak I'm desperate to fall over.

"Mhmm, Sawyer," I moan, my eyes closing. I'm almost there… just a little bit more.

As my body tightens and my orgasm is so close I can practically taste it, Sawyer slows down. "Who's John?" he rasps.

The words are like cold water on my hot skin. "What did you just say?"

He doesn't answer me, instead he grinds into me faster and harder. The tip of his cock hitting me just right. Once again, I feel my pleasure building.

"Who's John?"

I cry out in disappointment and anger when he robs me of my orgasm again. "You bastard!" I scream, balling my hands into fists. "Get off me."

He continues the unbearable torture, taking me right to the edge before repeating his question. I try to hide when I'm close both by holding my breath and forcing my limbs to remain unmoving. But he knows. I don't know how, but he fucking knows and stops every time before I can come.

"Suit yourself," he smirks when I deny him for the sixth time.

Shifting, so his cock isn't hitting my clit, only my opening and lips, he groans. Then he continues rutting against me until he curses and becomes tense. It takes me a second to realize he just came. The bastard fucking came without giving me the orgasm he promised me, and has been teasing me with for God only knows how long.

"You're such a fucking jerk," I hiss, pushing against his chest.

He laughs, but doesn't budge. "I gave you the opportunity. Not my fault you didn't take it, baby. But I'll give you one last chance."

Before I can ask him what he means, he shuffles down until his head is perched between my spread legs. "No," I shriek, panic setting in. I try to close my legs, but of course I can't do that when he's resting there and has no intention of stopping his torture.

Sawyer frowns. "Calm down," he says so matter-of-factly, I would laugh if I wasn't busy fighting the dread I'm feeling.

"Not again," I cry. "Please, Sawyer. I'll tell you anything you want to know, just... please don't do this."

"Lucia." I can barely hear him over the thundering beat of my heart. "Lucia. Hey, it's okay."

It's not okay. He's still down there, and the last time anyone was in that position... no, I can't think about it.

Breathe, Lucia.
You're stronger than this.
Don't let him see you like this.
Pull yourself the fuck together!

"Lucia!"

Wait, this is Sawyer and not Fabian.
Doesn't matter, I can't fight him in this position.
I can't let him get that close.

"No!" I scream again, thrashing and bucking to get him to let go.

I'm vaguely aware I'm being jostled, and then I feel warm arms engulf me, holding me tight while he whispers my name over and over. "Come on, Lucia. Breathe for me. I'm sorry, okay? I didn't know."

Slowly, I peel my eyelids back, and as I look around, I realize it's Sawyer holding me. But it wasn't him before, was it? Yes, I think it was. Fuck, that means I just allowed my trauma to show my weakness to someone who can't be trusted with it.

"I'm sorry," I whisper. "I don't know what happened." It's a pathetic lie, but right now, it's all I've got.

"You don't know what happened?" he asks, incredulously. "You just freaked the fuck out and screamed bloody murder. That's what happened."

Taking a shuddering breath, I admit, "I know."

He strokes my hair. "Wanna tell me what that was all about?" I shake my head vehemently. "Okay. Do you just want to go to sleep?"

"Please," I croak, feeling too out of sorts, too emotionally exhausted to continue this conversation. When I feel him shift, I take his hand and hold it. "Don't go, please."

I have no idea where the words come from, and frankly, it doesn't matter. My guards are down, exposing me, making me vulnerable. Tomorrow I'll rebuild my mental walls and make them stronger. But for now, I need someone to stay with me so I'm not left with my own thoughts. And even though it's not ideal, Sawyer's better than being alone.

Sawyer stills. "Just for tonight."

Yeah, just for tonight.

His big hand rests on my stomach, gently stroking the soft skin, and I gradually relax, counting his breaths. We're both ignoring his growing hardness nestled against my ass. It's... I don't think I've ever laid like this with someone else, and a part of me is happy it's Sawyer.

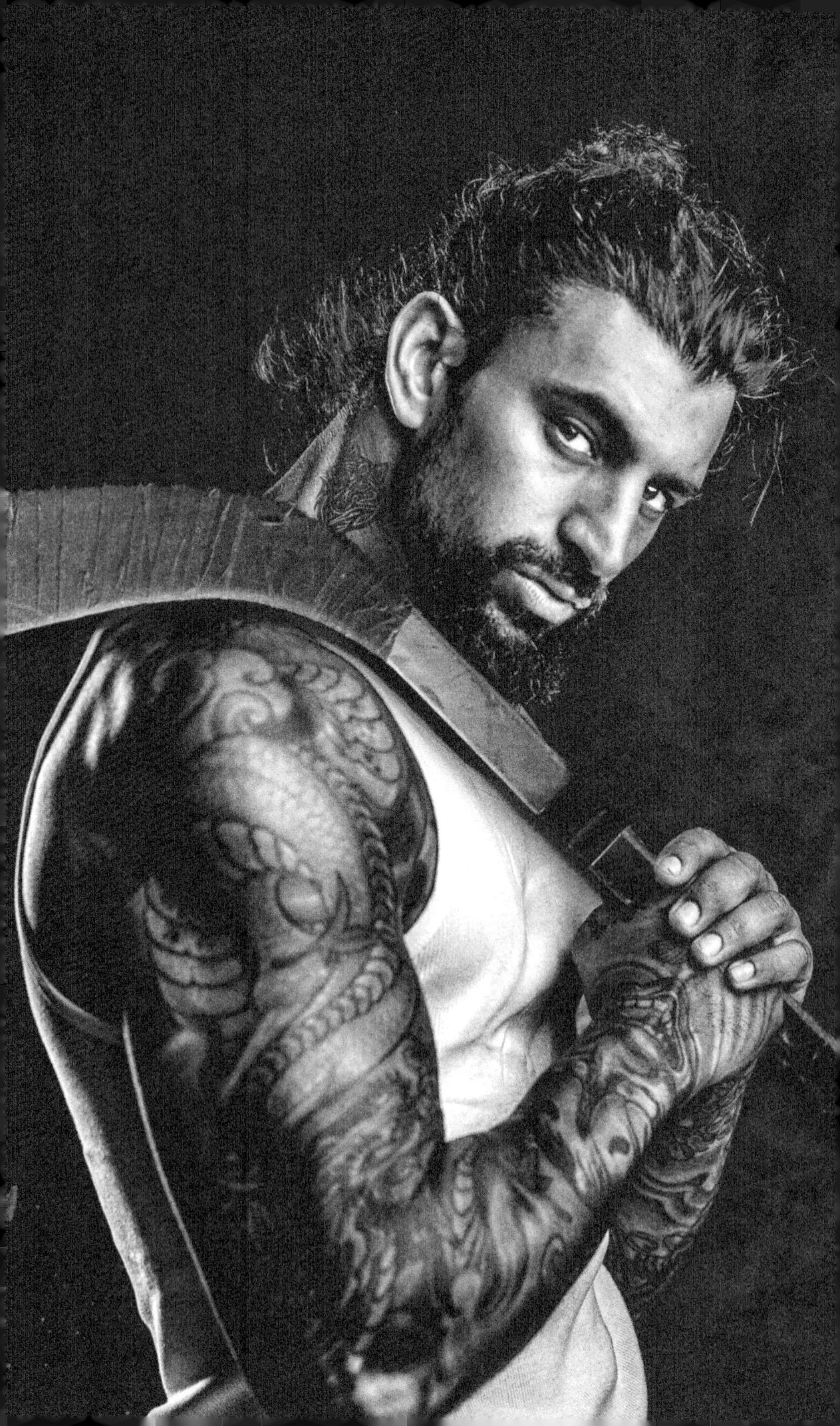

CHAPTER 12

Sawyer

I wake up with my arms around Lucia, and for a moment, I allow myself to savor the warmth of her body against mine. Surprisingly, I don't want to let go just yet. My mind drifts back to last night—the second time she looked like she was having a panic attack. I've spent most of the night trying to pinpoint what I did to trigger her, and I think I've found my answer.

Lucia stirs beside me, turning onto her back and blinking awake. For a split second, she looks relaxed, but then a shadow falls over her expression. Her eyes dart between me and the door, and she resembles a deer caught in headlights while she contemplates making her escape. It's very different from the sharp PR woman I know her as.

"Morning," I mumble, trying to break the silence between us.

"Hey," she replies, her voice barely above a whisper.

I study her carefully, noticing the furrow in her brow and the way she avoids meeting my gaze. It's as if she's a million miles away, lost in her own thoughts.

"Are you okay?"

She hesitates before answering, her words coming out in a rush. "Yeah, just... didn't sleep well, I guess."

I know that's a lie because, unlike her, I've barely slept. Too busy making sure she was okay and didn't bolt in the middle of the night. Knowing she's lying to me makes me annoyed, and I refuse to let her brush it off so easily.

"Lucia," I say, my tone firm. "You can't keep hiding things from me. Whatever it is, you can tell me." I can admit I haven't given her much reason to trust me, but we're kind of stuck together for the next year and a month, so whether I want to or not, I have to make sure she's okay.

Her eyes widen in surprise at my persistence, and for a moment, I see a flicker of vulnerability in her expression before she quickly masks it. "There's nothing to talk about," she insists, her voice tinged with frustration.

I reach out and gently take her hand in mine. "Okay, if you don't want to talk, I will." She looks expectantly at me. "We've made a commitment, one we can't just get out of. So even if either of us has regrets, we need to see this through. Do you understand that?"

Her voice is anything but steady as she whispers, "I know that," and frankly, it pisses me off. No one else but me has the right to make her feel like this. At least not for the next year and one month. For that time, she's mine to do with as I please, and I don't share my toys.

My hand is still splayed on her lower stomach, close to her left hip. Absentmindedly, I run it up and down. Lucia's eyes widen when my hand lands on rough skin, and I frown—both at her reaction and the feel.

"Don't," she says at the same time as I pull the sheet away to inspect her body.

She tries to bat my hand away, but I don't let her. "What the hell is that?" I ask, zeroing in on the weird tattoo on her hip. Without meaning to, I move my hand to the similar tattoo on my neck when I realize what it is; a wolf head, and below hers are some letters. "S.P.Q.R." I read them out loud, confused. "What does that mean?"

"Senatus Populusque Romanus." Lucia's accent completely changes as she speaks the words, making them sound more foreign than they already are. The words are barely out of her mouth before she slaps her hand across her mouth. "I shouldn't have said that," she says, her accent now sounding like it usually does.

What the fuck? I've never heard anyone change their accent like that. "Huh?" I muse. "So you're into gladiator shit? Never would have guessed."

"I am," she confirms. "It's a… passion of mine."

Lucia's tense as fuck while I trace the indented pattern, giving it more attention. My brows furrow in confusion because it doesn't feel like a tattoo at all. "Wait a second," I grunt as realization dawns. "This isn't a tattoo at all. Is this branded into your skin?"

"Yeah."

I look up at her, determination shines in my eyes. "There's a story there."

"One for another day," she replies. Then she removes my hand, and I let her, too stunned to stop her.

I'm struggling to make sense of any of this. But one thing is clear, Lucia has a very high pain tolerance. I've never been branded, but I've seen it done, and judging by the pained screams, it hurts like a motherfucker. And Lucia's brand is big compared to what I've seen. Hmm, maybe she would be receptive to what my beast craves.

After showering and getting dressed, we have breakfast together. Well, Lucia has a granola bar, whereas I eat enough for a family since we have a game tonight. Then we head to Lucia's place so she can change. I wait by the door, giving her some space. I discreetly look around, trying to find any evidence about who John is, but nothing sticks out.

Judging by the design and the knick-knacks, no guy lives here with her and Gail.

When Lucia emerges, her PR mask is firmly in place. "I'm ready," she says, her words robotic and her smile doesn't reach her eyes.

"Can you not do that?" I ask, annoyed she uses that shit on me.

"What?"

Sighing, I run my hand down my cheek and through my beard. "Don't use that professional shit on me." She looks taken aback, like she doesn't know what I'm talking about, so instead of carrying on, I hold the door open for her and wait while she locks up. "Where's your roommate?" I ask the question as we walk down to my car.

"She's visiting her brother for a few days," Lucia answers. There's a fleeting look of hurt in her eyes, one she fails to mask completely. Gail's a sore spot, got it.

As we drive to the arena, the air between us has shifted, the tension easing slightly as we fall into a comfortable silence. It surprises me that I like it, which I shouldn't. "So, uh... anything exciting on your agenda today?" I ask. It's easier to talk with Lucia than being quiet with her. Because when there's no conversation to focus on, I start noticing little things about her. Like how she tends to gnaw on her bottom lip when she's deep in thought. Basically, things I don't want to know about her.

She hesitates for a moment before replying, her voice tinged with nervousness. "Actually, I got a text from Jo last night after the interview. I'm supposed to meet with her in..." she pauses and looks at her phone. "... shit, in ten minutes."

I glance at her. "Well fuck. There's nothing I can do about that now, and we're still twenty minutes away."

Lucia waves me off. "I'm sure it'll be fine." She doesn't sound convinced, which I guess is good, since Jo is a stickler for promptness. It's better that Lucia knows being late isn't helping.

"So what's the meeting about?" I ask, curious as to why she'd be nervous.

Lucia hesitates for a moment before unlocking her phone and scrolling through something. I try to look, but she's angling the device away from me. "She told me to be in her office at 9am or to kiss my job goodbye."

Laughing, I ask, "Are you sure she meant it? Jo can be fucking dramatic. Trust me, if I took every threat from her seriously, I'd be guarding my balls 24/7."

"That's how she speaks to you players, not me or the other people on the PR team. She's never spoken or written to me in that tone before."

When we finally reach the arena, I put my hand on her knee to stop her before she jumps out of my car. "Do you want me to come with you?" I offer. "I could back you up if you think you need it?"

She shakes her head, a small smile playing on her lips. "Thanks, Sawyer. But I think I'll be okay. It's probably nothing."

Well, thank fuck for that. I want to be there and help her, which is exactly why it's good she doesn't want me there. I have no fucking business fighting her battles for her, let alone wanting to do it. And Jo's her boss, not mine.

"Alright. I'll talk to you later," I say as we're about to head in different directions. Then I think better of it, and even though there's no one around, I pull her into a hug. "Text me how it goes."

Her expression is stunned when she looks up at me. "Umm... are you sure? Won't you be busy preparing for tonight's game?"

"Text me," I repeat. "I'll answer."

After parting ways with Lucia, I quickly make my way to the locker room where my teammates have already gathered. The atmosphere buzzes with excitement and anticipation of the home game this evening.

"Hey Sawyer, you ready to tear it up tonight?" Soren grins, giving me a fist bump.

"Damn right," I reply, returning the gesture. "We're gonna crush 'em."

Mickey nods in agreement, his expression serious. "We need to stay focused out there, boys. No room for mistakes tonight."

I give him a mock salute, my mind already running through the game plan Coach has laid out for us. He's a tough taskmaster, but he knows how to get the best out of his players.

"Dude, are you engaged?" one of my teammates asks me casually.

"Yeah, the internet is buzzing with your hidden engagement," another says.

I look at Soren. "It's everywhere."

Mickey moves closer and lowers his voice. "If you want my opinion, you should just do it. What's the worst that could happen?"

The actual fuck?

Soren leans in, murmuring, "I agree. Give the press what they want. What does it matter anyway? You're going to be the one coming out of this looking good. Besides, don't divorced men get a lot more tail?"

Mickey nods enthusiastically. "Yup. I hear sympathy sex is better than makeup sex. Like, the chicks are so eager to make you feel good they'll do anything."

I run my hand down my face, mentally begging for Coach to show up so I don't have to listen to this bullshit any longer.

Speaking of Coach, he enters the locker room just as we're finishing our preparations. "Alright, boys, listen up," he says, his voice commanding attention. "We've got a big game tonight, and I expect nothing but your best effort out there. Stick to the game plan, play smart, and leave it all on the ice."

We nod in agreement, already feeling the adrenaline pumping through our veins. It's moments like these—standing shoulder to shoulder with my teammates, ready to battle it out on the ice—that remind me why I love this game so much.

Heading out onto the ice for warm-ups, I glance in the direction of the offices. I know Jo's and Tom's overlook the rink, and I wonder if Lucia is in one of them now. Fuck, I shouldn't be worrying about her. She's not my fucking concern. So why the hell can't I stop thinking about her? Wondering if she's okay? Nope, this has to stop. She's a grown woman, I'm sure she'll be fine.

Lucia

I sprint down the corridor to Jo's office, my heart pounding in my chest. Without pausing to catch my breath, I burst through the door, panting slightly. "Sorry I'm late," I gasp out, but Jo barely acknowledges my apology, her expression tight with irritation.

"Sit down, Lucia," she says curtly, gesturing to the chair opposite her desk. I comply, feeling a knot of anxiety forming in the pit of my stomach as I meet Jo's steely gaze. "Who the hell was that guy at the interview?" she demands, her tone sharp. "And don't you dare lie to me."

I swallow hard, feeling a surge of panic rising within me. I can't tell her the truth about Fabian, not when it could jeopardize everything. So instead, I try to play it off. "Oh, uh... he was just... someone who showed up," I stammer, my voice faltering.

Jo's eyes narrow, her frustration palpable. "Don't play dumb with me, Lucia. I want answers, and I want them now."

My heart sinks as I realize Jo will not let this go easily. Obviously, I can't tell her the truth, but I also can't afford to raise any more suspicions. Maybe I should have taken Sawyer up on his offer to join me. I bite my lip, struggling to find the right words. "I honestly don't know who he was, Jo." Fuck, I need to lie better. "We weren't really introduced. So I assume he was just a random person in the audience."

Jo nods, like she expected me to say all of this. She opens her laptop and shoves it toward me. "Why do you look scared?" she asks, her tone less accusatory now. "Has this man harassed you in the past or something?"

Balling my hands into fists, I dig my nails into the soft flesh on my palms. "He just reminds me of someone I used to know. But when he talked, I realized it wasn't him."

"And you're sure that's all there is to it?" Jo asks, cocking an eyebrow. "Now is the time to come clean, Lucia."

I swallow audibly. "As far as I know, there's nothing more to it. But as I said, I don't know him, and the likeness to someone from... err, back home just took me by surprise." I'm relieved when Jo's expression softens, and I hope that means she believes me.

Jo leans back in her chair, studying me intently for a moment before sighing heavily. "And what about the engagement news? You do realize it's everywhere, right? Thanks to the live interview, there's no way to contain it."

"I didn't know," I say, mentally cursing myself for not checking mine and the team's socials before coming here. "But there's nothing to it."

"Why did you wear the ring?"

Shrugging, I explain, "You guys wanted Sawyer to look more... stable, I guess. So I thought it was a good way to hint at how serious we want them to think the relationship is. Give them something to guess and gossip about."

I try my best to act like it was all done in service of the greater good. Which I suppose it was... *my* greater good that is. I'm the one who needs the rumors flowing. It's not like I can walk right up to Sawyer and ask him to marry me.

But maybe public opinion and, yeah, gossip can help nudge him in the direction I need.

The more I think about it, the smaller I feel. I know I'm manipulating Sawyer, playing him big time in a way I have no right to do. But... I'm not willing to stop. My freedom hinges on me getting us to the altar, and that's something I've wanted for too long to give it up all because of my pesky conscience.

"Fine," she says. "But for your sake, I hope you're telling me the truth. I don't have to tell you what will happen if this comes back to cause problems later."

"Maybe you should," I volley, unable to keep my temper locked down. "What have I done to deserve you treating me this way, Jo?"

She gapes. "Excuse me?"

I shake my head. "No, not anymore. First, you deliberately make me late for the meeting with Tom. Then you make me sound incompetent, and now, after making the world see Sawyer as a doting boyfriend who's about to move in with the love of his life, you threaten my job because of a random person in the audience. So I ask you again, what have I ever done to you?" I'm shouting at the end of my tirade, but I don't care. She owes me some answers.

Jo is quiet for a few moments, her expression unreadable as she considers her response. When she finally speaks, her tone is softer, but there's a hint of sadness in her voice. "Lucia, you have to understand," she begins, her words measured. "Before the meeting with Tom, I knew he wanted the PR team to find a fake girlfriend for Sawyer. And I also knew that you were already his top choice."

I blink in surprise, taken aback by Jo's revelation. "Wait, what? Tom wanted me to be Sawyer's fake girlfriend?"

Jo nods, her gaze steady. "Yes. And when I found out, I... I was trying to protect you, Lucia. I knew it wasn't fair to put you in that position, so I tried to shield you from it as much as I could."

I feel a mix of emotions swirling inside me—shock, anger, confusion. How could Tom do this to me? And why didn't Jo tell me sooner?

"Why didn't you tell me this before?" I demand, my voice tinged with frustration.

Jo sighs, her shoulders slumping slightly. "I wanted to, Lucia, I really did. But I didn't know how you would react. And I was hoping that maybe... maybe I could find a way to fix things before you had to find out."

I shake my head, feeling a sense of betrayal creeping in. "So you kept this from me, just to protect me?"

Jo nods, her eyes pleading for understanding. "I know it was wrong, Lucia, and I'm sorry. But I was just trying to do what I thought was best for you."

I take a moment to process Jo's words, feeling a mix of gratitude and resentment swirling inside me. It's clear that Jo was only trying to look out for me, but I can't help but wish she had been more upfront with me from the beginning. How fucking ironic when my life is nothing but one lie after another.

Yeah, I really don't have a moral high ground at all. I'm willingly whoring myself out for my freedom, all while pushing away my best friend, and deceiving everyone who comes into contact with me. What a fucking treat I am.

"But I hope you know how proud of you I am," Jo continues, pulling me out of my thoughts.

"Huh?"

She nods eagerly. "Yes, it's a big step. But I have to ask, are you okay with living with him?"

I rub my fingers against my temples and exhale slowly. "Yeah, I am. We've already discussed it, and I'm moving into his place."

"Okay," she says. Then turns her laptop back toward her and begins to write something. "I'll make sure a moving company comes to your place on Monday. You should probably stay at Sawyer's until then to keep up pretenses.

But I'll have people at yours on Monday at noon to help pack up your stuff and get it all moved."

Shaking my head, I decline her offer. "That won't be necessary. I don't want to leave my roommate with nothing. All I need are my personal belongings."

"Nonsense," Jo says, waving me off. "It's not up for discussion. The two of you need to be at your apartment at noon."

The day passes by in a haze. Although I'm not physically packing boxes, my mind is constantly buzzing with lists and mental catalogs of the items I'll take with me tomorrow. It's not until mid-afternoon that I remember I promised to text Sawyer, and when I do, his reply is almost instantaneous.

Sawyer: Glad to hear it's all sorted. You doing alright?

I frown at the text. He shouldn't be asking me that. We both know that what's happening between us is nothing more than an arrangement we're both benefiting from. Sure, he doesn't know what I'm getting out of it. Then again, considering I've now freaked out on him twice, it's not that odd he's asking. I really need to get my shit together fast.

Me: I'm fine.

Sawyer: Then stop frowning.

I look up from my phone and turn my head, but I don't see him anywhere.

Sawyer: Don't forget to wear my number tonight!

With a sigh, I tug my phone away and grab the package that was delivered a few days ago. Then I go to the bathroom to change into something a little less business-like and a lot more girlfriend-like.

The custom-ordered, tight, low-neck sweater fits me like a glove. It's made in the Sabertooths' color and has their logo on the front and Sawyer's number on the back. With my dark jeans and ankle boots, I'm pretty sure I'm looking the part. After touching up my makeup, I pull a sharpie out of my bag and draw Sawyer's number on my cleavage. There, now there can be no doubt about who I'm there to support.

Before leaving the bathroom, I text Gail. I don't know if she's seen the interview since I still haven't heard from her, but I owe her to hear it from me, too. As with all the other texts, it shows as read almost immediately, but no reply comes through.

When it's finally time, I make my way into the arena, taking my seat among the other girlfriends and wives, who greet me with big smiles and cheers. At first I was really nervous about having to sit with them, but the way they welcome me instantly puts me at ease.

"I never thought I'd see the day one of these seats was taken by Sawyer's girlfriend." The woman speaking grins widely.

"Seriously. I'm glad we didn't have bets going, or I'd have lost everything," another jokes.

Grinning, I reply, "Trust me, even while living it I would have been betting against us." That earns me a loud round of laughs, making it even easier to be around them.

The arena fills with excited chatter and the shuffling of feet, bringing the atmosphere alive with anticipation. The hum of conversation grows louder, punctuated by bursts of laughter and the occasional roar of excitement. Fans clad in team jerseys and scarves stream in, their faces painted in team colors, adding to the vibrant tapestry of the crowd.

The energy in the air is palpable as the countdown to game time draws near. The lights dim, and a hush falls over the crowd as the familiar strains of the national anthem echo through the arena, accompanied by the fluttering of flags and the sound of applause.

As the anthem fades into silence, the tension mounts, building to a crescendo as the players take to the ice. When Sawyer comes onto the ice, skating a circle around Mickey and Soren before shoulder bumping them, I jump to my feet and chant his name along with the fans.

Sawyer scans the stands, and when his eyes land on me, he smirks. I turn around to show him his number printed on the back of the sweater. Then I spin again, pointing at my cleavage. I'm not disappointed by his reaction when his eyes widen and he licks his lips. My breath hitches as our eyes lock, making it feel like we're the only people here.

Our bubble bursts as the roar of the crowd swells to a deafening height as the puck drops, signaling the start of the game. With a flurry of skates and sticks, the players race across the ice, the intensity of the game unfolding before our eyes.

In that moment, as the game begins in earnest, the arena pulses with energy and excitement, uniting fans in a shared passion for the sport. As I watch from the stands, caught up in the thrill of the moment, I can't help but feel a sense of belonging—a part of something bigger than myself, even if it's just for tonight. What a fucking high.

Though it isn't, this almost feels like my first game. The other times I've watched, I've always felt like the spectator I was, and this time... this time it felt different. Don't get me wrong, I love the game and the organization, but I wasn't *in* love with it. Not until now.

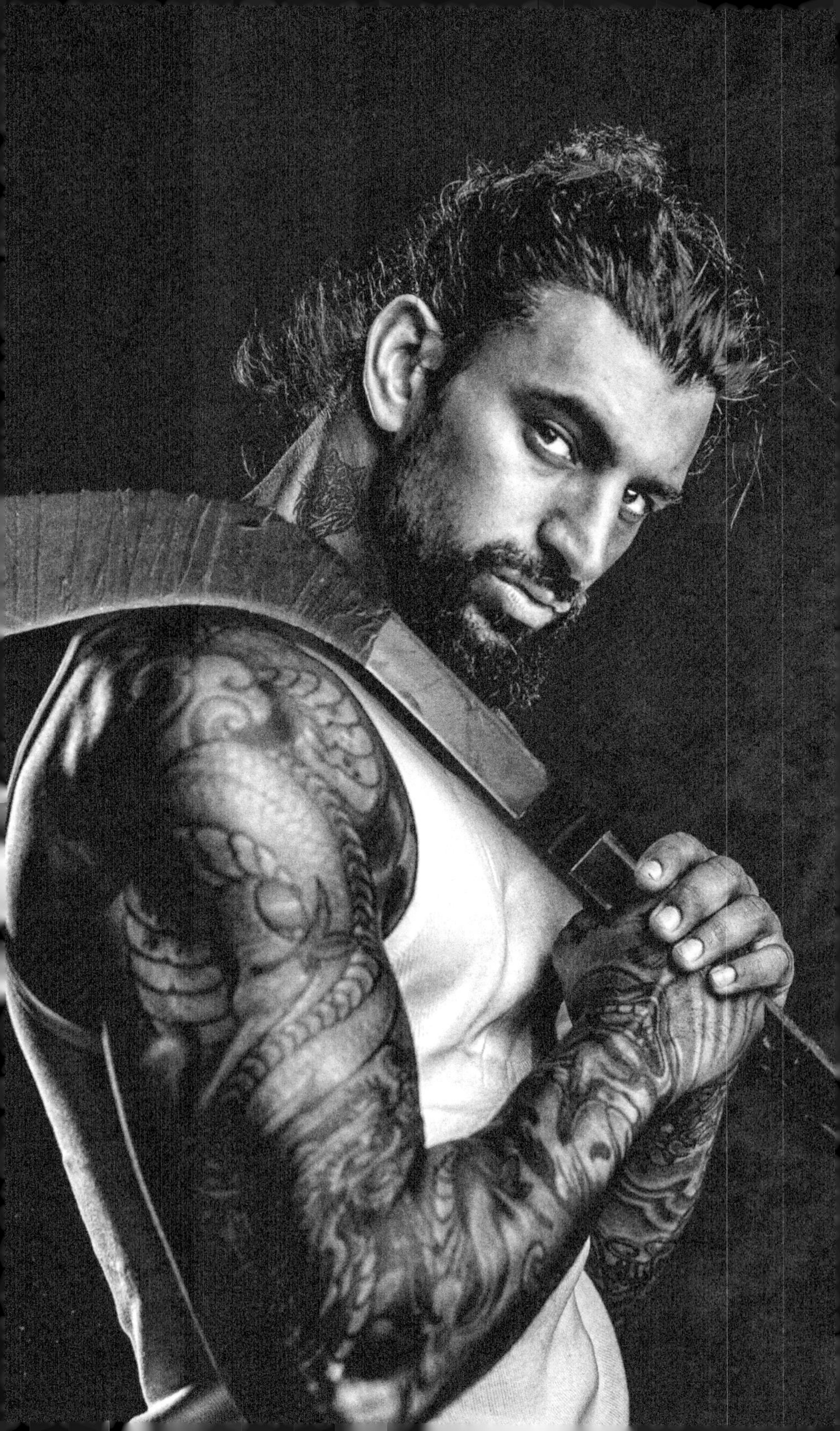

CHAPTER 13

Sawyer

The energy in the locker room is electric, pulsing with the high of victory. The Sabertooths have emerged triumphant once again, and the sense of elation is palpable among the team. As we gather around Coach, there's a buzz of excitement in the air, a shared sense of accomplishment that binds us together as a unit.

"Great game, boys!" Coach booms, his voice echoing off the walls of the locker room. "That was a hard-fought win, and each and every one of you played your hearts out on the ice tonight."

The room erupts into cheers and applause; the sound reverberating off the walls as we celebrate our victory. High-fives and fist bumps are exchanged all around, smiles stretching from ear to ear as we relish in the sweet taste of success.

To some, it means more to win a home game, but that's not how I see it. Winning on our turf is just how it should be. Beating another team in their home, that's the sweetest victory of them all. Still, none of that matters as I celebrate with my teammates.

Coach's eyes scan the room, his expression one of pride and satisfaction. "But let's not get complacent, boys," he continues, his tone serious now. "We've got a tough road ahead of us, and we need to stay focused if we want to come out on top." I roll my eyes while smiling wider. Of course, the old bastard would use a win to remind us we're not unbeatable. That's just how he rolls.

My teammates all nod in agreement, a shared determination to keep pushing forward and striving for the ultimate reward. Despite the exhaustion that lingers in our bones, there's a fire burning within each of us, driving us to keep pushing, keep fighting, keep winning. This team, this brotherhood, is something special, and I wouldn't trade it for anything in the world.

"Right, I'm going home to fuck my wife," Henry, our right defender, says.

"Hell yeah," Peter chimes in.

The two of them are always vocal about how much they crave sex after a win—hell, we all do. In the past, I usually found a puck bunny or two to celebrate with, but tonight I won't be doing that. My thoughts stray to Lucia, and the image of her sitting among the other girlfriends and wives during the game flashes through my mind. I wasn't prepared for just how hot she'd look wearing my team's color and my number. Really. Fucking. Sexy.

Distracted by my thoughts, I almost run into the group of women waiting for their men. "Sawyer," Amy greets me. "You played great tonight. Well, not as amazing as Peter, obviously."

"Obviously," I chuckle in agreement.

"I wanted to say I got to sit with Lucia. She's so sweet. You're going to bring her around more often now, right?"

Speaking of the woman in question, I look up and my eyes lock on the stunning redhead the world believes to be my girlfriend—fuck, fiancée. Her green eyes have a hazy quality to them. She wobbles slightly while biting down on her bottom lip. I wonder if she's been drinking, or if she, like me, is high on the atmosphere.

I don't even excuse myself, I just leave Amy right there and push my way over to Lucia. The closer I get, the more I feel the pull. We're still looking right at each other, and the moment I reach her, she throws her arms around my neck while I pull her into me.

"Sawyer," she breathes.

Slamming my lips down on hers, I steal her words. I slide my tongue into her mouth, kissing her hard. Hmm, I don't taste alcohol, so she's definitely not drunk. She moans into my mouth and fists the lapels of my suit jacket. It's the first time I've kissed her for real, and fuck me, Lucia is an epic kisser. Seriously, if I'd known she was this good, I'd have done it a long time ago.

We're interrupted by Mickey, Soren, and other teammates as they burst from the locker room. "Hey we're going to celebrate, right?" Soren asks.

"Lead the way," another guy says. "The usual place?"

I tear myself away from Lucia. "Let's go," I say, wrapping my arm around her so she has no choice but to follow.

We end up going to Magnitude, the club we always go to after a home game. Amidst the pulsating lights and throbbing music of the club, the celebration for our victory reaches a fever pitch as more teammates join us, their raucous laughter filling the air as we settle into the VIP section.

Soren raises his glass. "When's the big day, Sawyer?"

Mickey chimes in, his grin wide. "Yeah, spill the beans, man. Don't leave us hanging."

I chuckle, feeling the effects of the alcohol warming my veins. "Who says there's a big day? Maybe we already tied the knot."

Lucia's eyes twinkle mischievously as she leans in, playing along. "Oh, you didn't hear? We had a secret ceremony last week. Just the two of us and a bottle of tequila."

Everyone howls with laughter. "Seriously?" our backup goalie asks, shoving the woman in his lap away. "Are you two already married?"

"No," Lucia answers, winking.

As the adrenaline of the game still courses through my veins, I find myself unable to shake the comments from Mickey and Soren echoing in my mind. The weight of their words are on a loop in my mind, mingling with the euphoria of victory and the alcohol in my system.

It's more than that. Everyone sees me as an irresponsible forever-bachelor. I'm known as the bunny chaser, Mr. Fuck-Em-And-Leave-Em, the Sabertooths' Casanova, and whatever else the press have called me. Though it's never bothered me in the past, now that I've distanced myself from it and taken a good look at my life, it does. It makes me seem unreliable; the sponsors are right about that, and it fucking stings if I'm being honest.

It strikes me that marrying Lucia might be the very thing I need to do. It'll prove to both myself and the world that I'm not that fucking bad. I'm not my mom; unreliable and uncaring. And since it isn't love, but purely convenience, it seems like a brilliant idea to my alcohol fueled brain. It would also give me some serious brownie points when this charade is over.

Overcome by the sudden impulse, I don't pause to consider the implications before turning to Lucia. The words tumble from my lips in a rush of reckless abandon. "Let's do it" I say, low enough that only she can hear me. "Get married and to hell with the rest."

She pulls back, shock written all over her features. "What?"

Smirking, I move a loose tendril of hair behind her ear. "Don't pretend this isn't what you want, bunny. You wore the ring on purpose. Besides, when you break my heart in a year's time, it'll look even better for me."

Her eyes widen like saucers. "I-I..." Shaking her head, she clears her throat and gives me a defiant look. "Sure. Why the hell not." Despite her attempt at sounding nonchalant, she seems eager.

"Tonight?" I ask, mostly to test her.

Shrugging, she replies, "Sure. I know someone that can do it."

"What are you two whispering about?" Soren shouts, pointing between me and Lucia.

Ignoring him, I watch as Lucia pulls her phone out of her purse and frantically taps away on it. When a triumphant smile spreads across her face, I take a second to think it through. But no, I'm not fucking backing out. This is perfect.

"One hour," Lucia says, giving me a pointed look.

"Fine by me," I reply.

I spend the next hour with a bottle of bourbon practically glued to my mouth, and when it's time to leave, everything is spinning. I'm in the perfect state to enter a sham marriage; drunk off my ass, and horny from having Lucia in my lap.

Just as I'm about to ask if she's noticed it's been an hour, a well-dressed bodyguard kinda looking guy comes into the VIP section. "Who the hell is that?" I ask Lucia.

"One of my cousin's, umm... guards," she replies, getting out of my lap.

"Your cousin?"

"My cousin Remus is the one who can marry us."

My brows shoot up high on my forehead, but I quickly school my features and turn to Soren and Mickey. "I need your help," I say, pitching my voice low enough that the rest can't hear what I'm saying. "I'm going to do it, and I need you to be my witnesses."

"You're going to do what?" Soren asks, frowning.

"Well shit," Mickey breathes, looking between me and Lucia with a grim expression. "You know we were just joking around, right? You don't have to marry anyone—"

I cut him off. "I know I don't *have* to. But this... this works out in my favor."

They shrug, not objecting further as we follow Lucia and the bodyguard into a quiet room. The guard or whatever closes the door behind us, leaving us alone with a dark-haired guy who looks nothing like my soon-to-be wife.

Walking over to him, Lucia bows and does something weird with her hand. "Remus," she says. "Thank you for doing this. It's... umm, Sawyer wanted it over with quickly."

"Sawyer," Remus says, holding his hand out. "Lucia's told me this is urgent."

I look between the two of them, then, finally, I take Remus' hand. "It is," I confirm.

Just as I'm about to introduce my friends, Remus looks at them. "Soren, Mickey, it's good to meet you. I watched the game tonight and I have to say I'm impressed."

"Yeah, thanks man," Mickey says, looking straight at me.

Turning to me and Lucia, Remus asks, "Those are your witnesses?"

"Yep," I confirm sharply.

"Umm not to be a dick or anything," Soren says, "But don't we need a prenup or something?"

Well, that's definitely something I should have thought about. It's not that I think Lucia's a golddigger, and the contract with Tom already makes sure I'm going to be the one to profit once we end our bullshit relationship. That's in terms of reputation, not goods. And I won't risk Lucia getting her hands on anything I've worked hard for. I'm not all that materialistic, but this is a matter of principle.

"Already got that covered," Remus says smoothly.

Hmm, maybe drinking so much wasn't a good idea because that should sound sketchy as fuck. Yet, I nod and accept the papers he hands me. Flipping through the pages, I find what I'm looking for. Each of our assets is clearly delineated, ensuring there's no confusion about ownership. My estates, my money—all listed under my name. Lucia's belongings likewise belong solely to her. There's no room for ambiguity or dispute.

"Can I take a look?" Soren asks, and when I wave him over, he reads over my shoulder.

He wordlessly points out a paragraph that reads; *Upon entering holy matrimony, any previous marriages are nullified.*

"What the hell?" I mumble, looking over at Lucia who's wringing her hands together while talking with Remus.

Deciding it doesn't matter right now, I put pen to paper and sign everywhere needed. Then I hand the papers to Lucia, who smiles robotically. While she reads through it, I glance up at Remus, who meets my gaze with a reassuring nod.

"As smooth as silk," Remus remarks, a faint smile playing on his lips.

"Yeah, it looks good," I reply curtly.

Remus nods once more before turning his attention to Lucia. "Shall we proceed, then?"

After signing the last paper, Lucia nods, her eyes shining with determination. "Let's do it."

With a solemn nod, Remus begins the ceremony. "You're both agreeing you want to get married?"

"Yes," we reply at the same time.

"Very well."

Remus begins to talk about marriage, holy matrimony and yada, yada. Honestly, I space out. This isn't romantic, it's convenient and nothing else. So I don't care. "Sorry, can we just skip to 'I do'?" I ask, interrupting Remus.

His eyes flash with annoyance, softening as he looks at his cousin. "Do you agree?"

"Yes," she says stiffly. "Just get to the binding part so we can be done."

"Sawyer Perry, do you take Lucia Carter as your—"

"I do," I reply, interrupting him again.

"I do, too," Lucia says exasperated.

Remus scoffs. "Whatever. By the power vested in me by the Vatican, I now pronounce you husband and wife. You may kiss or not kiss. I couldn't care less."

Despite myself, I chuckle. Remus isn't that bad. Or maybe he is, since he just married his cousin to someone who doesn't care about her at all.

After signing the marriage certificate Remus lays out in front of us, it's done. I'm now a married fucking man. The hollowness and despair I always thought would accompany me if I crumbled and tied myself to a woman is nowhere to be felt. I feel the same. I'm still me, Sawyer Perry. Some papers and meaningless promises aren't going to change a damn thing.

I know I've made a rash decision tonight, I feel good about it though. Tom might be the one who forced me into this lie of a relationship, but I'm the one who made it on my terms. And now I'll never again be the lifelong bachelor, in a year I'll be divorced. The thing nagging at me now is that while I know why I've said yes, I don't know Lucia's reasoning. Then again, I have plenty of time to find out.

"Are you taking Sawyer's last name?" Mickey asks, interrupting my thoughts.

Lucia looks at Remus who just shrugs. "No," she says. "I like Carter."

"Should we send out a press release or something?" Soren already has his phone in hand as he asks.

Shaking her head, Lucia rushes to explain. "I think it's better we keep it under wraps. If we leak the information it's going to look like we... umm... planted it and the press will dig. But if it just comes out organically, it'll look like we tried to keep it secret."

I'm actually okay with that. Mostly because I don't feel like explaining to Tom why I married Lucia just after announcing we're moving in together. But before I can agree, Mickey says, "Agreed. Just go on as you guys have, and when the time is right, you can announce it. I think the fact you had a small, intimate wedding will play in your favor."

The smile Lucia gives him grates on me for all the wrong reasons. It might be a fake marriage, but that doesn't mean I want her to look at my friend like he hung the fucking moon. "We're leaving," I grind out, pulling Lucia to my side.

"Just one second," Remus says, and I stop. He hands Lucia a small box. "I didn't know if you'd have a wedding band, so I brought you this."

She eyes the box like it's toxic. "It better not be—"

Throwing his head back, Remus lets out a booming laugh. "It's not. Christ, cousin, what do you take me for?" When Lucia glares at him, he chuckles. "Don't answer that. Just believe it's not what you think it is."

Taking the box, Lucia opens it with shaking fingers. Inside it is a small gold band. As she holds it up, the letters S.P.Q.R. glint in the light from where they're engraved into the jewelry. "Thank you," she says, bowing and doing that weird thing with her hand again.

"Senatus Populusque Romanus," Remus says, and Lucia replies, saying the same words.

Like last time she said them, her accent changes completely, making it sound foreign. Remus pronounced the words the same way, coated heavily with the exact same accent. Hmm.

"Right, I'm gonna go find my fuck for the night," Mickey says, classy as always. "This has been… not a pleasure."

Soren laughs as he follows him, leaving me alone with Lucia and her cousin. "I'm off as well. You two should go… consummate the marriage," Remus says, grinning.

I roll my eyes, but shake his hand and thank him for coming here. I still can't believe I'm married, or that it's a secret. If I'd known how exciting it would feel, I might have made a habit out of it just to feel the thrill coursing through my veins right now.

"We should leave," Lucia says, looking down at the wedding band with lust in her eyes.

My dick wakes up, loving her sultry tone. "We should," I agree. "I've never had a wife before so this should be interesting."

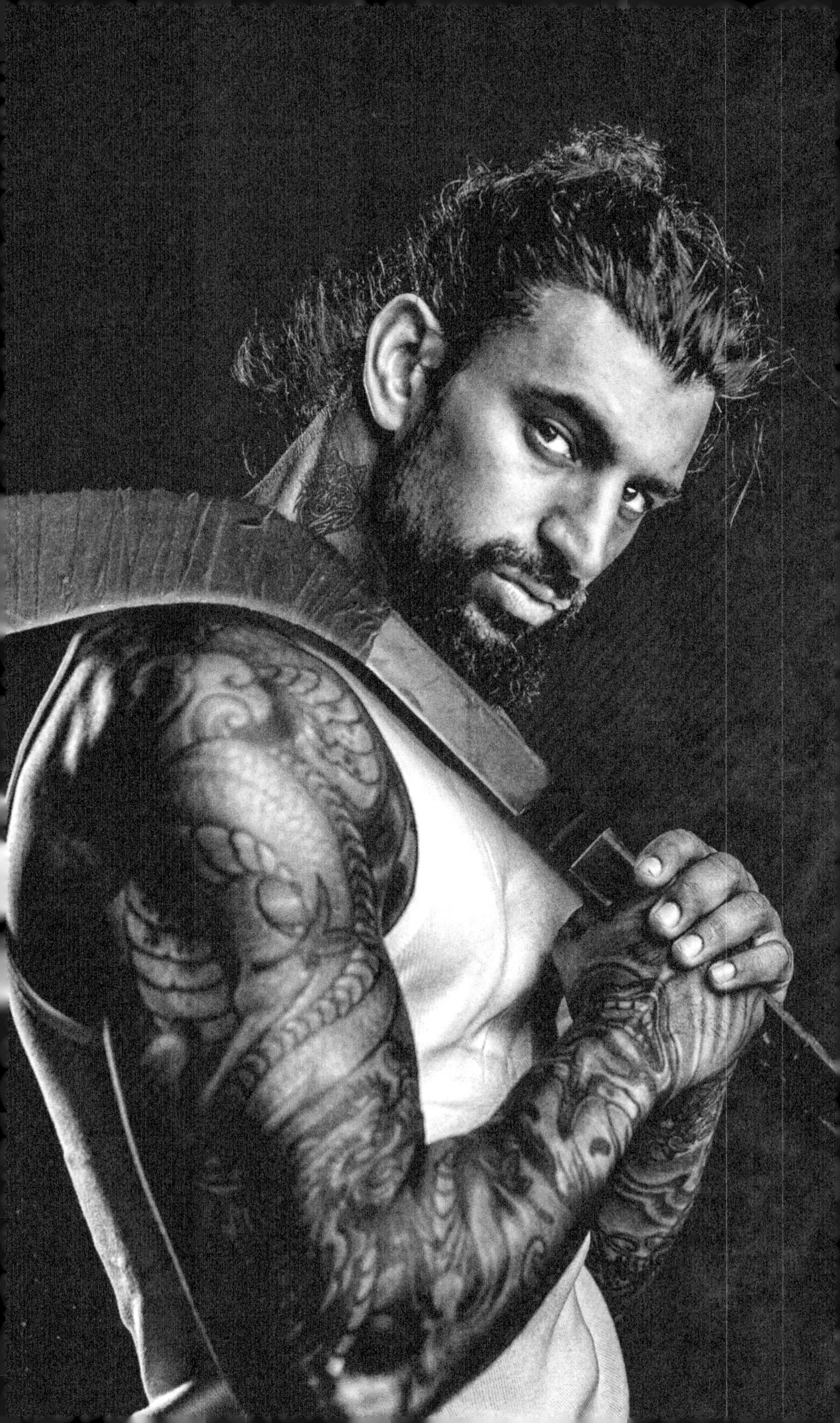

CHAPTER 14

Sawyer

With my arm slung over Lucia's shoulder and hers wrapped around my middle, we make our way out of the club. Neither of us pay attention to the cameras and reporters as we get into the car Remus promised would take us back to my place.

The drive back to my place with Lucia is filled with silence, it's a palpable presence, like a living, breathing pulse that seems to grow stronger with each passing moment. Glancing over at Lucia, I can't help but notice the way the streetlights cast shadows across her features, illuminating her in a soft glow.

After getting out of the car, I take her hand and drag her over to the elevator. The doors barely manage to slide close before I have her off the ground and pinned against the wall. Her legs wrap around my waist, and she moves her hands under my shirt and practically claws at me.

"Sawyer." My name is like a prayer.

My lips descend on hers again. I waste no time sliding my tongue into her mouth, stroking hers while we both pant. My dick is throbbing in my suit pants, and I grind myself hard against her cunt. It's taking all my self control not to rip her clothes off right now and bury myself in her tight heat.

We stumble out of the elevator when it reaches my apartment. Well, I'm the one doing the stumbling since I'm carrying Lucia, who refuses to stop kissing me. At the back of my mind, I remind myself this is a one-off. It's only because it's game night, and because we got married, and because I really need to fuck her.

"Fuck. You're kissing me like you want to consume me," I groan.

"You caught me," she purrs, undulating her hips. "That's my master plan. Now shut up and kiss me back." This bossy, take-charge side of her is so fucking hot I groan into her mouth.

Reaching my bedroom, I set her down on her feet and loosen my tie. "What do you want, Lucia?" My tone is gruff.

I continue to undress while she looks up at me through hooded eyes. Then she kicks off her shoes and undoes her pants, pulling them down her long legs. Her thong is next to go, and she doesn't break eye contact.

"Leave the shirt thingy on," I rasp when she reaches for the hem.

"Oh, this old thing?" she pulls at it and does a little twirl so I can take it in from the back as well. "Yeah, I guess I can keep it on."

Fuck, it looks good on her, and I might just fuck her while she's wearing it.

Her eyes fall to the outline of my erection, and the way she licks her lips makes it grow harder. "Come over here and undress me," I rasp.

Lucia hums when she reaches me, her hands going straight to my suit jacket. She painfully slowly pops each button before reaching up and pushing it off my shoulders.

While I shrug it all the way off, she repeats the motions with my shirt. Her movements grow more and more impatient, making me smirk.

When she finally reaches my belt, she hums as she tugs it through the loops on my pants. Then she drops to her knees, looking up at me. "I want this," she pants, answering my question from earlier.

Shaking my head, I grab her shoulders and pull her back up. "No," I say, sternly.

"Why?" The incredulous look on her face makes me smirk down at her.

"I think we need to talk about boundaries." I slowly open my pants, tug them down, and get rid of my socks. Leaving my boxer briefs on. "You like sucking cock, don't you?"

She licks her lips again. "I liked sucking yours."

I grunt in agreement because let's be fucking honest; it was incredible. "Well, too bad. It's not happening."

She rears back like I've slapped her. "Don't tell me you didn't like it." Heat burns in her bright, green eyes.

Unbothered by her reaction, I stroke my cock until it's peaking out of the top of my boxer briefs. Precum leaks from the tip and onto my stomach. Sliding my finger through it, I hold it up and show it to her. "What do you like about it? The control or the taste?"

Her cheeks become red, but she doesn't back down or look away. "Both," she admits breathily.

Nodding, I wipe my finger on my boxer briefs and tug them down. My cock springs free, jutting out from my body. "I love eating pussy, Lucia. I fucking love the taste, and I'm the kind of guy who wants to play with his food."

Realization dawns on her face, making her take a step back. Her eyes flick nervously between mine, like she's looking for something in my gaze but isn't finding it. "I-I can't..."

"I know," I rasp. "But it doesn't seem right that you get to have my cock in your mouth if I can't have my tongue deep inside your cunt."

It doesn't take a fucking genius to work out the link between Lucia's aversion to my face being near her cunt and the scars on her thighs. I get it. Something really shitty happened to her. But she should have fucking told me upfront, so I knew what I was signing up for. Panic attacks and snuggling aren't part of the package. So if that means we can only fuck and nothing else, so be it.

I wasn't lying, though. I fucking love eating pussy.

"Get on the bed, Lucia. I want your ass in the air, and I want you to spread your ass cheeks for me." Without hesitation, she gets into position, her head resting on the mattress. I chuckle when I see her lower lips are already swollen and glistening with her arousal. "Are you already wet for me?"

"Yes," she moans.

I slowly move over to my nightstand, grabbing a condom before positioning myself behind her. I place one knee on the bed, and after I've rolled the rubber on, I nudge my cock against her wet opening. "Does this bother you?"

She shakes her head. "No." Gripping her hips, I slowly feed her tight cunt inch by inch of my cock. She moans and wiggles her ass invitingly. "Don't toy with me, Sawyer," she pants in protest.

"You said I could use your body however I wanted," I remind her. "Turns out you lied."

Lucia freezes and lets go of her soft globes. Then she slowly pushes off the mattress so she can look back at me. "I didn't know."

I push further into her. "Didn't know what?"

"That you wanted to eat me out." Her eyes flutter closed when I bottom out inside her.

"Eyes open," I command, wanting her to watch me fuck her. "Why didn't you think I'd want to feast on your cunt?" Her pussy squeezes me tighter at my words.

"It's never been... I mean..." She trails off, and I stop moving. When she finally speaks again, I ease my cock in and out of her. "No one has ever wanted to do it. It was either used as a punishment or... to control me." Her eyes are glassy and her voice cracks on the last part. Still, her pussy squeezes me, and I groan.

"Is that the truth?" I rasp, thrusting into her at a steady pace.

"Y-yes."

A single tear falls from her eye, and I lean forward, catching it on my finger. I stare at it like it's a rare treasure, which I suppose in some ways it is. Lucia's showing actual emotions, and this time she isn't freaking the fuck out. I lick the salty droplet from my finger before I pick up my pace, slamming into her so hard she's shoved forward and has to use her arms to steady herself.

The sounds of our bodies slapping together and moans are like a fucking symphony of destruction. One where I'm dishing it out while she takes it, escalating the punishing rhythm by pushing her ass back against me for more. My body is covered in sweat, and my hair has come loose from the bun I had it tied in. I'm gripping her hips so tight I won't be surprised if I'm leaving bruises.

"I'm so close," Lucia cries out. Then she moves one hand between her thighs, but I slap it away. "What? I want to come."

I feel fucking feral for this woman, and I'm far from done with her yet. "Not yet, baby."

Leaning forward, I take her hands and force them backward. She willingly lets me, trusting me to hold her up. "And I want you to come from my cock inside you. Can you do that for me, bunny?"

She doesn't answer, but her moans turn to nonsensical words when I fuck her harder, ramming my cock all the way inside her with each thrust. Her cunt spasms, sucking me in deeper and tightening like it wants to keep me all the way inside her. I fuck her through her orgasm, then, without giving her time to come back down, I let go of her arms so she slumps forward.

"What the—"

I interrupt her panting moans. "Take your bra off and ride me," I groan as I climb onto the bed and lie down on my back. "Show me how much you want my cock."

It looks awkward for her to unclip the bra and slide the straps down her arms through the sleeves, but she does it and when done, throws it on the floor with a sinful smile. Then she straddles me while fisting my base, angling the tip toward her soaking cunt. Instead of slowly lowering herself, she slams down on me, completely sheathing me in her heat. Lucia tucks her legs beneath her and begins to move up and down on me, and I groan, loving the way her tits bounce in the sweater.

I'm tempted to have her take it off, but decide against it. There's something so fucking dirty about fucking her while she's wearing it. "Faster," I groan, reaching under her sweater so I can palm her tits.

Throwing her head back, Lucia moans loudly. She begins to move faster, angling her hips so my pubic bone adds stimulation to her clit. I squeeze her tits, unable to just lie there while she fucks me so good. Every time she comes down, I thrust up and into her.

"Fuck... Lucia. Fuck!"

"Sawyer," she cries. "Please... I need to... I have to—" she cuts herself off with a desperate moan.

I find her nipples and pinch them. "Come for me, wife." My tone is so fucking husky. "Come all over my cock. Soak me in your wetness."

A tingling sensation builds from my groin to my spine, building as my balls tighten. "Fuck," I curse, viciously. My entire body tenses, and while I empty myself into the condom, Lucia cries out and her cunt holds me in a vise grip, not letting go until I'm spent.

Lucia collapses onto my chest, and before I know what I'm doing, I wrap my arms around her back, holding her closely. All I can hear are our panting breaths and the thundering beat of my heart. Fuck me, I don't remember the last time I came that hard.

I reach for the condom and slide it off, careful to keep my jizz inside it. Then I tie it into a knot and throw it toward the bathroom door. I'll deal with that shit in the morning. I'm way too tired and comfortable to move right now.

Once our breathing returns to normal, I ease her to the side and lazily move my hand up and down her back. That's how we fall asleep; a married couple, with her head on my chest and her leg thrown over my hip.

I wake up with Lucia still in my arms. I can still smell her wet cunt, the scent lingering heavily in the air. De-fucking-licious. No wonder I have a raging boner right now. But it's more than that. Her body fits perfectly against me, making me feel all... content and at peace.

Without a word, I roughly push her away. I don't fucking cuddle. I'm a fuck them and leave them kinda guy, and just because the world thinks we're in a happy relationship doesn't mean I'm okay acting like it behind closed doors. But with the way my body's reacting and my thoughts focusing on how good it feels, my brain isn't getting the memo that the marriage isn't real. So it's time to end it. She complains in her sleep, but I don't pay attention to her words, and instead of hanging around, I lock myself in the bathroom.

There's a dull ache in my muscles from last night's game, but the euphoria of the win courses through me, driving away any hint of discomfort. As I shower, I think back to the game. It wasn't even a hard one. Well, not as hard as we thought it was going to be. But a win is a fucking win.

Getting dressed, I head to the kitchen. My stomach is growling for food, and I consider ordering a big fucking meal from somewhere. But decide against it, not wanting to wait for delivery. So I throw together some eggs, bacon, and toast. The sizzling of the frying pan almost masks Lucia's quiet footsteps.

"Good morning," she chirps. She looks sleepy, her red hair in disarray, but she's still wearing the sweater from last night. In other words, she looks amazing. Having her around like this is definitely something I could get used to.

Fuck, no. There's no getting used to anything. This. Is. Not. Real. It isn't real now, and it'll never be more than a fucking sham. So no matter how sexy she looks, or the fact we're legally married, this has to stop.

"You hungry?" I ask, and when she nods, I crack a few more eggs open and add more bacon to the mix. "Coffee's ready."

She wordlessly opens cupboards, looking for my cups until I sigh and point to the correct one. She pours us both a decent amount before asking, "How do you take yours?"

"Black."

When I'm done with the food, I carry it over to the island where she's sitting, opting to stand opposite of her instead of sitting.

"Why are you still wearing that?" I ask, pointing at her sweater. She's put on a sorry excuse for panties that barely cover her ass, but her legs are bare.

She frowns around a piece of bacon. "I thought you liked it."

I run my hand down my face and reach for my coffee, gulping it down. "It's not game night, so you don't have to wear my number. Besides, didn't I tell you to be naked when you're in my apartment?"

Hurt flashes across her green eyes, but she lifts her chin up. "Fine," she snaps. Red spots break out on her neck and chest, probably from anger.

I don't look away while she pulls it off. Fuck me, her tits look biteable. I really should have made her take the sweater off last night. Oh well. Tilting my head to the side, I look at her. "And your panties."

"Don't push me, Sawyer," she growls, and dammit, it's hot.

"Are you going back on your word already, wife?" I don't even pretend to hide the fact I'm eye-fucking her so hard as she slides off the stool and tugs her panties down. "There we go. That wasn't so hard, was it?" I say, secretly loving the daggers she glares at me while she sits her perky ass back down.

"You're such a jerk," she hisses.

I shrug because she's not wrong. "You didn't think anything had changed because of last night, did you?" I know I sound like a condescending dick, I just don't care enough to do anything about it.

"Why would I think that?" she asks saccharinely, baring her teeth. "Because you kissed me? Or because you were actually somewhat... nice? Or maybe because you married me?"

Throwing my head back, I laugh so hard my entire body is shaking. Oh shit, this is too fucking funny. The way she curls her upper lip in distaste and the anger in her eyes is strangely adorable. Just as I get my laughter under control, she scrunches up her nose like a fucking bunny of all things, and the thought makes it hard to stop laughing.

Lucia continues, ignoring me completely. "Or maybe it's because you told me to keep the sweater on. No, that couldn't be it, could it? Tell me something, Sawyer." She narrows her eyes. "Why did *you* think I would think that anything had changed?"

I run my hand down my face, trying to wipe the amused grin away. Not that I succeed. "Awww, bunny," I coo. My grin grows as more red splotches of anger spread across her neck and chest. "Let me make myself perfectly clear. Apart from thinking about sinking my dick into your tight cunt, I don't think about you. Drop the mind games and, for your own sake, don't read too much into anything. You'd just be wasting your time."

"So that's how it's going to be?"

Nodding, I fold my arms across my chest. "'Fraid so, bunny. I thought I'd made it more than clear that when we're here, I only care about what's between your legs. And when we're out there..." I gesture toward the windows. "...I only care about my image."

"You're disgusting," she spits.

I shrug again. "Maybe so. But you're the one who sought me out and married me. Don't fucking forget that." Leaning closer, I take her hand and pull it onto my hardening cock. "This is what you sold yourself for, bunny. Don't start crying about it now. Especially not when you creamed all over me while I fucked you like a whore last night."

"Do. Not. Call. Me. Fucking. Bunny." With those words, she picks up her cup and swirls the now cold coffee in my face, making me burst out laughing again. "Dick," she growls as she spins around and marches away.

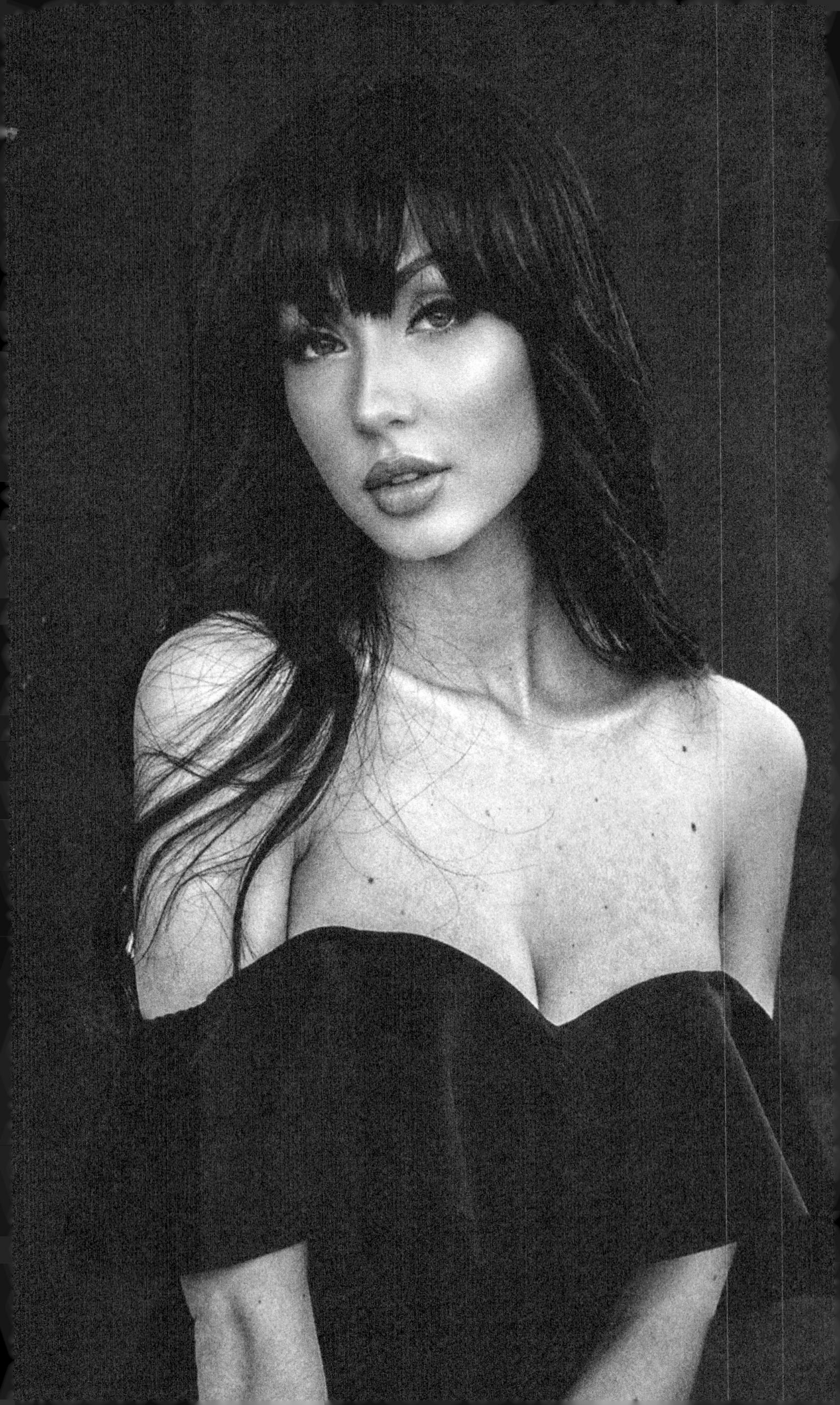

CHAPTER 15

Lucia

Who the fuck does he think he is?

That arrogant fucking son of a bitch just crossed a line I didn't even know existed. Seriously, I thought I could keep my cool and play the dutiful girlfriend... wife. Hell. Fucking. No. I can't. Everything in me screams for me to lash back, to get even—to show him I'm not a fucking puck bunny, like he insinuated.

Storming out of the kitchen after the incident, I seethe with frustration. Seriously, what makes him think treating me this way is okay? Like he has the right to push me away, dismiss me like a common puck bunny whenever he feels like it? It's bullshit, plain and simple.

I'm Lucia fucking Russo, and this... nope. We don't do that shit here; least of all to me.

Like the pissed off drama queen I am right now, I slam the bedroom door behind me. My breathing becomes labored when I hear his infuriating chuckle. Why isn't anything fazing him? Wait... that's not entirely true. My body very much fazes him. Right, that settles it. I need to get to my apartment so I can get the dress I need for tonight.

With a smirk grazing my lips, I walk into the adjoining bathroom and switch on the shower, the hot water, obviously. Might as well cost him a few bucks while I'm pretending to be in here. Then I sneak back out to the kitchen, glad to see he's gone. As I get closer to his bedroom, I hear the water from his shower which is weird since he just showered before breakfast. Oh well.

I stealthily enter Sawyer's bedroom, and yes, he isn't there. Wasting no time, I gather my things and steal one of his shirts because there's no way in hell I'm putting that sweater back on. As soon as I'm dressed and have my things, I leave the apartment, even ask the doorman to call me a taxi, which he happily does.

Entering the apartment, I'm hit with Gail's absence. It's all-consuming. The lack of her presence vibrates from every room, hell, from every corner of the home we share. Until tomorrow... the home we share until tomorrow. Then it'll all be over; the end of an era.

Our place isn't big by any means, but right now, as I'm the only one here, it might as well be the enormous mansion I grew up in. My texts to my best friend are still going unanswered. Actually, she never even opened the last three I sent. My finger hovers over her brother's contact information on my phone. I'm itching to call him. If for no other reason, then just because I need to know she's okay. And to tell her... how sorry I am for lying to her for all those years.

I miss her so badly my heart tightens at the thought of never speaking to her. Knowing that now isn't the time, I let go of the idea and instead head to my closet, rummaging through it until I find the dress I want for tonight. Then I enter the bathroom and take a long shower. I stand under the hot sprays, scrubbing my skin red like that's going to help me shred the layers of shit I've found myself in.

Done with my pity party, I set about getting ready for my big night out. I shave, scrub, use both a hair and a face mask, and even waste some of my expensive and luxurious coconut bath oil. Sawyer isn't worth it, but I am. And since my legs are going to be on full display tonight, I want them to look their best.

Back in my room, I begin curling my long red hair until it's all a mane of soft curls falling down my back. Then, because I still haven't been to the damn hairdresser, I blow dry my bangs to give them a bit of volume, which makes them a tiny bit shorter, so they're no longer shielding my green eyes.

My phone won't stop ringing, but I ignore it. I refuse to let Sawyer ruin my me time. Especially since I feel a little better after my shower.

Taking a deep breath, I settle in front of the vanity mirror, ready to do my makeup. I spent hours in the shower, so by now, the sky has started to darken. I've already switched all the lights on in my room, and they're enveloping me in a warm, familiar aura.

I begin by smoothing a light layer of primer over my skin, the cool, silky texture calming the simmering anger within me. Next, I apply a flawless coat of foundation, carefully blending it into my complexion. As I work, I catch glimpses of my reflection—a cascade of long, red curls framing my face, complementing the emerald green cocktail dress waiting for me.

For my eyes, I opt for a palette of shimmering emerald greens, carefully blending the shades together to create a sultry, smoky effect. With each stroke of mascara, I enhance the intensity of my green eyes, the color seeming to dance and shimmer with every blink.

A bold swipe of deep red lipstick completes the look, adding a touch of sophistication and glamor. With a satisfied nod, I take one last look in the mirror, the reflection staring back at me radiating confidence and poise. Tonight,

I'll make sure Sawyer knows exactly who he's messing with... kinda.

I can't tell him exactly who I am, of course. But I can show him a side of myself that I've kept hidden so far. The one that's far less agreeable, the one that knows he's fucking trapped and can't get rid of me even if I stop obeying his stupid rules.

Game on, motherfucker.

The sounds of someone trying to break down my door by fist startle me. Before I can decide what to do, I hear him. "Open up, bunny. I know you're in there." I curse when Sawyer's angry tenor reaches me. Who the hell does he think he is coming to my place like that? I have neighbors that absolutely don't need to think there's trouble in mine and Sawyer's fake paradise.

I reach for my silk robe, barely managing to tie the belt before I rush to the door and throw it open. Sawyer's hand is in the air, poised for another angry knock. "Get in," I hiss. I look around to make sure no one is watching us before I close the door behind him.

Sawyer isn't hanging around, waiting to be invited further into my apartment. He's already making his own way into the living room. I follow, hot on his heels, my anger at his rudeness and total disregard for my home lengthening my steps.

He turns, his upper lip curled. "You fucking left—"

I hold my hand up, silencing him. "Stop right there," I whisper-yell. Though I want nothing more than to scream at him, I deliberately keep my voice pitched low. Gail and I have never had any real problems with hearing the other tenants in the building, but that doesn't mean I'm willing to risk a screaming match. "You're in my apartment now, Sawyer. My home, my fucking rules. And I don't like people forcing their way in here and trying to throw their weight around."

His eyebrows shoot up his forehead, and his lips part, but he doesn't speak. He clenches his jaw tight while narrowing his eyes like he can intimidate me telepathically. I meet his gaze straight on, lift my chin, and place my hands on my hips.

"Got it," he chuckles, the sudden change in him surprising me. "I only get to make demands when we're at my place."

There are many things I'll bend on, but I will not allow him to intimidate me in my own fucking home. "That's right," I shoot back. I don't like the smile that spreads across his face.

Sawyer schools his expression and looks around the living room. I try to imagine what he's thinking as he takes in the place that screams home. Gail is big on knick-knacks and keepsakes. So we have Polaroid pictures littering one wall, all of which are of us doing everything from eating ice cream, walking on the beach, to the day she won a beer drinking contest. My home is everything I never allow people from work to see in me; it's soft and oh so personal.

"This is different from what I imagined your home to look like," he says. I watch as he moves over to the wall and runs his index finger over a picture from the day we moved in here. "Guess you don't have a stick up your ass all the time."

I shrug, refusing to take the bait. "Only when some jerk shoves one up there," I retort.

He nods as though he agrees and finds my statement reasonable. "Tell me why you left," he probes, still staring at the Polaroid pictures.

"Because I had to get ready," I answer, opting for a half-truth.

A smirk splays at the corner of his mouth, and he runs a hand through his untamed hair. It looks wild and free when it isn't constricted by an elastic band. Just like his beard. "Another half truth. Do you want me to start putting them together like a damn jigsaw puzzle and draw my own conclusions?"

I purse my lips, trying to come up with a deflective retort. But nothing comes to mind, so I say nothing.

"Well?" he prompts, impatience coating that one word when I still haven't answered him.

Licking my lips, I meet his gaze. "You pissed me off with your stupid demands, and I needed my dress, Sawyer. There's nothing else to it."

At the mention of his demands, his eyes leisurely peruse my robe covered body. He isn't even trying to hide the way he studies my bare legs all the way up to my mid-thigh, where the fabric covers the rest of me. The belt is keeping the robe mostly closed, but my cleavage is still on display. Is he aware he licks his lips and that his pupils widen? Clear signs of arousal.

I momentarily consider distracting him with another blowjob. Definitely not because I regret not taking my time the last time I had him in my mouth. But more to get rid of the tension that's building in the room. I decide against it and tell myself it's because he took them off the table.

It feels like I'm being doused in cold water when he rips his gaze away and says, "Okay," like he isn't affected at all. "I need to go home and change. Pick you up in an hour or so?"

"Fine," I say, reluctantly.

Sawyer slowly moves closer until our bodies brush against each other, and he bends down to rasp into my ear, "Don't wear any underwear. Those sponsor events are boring as fuck, so I plan on making you keep your promise tonight." I shiver as his lips graze the shell of my ear.

"We can't," I squeak, hating the effect he has on me. "The whole point of living this lie is to endear you to the sponsors."

He chuckles darkly. "Then we better not get caught, bunny."

I stand there, gaping and frozen in place as he leaves and bounces down the stairs. I'm feeling both schooled and... I don't know how to describe the way he's managed to unsettle and excite me with just a few words.

This isn't going how I want it to at all. And what's worse is that this isn't me. I'm in charge of my career, and the way people see me. Only very few people know the real me. Gail's probably the one that's got the closest. With her, I don't have to wear a mask of indifference. She's seen me laugh at silly things, cry at movies. During all our years of friendship, there's only one thing she didn't know; the truth about my family.

I hate how much Remus' presence has thrown me and my world off kilter. In barely any time at all, everything has changed. My best friend won't talk to me. I might have managed to make Fabian my ex husband by marrying Sawyer, but it's not enough. The world still needs to know, and then he'll need to come to the Vatican with me, so we can stand in front of the Senate. I don't know what the hell I'm doing. I'm winging it, one shitty decision at a time.

My legs shake and I feel like they might give out at every moment as I stagger back to my room. I look longingly at the green dress, but instead of putting it on, I lie down on my bed. I need a few minutes to calm myself down before getting dressed.

Every time I've wanted something big in my life, I've attacked it in stages. When I decided I wanted to be free of my family, I didn't approach my uncle straight away. I took my time, and came up with a plan for how and when to present it to him. Until then, I let my entire family, my parents included, think I was fine with my marriage. It wasn't until my seventeenth birthday that I asked my uncle for my freedom.

There are two paths to take in my family; either become my uncle's protégé at fifteen, which basically means you sign up to get trained by him, and have to follow the plan he lays out for you. Some of my siblings and cousins went down this path, all of them wanting the chance of being the next head of our family. Since I had no such aspirations, I chose path number two, and my uncle and parents chose a husband for me; Fabian. We got married on my sixteenth birthday, which was the single worst day of my life.

My family dabbles in many things, but the biggest is that almost every lead politician is a Russo in blood. Not just in Italy, but all over the world. And Fabian, who was in with the current Prime Minister of Italy at the time, was pushing his own agenda. He allowed deals my uncle worked against. When I got proof of that, I used it to barter my way to ten years of freedom, all with my uncle's blessing and funding.

I guess that's the blessing about your husband seeing you as nothing but a stupid little girl. For Fabian, his arrogance became his downfall, or so I thought. It's why I can't understand why or how he got a seat on the Senate. He should have been ousted for going against my uncle's orders.

Slowing my breathing, I force my thoughts to stay on track instead of running free and making me even more anxious. There's always been multiple steps to conquer, but right now I'm doing the opposite. I've jumped in at the deep end, attempting to tackle it all at once. That'll never work. I need to take it one step at a time. Starting with getting ready. I can do that.

I sit up and reach for my cocktail dress, and before my mind can conjure up things I need to lock down tight and never think about again, I get dressed.

My emerald green dress hugs my curves in all the right places, the luxurious fabric draping elegantly from my slender frame. The neckline plunges daringly, exposing my belly button. Delicate straps crisscross over my shoulders, holding the top together, while a gold chain accents the plunging neckline, adding a touch of sophistication.

As I move, the dress catches the light, revealing subtle hints of shimmer and sparkle woven into the fabric. The rich, jewel-toned hue complements my fiery red hair and brings out the depth of my green eyes. The fitted bodice cinches at the waist before flowing gracefully into a tight skirt that reaches only to my mid-thigh. With every step, the skirt clings to my curves, accentuating my figure in a way I know Sawyer can't ignore.

There's no way I'd ever wear underwear in this dress. It would be sacrilegious to do so. Not only because it has an inbuilt bra, but the lines from a thong just aren't sexy. I still want to tell him he isn't the reason I'm going commando. Just so he doesn't get any ideas, like thinking I'm gonna continue to let him boss me around.

Once I'm wearing my black pumps, which give me a couple of extra inches to work with, I finish the outfit with some jewelry—gold hoop earrings, and fifteen gold finger rings spread across one hand.

My phone pings with an incoming text.

Sawyer: I'm coming up.

Sighing, I put my phone, lipstick, and other essentials in my black clutch and head for the door. While I'm debating what coat to wear, he rings the doorbell, proving he can be civil when he wants to. Asshole.

I end up wearing my knee-length, black coat since you can never go wrong with black, right? Once it's buttoned, I open the door, greeting Sawyer with a sharp nod.

"Are you ready?" he rasps in that overly sexy voice of his.

"Yep," I say, trying to sound like I'm in charge. But the sad reality is it comes out as a croak because... damn.

Sawyer stands before me, his presence commanding attention as he exudes confidence and allure. He has pulled his shoulder-long hair back into a sleek man-bun, adding a touch of rugged charm to his appearance. Each strand falls perfectly into place, framing his chiseled features and drawing attention to his intense, dark eyes.

Dressed in a tailored dark green suit that fits him perfectly, Sawyer cuts a striking figure. Every detail of the suit highlights his body, from the sharp lines of the jacket to the perfectly pressed trousers that hug his bulging frame.

His long beard is neatly combed and trimmed, adding masculinity to his otherwise polished appearance. And fuck me, the way it accentuates the contours of his jawline is... it's turning me on, and making me want to lick his cheekbones.

As our eyes meet, I can see desire burning in his gaze, and I'm pretty sure the same lust is reflected in my eyes.

"You look stunning," Sawyer says, his voice low and husky, his dark eyes lingering on me with a mixture of admiration and desire.

I want to laugh since he doesn't know what I'm wearing under the coat, and he already saw my hair and makeup when he was here only an hour ago. "Thank you," I reply, licking my lips.

With a nod, Sawyer gestures toward the stairs. "Shall we?" he asks, his tone casual yet tinged with an undercurrent of anticipation.

The words sound so oddly stiff and formal from him that I let out a nervous giggle. I quickly pull myself together and nod as I take the first step. When we reach the bottom, Sawyer takes my hand, squeezing it. Though it's nothing more than what I'd expect, it doesn't feel like a role he's playing when he looks at me. And when he squeezes my hand a second time, it almost feels like a reassurance that we're in this together. Or maybe that's just wishful thinking.

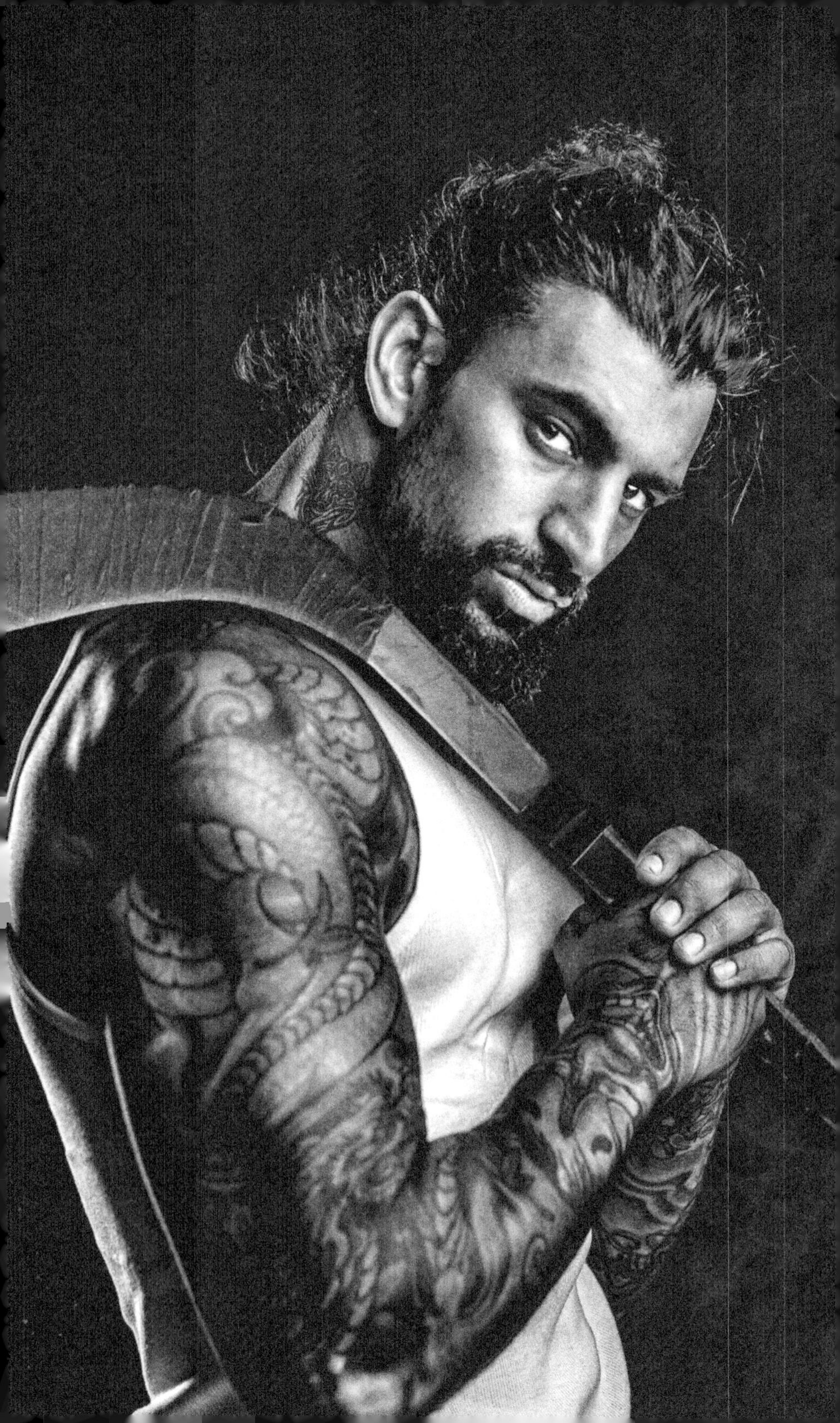

CHAPTER 16

Sawyer

We arrive at the venue where the sponsor event is being held. Sometimes it's at the arena, but this time Tom wanted to go all out and make sure there was enough room for everyone. Which is why we're finding ourselves at a place with a valet that doesn't look old enough to be driving.

"One scratch on my car and I'll hold you personally responsible," I threaten, throwing the keys to the boy.

"Y-yes, sir," he stammers.

Lucia makes a clicking sound with her tongue and rolls her eyes. "I'll pay you to knock off the side mirror," she smirks, not looking away from me.

I arch an eyebrow at her. "I'm not sure you can afford it, bunny." Her nostrils flare, but I ignore it and take her hand, lacing our fingers together. I watch the guy drive away, grinding my teeth while he grinds the gears. "Fuck's sake," I curse.

Lucia pats my arm. "It's not like you can't afford to fix what he damages," she sing-songs.

"That's not the point," I retort. "If he can't drive a fucking stick, he shouldn't have a job parking cars. That would be like me trying to get a job at NASA without knowing anything about space."

Her laughter stuns me, as in actually makes me come to a halt. It's not the polite sound I've heard around the arena. No, it's more like the cackle you'd expect from a Disney villain. I shake my head and ignore her little outburst, chalking it up to… yeah, I got fucking nothing. Nerves? PMS?

We slip through the entrance, and after handing over my coat, I help Lucia with hers. "Fuck me," I praise when the scrap of a dress comes into view.

She runs her hands down the skirt. "You like?" she asks, her tone low and sultry.

"It's alright," I say, shooting her a glare and correcting my dick that just arrived at the fucking party.

Really, that dress is more than alright. It's indecently fucking perfect. One of the sexiest things I've ever seen is Lucia naked; second sexiest was her wearing my number while riding my cock. But this… this is definitely sliding into third place. Her voluptuous tits and toned stomach are as impossible to ignore as the way her bubble ass sways with each step.

"Hey," I snap my fingers when it becomes clear I'm not the only one noticing how sexy the siren at my side is. "Don't fucking look at my wife like that," I snarl at the guys manning the door. They both shrug and mumble half-assed apologies. Fuck… I didn't mean to call her that.

"Let them stare," Lucia says, shaking her ass a little. "It's nice to know my hard work is being appreciated."

I take Lucia's hand again, squeezing it tighter than before. "What's gotten into you?" I seethe under my breath.

"You," she answers simply. "Your dick was in me, and that was quite the revelation."

Smirking, I say, "Well, I can't say I've been told that before."

Lucia keeps her smile firmly in place, even waving at some of the people we pass. "It's not a good thing, Sawyer. While your dick might be magic, you're nothing more than an asshole looking out for himself. So I figured I ought to do the same."

"Lucia—" I'm interrupted as we walk into the large room we're occupying this evening.

Music fills the air, mingling with the chatter of guests as they mill about, all dressed to the nines for the occasion. It's a stark contrast to our usual routine, but there's an undeniable energy in the air that's infectious. Lucia and I exchange a glance, our silent communication speaking volumes as we take in the scene unfolding before us.

"Time to behave, bunny," I remind her, ignoring her answering hiss.

As we navigate through the crowd, I spot familiar faces among the sea of guests. The team sponsors and GM are here, along with a multitude of other attendees, all eager to shake hands and make small talk.

"Sawyer, glad you could make it," one of the sponsors says, extending a hand.

"Thank you, it's great to be here," I reply automatically, returning the handshake.

"And who might this lovely lady be?" another sponsor asks, gesturing toward Lucia with interest.

"This is Lucia Carter," I introduce her with a smile. "She's my…" What the hell do I call her? Fiancée? Wife? "… mine."

"Ah, so this is the lucky lady we've been hearing about," the sponsor remarks, turning to Lucia with a warm smile. "It's a pleasure to meet you, Lucia."

"The pleasure is mine," Lucia replies graciously, offering a polite smile.

We engage in light conversation with the sponsors, discussing the game, upcoming events, and the excitement surrounding the team. Despite the formalities, there's a genuine warmth in the air as we mingle with the sponsors. Tonight, there are none of the disdainful gazes or strained smiles I'm used to from these people.

"Tell me, Sawyer, how's the season treating you so far?" another sponsor inquires, leaning in with interest.

"It's been great so far," I respond. "The team's been performing exceptionally well, and we're all excited about our prospects for the cup this year."

"Where are my manners?" the sponsor says, smiling widely at Lucia. "I'm Edmond—"

"Edmond Francis," Lucia says, interrupting him with a charming smile. "Sawyer made me memorize everyone's names, so I know who you are."

"You didn't," Edmond laughs.

Lucia giggles and shakes her head. "No, he didn't. But he did tell me about how important you guys are, and how much he looked forward to tonight. I hope you'll forgive me for prying, Edmond, but I have to ask. How is your daughter doing? Sawyer and I were both so happy to hear the accident wasn't serious."

I try not to gape at the woman at my side, as she charms the old man with intimate knowledge about his family. Knowledge I have no fucking idea how she got or why she bothered remembering.

"It's so sweet of you to ask. Yes, she's doing much better. It was nothing more than a concussion."

While looking like she's listening intently as Edmond explains about his daughter's fall off a ladder while cleaning her roof or what-the-fuck-ever, Lucia digs her nails into my hand. Right, I should probably say something. "Glad she's okay," I add, trying my best to sound like I care.

"Yes, Sawyer asked me to send a gift basket, but I forgot. I'm so sorry, Edmond. But maybe..." She trails off and opens her clutch, pulling out a small envelope. "...she'll enjoy these once she's on the mend."

Edmond takes the envelope and opens it. "Oh my," he says, his eyes twinkling with delight. "She'll love those. How did you know Giselle is her favorite?"

Instead of asking what the fuck a Giselle is, because the only one I know is Bündchen, I pull Lucia closer and wrap my arm around her middle. "Don't let her fool you," I say jokingly. "This is all her. I don't even know what Giselle is."

While Edmond explains that the ballet is his daughter's favorite, I pretend to kiss Lucia's cheek. "What the fuck are you doing? You can't buy the sponsors. You're crossing the fucking line," I whisper directly into her ear.

Her smile doesn't slip once, that's how good she is.

Before we can make our escape, another sponsor joins us. Jeffrey. "There you are," he bellows, like he's not standing right next to us. "I hear you and Lucia are making headlines. Who would have thought you even knew how to stick to one woman." Then he laughs boisterously, not realizing no one else is joining in.

Lucia raises an eyebrow with a playful grin, but before she gets the chance to speak, I say, "Watch it, Jeffrey. You should show Lucia some respect."

The jerk has the balls to leer at her tits. "Didn't mean no offense," he says, not even bothering to hide his lingering eyes.

I clear my throat and give a polite nod to Edmond and the others. "If you'll excuse us, I promised Lucia a drink."

When I look back, Jeffrey is staring at Lucia's ass, while Edmond is busy showing the ballet tickets to anyone who will listen to him.

"What the fuck was that?" I hiss. "You can't just—"

Lucia shoots me a glare and drags me over to the wall. Then she winds her arms around my neck, moving closer so it looks like we're sharing an intimate moment rather than gearing up for a fight. "I can, and I just fucking did," she hisses back. "Did you know Edmond and Daniels are the two sponsors who have been most vocal about not wanting to stand for your bullshit?"

I shake my head because no; I didn't fucking know that.

"Now that they've seen you with me, they'll buy the girlfriend story. And with the tickets and my knowledge, it looks like you give a shit about someone that isn't you. So you're welcome."

A growl bubbles up my throat and I don't even try to contain it as I look at the woman who's more fox than bunny. "You're not my fucking girlfriend," I spit. "You're my wife." I have no idea why I'm getting hung up on that shit right now, but it feels important to clarify.

She sighs and opens her mouth, likely to argue. But instead of giving her the chance to say anything, I wrap my hand around her throat and pull her closer. Then I fuse our lips together, kissing her hard.

"Sawyer," Lucia gasps.

I use the opportunity to slide my tongue into her mouth, stroking hers. Remembering that we're in a room of people who I should care about, I spin us around so her back hits the wall, and she lets out a breathy 'oomph'. I still have one hand around her throat, squeezing lightly, while the other is on her hip.

Lucia's entire body is trembling as she returns my kiss with demanding strokes of her tongue. She isn't surrendering; she's meeting me stroke for fucking stroke. My cock is hard, straining against my suit pants and I fucking hate that I can't bend her over something and fuck some sense into her.

"Well, well, well," a familiar voice drawls. "Come have a look, Mickey. It looks like Lucia's face—"

I rip my lips from hers and stare daggers at my friend. "Not another word about her face," I growl.

"Dude." Soren throws his hands up and chuckles. "Everyone is staring."

Shaking my head, I repeat, "I don't fucking care. Don't talk about her."

I ignore his eyebrows that shoot so far up his forehead they're practically meeting his hairline. "You okay?" I mumble, only loud enough for Lucia. She looks up at me, her eyes hooded and her lipstick is smeared. If you ask me, it looks better this way, since I know it's my handiwork. But I already know she won't agree. "You should go to the bathroom and clean up." My husky tone makes it sound suggestive rather than a suggestion.

"Will you meet me there?"

Taking her hand, I bring it up to my mouth and bite two of her fingers teasingly. I don't stop until her breath hitches and she moans softly. "Do you want me to join you?" I ask.

"Y-yes."

"We'll be back," I say, winking at my friends. "Hold down the fort while we're gone."

Lucia blushes as they howl and laugh boisterously, but I don't care. Why would I when I'm about to play with the best cunt I've ever had.

No one pays us any attention as we weave through the throng of people. Luckily, the bathroom area is almost deserted, and I don't think anyone notices us ducking in there. As soon as I have the door closed and locked, I push Lucia up against it, wasting no time before I claim her mouth in a hot, languorous kiss. While our tongues snake around each other, I move my hands under her dress and roughly cup her cunt.

"Look at you doing what I said," I rasp into her mouth. "No underwear." I punctuate the words by sliding two fingers inside her.

She's already so wet no prep is needed, and the moment I curl my fingers, she breaks the kiss and moves her head to my shoulder to bury her moan. "I-I didn't want lines."

Her words make me chuckle. "Fashion over everything else, huh?" I taunt. "Not that I'm complaining. I love having easy access to your cunt."

While my fingers piston in and out of her, she spreads her legs even more. "Please fuck me, Sawyer."

I want to. Fuck, I want to so badly. But I'm not going to. "Not yet, bunny," I rasp.

She tenses. "What? Why not?"

"Don't worry, baby. I'm still going to get you off." I hike her dress up around her hips so I can look down at what I'm doing. Though I really fucking want to get on my knees and introduce myself properly to her weeping cunt, I stop myself. This isn't the time to push that issue. "Hold your dress up for me," I command huskily.

Lucia does as I say, holding the skirt of her dress so it's out of the way, and I reward her by fusing our lips together again. I swallow her moans, keeping them for myself while I use my fingers to fuck her.

As the heel of my hand grinds on her clit, her moans become deeper. She uses one hand to pull at my tie. "Sawyer." Fuck, I love the determination in her tone. "Make me come all over your fingers."

"Always, bunny," I rasp while wrapping my hand around her throat. I tighten my grip and fuck her harder. Her breath hitches and her eyes widen, but she doesn't try to stop me. "That's it. Don't fight it, just feel it."

My thumb is on top of her pulse, which feels fucking amazing. Like I can do anything, especially when she looks at me like she trusts that I know what I'm doing to her. "Do you trust me, wife?" I ask, needing her to say the word.

"Y-yes," she croaks.

I add more pressure, both on her throat and on her clit. She moans beautifully in response. Her tits heave as she tries to get the air her body is so badly craving, but that I'm denying it. Never looking away from her, I see it immediately when her eyes roll back in her head. Her cunt spasms, squeezing my fingers while sucking them farther into her.

When she lets out a strained whimper, I let go of her neck. Moving closer so my body is holding hers up against the door while she sags. There's a goofy smile on her lips, one that comes from being thoroughly fucked.

After checking the lid is down on the toilet, I take her into my arms and sit down so I can hold her steadily. Her eyes are still closed, the lids moving slightly as her long, dark lashes fan across her cheeks. I never noticed how long her eyelashes are until now. I wonder if they're real or fake. Yet another thing I want to know.

My heart beats thunderously in my chest while I hold her tight and watch over her. It's at this moment I realize what the fuck is going on. Lucia isn't my pretend anything, she's so much more than that. I don't know when or even how it happened, only that it did. And now... now there's no escaping it. Lucia Carter is mine—all fucking mine.

"Sawyer?" As though she's heard my thoughts, she slowly opens her eyes and looks up at me. "That was really something," she breathes.

"You did good, sweet bunny," I rasp, kissing the crown of her head.

"I'm glad," she says. "I like pleasing you." She snuggles closer and closes her eyes again. "Just give me a few minutes, and then I'll clean up so we can go back."

I want to tell her that she can take all the time she wants, but I don't—I can't. The words stay lodged in my mouth like a golf ball I can barely swallow around. I've never felt like this about anyone, so I'm not sure I know what it means. Not that it really matters since I have thirteen months to figure it out.

When Lucia no longer feels boneless, she gets up and I wait patiently while she fixes her hair, lipstick, and dress. But when she wants to wipe her cum away, I've had it. "No," I growl, startling her. "When we go back out there, I want to know you have your cum leaking down your legs."

To my surprise, she gives me a sly look. "Okay," she agrees. "You know you don't have to growl to get your way, right? You could have just asked and I would have done it."

Shaking my head, I take her hand and pull her out of the bathroom. "I shouldn't have to ask."

As Lucia and I return to the party, Tom, the GM, intercepts us with an eager grin, motioning us over to the bar.

"Sawyer, Lucia, perfect timing," Tom greets us, his eyes bright with excitement. "I want you to meet someone."

Intrigued, we follow Tom to the other side of the bar, where a man stands waiting. He doesn't look like the other rich and stuffy assholes. His white hair and blue eyes makes him stand out. He's shorter than me, but then again, at six-foot-five most people are. It's not like he's tiny or anything, probably around six-one.

"Sawyer, Lucia, this is Fabian," Tom introduces, his voice filled with enthusiasm. "Our newest sponsor. It's been a long time coming, but we've finally come to terms." Fabian doesn't speak. Hell, he doesn't even acknowledge that Tom did. "Sawyer is our star forward," Tom continues, oblivious to the fact that Fabian is ignoring us both. He's too busy looking at Lucia like she's a piece of meat. It takes every ounce of self control I possess not to snarl at him to back the fuck off.

"Pleasure to meet you both," Fabian finally says, his gaze lingering on Lucia. "Especially you, Lucia. I already feel like I know you from all the nice things Tom has said." I swear his accent changes slightly when he says her name.

"Yes… umm… you too," Lucia rambles, not at all sounding like her usually collected self. Instead her tone is shrill and her words are a mess.

Hmm, what the fuck am I missing here? And why do I feel like I've heard his voice before?

I shake Fabian's hand when he holds it out to me, and force myself to exchange polite pleasantries with him, but my attention remains on Lucia, whose reaction is far from normal. As Fabian extends his hand toward her, she stiffens beside me, her grip on my arm tightening as a soft whimper escapes her lips.

"You okay, bunny?" I ask, my concern evident as I meet her gaze.

Her eyes betray a hint of fear, and she instinctively seeks refuge in my embrace. Anger courses through my veins, demanding to be set free. But I can't just start punching sponsors, especially when I don't know why.

"I... I'm fine," she murmurs, her voice barely audible above the noise of the party.

She's clearly anything but fine right now. But with Tom and Fabian here, I can't outright ask her what's going on. I can, however, make sure the dickhead doesn't get closer to her. Shifting her slightly, I make sure his hand doesn't touch her when he moves closer, silently insisting on a handshake.

"Want to shake my hand again?" I force a laugh. Then I make a fist, awkwardly fistbumping his hand. "That's how we do it on the ice," I explain, doing my best to make it seem more natural. I fail. There's nothing fucking natural about this interaction.

Fabian laughs. "I like you, Sawyer. From what I heard, I expected you to be a lone wolf, but you seem fine to me."

I shrug. "What can I say, my bunny brings out the best in me."

As I lean down to kiss the top of her head, Fabian's eyes flash with anger. Interesting. I shoot Tom a questioning glance, but he just shrugs. Dick.

"Bunny?" Fabian laughs, echoing my fucking name for Lucia. "After everything I've heard about her, she sounded more like a wolf."

What is it with this guy and wolf anecdotes?

"Oh, God," Lucia whines. "I-I'm sorry... I think I'm... I don't feel well." One look at her, and it's easy to see she isn't lying. She's paler than a fucking ghost. Sweat beads on her forehead, and she's trembling.

Fabian shifts closer, his eyes glued on the wedding band on Lucia's finger. "So congratulations are in order," he says. His smile doesn't reach his eyes.

"Congratulations?" Tom asks, frowning in confusion.

Nodding, Fabian moves closer and grasps Lucia's wrist, causing her to cry out in surprise. "I know a wedding band when I see one," he sneers, giving up all pretenses about being nice.

"What the? No, that can't be right," Tom says. But as he looks down at Lucia's hand, he realizes just how right it is. "Sawyer?"

Holding Lucia tighter, I give him a strained smile. "We weren't going to announce it until after Christmas," I say, making it up as I go. "But yes, we're married."

Tom holds my gaze longer than he needs to, searching in the depths for... well, I don't fucking know. Whether it's a sham or real marriage shouldn't matter to him. He's the one who wanted me to date Lucia. "I see," he finally says. Looking away, his eyes sweep over Lucia. "Perhaps it's best if you call it a night," Tom suggests, with a forced smile, his disappointment clear.

"Of course," I reply smoothly. Though I note the tension in his voice, I don't give a fuck about anyone else but Lucia right now.

As we turn to leave, I overhear Tom's voice, his tone apologetic. "I'm truly sorry about that, Fabian. I hope it didn't spoil your evening."

Fabian's response is a low chuckle, tinged with amusement. "Not at all, Tom. These things happen, and I'm sure I'll get the pleasure of catching up with Miss Ru-Carter another time."

Lucia doesn't ease her hold on me, in fact, the further we get away from Tom and Fabian, the more she shakes. After getting our coats, I guide her outside. When she almost falls for the third time in just as many minutes, I give up and carry her to my car.

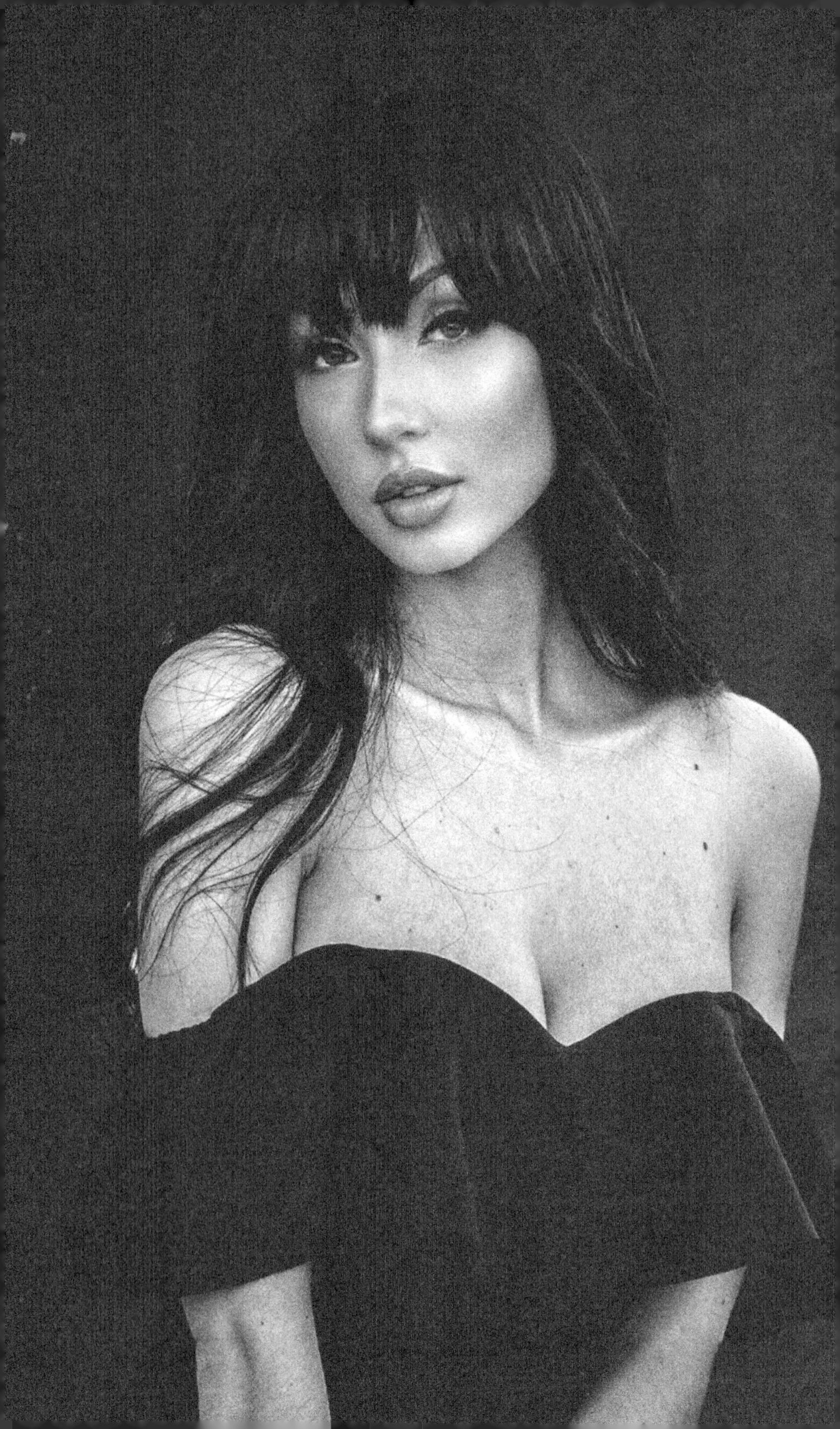

CHAPTER 17

Lucia

I don't think my body has ever been louder than it is in the silence of the car. My teeth are chattering, my blood rushes in my veins, and my heart is beating so violently I can barely hear the other two.

Fabian…
Fabian is…
Fuck.
Fabian is here.

I don't understand it. It's like there's a fog making it impossible for my brain to comprehend what just happened. Rationally, I know exactly what's going on; Fabian bought his way into my world and put himself in a position of pure power. Irrationally, my brain rejects the idea. Scoffs and tells me it's not possible. But not only is it possible, it happened.

"Was his name really Fabian?" I ask again, hoping beyond belief that Sawyer is going to look at me with a smile and tell me "gotcha."

"That's what he said," Sawyer replies, his tone as strained as the veins on his arms.

Despite the turmoil in my mind, I can't stop looking at him as he sits there, bare-chested and tense and so handsome it's hard to look away. Since I'm still shaking, he gave me his suit jacket and shirt to cover me. And since I didn't have the words to explain I'm not freezing because it's cold, but because I'm scared to the very marrow of my being, no amount of fabric will make me warm again.

The one thing I remember the most from living with Fabian and being his wife is how cold I always felt. Even during the hottest summer day in Rome, I'd be cold all the way into my bones. No amount of sun or Roman baths could heat me up. I didn't feel warm again until my uncle took my deal and granted my wish; saving me from Fabian's cruelty.

"Goddamn it, Lucia. What can I do?" I turn my head sluggishly, just in time to see Sawyer punch the steering wheel. "We'll be home soon. Just hang in there. Please."

His words don't make a lick of sense to me right now, so I just look at his many tattoos. His upper body is completely covered, but I've never really looked at them. As my eyes slowly trail up to his neck, I almost jump in my seat. That can't be...

"Is that a wolf?" I lean closer, my eyes locked on the animal resting on his neck.

"Really?" he barks. "That's the first thing you say, and you want to know about my tattoo?"

I roll my eyes. "Is it?"

"Yeah," he replies. "Got it years ago. When I was eighteen, I think."

Without meaning to, I reach out to touch it. Sawyer's skin pebbles under my fingers, and I once again feel his eyes on me. It feels intimate, more so than any time he's been inside me. Which is weird, but also oddly... nice.

"Why a wolf?"

He shoots me a strained smile. "Because I wasn't emo enough to get a fucking butterfly." His words make me want to smile, but I don't. I don't know how to. It's like I've forgotten how to use the muscles in my face. So I just sit there, doing and saying... nothing.

When we arrive at Sawyer's place, he tells me to stay put. I watch him summon the elevator and place his shoe in the door so it can't close. Then he comes back to the car, opening the passenger side door, and lifts me into his arms. I snuggle into him, breathing in his unique scent while he carries me with my head resting on his chest.

I've never paid much attention to how he smells, but right now it's all I can think about. It's... everywhere. Sawyer's scent envelops me like a warm embrace, a blend of sandalwood and fresh pine that tingles my senses. Beneath the earthy notes, there's a hint of leather, adding depth to his fragrance. It's a comforting aroma, masculine yet soft, drawing me in with its subtle allure. Every time I catch a whiff of his cologne, it's as if I'm transported to a tranquil forest, lost in the rugged beauty of nature and the promise of adventure that Sawyer embodies.

Jesus, my mind is basically waxing poetry about his smell.

The elevator dings and the doors slide open, revealing the inside of Sawyer's apartment. Even though this isn't my first time here, I feel like I'm seeing it through fresh eyes. Previously, I never paid much attention to how bright and open the place is. Whoever the interior designer is, they've done a great job. It's just the right amount of stylish and homey, without being too much of either.

I know I shouldn't focus on trivial things like Sawyer's smell and home decoration, but the way my mind is latching on to any distraction makes it impossible to let it go.

"Who decorated your home?" I ask as I take in the paintings on the wall.

Sawyer gives me a curious look, like he isn't sure why I'm asking. "My mom did."

"Is she—" I stop talking when he presses a finger against my lips to silence me.

"I don't want to talk about her."

Right, we don't talk. Knowing what comes next, I wiggle until he puts me down. As soon as my feet touch the carpet, I shrug his shirt and jacket off. Then I unzip my dress and let it pool around my feet. Since I'm not wearing any underwear, I stand naked in front of him.

"What the fuck are you doing?" Sawyer asks, incredulously. "Why the hell are you getting naked when you're so cold?"

I stare at him, uncomprehending. "Your rule," I whisper, reminding him.

He scoffs angrily and rolls his eyes. "Fuck the rules, bunny. All I care about right now is getting you warm."

Now that he's mentioned it, I realize I'm still shaking. Not as bad as before, but still enough for him to notice it. I sigh and look up at him. "I can't get warm as long as Fabian's around."

"You do know him." It's not a question, but I still nod. "How do you know him?"

"I-I can't tell you." My voice cracks, and tears form in my eyes. I blink rapidly, refusing to let them fall. Though it's been a long time, I still intend to keep my promise to myself about not allowing Fabian to be the reason for more tears.

Sawyer swallows harshly, and I can't stop looking at his Adam's apple as it bobs in his throat. "How about we get you into a warm bath, and then you can tell me... at least something."

Before I can answer, he picks me back up and carries me to his spacious bathroom. I feel a little ridiculous as he sits me down on the toilet while he fills the tub that's big enough for three people. The splash of the water is soothing, and I feel even more relaxed when the scent of eucalyptus reaches my nostrils.

I eye the fancy glass bottle holding the green liquid. The smell itself isn't feminine by any means, but the bottle doesn't seem like something a guy would buy. If it's leftovers from some puck bunny, I'll fucking lose my shit. Tonight's not the night. I don't care if we're only faking our relationship—our marriage. I still want the respect, even if it's faked.

When I look up, Sawyer's watching me with an amused grin. "What made you look so murderous all of a sudden?"

"Who does that belong to?" I ask, pointing at the bottle.

"Me," he answers. His brows furrow together. "Why?" Before I can say anything, he throws his head back and roars with laughter. It's so infectious the corners of my lips turn upward, twitching into a semblance of a smile.

I raise an incredulous eyebrow as I perch on the toilet lid, naked and… I don't even know, while Sawyer stands nearby, his eyes crinkled with laughter. "What's so funny?" I remark, my tone laced with disbelief.

Sawyer's lips curl into a playful grin as he leans against the bathroom counter, his gaze fixed on me. "You're jealous," he replies, his voice tinged with humor.

I scoff, my eyes narrowing. "Jealous? Of what?" He doesn't need to know he's right. It's an irrational and ridiculous feeling—one I have no right to harbor, one I definitely won't own up to.

Sawyer chuckles softly, the sound warm and infectious. "Sure thing, bunny," he quips, his tone making it clear he doesn't believe me at all.

I huff and pointedly stare at the bathtub. "Can I get in now?" I ask.

"Yeah," he rasps, his eyes trailing all over my naked body as I stand and allow him to help me into the massive tub.

I moan softly as I lower my body into the water. It feels amazing. While we were talking, I forgot all about feeling cold, and now, well, I don't feel cold at all. The hot water is like a soft blanket cocooning me, warming me from the inside out.

Once I'm comfortable, I lean my head back against the edge and look up at Sawyer. He's grinding his teeth while looking at me like he wants to either fight or fuck me. "I don't really have any other bath products," he explains, sitting down on the edge of the tub. "This is the shit Coach wants us to use for our muscles."

Oh... now I feel a bit stupid for jumping to conclusions. I close my eyes, soaking up the warmth, loving the way I can feel it all the way into my bones. When I open my eyes again, Sawyer has lowered himself so our faces are almost touching. I let out a surprised gasp, but don't look away. The longer we stay locked like this, the less cold I feel. That's when I realize it's not the water chasing away the dreadful feeling; it's Sawyer.

Sawyer Perry, of all people, is the one to make me feel better. Huh, I guess life really has a sense of irony after all, considering how many times he's made me feel like shit.

"Aren't you getting in?" I barely recognize my voice. It's all sultry and low, like I'm trying to seduce him with my voice alone.

"Do you want me to?" he asks, quirking an eyebrow.

Feeling suddenly shy, I bite down on my bottom lip and nod. Then I proceed to ogle him, which is a complete contradiction since I don't hide the way my eyes caress his body while he first removes his shoes, pants, and then... wait, when did he put his shoe back on after using it to keep the elevator doors open? I shake my head, that's so not the right thing to focus on as he gracefully steps into the tub.

"Move forward," he rasps before sitting down. I feel him move and shift behind me, making himself comfortable. Sawyer palms my hips and pulls me back, so I'm nestled between his long, muscular legs. His hard-on prods me in the back, and I wiggle my ass against him. "Ignore that for now."

"What if I don't want to ignore it?" I ask, slightly breathless.

"I want to talk, bunny. Really talk." He tugs at my hair until I relent and lean back against him. "We're married for fuck's sake, and if tonight's taught me anything, it's that we know hardly anything about each other."

Taking my hand, he lifts it into the air, his fingers gracing the Russo wedding band heirloom. It looks simple enough if you don't know what to look for. It's gold, with the letters S.P.Q.R. engraved, and at the front there are two white diamonds, symbolizing the eyes of the wolf. I know Fabian recognized the design when he saw it. Shit... he knows... he knows I'm married to Sawyer. For the first time, I'm scared of what this will mean for my husband.

Fabian is bound by the laws of our family, and he isn't allowed to interfere. But he obviously doesn't give a shit about that since he's now a sponsor for the Sabertooths. I wonder how long he's been here, watching me... shit. Oh no, the things I accused Remus of... sending the weird presents and painting my door. Fuck. It wasn't Remus, it had to be Fabian, I was just too stupid to see it.

And just like that, the coldness returns. Not as much as before, but enough that I feel it seeping under my skin. A part of me considers reaching out to Remus to ask if he's told Fabian about my marriage, and... it doesn't matter. I fought so hard to get away, and I won't let myself be roped back in by asking our Don to interfere or for an update.

"Lucia," my husband growls, reminding me I've just been sitting here, too lost in my thoughts to speak.

"I don't want to talk," I say, almost petulantly. But dammit, I don't want to. Not even a little. Because right now, I'm not sure I can filter myself enough. So if I start talking, I don't think I'd be able to stop.

"Because you don't trust me." There's no accusation in his tone. "And that's fair. But I trust you."

"You do?" I gasp, surprised by the revelation.

He bends so his lips graze the shell of my ear. "Why wouldn't I? You're playing your part well and making me look good even when you don't have to. You're living up to your end of the deal."

Well, when he puts it like that, I do sound like one helluva catch. "But you don't know me," I insist.

I'm not sure why I'm trying to talk him out of trusting me. Gaining his trust is exactly what I need, and what I've tried to achieve. Yet it doesn't sit right with me that he's declaring it when I'm lying… maybe not lying, but I'm definitely not being honest, and I am going out of my way to play the situation to my advantage.

Deciding to give him something, a small yet poignant truth, I say, "That guy from the interview… John is… well…" Shit, I don't know how to explain this. Maybe I just need to rip off the Band-Aid. "It was Fabian. He was the one who asked about me being honest at the interview."

"I figured," he says. "Your reaction tonight was worse than at the interview, but pretty damn similar." Sawyer runs his big hands up and down my arms in a soothing motion while he licks and kisses his way down my neck to my shoulder, then back up again.

My skin pebbles, and I do my best to hold back any sounds, giving away how amazing it feels. "Do you, umm, have any follow up questions?" I don't know why I'm asking that. But a part of me feels like I should open the door, allow him to ask any questions he might have.

"I know enough," he finally says. His hand snakes down my body until it rests perfectly on top of my brand. "I know you're loyal." I shiver as he moves his hand down, down, down. But to my disappointment, he doesn't touch my pussy. Instead, he trails his fingers over the scars on first one thigh, then the other. "And I know someone has taken advantage of you."

Tears pool in my eyes as I choke back a sob. Sawyer has noticed a lot more than I've given him credit for. The intensity in his voice is like a current, threatening to pull me under if I let it. "The same can be said for most people," I say. My voice cracks, so I clear my throat before continuing. "No one can survive without loyalty, even if it's just to themselves."

Sawyer presses his hand tighter against the brand on my hip. "And who are you loyal to, sweet bunny?" he asks.

"Myself," I retort. This time, my voice holds steady, making my answer strong and almost unyielding. I stiffen, feeling defensive when I feel him nodding. "I wasn't always like that, Sawyer. If you'd met me before... well, just before, you would have seen how much I cared about other people."

I don't know why I'm justifying myself to him, of all people. The only reason I have is that I don't like him thinking of me as a completely selfish person. I mean, I am... but for some reason, I don't want that to be how he sees me.

"I know what it's like not to have anyone to be loyal to," Sawyer rasps. He leans forward, bending me like a rag doll as he reaches for the tap and turns the hot water back on. "Sometimes it's not about whether we're loyal or not, but whether we have anyone in our lives that deserves our loyalty."

Hmm, that's... profound. Not something I'd expect to come out of his mouth. "You have your team," I say. "You're loyal to the Sabertooths."

"They're my family," he replies. "So yes, I'm loyal to them on and off the ice. But they're also the only family I have."

"And your mom," I say, almost on a scoff. Then I slap my hand over my mouth, immediately regretting the words. "I'm sorry, I shouldn't have brought her back up." He did say he didn't want to talk about her, and as someone who doesn't want to talk about my family, I should respect that.

He chuckles. "No, you shouldn't have. But you're right. I have my mom. Except, she's nothing to me, and I'm even less to her." Try as he might to hide it, I can hear the underlying hurt in his voice. It doesn't sound fresh, but more like it's something he has carried around for years.

"My mom is my blood," I say, deciding to give him the tiniest bit of information. "But she's not family. She hasn't been for years, and she never will be again. If the Sabertooths are your family, I guess Gail is mine."

"That's your roommate, right? The one you've taken with you to most games?"

I stare up at the ceiling, trying to ignore the way my heart hurts. I miss Gail, and nothing feels the same without her. "Yeah, that's the one," I breathe.

"Why wasn't she with you the other night?"

"Because I fucked up." Now it's my turn to bleed my emotions everywhere. My voice betrays the pain I'm carrying around. I'm sure Sawyer will find a way to use it against me at a later date. Yet I don't regret saying it.

I don't know what it is about Sawyer. The more time I spend with him, the more I wonder what it would be like if he knew the real me. If we'd met under different circumstances. If, if, if... I let out a wistful sigh and squeeze my eyes shut. Ifs and buts don't matter. This isn't a fairy tale where a genie can give me a do-over. It's life, and there's only one direction; forward.

As though he can sense my inner turmoil, Sawyer holds me tighter. His hands aren't seeking my pleasure spots, he's just... caressing me in an assuring way. It's both unsettling and just what I need. I rest against him for a beat longer, then I stretch my leg and use my foot to turn the tap back off. The hot water is like a cocoon, keeping us in this moment of bliss where nothing can hurt us.

I'm half asleep when Sawyer asks, "Are you ever going to tell me about Fabian?"

My body reacts on instinct, and I sit up, ramrod straight. I hide my trembling hands between my thighs, squeezing them between the skin he marred. "Absolutely not," I hiss. Then I realize that was the wrong reaction; the worst, in fact.

"He's the fucker who cut you." Sawyer's tone has dropped several degrees, making it practically icy. Since it's not a question, I don't answer. "Tell me it wasn't him," he growls.

Since I don't have a reply, I jerk forward and rush out of the bathtub. Then I reach for the closest towel, and wrap it around me. "Who it was or wasn't isn't any of your business, Sawyer," I seethe. "I appreciate that you took care of me tonight, and I'm glad to know you're not a complete jerk. But none of that gives you a right to my secrets."

His nostrils flare, and when he stands, his hands are clenched at his sides. Despite the anger brewing between us, I can't tear my eyes away from his body. This man... Jesus. The statues back in Rome have nothing on Sawyer's chiseled, rough, unpolished beauty. Yeah, he isn't merely handsome—he's whatever the male equivalent of beauty is.

"What did you just say?" His tone is deceptively low, sending shivers down my spine. Not of fear, like with Fabian, but with... excitement.

"I said—"

He waves me off. "I fucking heard you, bunny. I'm giving you the option to take it back before it's too late."

Rather than heeding his warning, I shake my head stubbornly. "I said what I said," I retort, lifting my chin like a bratty teenager instead of the almost twenty-eight-year-old woman I am. When it comes to Sawyer, I can't help myself. He's awakening a side of me I'd long since forgotten ever existed. "I'm not your fucking toy."

He throws his head back and laughs loudly. "Aren't you, though?" When he steps out of the tub toward me, I instinctively take one back. "You gave your body to me, bunny. That very much makes you my fuck toy. And since you were never specific about your terms, I also happen to think that whatever happens or happened to your body is my business."

"No," I croak, sensing where he's going with this.

"Yes," he says, taking another step closer.

My heart thunders in my chest, as I give up on holding the towel together and spin around. I dart out of the bathroom so fast I almost trip over my own damn feet, but I manage to right myself at the last minute.

"Where are you going, sweet bunny?" he calls after me. I ignore his taunting voice and focus on avoiding the furniture in his dark living room.

I don't even know why the hell I'm running, or what I think I'm going to get out of it. I'm stark naked, which means I'm confined to this apartment. It might be big, and have rooms I haven't even been in yet. But that doesn't mean it's too big to find me. It's only a matter of time before Sawyer catches me. We both know it.

"Lucia!" Sawyer sounds less amused now. "Stop fucking running and behave like a grown ass adult instead of playing games."

"I'm not playing games," I squeak. Fueled by a stubborn need to get away, I try the door next to the guest bedroom I've slept in.

To my surprise, it opens and I dart inside. Now what? The room is nothing like the one I've been in. Sure, it's another bedroom, but it's so much more… I don't even know how to describe it. Personal? Yeah, I guess that's it.

On the wall hang pictures of what looks like a family. Mom, Dad, and… oh my God, is that kid Sawyer? I move closer, running my fingers across the frames. They all look so happy. One picture is of the woman and man watching as a small Sawyer rides his bike. I wonder if it's his first time riding it by himself?

"You have no right being in here."

I let out a bloodcurdling scream and spin around so fast I feel dizzy for a second. "Don't do that," I scold.

Sawyer quirks a brow and stares unamused at me. "Don't do what? Don't go snooping in your home? Oh wait, that's you and not me."

Ignoring his admonishing tone, I shake my head and explain. "No. I meant, don't sneak up on me." As my breathing calms down, I consider what he just said. "And I'm sorry. I didn't mean to go snooping..." I scrunch my nose in distaste at the word. "... I only tried to get away from you."

When Sawyer moves behind me, I feel it more than hear it. He's like a magnet, and my body is ready to obey him in every sense of the word. My mind, however, is fighting to stay clear of the erotic fog that seems to take over whenever we're together. Especially when we're naked, which we both are.

"Lucia—"

Although I like the way he pronounces my name, I interrupt him. "Are those your parents?"

Sawyer moves closer, not stopping until his hands are on my hips and his hardness nestled in the crevice of my ass. "Yes." His hot breath fans across my shoulder.

He bites down on my shoulder. It's not hard enough to break the skin, but enough to make my back arch, pushing my ass against him. "Sawyer." My voice is all breathy and low.

"Those pictures are some of the few memories I have of us being together as a happy family," Sawyer says. It's hard to focus on his words when he tightens his hold on my hips and grinds against me. "I don't think my mom was cheating yet. But she did not long after."

His words clear the fog from my brain. "Y-your mom cheated on your dad?" I ask. I don't know what's shocking me more; finding out that this is like some kind of shrine to a time that's long gone, or that he's opening up, sharing with me.

"She did," he confirms. His voice is gravelly and his breathing ragged as he grinds harder against me. "For years, until he finally had enough and left."

"Oh shit," I mutter as something clicks together in my head. "That's why you punched that guy, isn't it? Because he accused you of cheating."

"I don't fucking cheat. And I don't fuck anyone who's married."

Well... shit. Now I definitely can't tell him about Fabian because judging by how hard he's gripping my hips and the tone of his voice, fucking a married woman is a hard pass for Sawyer. One he wasn't aware he was breaking, but I was. I consider telling him the truth, but then I shut that shit down fast. Sawyer is my ticket to freedom. Even if I'm slowly growing a conscience, I can't allow it to change anything.

Sawyer grunts in annoyance when I turn around, and when I see the look on his face, I kind of wish I'd stayed with my back to him. He looks... haunted. There's no other word for it. I stretch and wrap my arms around his neck, adding pressure until he bends so I can fuse our lips together. He kisses me like he fucks; hard and so demanding, he starts a fire in my lower stomach.

I jump and wrap my legs around him. "Take me to bed," I murmur. His hands squeeze my ass cheeks, holding me in place while he carries me back to his bedroom.

As soon as we enter the room, he walks over to the wall, so it's at my back. We're still kissing, and I'm gyrating my hips so his cock slides between my pussy lips. When he breaks the kiss and puts some distance between us, I don't open my eyes. I'm too scared I'll see the haunted expression on his face.

"Look at me," he commands. I shake my head. "Fucking look at me when I'm speaking to you, bunny."

My eyes flutter open. Our gazes lock; his dark one on my green orbs. It feels as though time stands still while we look at each other, locked in something unspoken that I'm not sure I understand.

"Do you want my cock inside your cunt?" he rasps, moving one hand between us so he can swirl my clit around.

"Y-fuck." A moan bubbles up my throat as he adds more pressure, working my clit like a pro.

"Answer me, bunny."

"Yes... oh God. Yes. Please."

With each swipe of his finger, it becomes harder to think. Harder to focus on anything but the pleasure growing inside me.

I whine in protest when he stops and removes his finger. But as quickly as he stopped, he angles the fat tip of his cock against my drenched opening. "Say please."

"I already did," I huff, frustrated and so damn horny.

"Mhmm, I know. I love it when you beg. So I'm not fucking you until you tell me how much you want me inside you."

"Please fuck me, Sawyer," I purr. He shows his approval by sliding the tip inside. "Don't stop until I feel my pussy stretching around your big cock. I want... fuck. I want—" Sawyer slams all the way inside me, effectively rendering me speechless.

I moan as my pussy does just what I said I wanted, and I feel it stretching to accommodate Sawyer's huge dick. I pant through the burn, relishing in the exquisite pain that quickly morphs into pleasure.

"That's it, wife. Open up for me so I can fuck you deeply," Sawyer groans. "Fuck. Your cunt is so tight. Relax."

I try to answer, to tell him I'm as relaxed as I can be, but the words are a garbled string of nonsensical noises. He moves his hand between us so he can touch my clit again. With each flick, I become more boneless. My moans grow louder and louder until he finally stops teasing me with his shallow strokes, and bottoms out inside me with every thrust.

"Sawyer!" I scream his name as my pleasure skyrockets, sending me hurtling over the edge and into an intense orgasm.

"Fuck! Bunny!" He punctuates each word with a thrust. "I love feeling you come on my dick."

I'm too far gone to master the art of speaking, so I just look up at him with a goofy, satisfied grin on my lips. Christ, the orgasm he doles out should be illegal with the way it leaves me unable to control myself. I'm pretty sure that if he asked me about my past now, I'd spill every dirty secret without blinking.

Sawyer doesn't pause while I recover. If anything, he fucks me harder. I can feel the brick wall dig into my back, but I don't move or shy away from it. Knowing that it's scratching my skin because of what we're doing makes it delicious.

Wanting Sawyer to feel what I'm feeling, I run my hands down his shoulders to his back. Then I dig my nails in just as he thrusts deep inside me, touching that magical spot that has me crying out his name in sweet agony-filled pleasure.

"Fuck. Wife," he groans. "Harder." Doing as he says, I scratch him harder. "Fuuuuck!"

I can barely breathe with how full I am. My senses are working on total overload, making it hard to think. Good thing I don't need my wits about me for something as basic as what we're doing.

Sawyer moves his hand around my throat, and just like earlier tonight, he robs me of the ability to breathe. I know I should panic, yet I don't. It makes me fly higher, makes my pleasure reach higher than ever before. As darkness settles around me, he groans my name and paints my insides with his cum.

"Come for me, bunny."

Again, my body obeys him and I scream his name while fighting the need to pass out. As soon as he lets go of my neck, I take in air, greedily gulping it down in huge gasps. Despite my sore pussy and throat, I feel better than I think I ever have before. I feel free and... powerful.

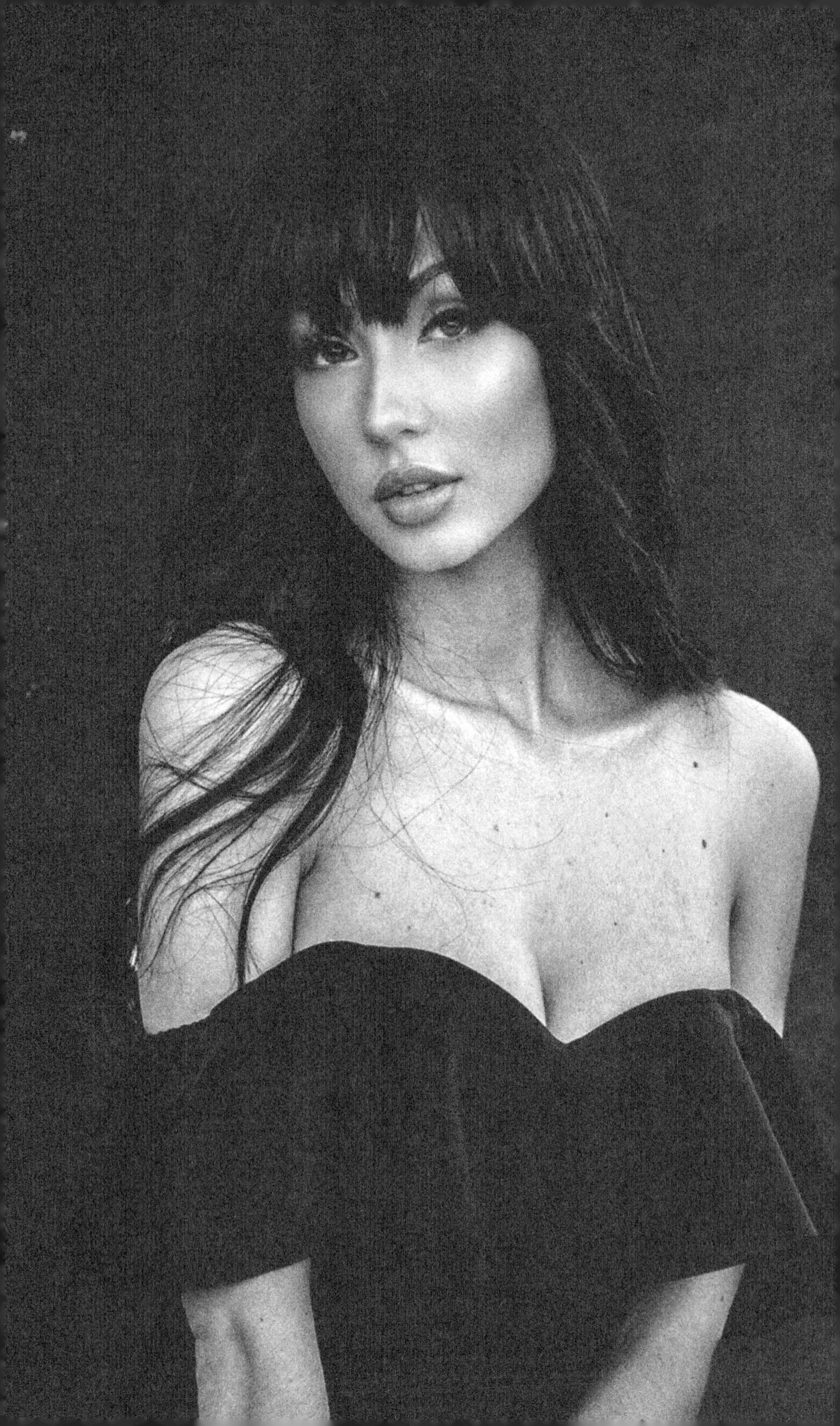

CHAPTER 18

Lucia

Four days have passed since the sponsor event, and it feels like a whirlwind of change. The day after, Monday, I officially moved in with Sawyer. Jo orchestrated the whole thing, ensuring that the press captured every moment of our supposed domestic bliss. It was surreal, to say the least.

We've only spent two days living together before Sawyer had to hit the road for an away game, leaving me alone in his apartment. Maybe I should have joined, but since not all the wives/partners/girlfriends did, I stayed back.

Right now, I'm kind of regretting it because the silence feels deafening, and the emptiness of the place echoes with the weight of our arrangement. It's strange, being here without him, after all the chaos and intensity of the past few days.

Having the t-shirts he left me isn't enough. Though I do love having his smell with me when I go to sleep, it's such a hollow feeling when I wake up alone. Even the small, sweet handwritten notes I've found in random places like on the fridge, and on the coffee maker aren't enough to fill the void he's left behind.

Weirdly enough, my biggest comfort is the burn on my back from when he fucked me up against the wall. The next day I made him take a picture to show me the damage, and I'm still surprised by the surge of desire that followed after seeing my back all red. There were even parts where my skin had split open. But knowing it happened at Sawyer's hands, doing what we did, made it hot instead of scary. And now... now I can't stop fantasizing about how it would feel to do it on purpose.

As I sit alone in the apartment, I can't help but feel a sense of unease creeping over me. It's not just about living with Sawyer or the media attention surrounding us. It's about the ticking clock, the ever-looming deadline hanging over my head. Every moment spent here feels like a countdown, a reminder that my time is running out.

I try to push aside the anxiety gnawing at me, focusing instead on the tasks at hand. But no matter how much I try to distract myself, the sense of urgency remains. I know I need to make the most of this opportunity to secure my freedom and escape the suffocating grip of my past.

But with each passing day, I can't shake the feeling that time is slipping through my fingers like sand, and I'm running out of chances to make it right. I guess that's not exactly true, something I need to come to terms with. I've managed what I thought would be the hardest thing; I'm married. The next part is taking Sawyer to the Vatican with me, standing in front of the Senate. Something I really don't want to do. I... I'm protecting Sawyer, possibly at the expense of my freedom.

Fuck.

I pick up my phone, looking at the last two contacts I've used that aren't work related. Gail and Remus. My fingers hover over the keys as I decide to text my cousin, something I should probably have done right after the interview where Fabian showed up. But fuck, I didn't want to. I wanted to handle all of this on my own, a way of showing I don't need him.

Me: Are you aware that Fabian has found me?

My cousin's reply is instantaneous.

Remus: Yes. Nothing I can do about it unless you're ready for the Senate.

I grit my teeth together. This is exactly why I didn't text him earlier. I knew he'd give me some bullshit about family politics, and how this is my fight. I mean, it is my fight, but it still doesn't seem fair that Fabian uses his spot in the Senate, and the influence that follows with it.

Me: You know I'm not. But how exactly am I supposed to do anything with him breathing down my neck?

Remus: What do you mean?

Sighing, I look down at my phone, letting my mind wander. Remus doesn't sound like he knows Fabian is now a sponsor of the Sabertooths. But even if he knew, I'm not sure he can do anything about it.

Me: Fabian's been sending me weird "presents", even spray painted my front door. And

now he's a sponsor for the team I work for. Don't tell me that's a coincidence.

Remus: I didn't know that, and it's definitely not with my blessing he's bought his way in. But there's still nothing I can do. This is your fight, Lucia. There are those in the Senate that believe my dad was wrong for letting you go, and they've sided with Fabian. The Senate is divided, so the sooner you bring your new husband home to meet the fam, the better.

Well... fuck. It sounds like a civil war is brewing, which means that even if Remus wanted to, he can't be caught helping me. He's right, though. I need to end this once and for all. Sadly, the person to help me figure my shit out is still not talking to me.

"Enough's enough," I say to myself.

I can't keep stewing in this anxiety-fueled solitude. I need someone to talk to, someone who understands me. I'm done with Gail ignoring me, pretending like everything's fine when it's clearly not.

With a resolute determination, I leave Sawyer's apartment behind and climb into my car. The engine roars to life, a fitting soundtrack to my determination. I know exactly where I need to go.

Driving with purpose, I navigate the familiar streets until I reach Gail's brother's house. Parking hastily, I practically leap out of the car and stride up to the front door, my heart pounding with anticipation and frustration.

I ring the doorbell, my patience wearing thin with each passing second. When the door swings open, Gail's brother stands there, a surprised expression on his face.

"Lucia, hey," he greets me, his voice tinged with confusion. "What brings you here?"

I brush past him, not bothering with pleasantries. "Where's Gail?" I demand, my tone firm and uncompromising.

His eyebrows shoot up in surprise at my abruptness. "Uh, she's inside," he replies, gesturing toward the house. "But I don't know if she's…"

I don't wait for him to finish, striding past him and into the house. I find Gail sitting in the living room, her expression guarded as she looks up at me.

"Gail," I say, my voice soft yet filled with urgency. "We need to talk."

Her eyes widen in surprise as she takes in my determined expression. She opens her mouth to say something, but I cut her off before she can speak.

"I'm not going to stand here and pretend everything's okay anymore," I declare, my voice tinged with frustration. "You've been avoiding me, ignoring my calls and messages, and I've had enough."

Gail's expression shifts, guilt flickering across her features. "Lucia, I…" she begins, but I raise a hand to stop her.

"No more excuses," I insist, the weight of disappointment heavy in my tone. "We've been friends for years, and this isn't how we solve shit. We get drunk and say all the things we wouldn't normally say. But we don't ignore each other."

There's a tense silence between us as Gail looks down, unable to meet my gaze, and I can sense the conflict within her, the struggle to find the right words. "I'm sorry," she finally whispers, her voice barely audible. "I've just been… you dropped a lot on me, Luce."

I take a deep breath, trying to temper my frustration with understanding. "I get that," I say softly. "But shutting me out isn't the answer. We're supposed to be there for each other, remember?"

Gail nods, her expression pained. "I know, Lucia. And I'm sorry. I'll do better, I promise."

As the tension begins to ease, I feel a sense of relief wash over me. "Good," I say, offering her a reassuring smile. "Because I need you now more than ever."

"I actually have tomorrow off," Gail says, shooting me a smile. "So if you're serious about getting drunk..." She trails off, but I don't need her to finish.

"Where?" I ask immediately.

Then we both say "O'Jackie's" at the same time, and burst out laughing.

As Gail disappears into her room to change, I lean against the wall, feeling a mixture of relief and anticipation. It's been too long since we've had a proper heart-to-heart, and I can't wait to finally clear the air between us.

"Heading out tonight?" I startle as her brother emerges. "Sorry, I didn't mean to scare you." His tone is casual, nothing like I imagine it would be if Gail had told him why she's hiding out here.

I nod, giving him a small smile. "Yeah, we're going to O'Jackie's for a drink or twelve."

"Need a lift?" Jamie offers, already reaching for his keys.

"That would be great, thanks," I say, relieved that we won't have to worry about driving.

"No problem," he says, flashing me a reassuring grin. "I'll meet you guys outside." With that, he heads toward the door, leaving me to wait for Gail to finish getting ready.

When Gail emerges, dressed in a casual outfit, I offer her a small smile, and she returns it with a hesitant one of her own. It's a start, I think to myself as we head outside to where her brother is waiting.

As we climb into the car, I feel a sense of gratitude wash over me. With Gail's brother behind the wheel, neither of us have to worry about driving, allowing us to fully indulge in the night ahead.

The drive to O'Jackie's is filled with a nervous energy, a mix of anticipation and apprehension swirling in the air. I steal glances at Gail, noting the tension in her posture, and

I can't help but feel a pang of sadness. This is all my doing, and I want to make it right.

I decide then and there that I won't allow either of us to leave the pub until we've dived headfirst into the realm of alcohol-fueled honesty and reach... I don't know. An understanding?

Tonight, nothing is off limits. Fuck NDA's and family obligations.

As we pull into the parking lot of the Irish pub, I take a deep breath, steeling myself for the conversations that we need to have, and for the honesty I owe her.

"Thanks for the ride," I call over my shoulder just before shutting the car door.

Gail's brother offers us a wave before disappearing into the night.

The moment we step into O'Jackie's, the lively chatter and clinking of glasses envelop us, drowning out any thoughts of the outside world. It's a welcome distraction from the weight of our troubles, and Gail and I waste no time making our way to the bar.

As we push through the crowd, I can feel curious eyes following our every move, whispers of recognition rippling through the room. It's hard to ignore the attention, knowing that I'm now labeled as Sawyer's girlfriend-maybe-fiancée, but I push the discomfort aside, focusing on finding a secluded spot where Gail and I can finally talk.

Before we can even order our drinks, Jackie herself appears at our side. Apart from when Sawyer took me to get my belongings, I don't think I've ever talked with her before. Hell, due to my evil hangover, I'm not even sure I could have picked her out of a lineup. But thanks to the pictures hanging around on different walls, she's easy to recognize.

Her sharp eyes take in the scene with a quick sweep. "Well, well, well, look who it is," she says with a sly grin, nodding toward me. "Sawyer's lass, huh?"

I nod, offering Jackie a wry smile. "Yeah, that's me," I reply, trying to keep my tone light despite the weight of her scrutiny.

Jackie's gaze lingers on me for a moment longer before she turns to Gail, a mischievous twinkle in her eye. "What's your poison?"

I blink. "Excuse me?"

Jackie rolls her eyes. "What will you be drinking?" She talks slowly, like I'm being difficult.

Resisting the urge to roll my eyes and snap something at the older woman, I turn to Gail. "Tequila, please," Gail whoops. "And lots of it."

With a sly smile, the older woman reaches behind the bar and grabs a bottle and two glasses. "Well, lucky for you two birds, I've got just the thing," she says, gesturing toward the back of the bar.

Intrigued, Gail and I follow Jackie through the crowded room, grateful for the chance to escape the prying eyes and probing questions. As we enter one of the pub's private rooms, I can't help but feel a sense of relief wash over me, knowing that we'll finally have the chance to talk in peace.

But before we can even settle in, Jackie leans in close, her voice low and intense. "Listen here, Lucia," she says, her eyes boring into mine. "You better treat Sawyer right. He's a good lad, and he deserves someone who appreciates him."

I nod, understanding the gravity of her words. "I will." It's an empty promise, one I don't feel good about making.

She huffs and turns to leave after leaving the bottle and glasses on the table. "Just use the intercom if you need anything. And if you puke, you clean it or pay for someone to do it for you. I ain't touching anything that's been inside your stomachs."

As we settle into the privacy of the room at O'Jackie's, the atmosphere shifts, enveloping us in a cocoon of quietude. With our drinks in hand, we sit in silence for a while, each lost in our own thoughts. The weight of the last time we were here together hangs heavy in the air, casting a shadow over our conversation. But as the minutes tick by, I can feel the tension between us slowly beginning to dissipate.

I know I should be the one to break the silence. Fuck it, I owe it to Gail. That doesn't mean I know where to start, or even what to say. So much has happened. Yeah, I need some liquid courage. I refill my glass, and without hesitation, I down it in one swift motion, the fiery liquid burning its way down my throat. Gail watches me with an amused expression, but I pay her no mind as I pour myself another glass.

With newfound courage coursing through my veins, I turn to Gail, my words tumbling out in a rush. "I'm sorry," I blurt out, the weight of my confession hanging heavy in the air. "I'm sorry for all the lies, for all the secrets. You have to know that I never meant to deceive you, Gail. It's just... I didn't know how to tell you the truth."

Gail's expression softens, her eyes filled with understanding. "I get it, Luce," she says gently, reaching out to place a comforting hand on mine. "I'm not proud of abandoning you. But I needed the time to... think everything through."

"And have you?" I ask.

"I think so. Look, no matter how pissed I am, I really do get it. Everything you could have said would lead to a million more questions."

I nod, grateful for... her. "Thank you," I whisper, feeling a sense of relief wash over me. "Okay, so what do you want to know?"

She empties her glass while looking at me, and I can tell from her expression that she's trying to decide which questions I'm likely to answer. "You moved out." It's not a question. "And you're now living at Sawyer's, right?"

Okay, I guess we're starting in the safe-zone. "That's right," I confirm.

Gail nods to herself. "Who was the man that asked you the weird question during your interview?"

So much for starting out softly, Gail's going straight for the kill. I brush some imaginary lint off my pants and fidget in my seat. When I can't ignore the question any longer, I meet her gaze. "My ex husband," I reply matter-of-factly. I freaking sound like we're discussing the weather rather than the guy that'll kill me if he ever gets me back.

"I.. uhh... what?" She forces a laugh and stares at me like she's expecting me to keep talking. I don't. I'm fine with answering her questions, but I'm not fine with volunteering information. It feels like betraying my fucked up family. "Ex husband? I thought you guys were still married."

"Right..." I clear my throat and hold up my hand, showing her my new wedding band. "Sawyer and I kinda got married—"

"Kinda?" she screeches, grasping my hand. "You did it? You got what you wanted, so you're free now, right?"

I hate having to ruin the hope in her voice. "Yes and no. Yes, we're married. But no, I'm not free. I have to take Sawyer to Rome with me and get my family's approval. It's... it's hard to explain."

Gail nods slowly. "I get it. I've seen enough mob movies to know how this works. So there's a chance they'll reject it? Can't you just talk to your cousin?"

"My cousin married us," I explain. "He's on board, and if it was only up to him I think he would let me go. But there's like... a council I guess you can call it, one who needs to approve."

"Well... fuck," Gail curses, looking like she might start crying. "So I might still lose you?"

I force a confident laugh I don't feel. "Nah, it'll be fine. I know exactly what to do."

She eyes me skeptically while sipping at her drink. "So let's circle back. If it was your ex in the audience... I mean, I get he isn't a nice guy. But why did you look so scared? And why was he hiding?"

Before I went to get Gail, I knew she'd ask all these questions. I told myself I was okay with it, which I was—past tense. As we sit here now, I feel cold again, just at the mention of Fabian. I'm not sure I have it in me to lay it all out there. "Because he's a scary guy," I deadpan.

Gail huffs and crosses one leg over the other. "Is this your idea of honesty, Luce?"

"I am being honest, Gail. Fabian is bad news, and he's fucking scary." My tone rises, and I have to stop myself from shouting. "Look, I'm all for a night of honesty. But maybe we need some ground rules?" I suggest.

"Like what?"

Taking a deep breath, I bite my bottom lip. "Like… I promise not to lie, but there are things I can't tell you. Things that… hurt too much to talk about." I do my best to lace every word with emotion so she knows I'm not trying to weasel my way out.

"Fine," she relents. "But you have to give me something. How old were you when you got married?"

I take a sip of my drink before answering. "Sixteen. We got married on my sixteenth birthday."

Her eyebrows shoot up her forehead. "What? Is that even legal?"

Shooting her a sad smile, I say, "Gail, remember all the things I told you my family orchestrated? Do you really think something as insignificant as my age matters?"

"I suppose not," she hisses. Her eyes flash with anger and indignation. "So you were forced to get married while you were basically still a child?"

"Yep. At fifteen, my uncle and parents began looking for a suitable husband for me. They chose Fabian because of his standing, which they felt was a good fit—"

Before I can finish, Gail interrupts me. "Was he forced as well?"

Her question makes me laugh bitterly. "Trust me, he was eager. I didn't know it at the time, but Fabian prefers his women young, so he has time to shape them."

"Well... fuck." Fuck's right. "Did he... Luce... did he... touch you?" Gail trails off, and when I look at her, tears stream down her face.

I want to scoff at the question because Fabian did a whole lot of touching. But since I get where Gail's coming from, and know she's asking out of concern, I force myself to take a moment to compose myself before answering.

While the age of consent is eighteen in the states, it's sixteen where I come from. Though, since the laws of common people don't matter to people like my family, that's neither here nor there. The thing that's making all this hard to explain is that I don't want Gail to know about all the things Fabian has done to me. She doesn't need those images in her head.

And... because I don't really want to admit how spineless I was. Back then, I'd told myself it was fine, that my family wouldn't force me to do it if it weren't okay. So much fucking bullshit.

"He didn't touch me until we were married and I was of age," I say robotically, opting for the simple explanation instead of explaining how badly he'd hurt me the moment he had a ring on my finger. "But he also didn't respect the word no."

Gail lets out a guttural cry and practically throws herself at me. She holds me so tight it's hard to breathe, but I don't mind one bit. I let her cling to me while she cries. Through it all, I don't shed a single tear. I've cried enough for the girl I once was, and for everything Fabian did and took from me. I'll never cry because of him again. Never.

"I get it," Gail hiccups. "Fuck. He broke you, didn't he? Or... he tried because no one can truly destroy you, Luce. You're too fucking strong."

"Gail..." I stop talking as my voice cracks. Instead of looking for the perfect words, I hug her harder, using the embrace to tell her what I don't have the words to express.

Once Gail's all cried out, she returns to her chair and I quickly refill our glasses. As we drink in silence, I'm hit by a sudden need to have Sawyer near me. While he's been gone, I haven't let myself admit how much I miss him. But dammit, I do.

I don't care how rude it is, I pull out my phone and activate it. To my surprise, there are missed calls and texts from Sawyer, demanding to know what I'm doing at O'Jackie's. Gail distracts me when she stands up, and tells me she's going to the bathroom. As soon as she's gone, I hit the call button.

"Why the fuck didn't you tell me you were going out?" Sawyer barks as a way of greeting.

"Hi to you too," I chirp.

"You okay, bunny? Did something happen?" I'm stunned into silence. How the hell does he know? "Put your camera on," he demands, and I do what he says.

Holding the phone at arm's length, I wave awkwardly. "Hi there."

Sawyer's having none of it, and gets straight to the point. "What's wrong?"

"I'm out with Gail," I admit. "And it... uhh... got a bit heavy."

His tone sounds relieved as he says, "Fucking hell, bunny. You had me worried."

"Sorry," I reply on a whisper. "I didn't know..." Didn't know what? That he'd be worried... that he'd care... the list goes on, but I don't know how to put it into words.

Proving he knows me better than I know myself, at least right now, Sawyer finishes my sentence. "You didn't think I'd care." I nod, knowing he can see the bob of my head. "I care about everything you do, bunny. Did you have cereal for breakfast? You tell me. Did you touch yourself in the shower? Show me. No, better yet, call me. When I say all that you do interests me, I mean it. I'm a greedy fucker when it comes to you, baby. So I want to know it all."

"O-okay," I stutter. The sheer magnitude of his gaze is enough to make me feel the depth of his words in every fiber of my being. "I didn't touch myself, by the way."

His breath hitches. "No? So you're telling me that you've only had the orgasms I've given you?"

I nod. Then a thought hits me. "Why? Have you been touching yourself?"

Sawyer's low chuckle and mischievous smile makes my nipples pebble, and arousal spread through my core. "At least twice a day," he confirms.

"Don't," I hiss, feeling irrationally annoyed. "I want all your orgasms, Sawyer. They belong to me."

"Is that so?" he rasps, his eyes hooded.

"It's only fair," I say, trying to reason my way out of the ridiculous claim I'm... well, claiming.

Before he can answer, the door opens and Gail comes back into the room. I hold my finger up in her direction, and she grins, mouthing, "Sawyer?"

"I have to go," I say, looking at the man who looks entirely too smug now that I've declared I want his cum. Or his orgasms... both.

"Okay," he rasps. "I hope Jackie is looking after you two."

My jaw becomes slack, and I gape at him. "That was you? You're the reason she gave us this private room?"

He grins. "Bunny, you're all over social media. The second I saw, I texted her and asked her to look after you."

"You checked your socials?" I ask, arching my eyebrow. "But you never do that."

He grins. "I do when I want to see what you're up to."

"Thank you," Gail pipes up, grinning widely. "For getting us this room."

It is sweet, but it's also annoying. All I wanted was a night out with Gail, which he had no right hijacking. I know my annoyance is irrational, and I know he didn't really do anything. It irks me all the same, though.

"Don't mention it," Sawyer says smoothly. "Once you're done, there's a car waiting outside and there is security waiting outside the doors to the room you're in."

I look at Gail, and she nods. "Yep. Saw the two beefy men when I went to the bathroom."

"Sawyer," I growl.

"Lucia," he says, mimicking my tone.

"Gail," my friend says, shrugging unapologetically when I shoot her a glare. "Hey now, don't look at me like that, Luce. I'm starting to feel left out."

I roll my eyes while Sawyer bursts out laughing. "Glad to know you approve, Gail." He grins.

My friend comes over, standing right behind me and looks at the screen. "Just to be clear, I approve of the way you're looking after Luce. I'm not sure I approve of you as a husband yet."

Sawyer laughs harder. "Noted. I'll do what I can to get your approval."

"You should," Gail says smugly. "My opinion is very important to Luce."

The smile is wiped away from Sawyer's face. "Speaking of approval, Gail. Don't ever fucking ignore my wife again. If you do, I'll make sure you never speak again."

Instead of taking offense, Gail smiles sweetly. "Noted," she says, echoing his sentiment. "By the way, you just got an extra point for being so protective."

The two of them grin at each other like proud children who have outwitted each other. "Okay then. Now that you're done setting the rules, I'm gonna go," I deadpan.

"See you tomorrow, wife," Sawyer rasps. Then he hangs up before I can say anything.

Ducking my head, I hide behind the curtain of my long red hair, taking my sweet time putting my phone away while Gail returns to her seat. I know I'm smiling, and I already know Gail's noticed it which means she's about to give me shit.

"Soooo," she drawls, dragging the word out. "When exactly did you fall for Sawyer Perry?"

I scoff at her. "I didn't. I'm just… just… it's not what you think, Gail. He's an ass and I'm a bitch. So if anything, I'm just making the best of a shitty situation."

She sighs audibly. "Right. And I've never lied to a one-night-stand."

"Huh?"

"Oh, sorry, buttercup. I thought we were spewing ridiculous lies. My bad." She wiggles her eyebrows playfully. "But seriously, though. When did you fall for him?"

"I didn't," I growl. "He has a nice dick, and he knows how to use it. That's it."

She laces her fingers together and raises her arms above her head, lazily cupping the back of her head. "I thought we weren't going to lie tonight," she says, arching an eyebrow. When I stare uncomprehendingly at her, she smiles even wider. "Oh my gosh, you don't even realize, do you? Well, well, well. This just got a lot more interesting."

"Whatever," I mumble, over this conversation.

Gail laughs. "Tell me about the wedding."

Knowing what she wants to know, I explain my idea of wearing the engagement-looking ring at the interview to stir up rumors. "I don't know what made him suggest it, only that the idea came from him. And then I had my cousin marry us, which was needed per the family rules."

"And the divorce?" Gail asks.

"It was hidden in the prenup. But as promised, Remus granted me my divorce just as I was about to get married."

She lets out a whistle. "Damn. Not even thirty and married twice. Go Luce." I shoot her a dirty look that makes her cackle. "Too soon?"

"Way too soon," I confirm.

Picking up my glass I drink the few drops left. I contemplate refilling it, but I'm starting to feel tired. Plus, the quicker I go to sleep, the quicker Sawyer's back.

We only stay for another hour, which we spend discussing possible outcomes and ideas of how to approach the trip to the Vatican that I need to gain my freedom. But no matter how much we talk about it, I don't see a natural way to bring it up.

"If he needs to stand in front of some kind of jury I don't think there's any sneaky way to do this," Gail says. "You just have to go ahead with it."

"I guess."

Shaking her head, she laughs as she stands. "Still denying having feelings for him? Because if you don't, you should just get it over with so you can be free to spread your wings or whatever."

"It's not that simple," I hiss. "Going to the Vatican could cost him his life. If the Senate doesn't approve, they could order his execution. Feelings don't fucking matter." Even as I speak the words, I know it's a lie.

Not the part about the potential consequences; the part about feelings. They matter, and it's the real reason I'm procrastinating. I want to have my cake, and eat it, too. I want my freedom to live my life with Sawyer, find out what that looks like without my family's interference.

"Is there anything I can do?" Gail asks when we get outside. We're flanked by the bodyguards Sawyer mentioned, and there are two cars waiting for us. Her shoulders slump when I shake my head. "I'm here if you need me, Luce. Day and night. And umm... if I think of anything that could help I'll let you know."

"You do that," I say, trying to sound as though I actually believe it's possible when in reality, I don't. "Talk to you tomorrow?"

"And the day after, and the next day, and the—"

I interrupt Gail's sing-song with a hug. After saying our goodbyes, I get into the second car, and sit back while the driver takes me back to Sawyer's place. My place... our place.

With every day that passes I know I'm getting closer and closer to the deadline. I can't keep ignoring the facts, which is also the real reason I went to Gail. I needed to make things right before my time is up. As for Sawyer... maybe I should just let myself enjoy what little time I have left.

No matter how many times I've gone over it in my head, I can't sacrifice him. I just can't—I refuse.

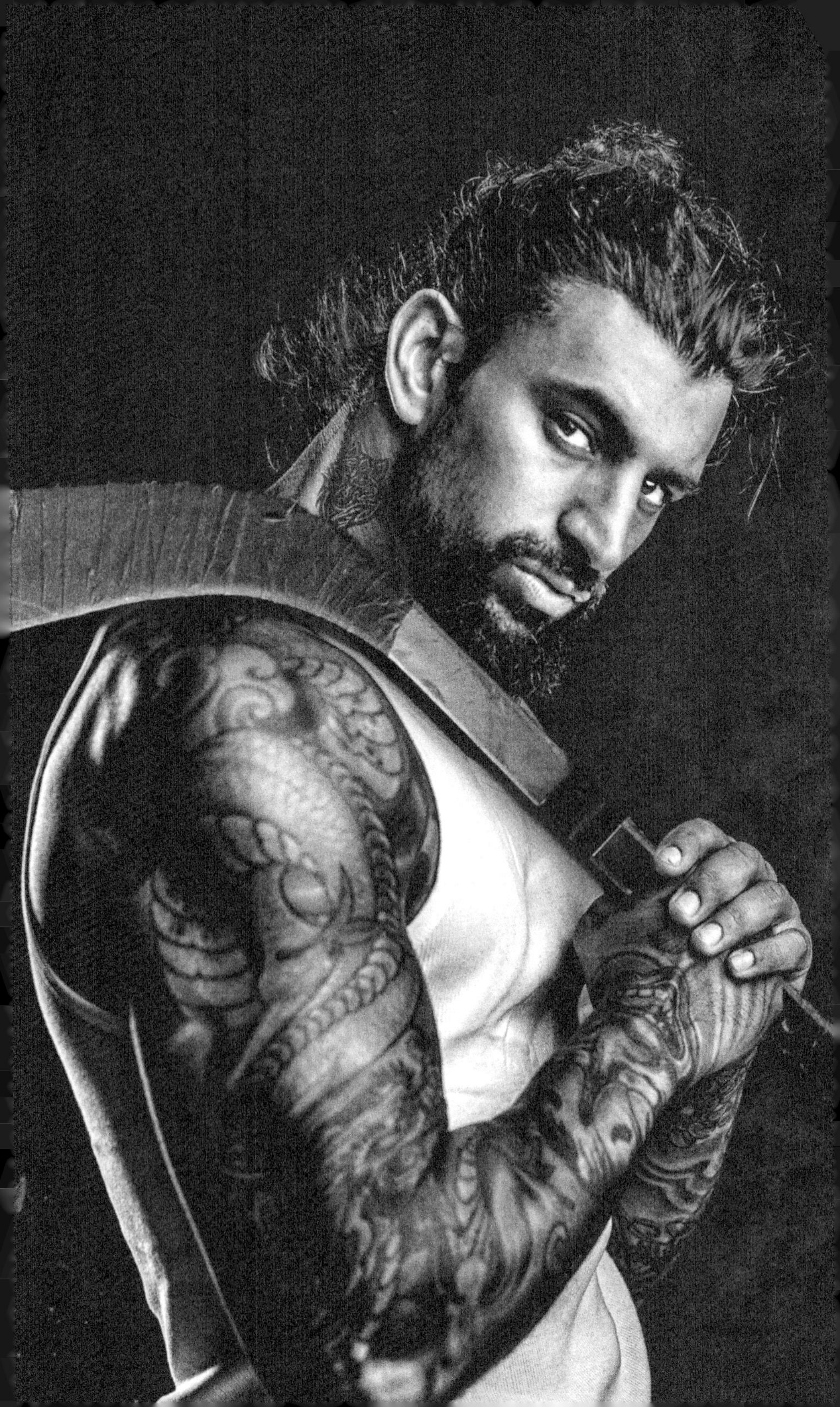

CHAPTER 19

Sawyer

As I pack my bags in a rush, Soren and Mickey hover nearby, their smirks practically audible in the dimly lit hotel room.

"You're really sneaking out in the middle of the night?" Soren jokes, his grin widening.

I shoot him a wry glance, zipping up my bag with fervor. "You bet your ass I am," I reply, my tone determined.

Mickey chuckles, shaking his head in disbelief. "Never thought I'd see Sawyer Perry whipped," he teases, his amusement clear.

Rolling my eyes, I sling my bag over my shoulder. "Call it what you want," I retort, feeling a surge of determination. The truth is that I can't control the part of me that's desperate to be with Lucia, to be inside her. It's an addiction only she can satisfy and I'm done fucking fighting it.

Soren claps me on the back, grinning. "You really like her, don't you? I mean, this is more than just the contract."

It's so much more than the deal I made with Tom. In fact, I don't care about that anymore. "She's my wife," I answer simply.

"Fucking caveman," Mickey chuckles.

"Well, better hurry then," Soren says, barely containing his own laughter. "Don't want her to forget who she belongs to."

I punch him on the upper arm. "Dick."

"We'll tell Coach something urgent came up," Mickey says.

"I never thanked you for being witnesses to our marriage," I say, looking between them. "Thank you."

"Was it real?" Soren asks, shifting his weight from one foot to the other.

"It is now," I admit. "So thank you."

Mickey chuckles. "Don't mention it."

With a nod, I stride out the door, driven by an intense need to be with Lucia. As I head to the airport, I feel a sense of urgency pushing me forward. I need her, and I need her now.

Flying from Vancouver to Minneapolis feels like an eternity. Restlessness gnaws at me throughout the flight, my thoughts consumed by Lucia. I spend the hours in the air glued to my phone, religiously watching the security cameras in my home.

Lucia's sleeping in my bed. Naked and starfished, which gives me a pretty fucking spectacular view of her body. Every now and then she mumbles in her sleep, but it's never anything that makes sense. She says something about a wolf, mentions her friend Gail, and then… she says my name. Pride swirls inside me, and I love knowing I'm starring in her dreams.

"Not long now," I mumble to the screen, wishing she could hear me.

As soon as the plane touches down, I'm out of my seat, practically sprinting through the airport. I completely ignore the fans calling out my name. Hailing a taxi, I throw an obscene amount of money at the driver, urging him to speed to my destination. Every passing moment feels like an eternity, my impatience growing with each second. All I can think about is getting back to Lucia. To my wife.

Call me whipped, call me emasculated... I don't fucking care about anything but burying myself in Lucia.

Finally home, I sneak into my apartment, careful not to wake Lucia up. As I enter the bedroom, a low groan escapes me when I see her lying naked on her stomach on my bed. My heart races at the sight, desire stirring within me. I quickly undress and approach her, unable to resist the pull she has on me.

As though she's sensing my presence, she lifts her hips slightly, showing me her perfect cunt. Fuck me, she's wet. Her lips are glistening with her arousal. The need to eat her out, to have her juices coating my tongue is strong. For a moment, I deliberate whether or not I should cross that line. The last thing I want is for her to wake up afraid, but on the other hand... fuck it. There is no other hand.

I slowly stroke my dick while watching her. I could just fuck her, she'd love that. No, I have to taste her first. Crawling onto the bed, I move closer until I can smell her arousal. I wish I fucking knew what she's dreaming about. It better be me.

Running my nose through her slit, I inhale sharply. Fuck, she smells as good as she tastes. She moans and lifts her ass higher when I lap at her pink opening. Her taste explodes on my tongue, making me groan in pure ecstasy.

"Fuck, bunny," I rasp. Licking the length of her perfect cunt, I harden my tongue as I reach her clit. My face is practically being smothered by her ass cheeks, and I fucking love it.

"Mhmm... Sawyer?" Lucia's tone is thick with sleep.

"It's me," I growl. I don't stop licking her. Pushing my tongue into her cunt, I greedily fuck her, loving the way my saliva and her juices mix.

"What are you... oh fuck!" She arches her back, pushing her ass more firmly against me. "Don't you dare fucking stop."

Huh, that's not the reaction I was expecting. I thought she'd be pissed I went down on her. "Is this okay?" I ask, needing to know. Then it hits me. "It's the position, isn't it?"

"Shut up and eat my cunt like you mean it," she demands. "Bury your tongue inside my tight pussy."

Fuuuck, I love the way the filthy words fall from her lips. She isn't asking, she's demanding, and right now, there's nothing I want more than to obey her.

I slap her left ass cheek. "Spread your legs wider, wife."

She immediately shuffles around on the bed, widening so I can slide under her. I move so I'm lying on my back, and then I grab her hips, using my hold on her to push her down until she's smothering me with her dripping cunt.

"Ride my face," I groan. I'm unsure if she's heard me until she rotates her hips. "That's it, bunny. Fucking use me." Moving my hands to the soft globes of her ass, I squeeze them tight.

"Sawyer," she cries.

"I want your cream, baby," I growl. "Give it to me."

Hardening my tongue again, I swirl her swollen clit. Her thighs around my ears muffle her sounds, but I can still hear her moans and cries for more. I continue to eat her like a starved man, and I don't stop until wetness gushes into my mouth.

"Sawyer! Fuck... I... I'm... Sawyer!" She screams my name so loud I'm glad I don't have any neighbors. Those sounds are for my ears only.

When she's no longer shaking, I lift her off me and throw her onto her back on the bed. Before she can protest, I hover over her. One knee between her legs, grinding against her soaked core. Lucia looks up at me through hazy eyes. She blinks once, twice. Then she rears up, winding her arms around my neck.

"Welcome home," she purrs.

I chuckle when I feel her tongue licking the wetness from my mouth. "Missed me?" I grin.

Instead of answering me, she claims my lips in a kiss that tells me everything she won't; she definitely missed me. "Lucia," I growl, breaking the kiss. "I told you I'm greedy. Use your words."

Laying back down, she gives me a coy look and bites her plump bottom lip. "Yes." Well, I can't say I was expecting her to be that honest. "I missed your cock," she purrs seductively.

"Only my cock?" I ask, arching an eyebrow.

Her cheeks flush a pretty red. It almost matches her hair, which is spread out beneath her. "Can you just fuck me already?" she snarks, making me laugh.

I feel like beating my fucking chest and roaring in satisfaction. Knowing my wife missed me as much as I've missed her is an incredible feeling. But, sadly she's not ready to admit that yet. I can be patient for a *little* bit longer.

"Sure," I agree. I lean back so I'm resting on my heels. Then I wrap my hands around her quivering thighs and drag her closer to me. Sliding my hands down her smooth legs, I throw them over my shoulders. I angle my hips so the head of my cock prods against her pink hole. "Hold on tight."

Before she can do or say anything, I slam all the way inside her. I groan as her warm, wet cunt squeezes me. "Fuck. Wife." I feel her stiffen when I look down between us, but I don't stop. I fuck her harder until the sounds of skin against skin and our moans ricochet off the walls. "Do you like me fucking you without a condom?" I rasp.

Before I went away, I fucked her three times without rubbering up, and neither of us have commented on it. But fuck if it hasn't played on my mind. How much better her cunt feels with no barrier. It makes it harder to hold back, all I want to do is rut into her like a feral animal.

"Yes," she cries, her back bowing off the bed as I lean forward and squeeze her nipples. "It feels fucking amazing. You feel amazing."

I slam into her over and over, loving the way she feels. She's so pliable when my thick cock's filling her up. "I'm never using one with you again," I grind out, tweaking her nipples. "Do you hear that, bunny? Never."

Lucia pulls her legs away from my shoulders and twists away from me. "The fuck," I growl.

She sits up and gets on her knees, moving closer until our foreheads are touching. "I want to be on top."

I chuckle breathlessly and slap her tempting ass. "Okay," I agree, laying down on my back again. Wasting no time, Lucia straddles me. She grabs the base of my cock and angles it toward her wet pussy. Then she slowly, painfully fucking slowly, sinks down. "Fuck," I groan.

Once she's taken all of me, she tilts her head to the side and looks down at me. "Do I please you, Sy? Do you like feeling my pussy squeeze your big dick?" Her tone is low, tempting.

"You do, bunny, and I fucking love *my* cunt." She moans at my words.

"Yours?" She moves her hands to my chest, gently caressing the skin with her long, sharp nails. "It's mine. I'm just allowing you to use it." I look down as her fingers trace my skin all the way to my nipple.

I groan when she squeezes my nipple with her nails. "It's *my* fucking pussy, baby."

She moans again. "Is your cock mine?"

"Of course," I groan. "All yours."

"Okay. My pussy's yours then."

Palming her hips, I hold her still as I begin to thrust into her. "It's mine," I snarl like she disagreed with me. "All. Fucking. Mine."

"Yes," she pants. "All yours, Sy."

I grin, which probably looks deranged. But I like that she's giving me a nickname, even if she is fucking butchering my name in the process. "I want to hear you moan that," I say as I buck under her.

"Stop being so bossy," she scolds. "Let me ride you."

Tightening my hold on her hips, I say, "I don't think so. You wanted to be on top, baby. So that's how I'm fucking you."

Her lips twitch in amusement while she simultaneously digs her nails deeper into my skin. I feel the moment she breaks through, and it causes me to let out a guttural groan. "Fuck yeah."

"You like pain with your pleasure?" she asks curiously.

At the mention, the scratches from Sunday itch on my back. She wasn't gentle, and the skin back there shows the proof. "I like everything you do." I punctuate my words by slamming up and into her, hard and unforgiving.

Sitting straighter, she lets her hands fall away from my chest and licks her lips. "I want to try that," she says, hesitantly. "I want you to h-hurt me while you're inside me."

I lean up and gently brush the hair away from her face so I can see her eyes. The green emeralds shine with determination. "Are you sure?" My gaze automatically drops to her thighs, to the scars.

She nods. "I want to know if it feels as good as you make it sound like."

We both look down at the crescent moon shapes she's left on my chest. They're red, and there's a little blood, but nothing serious—nothing like my back.

"Okay," I rasp, nodding. "But you have to tell me what you want."

Her breathing becomes labored, and she lifts herself slowly, easing off my cock. "I'll be right back." With those words, she turns and runs to the bathroom.

Lucia emerges only seconds later, clutching her pink razor. With a deep sigh, she hands it to me before she climbs back on the bed, immediately taking my still hard dick inside her. I fist the razor, turning it this and that way, which is a bit fucking stupid considering the darkness covering us.

"This won't do," I rasp, stretching so I can reach the bedside table. Opening it, I carefully feel my way around until I find the pocketknife I have in there. Bingo. I hold the knife up so Lucia can see the blade. Without moving her, I sit up so we're nose-to-nose. "Wrap your legs around me and sit still." She whimpers as I move my hand to her throat, squeezing until she stops moving.

"Will it hurt?" she asks, sounding so innocent my cock swells inside her.

"Yes," I rasp. "But if I do it right, you'll love it."

"How do you know?" she challenges. I chuckle and press my lips together. I'm not about to tell her how I know while I'm balls deep in her pretty pink pussy.

It's been years since I've had this dark need fed by anyone. Fuck, not since I entered the NHL. But before then, I frequented a whorehouse only one town over from where I lived. The women there charged a lot, but they also let you do whatever you wanted. Whatever. You. Wanted. I've been too scared to go anywhere since I became a public figure. Having the press find out about my kink isn't high on my to-do list.

Licking my lips, I let myself feel the dark anticipation running through my veins. Holding the sharp blade must be what it's like to smoke after taking a break. Or getting a steak after swearing off meat.

Lucia looks at me with so much trust I can barely stand it. "Are you sure?" I ask again, needing her to say the words. "I need to hear you say it."

"I want to try it with you," she whispers. "I-I trust you. At least I think I do."

With a growl, I claim her lips in a bruising, all-consuming kiss. Our tongues tangle, stroking each other while I flex my hand around her throat. Her breath hitches, and then she moans into my mouth.

I wait until her pulse under my thumb isn't running a million miles per second. With the other women, I loved watching my knife glint between their swollen cunt lips.

But given Lucia's past, I keep the pocketknife in my hand. While she's distracted by my mouth, I move the tool to her collarbone. I don't need to look to know what I'm doing, I've done it so many times my hands are practically my eyes.

"Sy." She moans my name sweetly as I add pressure, creating a thin line in her skin.

Unable to keep my need to watch the blood well to the surface at bay, I rip my mouth from hers and look down. "Look how prettily you bleed," I rasp.

Lucia takes a shuddering breath, gyrating her hips. Then she looks down. "Oh," she gasps. I don't know if she likes what she sees. "Mhmm, do it again." Throwing her head back, she arches her back, pressing her chest against the knife, and I'm not stupid enough to deny the invitation.

This time I slide the blade lower, cutting the skin at the top part of her left tit. I growl possessively when we both watch the blood seeping down her skin. "You're so fucking pretty," I groan. "So. Fucking. Delicious. Perfect in every sense of the word."

My cock throbs deep inside her wet heat. At the same time, my balls tighten, begging for a relief I'm not ready for yet.

Panting through parted lips, Lucia looks down, almost cross-eyed as she follows the blood slowly making its way down her skin. Yeah, she likes it. The evidence is right there in her hooded eyes and heavy breathing.

"This is honesty," I mumble, feeling something stir in my chest. "Blood doesn't lie, sweet bunny. This is the most honest a person can be."

She nods. "I can be honest." Looking up at me through her thick, dark lashes, I feel like she's looking into my soul.

"Give it to me," I rasp. The air around us is thick, and my skin is practically buzzing with anticipation. "Give me a truth, sweet bunny."

"I-I..." She pauses and straightens her spine. "I know Fabian. He's not a good person." Pain coats her words, and I feel it vibrating inside me like I'm absorbing her truth.

Though I'd already worked that part out for myself, I feel honored that she's choosing to tell me this. I lock down the part of me that wants to rage at the fact he's clearly hurt her, and instead I push the pocketknife into her hand. "Your turn," I say. "Claim your truth from me."

Lucia tightens her grip on the knife handle and hesitantly brings it to my chest. She chooses the spot right above my heart. My breath hitches when she rotates her hips, and my cock throbs in anticipation. I barely feel the cut, but I watch it, mesmerized as she parts my skin and blood flows down my body. She's cut me deeper than I did her, but not enough to do any real damage.

"Fuck," I grind out through clenched teeth.

Before Lucia, I've never wanted to be the one shedding blood or the one hurting. But the way she makes me fucking ache for her with a single look makes this oddly perfect.

"Give me your truth," she moans, her green eyes sparkling with determination.

I take a moment to consider what to tell her. Even though her truth wasn't a surprise, I know it was a big step for her to open up to me—one I want to reciprocate. I need to be smart about it. She might think I call her bunny as an insult, which I get considering the women looking to score with hockey players are called puck bunnies. But that's not why. It's because she's so fucking skittish, and the last thing I want to do is scare her off. Especially when my dick is inside her.

Taking a deep breath, I run a finger through the blood on her skin. I draw a small heart, grinning when she rolls her eyes. "You're the only person I'll ever bleed for," I answer, the gravel in my voice making it sound as sincere as it is.

Her eyes widen. Lucia holds my gaze for so long, I wish I knew what was going through that pretty head of hers. Then she lets out an almost animalistic sound; a mixture of a howl and a growl. Even though we're already tangled around each other, she lunges at me, knocking me down on my back.

"You're the only one I've ever bled for by choice," she mutters.

Before I can answer, she slams her lips to mine. Her tongue delves into my mouth in a kiss that's more bite than sweet. Her teeth knick my bottom lip, and within seconds the taste of blood hits us. Fuck me, this woman—*my* woman—is beyond perfection.

I pull my feet up, bracing myself so I can better fuck her from this position. "I need to fuck you now," I rasp. My hips piston, but it's not enough. I need another position, one where I can fuck her, so I'm as deep inside her as her blood is in me. It's not logical, it's pure fucking need, animalistic and raw.

Moving my hand up her torso, I close it around her throat again. I don't give her any warning before I throw her off me. "What the hell?" she screeches.

"Shh, I'll be back inside you soon," I growl. "Lie down on your side for me, sweet bunny."

I position myself behind her, hooking one arm under her leg so I can lift it up nice and high. She arches her back, wiggling her ass as though she's seeking my cock. My naughty bunny.

"Smear your blood on my cock," I demand as I nuzzle against the crook of her neck.

Doing as I say, she runs her hand down her bloody chest and wraps it around my hardness. Spreading her red essence all over me before guiding me to her entrance. As soon as the tip grazes her folds, I move my hips, sheathing myself inside her heat. Her cunt greedily squeezes me, trying to suck me deeper into her.

"Sy!" The way she screams her name for me, is music to my ears.

"Yes, sweet bunny?"

She pushes back against me, and it doesn't take us long to find a perfect rhythm. While our hips work in perfect tandem, I snake my hand between her legs, finding her clit. She moans and rotates her hips desperately.

"I need more. Don't hold back," she hisses, like she's annoyed by the mere thought.

"Are you all mine?" I ask, lazily rolling my hips.

"I... no... well—"

My hand around her throat shuts her up. "Hold your leg up," I say, flexing my hand. When she lifts it, I move so my lips touch the shell of her ear. "You are fucking mine, Lucia. Don't pretend otherwise."

"No... I..." I tighten my grip on her throat.

"You. Are. Mine," I growl, punctuating each word by pushing my cock in and out of her. "Admit it." Her pussy squeezes me tighter, and I groan, loving the feeling.

"Fine," she spits. "I'm yours, Sawyer. And you're fucking mine. Don't make me regret it."

I chuckle at her words. There she is, my red-haired spitfire. The woman I'm lucky enough to call my wife.

Our fucking turns frenzied, our moans primal. It's fucking beautiful and I can't wait to show her the security recordings one day. This, right here, is our claiming—and I'm completely fine with belonging to her as much as she does to me. Lucia Carter—one day to become Lucia Perry—is sinfully perfect, and now mine.

"I want you to come with me," my sweet bunny moans. When she places her hand on top of mine, I realize my grip has become slack.

My balls tighten at the same time as a warm sensation spreads across my lower back. "Come for me, baby," I groan.

"Sawyer! Yes! I'm... fuck, I'm gonna come. Your dick is filling me so good I'm gonna—" she cuts herself off with a guttural moan. Then her sweet pussy squeezes me, milking the cum from my balls.

"Fuck! Bunny!" I slam into her over and over, prolonging both our orgasms until I can barely move. That was, without a doubt, one of the most intense orgasms I've ever had. And it feels like it's going on forever, as cum keeps spurting from my spent dick.

As soon as I can move, I turn her on her back and slide two fingers inside her, eager to keep my cum there instead of leaking out. "What are you doing?" she asks lazily.

I smirk at her. "Until you're ready for me to either clean you with my mouth or watch my cum leak out, I want it inside you."

"Jesus," she murmurs. "Filthy fucker."

Grinning, I lean down and lick across the cuts on her chest. "You have no idea, baby."

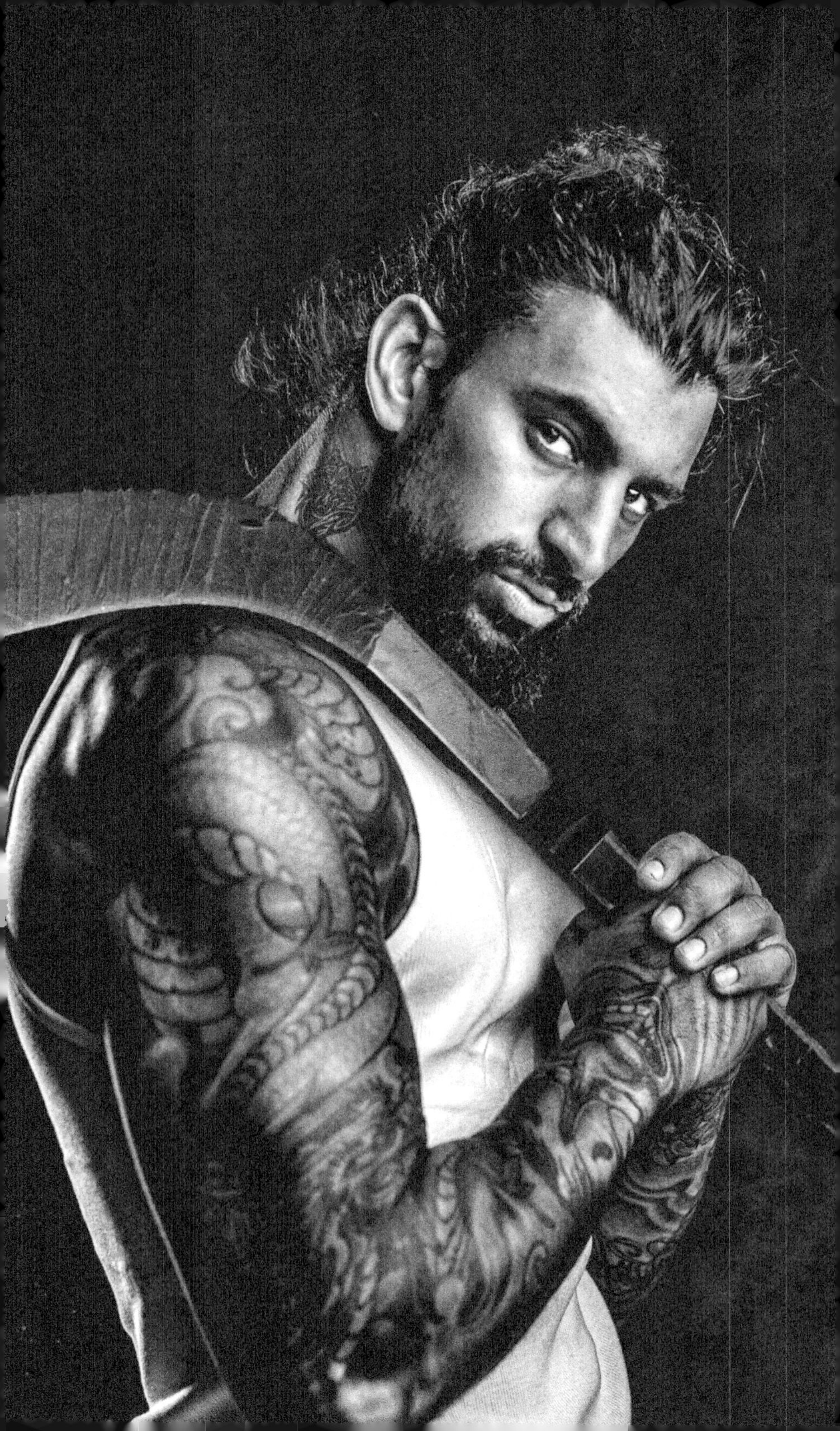

CHAPTER 20

Sawyer

Waking up with Lucia draped all over me is like heaven on earth. As I inhale deeply, I'm greeted by her intoxicating scent—a blend of sweet vanilla, very unlike the woman herself. There's nothing vanilla about my sweet bunny, or the sex we have. A grin spreads across my lips as I look down at her naked body, the dried blood on her chest a stark reminder of last night. Or this morning.

I've been awake for a couple of hours, content to just watch her. It's a weird feeling knowing even asleep, she's demanding my attention—calling to me in a way I never thought possible. The quietness has given me time to contemplate the way I woke her up when I came back, and as soon as she's awake, I'm going to need answers.

"I can feel you staring," Lucia murmurs sleepily. "Cut it out." She burrows her face against my chest and throws her leg around me.

Laughter rumbles in my chest. "Now, why would I do that when I enjoy watching you so much, bunny?" Bending my leg, I force the leg she has wound around me higher on my hips. It gives me better access to her core. Moving my hand down between us, I cup her cunt, letting one finger trail along the folds. "Your pussy doesn't seem annoyed with me," I observe as I push two digits inside her.

She whimpers as I curl my fingers, easily finding the spot inside her that makes her so fucking hungry for me.

"That feels so good," she moans, gyrating her hips.

"Yeah?" I rasp, continuing to push my fingers in and out of her so slowly I know it's going to drive her insane. "Better than waking up with my mouth on your pretty pussy?"

Her pussy tightens around my fingers at the same time as her breath hitches. "N-not better," she stutters.

Adding a third finger, I stretch her walls. "So my naughty bunny enjoyed being woken up like that?"

"Yes. I loved it."

She tilts her face up, and I waste no time claiming her lips. I bite down on her bottom lip, then suck it into my mouth to soothe the sting. "I thought you didn't let anyone eat you out," I ask, needing to know why last night was okay so I can ensure an encore.

"Really?" Lucia huffs, pulling back so she's looking at me. "You want to interrogate me with your fingers buried in my pussy?"

My bunny has such a way with words. "Seems like the perfect time," I smirk. Then I move my thumb to her clit, rolling it in perfect synchronicity with my fingers inside her.

"It's not the act but the position," she says.

"Explain."

She whimpers, chasing my fingers as I slowly pull them out before pushing them all the way inside her hole. "You've seen the scars, Sy. When I... when he... fuck. When he made them, I was on my back, my legs forcefully spread while he licked my pussy."

"Who?" I snap, hating that I don't know who this mysterious 'he' is. If I'm completely honest, what I hate is that neither of us are willing to say the name. But I need her to tell me so I know whether my suspicions are right or not.

Shaking her head, Lucia bites down on her lip. "Don't make me say his name."

"Bunny—"

"No," she screams. "I don't want to say it while you're making me feel so fucking good. Don't you understand? I don't want to taint what we have."

And now I feel like a fucking asshole for trying to get her to open up with my fingers buried inside her. "Sorry," I murmur. "Let me make it up to you."

Her pussy tightens around my fingers. "Make me come and we'll call it even."

I don't know whether I admire or hate the way she's able to compartmentalize. Both? Neither? Doesn't matter, though. She's earned the most intense orgasm of her life, and I'll be the one giving it to her.

"Ass in the air," I command, nipping at the skin on her neck. Lucia scrambles out of my embrace, getting on all fours with her ass up high. What a fucking sight. I line myself up behind her, reaching for her long hair and winding it around my hand, forcing her to bend her neck backward. Then, with no warning, I slam into her soaked pussy. "Christ, you feel fucking amazing."

Arching her back, she moans unashamedly as I fuck her in an almost punishing rhythm, and she meets me thrust for thrust, wanting as much of me as I do of her.

"Shit... I'm gonna... I'm gonna..." Her desperate moans turn to mewls. Her body shakes while her pink hole squeezes me so tight I know I'm about to join her.

"That's it, sweet bunny. Come all over my cock. Milk the cum from my balls," I grind out. A guttural groan is torn from my chest as Lucia orgasms, her cunt clenching around me like a vise. My dick swells and twitches inside her, and I pant her name as I find my own release. "Lucia. Fuck."

When I'm no longer coming, I let go of her hair and she immediately collapses onto the bed in a panting heap. I quickly join her, shuffling her so her head rests on my chest. We lie there, all tangled up, while catching our breath.

"My sweet bunny," I murmur, pressing a kiss to the top of her hair.

She's quiet for so long, I'm beginning to think she's fallen back asleep. Then she shifts so she can look up at me. "Why did you stop using a condom?"

Despite asking myself that question many times, I don't have a good reason. Well, I have a good one, just not a... logical one. "Because I wanted nothing between us," I answer truthfully.

"Aren't you afraid I'll get pregnant?" she asks, quirking an eyebrow at me.

I shrug. "Not really."

Her mouth becomes slack as she stares at me like she's trying to figure out if I'm joking. "Sawyer," she hisses. "That's not funny at all." Now that she's not using her nickname for me, I miss it.

Raising my hand, I sweep her hair back so it isn't covering her beautiful face. "I'm not laughing," I deadpan. "Why didn't you ask me to use one if you're scared you'd get pregnant?"

Lucia rolls her eyes, swirling a finger through the hairs on my chest. "I'm not scared of that. I'm on the pill. But you didn't know that."

No, I didn't. I just didn't care anymore. Shrugging, I place her hand on top of mine and move our joined hands to my heart. "You're mine, wife. If you become pregnant, I'm sure I'll love being a dad."

Scoffing, she pulls away, wrapping the sheet around her. I growl, annoyed she's hiding her body from me. "You don't love me, Sawyer. Stop trying to make this..." She gestures between us. "... More than a convenient arrangement by dressing it up as something romantic."

Before she can get off the bed, I reach for her and pull her back to me by the hair. "Let's get one thing straight, bunny," I say, my tone deceptively sweet. "Love is for teenagers or people who believe in fairy tales. I said I was yours and you agreed you're mine. What did you think those words meant? Maybe it's love, or maybe it's something more."

"Sawyer, that's not—"

Wrapping my other hand around her throat, I squeeze until her eyes widen. "That's not what? Hmm? You meant it as much as I did, baby. Don't pretend otherwise now just because you're scared."

Her nails dig into my wrist. I ease my grip, eager to hear what she has to say. "Fuck you," she spits. Hmm, guess I could have done without hearing that.

"Give me another few minutes to recover, and you can jump back on if you want another go," I smirk, gesturing at my crotch. "Is that what you need? My dick inside you, to be honest?"

Emotion dances across her green eyes, but it's not anger. It's... defeat? Longing? Fuck if I know. She takes a deep, shuddering breath and closes her eyes. When she opens them again, they're glassy with unshed tears. "Fine," she whispers. "You win. Is that what you want to hear?"

"It's not a competition, sweet bunny." Running a finger beneath her eye, I catch a tear. Looking at it, I feel like I'm watching part of her very essence. And being the greedy fucker I am when it comes to her, I lick it off the tip of my finger. "What I want to hear is the truth."

"I don't love you," she spits defiantly. "But I... ahh, I don't know. I do feel something for you."

"Are you mine?" I ask, not caring one bit about her ramblings.

"Y-yes," she admits. Then she lifts her chin, baring her teeth. "But you're mine too, Sy. I swear, if you make a fool out of me, you'll regret it."

Nodding, I lock my gaze on hers. "I've never claimed another person before. I've sure as fuck never said I belong to someone else. So trust me, baby. I'm taking this very seriously."

"How serious?" she asks, lifting her chin stubbornly.

I chuckle darkly. "You want me to measure my feelings for you? I'm not sure there are any measurements big enough, wife."

"Will you remain married to me when our time is up?" A tremor makes her shudder against me as she asks her question.

"Is that what you're worried about, hmm?" I cup her face, holding it still so I can look into her green eyes. Eyes that are swirling with emotions I don't understand. The last thing I want is for her to freak out, to bolt. "I'm never divorcing you, Lucia. You're it for me. You might not be ready to say it, but I want you to hear it. I love you."

Lucia stiffens, her eyes flutter closed. "You don't know what you're saying," she spits, sounding... insulted.

What the actual fuck is going on right now? "Look at me, sweet bunny."

Lucia

I shake my head, unable to look at him right now.

This isn't fair at all. Sy's just given me everything I wanted, yet I can't make myself take it. The icy grip around my heart and the hollowness in my stomach makes it impossible to accept the keys to my freedom.

Gail was wrong; I'm not strong and I've definitely been broken. My mind is hard-wired to think about survival, not love. And here I am with the perfect man, unable to believe or accept the fact he apparently loves me and... that I love him too. It's the only explanation for the way he makes my heart race and the loneliness I feel when we're not together.

"Lucia," Sy cajoles. "Look at me."

Shaking my head again, I let go of the tears building behind my eyelids. "Make me tell you," I whisper, too cowardly to look at him. "Do what you did last night. Bleed the truth from me. Please, Sy." My voice cracks, much like my heart does.

I don't want to tell him what's in my heart, but I need to. He's my husband, and I don't want to lose him before we even have a chance to see what we could be. I want him to hear the words, just as I want him to know the truth about Fabian. The mattress dips as he moves around, then he pulls me into his lap so my back rests against his front.

"Tell me the truth about who hurt you, sweet bunny," he rasps. I stiffen. That's not the truth I was referring to.

But as I feel a sting followed by the warmth of my blood, I feel compelled to answer truthfully. As I choke out his name, "Fabian," my voice trembles with emotion, each syllable a painful admission of the past I carry. "He's the one who... who did this to me," I confess, feeling the weight of his actions etched into the scars on my inner thighs.

My heart constricts with a tumultuous blend of sorrow and rage. Sorrow for the pain I endured, and rage directed at the man who inflicted such torment upon me. Sy wraps one arm around my middle, forcing me to stay in place. He curses viciously under his breath. "That fucking gutless piece of shit. I'll kill him for doing that to you."

His words thaw at the ice around my heart, the wall I erected years ago and only partially let Gail through. A sob escapes me. "You can't," I cry out. "He... he..." At a loss for what to say or how to explain this mess, I trail off and shake my head.

"Look at me." This time I don't hide behind my eyelids. Craning my neck, I look at my husband over my shoulder.

"I don't give a shit about who he is or what he can do. He hurt you. You. He'll pay, it's that simple."

A promise of violence and retribution shines from Sy's dark orbs. I let out a strangled cry and twist in his hold so I'm facing him. Then I finally give voice to what I feel in my heart. "I love you, too."

Our lips meld together in a fiery union, setting my senses ablaze with an intoxicating fervor. My fingers curl around the ends of Sy's hair, pulling him closer as I surrender to the electrifying sensation coursing through my veins.

Sy's embrace is possessive, his arms wrapping around me with a fierce desire that leaves me breathless. Lost in the moment's intensity, I savor the taste of his lips, the rhythm of our breaths syncing in perfect harmony.

"I love you," I murmur again. "You're my husband now and always, and I love you."

He growls, biting down on my bottom lip. "Now and always," he echoes.

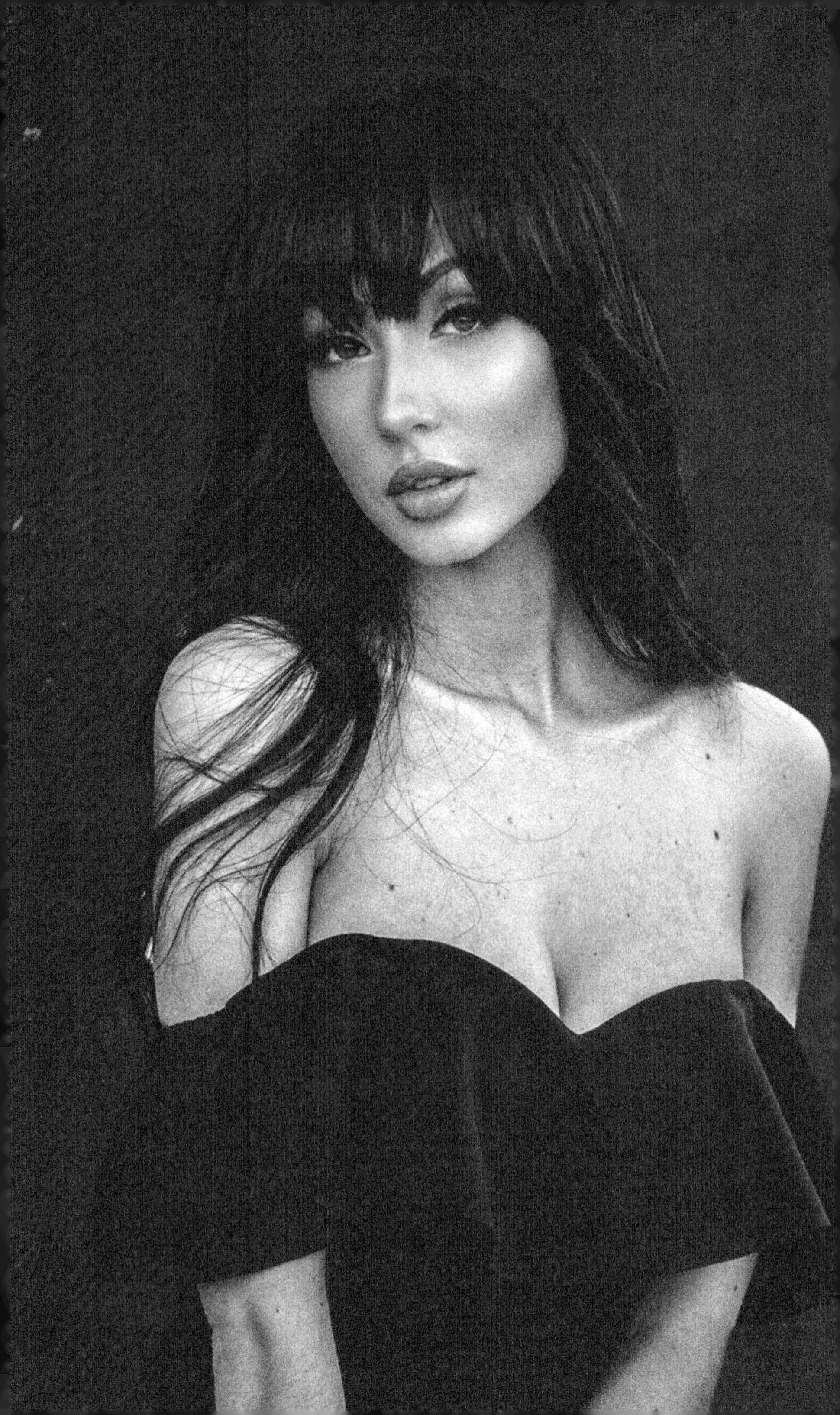

CHAPTER 21

Lucia

After tending to our wounds, taking a refreshing shower—individually, or we'd never leave the apartment—Sy and I, at his insistence, venture out for breakfast. Fortunately, we can use the elevator to go down to the parking lot unnoticed. But immediately upon leaving the car, reporters approach us. Their cameras flash as they throw question after question at us.

"Are the rumors true? Are you really married?"

"Why are you keeping your marriage a secret?"

"Sawyer, hey, look over here. Are you ashamed of Lucia? Is that why you kept the wedding a secret?"

A low growl works its way up Sy's throat. He grips my hand tighter and practically pulls me into the restaurant, his excitement faded. "Ignore them," I whisper as the door closes behind us.

"I won't allow them to insult you," he growls angrily.

Sy opens the door a second time and before I can comprehend his statement, he steps outside. "Please, just let it go," I plead, struggling to keep pace with his lengthy steps.

"Hey!" he calls, pointing straight at the guy who insinuated I was something to be ashamed of. "Show my wife some respect."

The reporter straightens up, a cunning grin appearing on his face. "So you're not denying it?"

Sy shrugs. "Are you hard of hearing or something? I just confirmed she's my wife." He reaches for my hand, holding it up for everyone to see my wedding band.

"So it's true?" another asks.

Throwing his arm around my shoulders, Sy pulls me to his side. "It is. I've married Lucia Carter."

"Don't you mean Lucia Perry?" a woman asks.

"Why would that be what he meant?" I ask, feeling as though I need to say something. "This isn't ancient times. I don't know if you've heard, but women actually get a choice nowadays. And I like the name Carter." I have no idea why I feel the need to defend myself.

Sy chuckles. "Maybe I'll change mine to Carter, seeing as I don't give a flying fuck what our last names are. The only thing that matters to me is that I'm with the woman I love." Looking at the reporter who insulted me, he narrows his eyes. "And if you ever insult her again, you won't be able to say you're sorry for a long time. A broken jaw takes a while to heal."

"Are you threatening me?" the reporter shouts, looking indignant.

"It was a warning," Sy snarls.

The surrounding crowd is growing rapidly, and there are questions coming from every angle. "Come on, I'm starving," I whine, tugging Sy toward the restaurant door.

He relents, and we head back inside. When some reporters try to follow us, a big guy gets up from one of the couches lining the walls. "No press," he barks, pointing at a sign on the door.

A server comes over, wasting no time finding us a quiet corner to sit in. One far away from the glass windows so we can't be seen by the people outside. After seating us, the guy leaves to get us some menus. When he returns, he's carrying a silver tray with two fresh OJs and our menus.

"Just let me know when you're ready to order," he says, smiling.

Perusing the menu, I find that everything is organic and fresh, and every single item looks delicious. "What's good here?"

Sy leans forward, pointing at my menu. "Their omelets are great."

Judging by the large portions of food being carried to the table nearby, I decide against it. So when the server returns and Sy orders a mushroom omelet, I ask for an avocado toast and a bowl of fresh fruit.

While we wait for our food, I study Sy while he's scrolling through his phone. His long fingers dance across the black device, so he's probably texting or emailing. From the little I know of him from working for the Sabertooths, he never looks at his socials. He's more than happy forgetting they exist. It's something I've tried to get better at recently. I don't want to see all the comments about me, and I know there has to be many by now. Luckily for me, the accounts I manage have been quiet the last few days, and I've actually managed to forget they even exist.

It's still weird to think of him as my husband, a term that's never meant anything but pain to me until I married Sy. My stomach churns as guilt settles deep inside me. Like a frigid cold, it spreads through my veins. I should have walked away without dragging him into my life. Yet, I can't make myself regret marrying him. I acknowledge my selfishness, yet my current state of mind disregards it completely. I deserve happiness, even if it's doomed to be fleeting.

"What's up?" I ask as he frowns down at his phone like it's offending him.

Before he can answer, the server carries our food over. "Oh my God," I moan, taking a bite of the avocado toast. "This is amazing."

Sy chuckles. "Been coming here for years. Can't beat the quality."

I raise an eyebrow. "And here I thought you only frequented fast-food joints."

He feigns offense. "Hey, I have a refined palate too, you know."

Our banter continues as we enjoy our breakfast, the atmosphere light and easy despite the tension simmering beneath the surface. I know he's going to demand answers about Fabian soon, and I'll either have to give them or... there isn't really another alternative anymore. Not now that we're married. But as both our phones buzz incessantly, our lighthearted conversation comes to an abrupt halt, replaced by a sense of foreboding.

"Ignore it," Sy grumbles when I go to get mine out of my bag.

I frown. "Why? Who is it?"

He shakes his head, locks of his long hair falling down his face. "Let's just enjoy our food." Agreeing, I finish up the toast and move on to the fruit, which is equally delicious. "If you lick that strawberry one more time, I'm going to drag you into the nearest bathroom and fuck you," Sy rasps, watching me through hooded eyes.

"Oops," I grin. Too busy enjoying the red berry, I hadn't even noticed I was playing with it.

The persistent buzzing of my phone is starting to make me nervous. I look longingly at my bag, considering what could be so urgent. "It could be Gail," I say, reaching for my bag again.

"It's not her," Sy rumbles. "Just leave it."

Reluctantly, I fish my phone out and answer without checking the called ID. I'm greeted by Jo's terse voice on the other end. Her tone is icy, her words clipped as she demands our immediate presence at the arena. My heart sinks, a wave of apprehension washing over me as I hang up.

"That was Jo," I say, wringing my hands.

"I know," Sy replies. "Tom's been texting and emailing me. They want us at the arena, but I say we blow them off. Fuck them."

"You know what it's about?" I ask, accusatory.

Sy finishes his food before leaning back in his chair, stretching before resting his hands on the back of his head. "They're not happy about the marriage."

Crap.

"Fabian wants proof it's real as he's apparently worried this will mean the Sabertooths' reputation will suffer if it's a stunt."

Fuck. The color drains from my face at the mention of my ex husband. "But it's not," I rush out. "It's a genuine marriage. They can't stop us."

Sy shifts in his chair and leans over the table, taking both my hands between his. "It is, and we know that. No, they can't stop us. No one can. But they can..." Shaking his head, he sighs deeply. "They can kick me off the team."

My shoulders deflate as I sag in my seat. "All this started so you wouldn't get kicked off the team," I whisper. "Now that we've delivered, they're still threatening you?" Tears gather in my eyes. I know this is my fault. Fabian is going to do what he can to get Sawyer removed, not just from the team, but possibly from the NHL and any other team.

"I know you don't want to talk about it, sweet bunny. But before we go into that meeting, I need you to tell me anything I should know. I need to be prepared, no matter how uncomfortable."

Looking up at him, I blink my tears away and nod. "O-okay."

"Is there anything I should know about you and Fabian?"

I take a shuddering breath, preparing myself. "We dated many years ago," I admit. The words taste like ash and I'm barely able to get them out. "My parents arranged it, so I never felt like I could say no. It wasn't so bad in the beginning, but the longer we were together, the worse he got."

"How long were you together?"

"About a year," I confirm, squeezing his hands tight.

Though I know I should, I don't admit to my marriage to Fabian. Like a coward, I decide to pretend it never happened and instead focus on getting to the arena so we can deal with Tom and Jo.

"And that's it?" Sy asks, his tone dark. "There's nothing else I should know?"

"No," I lie, forcing a smile. "That's it."

Sy looks like he wants to argue, but to my surprise, he lets it go and tells me to gather my things. On our way out, he pays the server, leaving a hefty tip.

Exiting the restaurant, we make our way to Sy's car. Luckily, the reporters have gone so no one disturbs us. With each step, I can't help but wonder what's churning in his mind, but I refrain from probing further, unwilling to divulge my own swirling thoughts.

Once inside the car, the tension is palpable, hanging heavy in the air as we navigate the familiar streets toward the arena. The rhythmic hum of the engine fills the silence, a stark contrast to the thoughts racing through my mind.

As we arrive at the arena, Sy cuts the engine and turns to me, his gaze piercing through my defenses. Before I can even open my mouth, he speaks, his tone firm and unwavering. "I know you're keeping something from me," he says, his words laced with a mix of frustration and concern. "This is your last chance to come clean."

I start to protest, but he interrupts me, his eyes holding mine in an unyielding grip.

"No more lies, sweet bunny. Just tell me this, is it something I should know before we go in there?" He points at the arena.

"I'm just nervous, Sy," I say, my voice tight with tension. "There's nothing else going on."

I can feel skepticism radiating off him like heat waves, but I hold his gaze steadily, refusing to back down. The truth is, I'm terrified of what might happen if he found out about my past, about the fact that I was technically married when we started fake dating. The last thing I want is to lose him, but the weight of my secrets threatens to crush me.

Sy's expression softens slightly, but the concern in his eyes remains. "I can't help you if you don't let me in," he says, his voice gentle yet firm. "Whatever it is, we'll face it together. I promise."

I swallow hard, grappling with the conflicting emotions swirling inside me. Finally, I nod, a silent acknowledgment of his offer of support. But deep down, I know that some secrets are too heavy to share, even with the person you love.

Forcing a smile, I say, "It's just nerves. Jo was really mad on the phone. So I just... I don't know what we're walking into." All of that is true.

Sy cups my cheeks while slowly moving closer until our lips touch. His lips mold the curve of my own with a surprisingly tender urgency that sends a shiver down my spine. I feel his warmth enveloping me, grounding me in the present moment amidst the whirlwind of emotions.

But beneath the surface, guilt gnaws at me like a persistent ache. I know I'm keeping secrets from Sy, and with every fleeting moment of bliss, that guilt only grows heavier. My fingers curl around the fabric of his shirt, anchoring myself to him even as I wrestle with the weight of my deception.

Breaking apart, we both get out of the car, and Sy takes my hand in his, his grip steady and reassuring. Together, we make our way into the arena, and head straight for Tom's office. When we reach it, I stop Sy from opening the door.

"Wait," I breathe. He stops his movement and looks down at me. Swallowing harshly, I meet his gaze. "I love you," I whisper. "Whatever happens, don't forget that."

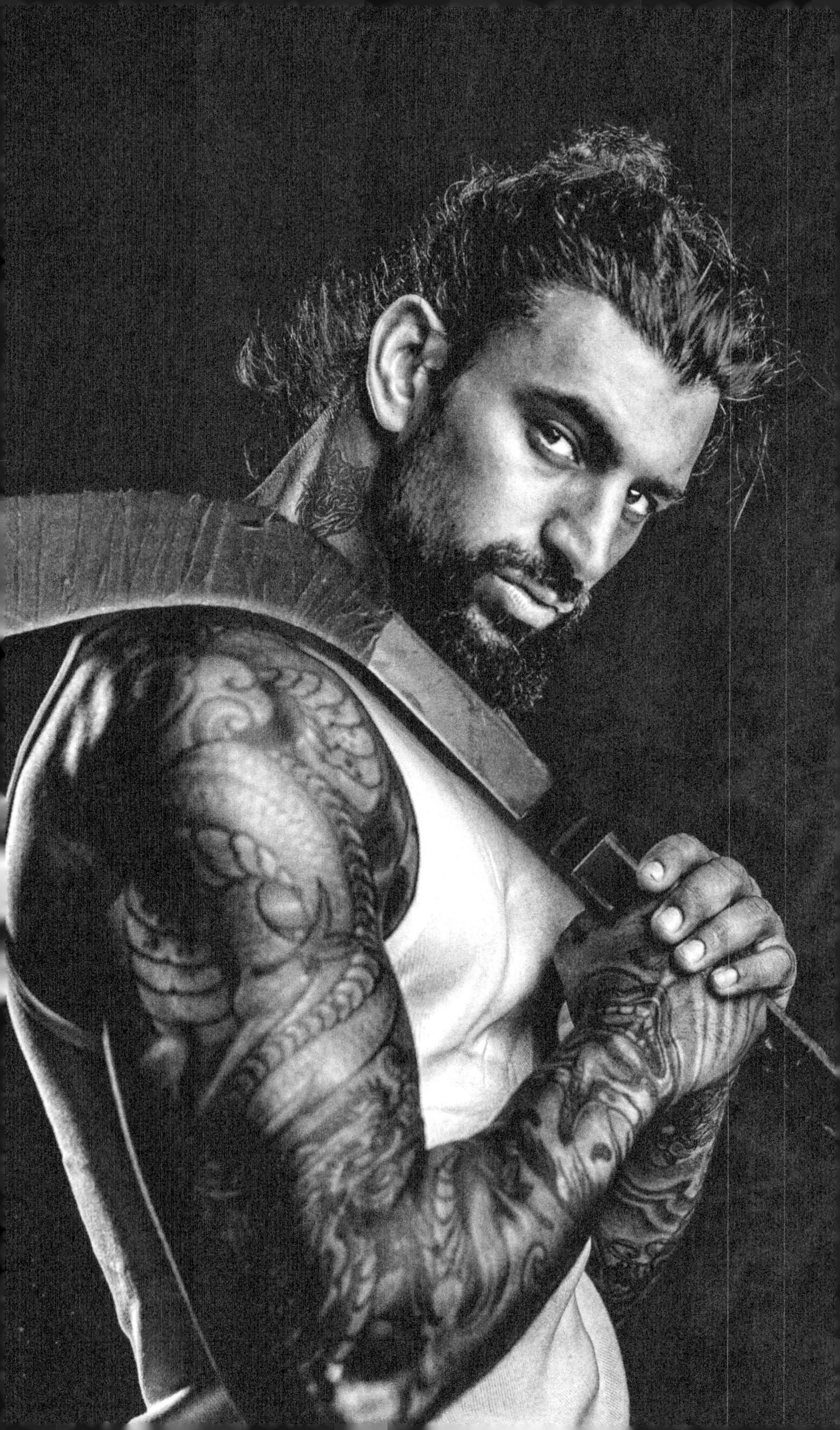

CHAPTER 22

Sawyer

The urgency of her whisper wraps around my heart in a way that makes me want to pull her into my arms and take her far, far away from here. Or get lost in her soft lips or her... nope. Instead of doing any of that, I knock on the GM's door, opening it without waiting for a reply.

Walking into Tom's office, I immediately sense the tension in the air. Jo's and Tom's expressions are grim, their eyes flashing with an intensity that sets my nerves on edge. But what catches me off guard is the presence of Fabian, lurking in the corner with a smug smirk playing on his lips.

Once again, I get the urge to whisk my wife away, but I know I can't do that. Not unless I want to kiss both of our careers goodbye. For a second I contemplate asking why Fabian is here, but what's the point? He's a sponsor and it's not the first time one of those is at a meeting.

My jaw tightens as I take in his arrogant demeanor, the way the fucker's gaze lingers on Lucia with a predatory hunger sends a surge of protectiveness coursing through me. I resist the need to confront him here and now, knowing that I need to keep a cool head in front of our team management. But one day... one day I'm going to make him fucking regret ever touching my sweet bunny.

Taking a deep breath, I steel myself for the reason we're here. I might have a good guess, but there's no chance I'm speaking first. They summoned us, so they can do the talking.

Tom's voice cuts through the tension like a knife. "What the hell is this, Sawyer? Why did you two get married?" His tone is accusatory, his eyes drilling into us with a mix of anger and disbelief.

I bristle at his words, instinctively pulling Lucia closer to me, as if shielding her from the storm brewing in Tom's office. "It's none of your business," I snap back, my voice laced with defensiveness.

But Tom isn't backing down. "None of my business? It is literally my damn business," he retorts, his frustration palpable. "You two are the faces of this team, and now you've gone and pulled this stunt without even consulting us."

I exchange a tense glance with Lucia, silently urging her to stay strong beside me. "Your contract didn't stop us from getting married," I reply firmly, trying to keep my voice steady despite the rising turmoil within me.

Tom's eyes narrow, his gaze flicking to Fabian before returning to us. "Maybe my contract didn't, but I never took you as someone who was okay with being a goddamn home wrecker."

I bristle and narrow my eyes on my GM. "No one is fucking cheating, and you already know I didn't know that woman was married." My nostrils flare and I squeeze Lucia's hand harder, hating that my past is being brought up around her, but happy to use her presence to keep me grounded so I don't do something stupid like punch Tom.

Running a hand down his face, Tom looks at Fabian, who gives him a curt nod. "So you didn't know?" he asks, raising an eyebrow.

"Know what?" I throw back.

"Do you want to tell him or should I?" Fabian says smoothly, not looking away from my wife. "What will it be, little wolf?"

"N-no," Lucia stutters, taking a step back. I watch as she closes her eyes, rolling her shoulders back before opening them. As I look into her green eyes, I recognize her PR persona. The one with a stick so far up her ass you can practically see the tip when she yawns. Well… fuck. She obviously knows what's going on, which means she lied to me. I asked her point-blank if there was something I should know, and she. Fucking. Lied. To. Me.

"Are you threatening my wife?" I ask, eager to keep the attention off Lucia. "Because that would be really fucking stupid."

"No one is threatening anyone," Tom cajoles, spreading his arms out wide. "But there are things we need to discuss. The day after the sponsor event, I received an email from Fabian with some very disturbing news," he admits. "I had to bring him in to address it. The longer we talked, I realized it was a discussion we should all have together. Normally, I would have wanted to do it right away, but with your away game it wasn't possible."

I look at Lucia, but she's completely rigid at my side. Even though she's looking straight ahead, I get the sense she isn't really seeing anything. "So?" I ask, doing my best to sound like I'm unbothered while mentally trying to work out what the hell Tom's talking about. "What was the news?"

Speaking up for the first time, Jo says, "It seems Lucia was married before."

She what? It takes all my control to keep my expression neutral and not look at my bunny, but it becomes hard when her next inhale is an audible gasp. I open my mouth, but snap it closed when Tom glares at me. "Everyone sit down. No one is leaving until I get to the bottom of this, so you might as well make yourselves comfortable."

Tom sits down at the head of the table, with Jo on his right and Fabian on his left. Since I don't think I can stop myself from punching the smug bastard if he's within reach, I sit down on Jo's side, leaving a few seats between us. Lucia follows me, but she doesn't look up as I pull the chair out for her. She just robotically takes her seat while keeping her eyes on Tom.

I don't like how pale she is, or the vacant, haunted look in her eyes. Or the way her hands tremble. She should have told me whatever it is Fabian has on her, and about her previous marriage to... fuck if I know. I ignore the voice in my head that's already put two-and-two together, because there's no way Lucia wouldn't tell me if Fabian is her ex husband.

"Right, where is it..." Tom pauses, rifling through some papers on the table before shoving a picture toward me. My eyes narrow as I see it's a picture of Lucia and Fabian on their wedding day. Judging by how young she looks, it's not recent. If I were to hazard a guess, I'd say it's over ten years old, which would make her... eighteen at the most. Fuck.

Lucia whimpers beside me, and I feel another surge of anger rise within me, directed squarely at Fabian. Snarling at him, I demand, "What the hell is this? Is it even real?"

Fabian merely shrugs, his smirk widening. "I take it you didn't know," he says, brushing some lint off his suit jacket. "I thought she would have told you by now. Since I disclosed it to Tom prior to signing the sponsorship paperwork, it never occurred to me that Lucia wouldn't be as forthcoming."

I resist the urge to lunge at him, instead turning to Tom with a steely gaze. "You knew about this?" I demand, my voice low and dangerous.

Tom nods. "I knew they'd been married, yes. What I didn't know is that when your arrangement with Lucia began, she was technically still married to Fabian."

"So you didn't find it weird when he pretended not to know her when you introduced us at the sponsor event?" I scoff, shaking my head.

"That was their business," Tom clarifies, though he does give Fabian a look of... I don't even fucking know.

Lucia

As Tom's words hang heavily in the air, I feel a surge of panic rising within me. My hands tremble uncontrollably as I struggle to process the implications of what he's just revealed. Married to Fabian when my fake relationship with Sy began. The truth hits me like a sledgehammer, shattering the fragile facade I've been desperately clinging to.

But my fear isn't for my safety; it's for the precarious bond I've forged with Sy. I know I've made a mess of things, and the thought of losing him sends a wave of despair coursing through me. I glance at my husband, searching desperately for any sign of reassurance, but all I see is a coldness in his eyes that cuts me to the core.

I've never felt so alone, so utterly helpless. I wish I'd had the courage to tell him the truth sooner, to spare him—both of us—this pain. But now it's too late, and I can see the walls building up around him, sealing me out.

As the tense silence stretches on in Tom's office, Sawyer's voice cuts through the air like a knife. "When did they get divorced?" he demands, his eyes burning with a mixture of anger and hurt.

Tom doesn't speak but instead reaches for another document, a second printout. He slides it across the desk toward Sawyer, who snatches it up with trembling hands. My heart sinks, I know he'll see the truth. That I got divorced and married at the same time.

The realization hits me like a physical blow. Not only did I keep my past marriage from Sawyer, but I also failed to disclose the fact that it ended the same day our relationship began. The truth hangs heavy in the air, suffocating me with its implications.

Sy's gaze flickers between me and the document, his expression a mask of betrayal and disbelief. Desperation claws at my chest as I reach out to him, but he recoils as if my touch burns him.

At that moment, I know I've lost him. Lost the only person who's ever made me feel truly alive and loved. Why the hell didn't I just tell him sooner? Right now, as I'm living my worst nightmare, I can't for the life of me fathom what scared me so much. If I'd been the one to tell him, I'd at least get to explain myself.

Jo's voice shatters the silence in the room, her words heavy with disappointment and frustration. "You're obviously fired, Lucia," she declares, her gaze unwavering as she locks eyes with me. "I need your keycard immediately. I'll pack up and send anything you might have left at your desk."

Tom nods in agreement, his expression grim. "I'm afraid Jo's right," he adds, his voice laced with regret. "This kind of deception is unacceptable, especially from someone in your position. You should also know that we disabled all your logins a few days ago. When you leave the arena today, you won't be welcomed back except for games."

Fabian's grin widens at the news, his satisfaction evident in every line of his face. "Oh no, how sad," he remarks, his tone dripping with malice.

Sawyer remains silent, his features carved from stone as he absorbs the blow of betrayal. His silence speaks volumes, a stark contrast to the cacophony of emotions swirling inside me.

I feel numb, disconnected from the world around me as the reality of my actions sinks in. The consequences of my lies are finally catching up to me, tearing apart everything I've worked so hard to build.

Sawyer's voice cuts through my thoughts, his words echoing with resignation and a hint of defiance. "What about the contract?" he questions, his gaze flickering between Tom and Jo.

Tom sighs heavily, rubbing his temples as if grappling with the weight of the situation. "The contract still stands," he confirms, his tone weary. "You'll both still need to maintain the appearance of a relationship until the stipulated time period is over."

A wave of despair washes over me at the realization that I'm trapped in this charade for even longer. The thought of pretending we're happily married when he won't even look at me fills me with a sense of suffocating dread.

Sawyer's jaw clenches as he processes the information, his frustration palpable. Despite his simmering anger, he nods in reluctant acceptance, his resolve hardening. With nothing left to be said, I rummage through my handbag and place my card on the table. I can't meet the gazes of Tom or Jo, but when I look at Fabian, I bare my teeth at him.

"I'd rather be hated by everyone than ever be tied to you," I hiss.

Then I follow Sy... Sawyer out of Tom's office. With each step, the weight of my deceit hangs heavy on my shoulders, dragging me down into the depths of despair.

I should have told him when I had the chance.

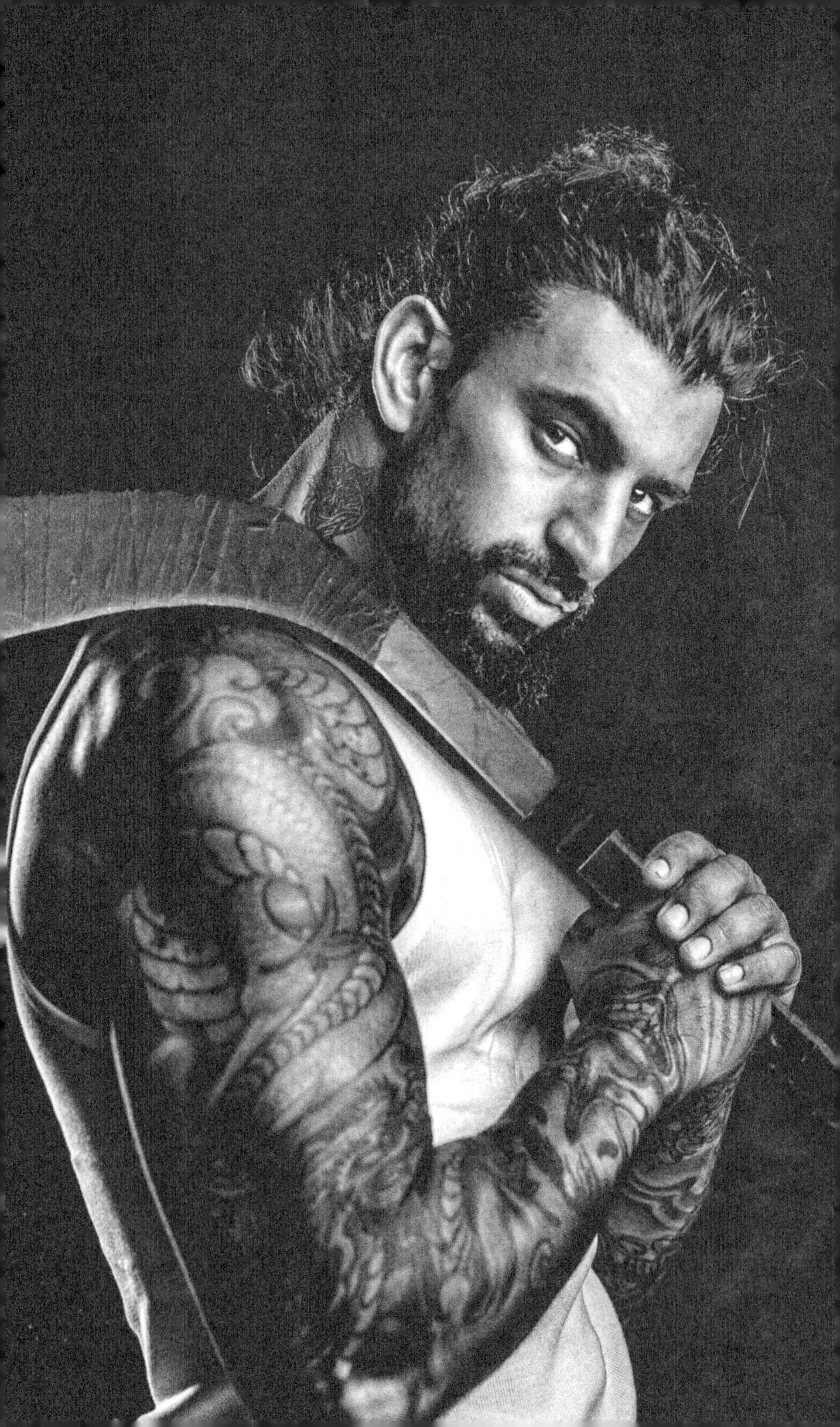

CHAPTER 23

Sawyer

"Get the fuck inside," I seethe, looking at the lying bunny through cold eyes as she comes to a stop, refusing to walk inside.

She shakes her head. "No."

"Get. The. Fuck. Inside."

I ignore the heartbreak and guilt written all over her features and in her glistening green eyes. She has no right to feel heartbroken. None what-so-fucking-ever. She lied to me even after I gave her the opportunity to come clean.

With her shoulders square, she finally walks over the threshold into my apartment. "What now?" she hisses. "Do you want me to get naked and kneel at your feet?"

I let out a mirthless laugh. "Keep your clothes on, lying bunny. No one wants to see that." We both know it's a lie, but the anger in my veins burns too bright for me to care. "Sit down," I say, my voice vibrating with the pent-up emotions swirling inside me.

Lucia scrambles over to the couch, sitting down so she's perching on the edge. "Sy—"

Holding up my hand, I cut her off. "My name is Sawyer. You should know, since you've screamed it enough times."

Red spots form on her cheeks and neck. "Fine," she bites. "Sawyer. What happened in Tom's office... it's... I mean, that's not how I wanted you to find out."

"No?" I quirk an eyebrow. Turning my back on her, I walk over to the minibar, pouring myself some bourbon. "That's a little hard to believe since you conveniently didn't tell me you were married to Fabian while I was fucking you."

"That's a technicality," she shoots back, darting to her feet.

I look at her over the rim of the glass as I take a large sip. Relishing the burn of the alcohol, I close my eyes and savor it for a brief moment. Then I pour myself more before sitting down in the closest armchair. Silence stretches between us, twisting, growing until it feels like it's consuming the entire room.

Where I'm using the quiet to make sense of everything, Lucia looks as though it's making her sick. She keeps shifting, crossing one leg, patting her hair, moving the other leg, twisting her hair. She can't sit still and if she doesn't let go of her bottom lip, she's sucked between her teeth, she's going to bleed soon.

Straightening, she looks at me, trying to catch my gaze. I continue to look at the spot just above her right shoulder, so I'm aware of what she's doing without looking directly at her. "Sawyer," she breathes, nervously wringing her hands in front of her. "I know this looks bad, and I'm sorry. I should have told you about my marriage to Fabian. But it wasn't real. We were never in love."

I don't acknowledge her words.

"He owned me," she goes on. "I-I was his property, and he never let me forget that. He would dress me up like a doll and parade me around for parties. Then, as soon as we were alone, depending on his mood, I'd either be his pet or his whore."

My mask almost slips as fury stirs inside me, but I catch myself and remain unmoving.

"P-please look at me," she cries. "Don't... please don't do this. Don't ignore me, Sawyer. Don't reduce me to nothing like he did."

Unable to ignore her heartfelt plea, I look into her green eyes. Without meaning to, I get lost in them. Noticing details I've been oblivious to until now. They're like two pools of liquid jade, drawing me in with their intensity. Flecks of gold dance within the verdant expanse. Her look is so intense it feels as though she's looking into the depths of my soul, searching for something.

"You're not nothing," I finally say, gravel evident in my tone.

Her shoulders sag with relief. "Thank you for saying that. I know I fucked up, but I want to make things right."

I continue, like she didn't speak. "You're a liar, a manipulator, and selfish. But you're not nothing."

She flinches with each word I speak. "N-no... I mean yes. Fuck. You're right. I did lie, and I did manipulate the situation between us. But it wasn't..." She shakes her head and swallows thickly. "It's not what you think."

"How do you know what I think?"

"I don't. But no matter what it is, it's not the truth. It can't be."

Nodding, I swirl the amber liquid in my glass. "What do you want, Lucia?" I ask. It's weird to use her name, but calling her bunny doesn't feel right anymore. She's not some scared prey.

She's quiet for so long I give up on getting an answer and stand abruptly. "Wait," she chokes out, reaching for me.

"I did," I say, shaking my head. "I waited for you to tell me the truth about Fabian. I waited for you to explain yourself just now. No more."

"But, Sy—"

"Sawyer!" I boom, hating that she flinches away from me.

As I walk over to the elevator with long strides, she follows me, rambling one excuse after the other all while begging me to stay. As I step into the elevator, she meets my gaze. Her voice trembling as she asks, "Is there anything I can do or say to make you stay?"

"You've already done enough," I say, my voice as gutted as I feel. "You made me care. Made me love you."

"I love you, too," she cries.

"And look where that got either of us," I scoff, just as the elevator doors close.

The look on Lucia's face haunts me during the descent, and even as I drive to Mickey's house on the other side of the city, it's not the traffic I see. It's Lucia's grief stricken expression.

Fuck!

I rap sharply on Mickey's door, my knuckles echoing the pounding rhythm of my heart. Mickey swings open the door, his eyes widening at the sight of me, recognizing the storm brewing behind my eyes.

"Hey, man," Mickey says, his voice tinged with concern as he steps aside to let me in. "Come on in. What's going on?"

I slump onto the couch, the weight of my emotions threatening to crush me. "It's a mess, Mickey," I mutter, frustration and anger seeping into my words. "Tom called me and Lucia into a meeting."

"Why?"

There's zero mirth in my forced laugh. "Oh, you know. The usual. He wanted to ask about our marriage, and then tell me Lucia was married when we got together."

"The fuck?" Mickey asks, echoing my thoughts perfectly. "To who?"

"Fabian," I sneer. "The new fucking sponsor."

Mickey's brow furrows in empathy, his understanding of my turmoil evident. "Damn, Sawyer. I can't even imagine. That's rough."

"Yeah, you could say that again," I bark. "She made me do the one thing I've always done my best to avoid. She turned me into a cheater, home wrecker. Whatever you wanna fucking call it."

Instead of letting me stew in my anger, Mickey tilts his head to the side. "You know I have a million questions, right?"

"Like what?"

"Like how she could be with you so much without Fabian knowing if they were married?" When I look at him with confusion written all over my face, he sighs. "Get your fucking head out of your ass long enough to look at the facts."

I run a hand through my hair, the feeling of betrayal burning like a wildfire in my chest. "The facts are pretty fucking clear," I argue, not really in the mood to listen to reason. "She. Was. Married. That's all there is to it."

Rolling his eyes, Mickey throws his hands up in the air. "Really? Then why did you come here?"

"What?"

"If you wanted someone to just agree with you and bitch out Lucia like a group of teenagers, you would have driven to Soren's house. So why are you really here, Sawyer?"

Sometimes I really fucking hate how perceptive Mickey is, and how well he knows me. I'm here because I want him to tell me I'm not turning into my mom, and to… I don't fucking know. Make sense of it all. Because I have no doubt if I'm left with my own thoughts for too long, I'll do something stupid. Like find Fabian and punch him.

"Fine," I agree after a lengthy silence. "Tell me what facts I'm overlooking."

Mickey looks up from his phone. Yeah, the second I stopped talking, he picked it up, happy to ignore me until I broke the silence. Mickey is one stubborn fucker. Seriously, if we didn't have practice, training, and games, we could sit here for days without talking.

"For one," he says, holding up one finger. "The thing I said about time. If her marriage to Fabian meant a damn thing, she couldn't be spending all that time with you."

I nod, acknowledging his words.

"Second..." He adds a second finger. "Where was her wedding band?"

"She could have taken that off," I growl.

Mickey shakes his head. "For years? What would have been the point of keeping it off for all the time we've been with the Sabertooths, and probably longer?"

This gets my attention. "What do you mean?" I ask, leaning forward, resting my arms on my thighs.

"If Lucia was married, the rumors would have reached the locker room. We both know she's been asked out many times by many different people. Why not just tell people she was married? It would have been the easiest way to let anyone down. Instead, she's turned every single person down in other ways."

That much is true. And Mickey is right. Lucia turning people down hasn't exactly earned her any bonus points. Where most will agree she's hot as fuck, most are also of the opinion she's so frosty her cunt would freeze anything that came into contact with it. Okay, it's not that bad. She isn't disliked or hated. She's just... no one would consider her cuddly or ask her to look after their pet.

"If you ask me," Mickey says, staring straight at me. "You're being an ass, and Fabian's a fucking rat and shouldn't be trusted."

"Yeah," I reluctantly agree, my head swimming.

"What would you do if you found out your wife—Lucia—was cheating on you?" Mickey asks, waving me off when I let out a low growl. "Down, boy. This isn't about your mommy issues. But think it through. You wouldn't go to Tom."

"Fuck no," I spit. "I'd find the fucker and punch his head in."

Even though it's not what's going on, anger swirls inside me at the thought of anyone else touching my wife. My. Wife. I might be too pissed to see reason right now, but that doesn't mean she isn't mine.

"Exactly," Mickey grunts. "But Fabian is a little bitch who went to Tom. Ask yourself why."

"Because he wanted him to know. If he came straight to me I could bury it."

Mickey annoyingly claps and lets out a sharp whistle. "Look at that, Sawyer. Maybe you're not too stupid to be a good husband after all."

Scoffing, I roll my eyes. "I'm not... I don't know." I run my hands through my shoulder-length hair, squeezing my eyes shut. "This is all so fucked up."

Mickey hums quietly to himself. "And I bet you just made it a million times worse."

"Probably," I admit. Lucia's stricken face jumps to the forefront of my mind. "Definitely."

"What your mom did was fucked," Mickey says, not bothering to sugarcoat the words. "But leaving your wife instead of talking to her, instead of listening, isn't much better."

"The fuck?" I roar. "I'm nothing like her."

"Aren't you, though?"

My nostrils flare as I clench and unclench my fists. "You're too fucking old to still believe she is the one who cocked everything up by herself—"

"Don't fucking use the word 'cock' in the same sentence as my mom."

Mickey guffaws. "Whatever. The point is that Dad Perry was no fucking prize. He left you. And he'd only contacted you after you made it big. And what does he say every time he calls?"

"That he needs money," I grumble.

Okay, I get it. I'm a dick, and instead of dealing with my issues, I've put it all on my mom. My mom, who also happens to be the only parent in my life, never asking for anything but my company.

"I get it," I finally agree. "But I'm not ready to forgive her."

"Which one?" Mickey asks, grinning. "Lucia or your mom?"

"Both."

He shrugs. "Hate to tell you... actually, scratch that. I love that I'm the one who gets to tell you this. Forgiving your mom is long fucking overdue. As for Lucia, I think you're the one who needs to be forgiven."

I arch an eyebrow, shooting him an unimpressed stare. "Really?"

"Yep. Really. You fucked up with both of them. Don't be such a pussy."

A wave of gratitude washes over me. This is why I came to him. Mickey is brutal in his honesty. "Thanks, Mickey," I say, my voice thick with emotion. "I mean it. Thanks for being here."

He shrugs again. "Technically, you're the one who's here since we're at my house."

I chuckle. "Dick."

We end up ordering pizza, the scent of melted cheese and tomato sauce enveloping us as we devour slice after slice. The distraction is welcome, providing a temporary reprieve from the turmoil brewing inside me.

Afterward, we watch a movie. Some stupid action shit that Mickey's into. As the credits roll on the movie we'd chosen, I find myself unable to face the prospect of returning to mine and Lucia's apartment. My thoughts are a chaotic whirlwind, and the idea of confronting them alone feels daunting, but it's still better than going home. I need some time alone to process everything I learned today.

Mickey seems to sense my unease, his gaze meeting mine with a silent understanding. "You're crashing here tonight, aren't you?" he asks, his tone gentle.

I nod in response, grateful for his intuitive grasp on the situation. "Yeah," I admit quietly. "I just... I need some time before I can go back there."

Mickey offers a supportive pat on the shoulder. "No worries, man," he says reassuringly. "You're welcome to stay here as long as you need to."

I manage a small, appreciative smile. "Thanks, Mick," I reply sincerely. "I really appreciate it."

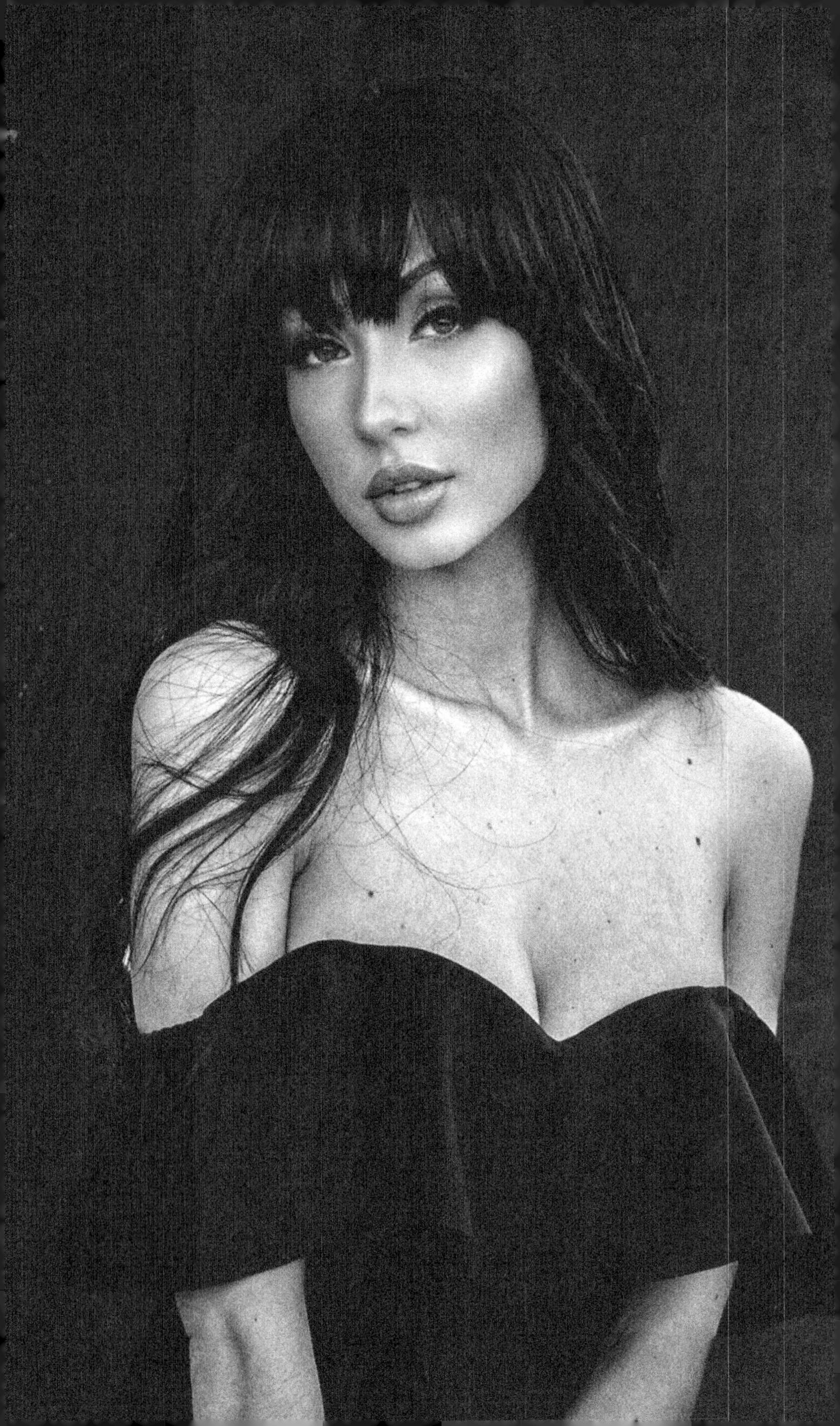

CHAPTER 24

Lucia

Four days.

That's how long it's been since Fabian dropped the bomb and Sawyer stormed out. Whomever said time heals all wounds was either a liar, or maybe ninety-six hours just isn't enough. Even if it feels like an eternity to me.

The first night, Sawyer didn't even come home. And just as I was about to try to track him down, Mickey texted me to let me know Sawyer was at his place and planned to spend the night. The surprising text from someone I mean nothing to, turned the hollowness in my chest into a liquid fire of anger.

Sawyer should have been the one to text me. He should have been the one who comforted me and assured me everything would be okay. Isn't that what a husband, someone who loves you, is supposed to do?

Maybe I should have asked him when he returned the following evening, but I didn't. Instead, I chickened out and hid in the guestroom. He didn't even bother to come and check on me. I heard him go straight to his bedroom, slamming the door behind him. The next morning he left again, still without coming to find me.

I haven't laid eyes on him for four days, and without my job, there's nothing to distract me. I'm left to grapple with the whirlwind of emotions that threaten to consume me. I miss him so bad it hurts, and at its worst, even something as mundane as breathing becomes hard. There's a heaviness in my heart I know only Sy-Sawyer can chase away.

When the hell did I become this dependent on him? In the grand scheme of things, the time we've spent together should barely register. Yet it's all-consuming; it's everything. Everything I miss, and everything I want. Everything I apparently can't have.

Despite knowing I shouldn't, I spend an ungodly amount of hours in the guest bedroom that feels like a glorified shrine—a tribute to a happier time in his life. I've studied every picture, smiled as I looked at the pictures of him riding his bike. His cheeks were chubby, but his eyes... they're the same, yet not. The boy is all smiles and giggles, whereas the man is intense. His gaze is like that of his predator; studying your weakness before pouncing.

Lying on the bed, I look at my phone, reading and re-reading the text from Sawyer.

Sawyer: Don't come to the game tonight. Fabian's here.

That's it. A handful of words after four days of no communication. Sighing, I get up and grab a quick shower. Then I quickly get dressed. Despite Sawyer's text, I have no intention of not showing up. Not only is it my duty as his wife, but I want to see him. And in public, he can't ignore me.

While making quick work of getting ready, I tell myself to leave my emotions behind. I can't show up with heartache written all over my face, or snarling at people because I'm spitting mad. But fuck... I have so much anger inside me. I'm angry with myself for failing to muster the courage to confess the truth to Sawyer when I had the chance, for allowing fear to hold me back from laying bare my secrets.

My anger is not solely directed inward. Remus' incessant reminders and demands for arrangements to transport Sawyer to Rome only serve to stoke the flames of my frustration. I resent his interference, his intrusion into our already tumultuous lives.

And then there's Fabian, the catalyst for this chaos, the one who tore open old wounds and exposed shit he had no right to expose. Though I should have seen it coming, his treachery took me off-guard. And now, my anger simmers to a boiling point, a fierce blaze of hatred that threatens to consume me whole. Despite my upbringing, I've never wanted anyone dead. Not really. That was then; the me living in the present very much wants his head on a spike.

"Enough," I tell my reflection as I stop, stealing a moment to make sure I look okay.

My long, fiery red hair cascades down my back in a loose braid, a stark contrast against the simple elegance of my outfit. I've opted for a pair of well-worn jeans, paired with sleek boots that add a touch of edge to the ensemble.

A crop sweater—another custom made item with Sawyer's number on it—its soft fabric hugging my frame in all the right places completes my choice of attire. It's a look that strikes the perfect balance between casual and put-together, allowing me to blend seamlessly in with the other women.

I can't help but feel a sense of satisfaction at the image staring back at me. My makeup is understated yet polished, enhancing my natural features without overpowering them. And then there's the glint of my wedding band on my finger, a constant reminder of the tangled web of secrets and lies that now define my life. But all in all, I look good, and not at all like a woman on the verge of giving up.

No, I can't think like that. I refuse to. I'm not giving up. Not on Sawyer, and not on my freedom. But... as I ride the elevator down, the thoughts I've done my best to keep at bay seep in. I have to face the fact that I might not be able to have both my freedom and my husband, not after I neglected to be honest. So if I have to make a choice... there's no choice at all.

I'll pick Sawyer because, without him, my freedom means nothing.

As I step out of the taxi, my heart races with a mix of nerves and anticipation. The arena looms ahead, a beacon of both excitement and uncertainty. I adjust the strap of my bag over my shoulder, my fingers fidgeting with the fabric.

Then I see Jo standing outside, her familiar figure standing by the entrance. I hadn't expected her to be here, and for a moment, I hesitate. But then I steel myself and approach her.

"Hey, Jo," I greet her, trying to keep my voice steady.

Jo turns toward me, a hint of concern in her eyes. "Lucia, I figured you'd show up. I'm here to escort you inside."

I nod, grateful for her presence despite my lingering unease. "Thank you," I murmur softly.

As we walk toward the entrance together, Jo speaks up again, her tone more gentle this time. "I wanted to apologize, Lucia. I know I was harsh the other day, and I regret the way things went down."

Her words catch me off guard, and I glance at her in surprise. "You do?"

Jo nods solemnly. "Yeah. You took me, all of us, by surprise, really. But despite everything, I care about you. I just want what's best for you."

I swallow, feeling a lump form in my throat. It's unexpected, this display of concern from Jo, but it touches something deep within me. "Thank you, Jo," I breathe, my voice barely above a whisper. "I appreciate that."

"Look, I talked to Tom and pointed out there's nothing anywhere in your contract that makes what happened grounds for firing you, and—"

"Jo," I say, cutting her off. "It's fine. I lied, so I get it."

Turning to me, she frowns. "Don't you want your job back?"

I shake my head. "If we're being honest, I don't care. The only thing that matters to me now is Sawyer."

Her eyes widen. "So it's all true. You really are in love." She says it more to herself than me.

"I love him," I confirm, deliberately not commenting on how he feels about me.

When we reach the area for family, she turns to me. "Okay, then."

"Okay," I echo.

"Let me know if anything changes," she says with a wry smile. "As far as I'm concerned, you'll always be a part of my team."

Before I can overthink it, I hug her. For a second, she doesn't react, and I almost pull back. But then I feel her arms close around me. "Thank you, Jo."

"Take care of yourself, Lucia."

As Jo leaves, I'm left standing alone for a moment, the echo of her words lingering in my mind. But before I can dwell on them further, I hear someone calling my name. Turning, I see Amy, Peter's girlfriend, waving me over.

"Lucia, there you are!" Amy exclaims, a bright smile on her face. "We've been waiting to hear all about your wedding to Sawyer!"

I offer her a small smile and join the group of women. Everyone is eager to ask me questions, not even pretending they aren't shocked about our marriage. "Tell us everything!" Sam, another one of the girlfriends, chimes in eagerly. "Was it romantic? Did Sawyer cry?"

Chuckling, I shake my head. "No tears. But it was... unexpected, to say the least," I reply, trying to keep my tone light despite the weight on my heart.

"I still can't believe it," Mandy says. "I don't think any of us thought we'd ever see Sawyer settle down."

"Why not?" I ask, feeling a touch of defensiveness. "I mean, it's not like he's a monster or anything."

Amy links her arm with mine. "That's not what we mean," she assures me. "We're just surprised he found someone that was around long enough to see past his... facade." She says the word like she isn't sure it's the right one to describe my husband, and she's right.

"I get it," I say, softening my tone. "I just hate that everyone seems to have such a negative opinion about him. Underneath it all he's really... not sweet, but..." Trailing off, I search for the right word.

"Hot? An alphahole?" Amy laughs as she unhelpfully makes suggestions.

"You're not wrong," I say, unable to hold my own laughter at bay. "I can't explain it because he isn't nice, and he isn't the heart and flowery kind of guy. But he's everything that matters, you know?"

Winking conspiratorially, she nods. "I get it. Peter's the same."

We're interrupted when the buzzing anticipation around us reaches new heights as the players file onto the ice, their skates carving sharp lines on the pristine surface. The crowd erupts into cheers as the starting lineup is announced, each player skating out with purpose and determination.

Sawyer takes his place among his teammates, his movements fluid and confident. His eyes gleam with intensity as he scans the opposing team, his focus unwavering. When some of the wives and girlfriends jump up, all calling their man's name, I join them.

The referee blows the whistle, signaling the start of the game, and the puck drops with a resounding thud. The players spring into action, their bodies colliding in a flurry of motion.

In the midst of the chaos, Sawyer stands out for his aggression. He's relentless in his pursuit of the puck, barreling through the opposing players with brute force. At one point, he delivers a bone-jarring hit that sends an opponent sprawling to the ice, earning him a penalty and igniting a scuffle between the teams.

Despite the tension on the ice, Sawyer shows no signs of backing down. He's determined to assert his dominance, engaging in several more heated exchanges with the opposing players. Each confrontation only seems to fuel his intensity, driving him to push himself even harder. The crowd loves it. They cheer him on, making it known they love that he's showing the Canadians up.

When he scores his third goal, the crowd goes wild. Everyone throws their hat onto the ice in celebration of the hat trick. Since I'm not wearing one, I just jump up and down with the others while screaming myself hoarse.

The spectacle from our area gets Sawyer's attention, and he looks up. Shock registers on his handsome face, but then an opposing player strikes him with his shoulder, breaking the moment. I want to curse at myself. I shouldn't have looked at him like that. Or, at least, I should have looked away. He needs his head in the game and not on me.

As the game reaches its climax, Sawyer's aggression becomes more pronounced. He's in the thick of every scrum, throwing punches and trading blows with anyone who dares to challenge him. It's clear that tonight he's not playing to win—he's playing for the fight.

"Did you criticize his stick or something?" Sam giggles, elbowing me gently.

"He seems more aggressive than usual," someone remarks, voicing what we're all thinking.

"Yeah, I wonder what's gotten into him," Sam adds, apparently not willing to let it go.

Unable to answer, I pretend I don't hear them as I stare straight ahead at the ice.

"They're all like that sometimes," Amy says with a shrug. "I swear they're like kids on the ice. Sometimes all it takes is a glare and they refuse to back down."

"Alphaholes," I giggle, repeating her word from earlier.

I glance at Sawyer, my heart tightening with worry. I can't shake the feeling that his behavior is somehow connected to the recent revelations about our marriage.

As the game progresses, the women continue to chat, but my mind is elsewhere, consumed by thoughts of Sawyer and the turmoil swirling between us.

"Good evening, ladies." I'm so focused on what's happening on the ice that I barely register the voice. "Are you enjoying the game?"

The second the voice registers, I become rigid. But this time, it's not cold that spreads through my veins; it's red-hot fury. How fucking dare he show his face? How dare he show up when Sawyer's playing?

"Yeah, we are," Sam says, answering Fabian's question. Then she winces as Sawyer glares in our direction before ruthlessly pursuing an opponent.

"Do you mind if I sit with you?" Fabian asks, already moving toward me.

No one seems to think it's weird that Fabian is here, in the family section so I don't comment on it. Even though I know it's frowned upon, I get up. "Take my seat. I was just leaving."

Without looking back, I hurriedly walk away, doing my best not to block anyone. Most hockey arenas don't allow spectators to get up during a game since it blocks the view of the fans behind you, which in turn puts them at risk of being hit by a puck. But fuck it, this is a special circumstance.

I hope Sawyer's watching, seeing me leave Fabian in the dust where he belongs. Despite acting cool, my heart thunders in my chest. I don't think I'll ever be able to not feel at least some sense of panic whenever my ex husband is near.

As I look across the rink, my gaze locks with Sawyer's, and he gives me a subtle nod. I breathe a sigh of relief, happy he saw me leaving the group. Maybe it's too much to hope for, but I can't help hoping he knows this is me choosing him. Now and always.

I watch the rest of the game standing. Though I'm alone, I don't feel it. Not when Sawyer looks at me every chance he gets. It's like a security blanket; comforting.

When the final buzzer sounds, signaling the end of the game, he skates off the ice with a smirk across his kissable lips. Despite the penalties and the physical toll, he looks happy about the win. As he should be. The Canadians are always favorites, but tonight the Sabertooths showed the league why they shouldn't be underestimated.

I'm just about to leave when movement in my peripheral vision catches my attention. "Oh, my God!" I exclaim as Sawyer gracefully skates right for me.

Without missing a beat, he runs through the opening in the barrier. People have stopped moving, and when he takes me in his arms, dipping me before fusing our lips together, the spectators clap and whoop with excitement.

At first, I think he's doing it for show. But the longer we kiss, I know it's more than that. The chemistry between us can't be fabricated any more than the passion and need in our kiss. And the kiss is one that could burn down forests and make the earth crack.

"My sweet bunny," he rasps against my lips.

Winding my arm around his neck, I pull at his hair. "I love you, Sy." I deliberately use my nickname for him, refusing to go back to a place where we act like strangers. "And I'm done with you ignoring me."

He helps me back up, smiling widely. "Yes, ma'am," he drawls, saluting me. As he looks at something—someone—behind me, his smile disappears. "What do you want?" His tone is no longer playful.

"I just came to congratulate you on your performance tonight," Fabian says. His beady eyes shift between us like he's trying to work something out.

Sawyer tries to push me behind him, but I stubbornly stay in place, refusing to hide from Fabian any longer. Canting my head, I stare at him through cold eyes. "Vattene." *Leave.* "Levati dal cazzo. L'ordine del nostro Don è di lasciarmi in pace. Questo è il tuo ultimo avvertimento." *Get the fuck out of here. The orders of our Don are to leave me alone. This is your one and only warning.*

Fabian narrows his eyes as his mouth opens and closes over and over. But he doesn't say anything. Only stares at me like he's imagining the ways he'd like to punish me for finally taking a stand.

"Cagna," he spits, making me laugh.

"What did he say?" Sawyer asks, not taking his eyes off of Fabian.

Together we watch him retreat, and it's not until he's out of sight I answer. "He called me a bitch."

Nodding, my husband looks down at me like that's what he thought. "And what did you say, sweet bunny?"

Though I was expecting him to ask, I still gulp. Not because I don't want to tell him, but because I'm scared he'll get pissed at my answer. "I can't tell you here," I murmur. When he takes half a step back from me, I hurry to explain. "I'll tell you the second we're home, Sy. But..." Trailing off, I look around. "Not here."

He looks around, obviously noticing the people still milling around. "The second we get home," he growls, clearly feeling the need to clarify.

I suck my bottom lip between my teeth before letting it go with a deep exhale. "I promise."

Thoughts about Fabian's anger assault me, and the memories of the ways he punished me makes it hard to think about anything else. It takes all my willpower to replace his face with Sy's in my mind's eye, and that's when it hits me. I know how to make up for my lies. It won't be pleasant, but that's okay. He's my chosen husband, and I can endure some pain for him.

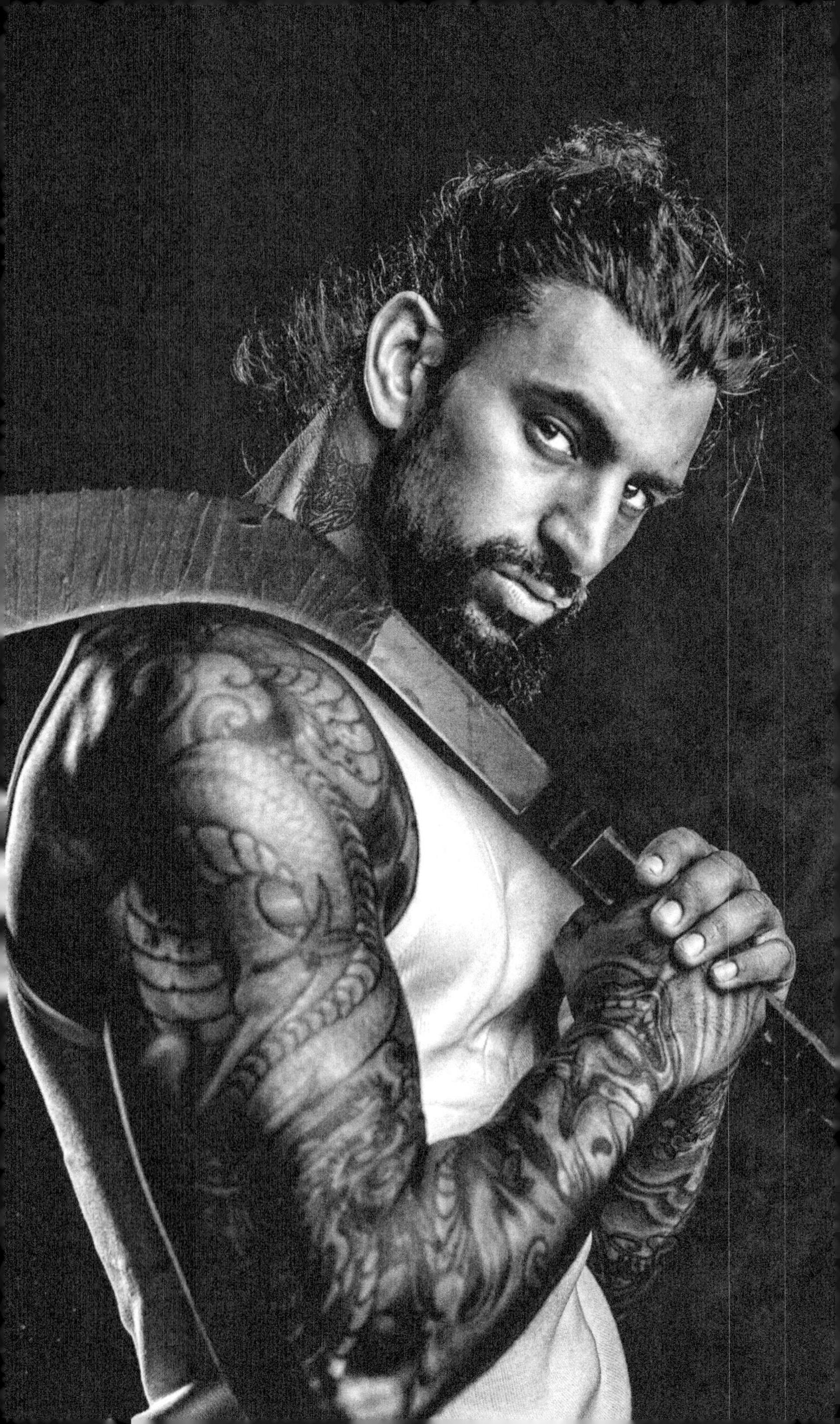

CHAPTER 25

Sawyer

I don't think I've ever showered and changed this quickly before. While Coach talks about our win, I can't keep my eyes off the door. All I want to do is leave with my sweet bunny, and not having her at my side is making me restless.

Seeing her tonight made me realize how much I've missed her. And for once, I'm glad she didn't do as I said, because seeing her here, in that crop-sweater or whatever... cheering for me. Not only was it hot as fuck, but it also made me realize just how much I've missed her. Sure, four days without her pussy has left me with blue balls, but it's more than that. I've missed her; her laughter, the way she hogs the sheet, the cute noises she makes when deep in sleep.

Mickey was right; I needed to get my head out of my ass and see the truth. I'm so fucking in love with my wife, consumed by her in ways I never thought possible. I need to tell her I'm sorry.

"Good game, guys. The press are waiting for us, so we should get out there," Coach says, walking over to the door and holding it open for us as we file out.

When we walk around the corner, I discreetly fall behind, and the moment everyone is in front of me, I double back and walk out the opposite door where I know Lucia's waiting for me.

"Sy," she breathes, her whole face lighting up as she speaks my name.

"Sweet bunny." I grin, taking her hand. "We have to leave quickly or they'll come looking for me."

Lucia looks up at me. "Huh? Why?"

What does she mean why? She knows my schedule, as everyone on the PR team does. As soon as I think that, I realize just how much I've messed up. I forgot she lost her job the day Fabian outed her to Tom and Jo. The thought makes me feel even worse about ignoring her. I should have been there to make sure she was okay. "There's a press conference," I explain as we leave through the back door.

We make it to my car without anyone stopping us, and we waste no time getting the hell out of there. As we drive through the mostly empty streets, I can't shake the weight of my own actions, the guilt that gnaws at me for avoiding my sweet bunny for days on end.

I steal a glance at her, the woman who holds my heart in her hands. "I'm sorry," I rush out.

"You're sorry?" she scoffs. "I'm the one who's sorry."

Shaking my head, I take her hand and press a kiss to the back. "No, baby. I'm the one who's sorry for running away like a fucking pussy. I should have stayed so we could talk. I should have been there for you after you lost your job."

I can feel her eyes bore into me, but she doesn't speak until I've parked and we're in the elevator. "I don't care about the job," she finally answers. "All I care about is us, Sy."

No words can express the way it feels to hear those words. So instead of cheapening the moment, I push her against the elevator wall and press my lips to hers. Her arms immediately wrap around my middle, and she's tangling her fingers in the fabric of my suit jacket like she's afraid I'll leave her.

I want to laugh at the absurdity of that thought. I can't leave her any more than I can cut out my own heart and continue breathing. She's it for me, and I want—crave—to be the same for her. Each swipe of my tongue is my way of telling her exactly that.

We end the kiss when the elevator doors slide open, and together we enter our apartment. After closing the door behind us, Lucia stays near it. Her eyes dart between me and the bedroom. Furrowing my brows, I sit down on the couch, patting the space next to me. "Come over here," I rasp.

Lifting her chin, she looks at me. "Are you going to shout at me?"

"What?"

I only now notice the way her clenched hands tremble. "I won't fight with you, Sy," she whispers. "So if you're angry you can..." Pausing, she swallows audibly. Then her eyes lock on to mine. "If you promise not to leave a scar you can take it out on my body. I won't tell anyone."

"Where's this coming from?" I ask, trying my damndest to keep my tone calm. "Tell me what you're thinking, sweet bunny. I don't want to hurt you and I don't want to fight. I want us to talk like equals."

She shakes her head. "I lied to you, Sy. I manipulated you and tried to... I was going to use you as a pawn in my game. We can't be equals until you make me pay for that."

Despite her words, uncertainty flickers in her eyes as I stand and make my way over to her. Her breath hitches as I reach for her, gently cupping her cheek. "You're my wife," I rasp. "I don't give a fuck how it came to be. It happened, and I won't change it for the world."

Looking into her green eyes, I feel as though I can see the version of her that's scared. The one Fabian obviously created by mistreating her. I hate him. Hate him for having had her, for hurting her, and for daring to speak to her at the game. The mere idea of him near her fills me with a primal rage that I struggle to contain.

"What did he do to you?" I ask, needing to know the full truth. Not bits and pieces, not a watered down version. All of it.

Taking a deep breath, she closes her eyes, stealing herself. When she opens her eyes again, they're emotionless orbs of nothing. There's no hint of my bunny in there at all. "I was given to Fabian, and on my sixteenth birthday, I married him—"

"You fucking what?" I roar, letting go of her so I don't accidentally hurt her. "You were just a child." Disgust coats my words as anger licks at my insides.

Ignoring my outburst, Lucia keeps talking. "My mom was excited by the match, my dad not so much. He actually tried to get me out of it, which cost him his life."

My breath hitches. What. The. Actual. Fuck.

"Mom turned my dad over to my uncle, who executed him for treason against the Russo empire after he tried getting me out." She lets out a dry, forced laugh. "We didn't even reach the city borders. Mom was on to us straight away."

I want to say something, do something as she moves around me, tearing at her clothes with violent movements. My brain isn't working, so I just stand there, watching her undress.

"This," Lucia says coldly, pointing at the brand on her hip. "Is a reminder of who I belong to. Of who I should always belong to. My family. In my family, freedom is an illusion. But I changed the rules. I bought my freedom. I, Lucia Russo, managed what no one else has. I. Got. My freedom."

Her words are stiff, formal. This is much worse than her PR persona, because the broken woman standing in front of me is nothing more than a statuesque husk of the woman I've seen, felt coming to life at my touch. The woman I opened my heart to. The woman I love.

"Let me get this straight," I growl. "Your family married you off while you were nothing more than a child. Is that correct?"

"I was sixteen," she volleys. "I haven't been a child since... well, I'm not sure I ever really was allowed to be one."

"Baby," I breathe, pulling her to me. Swallowing thickly, I search her eyes for... I don't really know. Signs that she knows how terrible her family treated her, perhaps. Whatever it is I'm looking for, I don't find it.

Looking up at me, she licks her lips. "T-there's more," she stammers.

I nod, having already deduced that much. "I have something I need to do first," I rasp.

"O-okay."

Dropping to one knee I take her hand while searching the pocket of my suit pants for what I need. "Lucia Carter... or Russo... whatever the hell your name is. Will you continue to be married to me?"

"Sawyer—"

"I know our beginning was bumpy and imperfect. But so are we. I don't want what the world perceives as perfect. I want you, because you're perfect for me and because I'm too selfish to ever give you up." Her green eyes fill with tears as I gently remove the wedding band Remus gave her, replacing it with the one my mom gave me many years ago.

"I-I can't," she cries out. "You need to hear everything first."

Shaking my head, I kiss her hand. "No, sweet bunny. I need to ask you now because you need to know that whatever you're about to tell me won't change anything. Will you stay married to me?"

"Y-yes," she hiccups. "Now and always."

"Now and always," I echo. Sensing that the ring from Remus is more than just a piece of jewelry, I slide it back on her finger.

Standing back up, I waste no time wrapping my arms around her shaking frame, holding her firmly against me. She hesitantly hugs me back, resting her head against my chest. Her tears soak my shirt, and I hate knowing she's in so much pain. I want to wage war on everyone who's ever made her feel like she's an object rather than the amazing woman that she is.

Fuck... married at sixteen because her family told her to. If I ever see Remus again, I will fucking punch him. I might not know what his role is, but my gut tells me he has one. And Fabian... I don't know. I've always believed that everyone is capable of murder given the right circumstances, and this, knowing he abused her definitely qualifies.

Once my sweet bunny has calmed down, she loosens her embrace. "Do you mind sitting back down?" she asks nervously.

Yes, I fucking mind. A lot, actually. "Of course not," I reply. Though I don't want to, I know this isn't about me but what she needs.

Sitting down on the chair, I watch her as she paces back and forth, seemingly lost in thought. Then she walks over to her pile of clothes, finding her handbag among the fabric. I see the gleam of the knife before she holds it out to me. "Make me tell you the truth," she pleads. "You need to know I'm not hiding anything, and this is the best way I can think of."

"Baby," I rasp. "I'm always up for cutting you when you need it. But I'm not going to do it if you think it's some kind of punishment."

She stands back up and comes over to me. "No, that's not what it is. But I..." Pausing, she swallows thickly. "I need you to know I'm not lying or holding anything back from you."

I take the knife from her outstretched hand and press it against the inside of her upper arm. "Here?" I ask, not taking my eyes off of hers.

"Yes," she breathes.

Moving the blade down her arm, I make sure the cut is shallow so there's no permanent or serious damage. She doesn't hiss or show any outward signs that it hurts, not even when I make the cut longer than I probably should. My eyes trail the cut, zoning in on the redness of her blood as it pebbles to the surface and begins to trail down her arm.

I stand up and remove my suit jacket and then shirt. Then I hold my arm out to her. "I'm not going to hold anything back either," I say, pushing the handle toward her.

She wordlessly takes it, holding the metal against my upper arm. "Are you sure?" she asks, her tone low and almost sultry.

"Absolutely."

A shudder runs through her as she leans closer and slowly cuts my skin open. She stares at it with a euphoric expression on her face. Then she takes a few steps back, putting the distance she needs between us. Sitting back down on the chair, I watch her mask of indifference slipping back into place. Even though I hate when she's wearing it, I won't ask her to stop. I have no idea what she's about to divulge, only that it's bad. So if this is what she needs, I'll let her have it.

"When this all started," she gestures between us. "I saw you as my ticket to freedom. If I got married before my twenty-eighth birthday, I'd be free forever. So when Tom wanted us to find you a fake girlfriend, it had to be me. I was set on manipulating the situation for my own gain. That's the kind of person I really am, and you should never forget that." She sounds like she's reading off a script rather than sharing details about herself.

I stand abruptly, sending the chair skittering behind me. "Let's get one thing straight," I say, my tone low and dark.

I take a step toward her, causing her to take one backward and away from me. But she meets my gaze head on, even lifting her chin. I love how defiant she is, even when her instinct is to retreat, she does it in a way that shows strength.

"I'll never allow anyone to speak badly about what's mine. Not even you."

Another step, and this time she doesn't back away from me.

"Do you understand?"

She gulps. "Y-yes."

I close the distance between us, using my body to push her back until her back hits the wall. Then I gather both her wrists in my hand, moving them above her head while pinning her in place with my hips. "I thought you weren't going to lie to me," I observe, wanting to provoke her.

"I'm not lying," she spits.

As I look into her eyes, I notice her fire is back. Sighing with relief, I tighten my grip on her wrists. "Are you sure about that?" I challenge. Using my free hand, I run my fingers through the blood still trailing down her arm. Then I swipe it across my lips before repeating the motion with my own blood, painting it across her lips.

"I-I..."

"That's what I thought. Tell me I'm nothing more than your glorified key to the shackles of your fucked up family. Now, Lucia. Tell me, and I'll let you go."

Her nostrils flare as she presses her lips together.

"That's what I thought," I growl. "You're lying to yourself and to me. But why? Hmm? Do you want me to leave you?"

"No," she whimpers. "But you're going to. I know it. And I... I..."

"You what?"

"And then I have to go back to Fabian—"

"The fuck you do," I interrupt with a growl. "You're mine, sweet bunny. I've already fucking told you that. What do you think those words mean?"

Shaking her head, she admits, "I don't know."

Her words feel like a punch to my heart. How can she not know what being mine means? "It means I'm not giving up on you—on us. I'm not letting you go, and you're never going back to that sick bastard."

After hearing her out and seeing how deep her scars run, I want nothing more than to kill the bastard with my own hands. I'm not talking about her physical scars, though I'm still curious about those. No, it's her mental ones that are the worst. She might act self assured and like she's not broken, but she is. My sweet bunny was broken and I'll be damned if I'm not going to be the one to put her back together.

"I was so fucking pissed at you," I say. My soft tone contradicts the words. "You should have trusted me with the truth instead of allowing that fucker to blindside me."

"I know," she whimpers.

Reaching out, I catch a tear on my finger and lick it off like I've done before. I don't know why I crave her tears, only that it feels like a waste to let them run down her face and become nothing. "I can understand why you didn't."

"You can?" she asks, hope coating her words.

Nodding, I assure her, "Yes. I can. And if I'm being honest, I'm not sure I would have listened to anything you said beyond already being married. But I'm listening now, sweet bunny. So tell me."

"I... I thought I was divorced from Fabian," she confesses, her voice shaky with uncertainty. "But Remus... he told me we were only separated." I meet Lucia's gaze, seeing the turmoil in her eyes, and my heart clenches.

"Remus," I repeat, my voice barely a whisper. "He's the one who set this up?" Lucia nods, her eyes pleading for understanding.

"Yes and no. When his dad died, Remus took over as the new Don, or Head, of my family."

My mind whirls with disbelief. "Head of your family?" My bunny nods.

Taking a moment, I sort through everything she's told me, as well as everything I've picked up. She's Italian, that much I've worked out. Okay, that makes me sound more sure than I am, but what she said to Fabian sounded Italian, and the way her accent changed when she first told me what the letters in her brand mean.

"Are your family members of the Mafia?" I finally ask, having no other conclusion.

The corners of her lips turn upward in an almost-smile. "In the Mafia?" she asks, tilting her head to the side and looking up at me from beneath her long, black lashes. "My family is *the* original Mafia. We're the very reason for every hair that raises in fear when people use hushed tones to discuss the crimes of the very institution I was born into."

I thought I was prepared for her answer, but now that I have it I know I wasn't. What the fuck do I say to that? "And Remus is the Don?" I ask. When she nods, I continue. "But it was his dad that forced you into the marriage with Fabian, and then later helped you out of it?"

"Yup," she confirms.

"Why?"

"Why what?"

I tighten my grip on her wrists. "Don't play dumb with me, sweet bunny. You're much too clever to pull that off. Why did he set you free?"

She swallows audibly. "Fabian was... well, he was plotting against the reigning Prime Minister of Italy. Someone who had Romulus', my uncle's, backing. I gave him evidence so he could stop the coup in time, and as a thank you he granted me a favor."

"A favor?"

"Yes, and I used it to ask for my freedom from Fabian and the Russo family."

"Why did he go back on his word?"

She lets out a hollow laugh. "He didn't. I guess I just wasn't specific enough in my wish. I did get my freedom both from Fabian and the family. He took me away when I was seventeen, and sent me to America when I was eighteen. Set me up with a fat bank account and made me almost untraceable. But—"

I cut her off. "But you didn't get your divorce." As soon as the words leave my mouth, I hear the mistake. "You didn't ask for a divorce. You asked for freedom."

"Exactly. And I didn't ask for it to last forever, which I'm assuming is the reason for the ten years I got."

Right, so the devil really is in the details, even when dealing with family. "What happens now?"

"Remus told me we have to stand in front of the Senate. It's a… counsel of sorts. And they have to approve of my marriage to you. If they do, that's it. I'm free forever and they can't ever take it back."

My tone is grave as I ask, "And what happens if they don't approve? Because I don't care who your family is. You're *my* wife."

She gulps. "Then they kill you and give me back to Fabian." Her voice quavers, betrays her nerves.

"So you really weren't in a relationship when we got together?" I ask, frustration creeping into my voice.

I know it shouldn't matter, but I can't help the need to get absolute clarity. I have to know she didn't cheat on her husband with me, even if her husband is… *was* someone as sick as Fabian. Shit, this entire situation is so messed up and I'm focusing entirely on the wrong things.

"No," she almost shouts. "I've been separated from Fabian for almost ten years. We hadn't spoken until he showed up at the Sabertooths' sponsor event, and we sure as hell haven't been intimate or anything."

I search her eyes for any hint that she's lying to me. But there's none. She looks back at me with complete honesty written all over her features. "Okay," I relent. Taking a deep breath, I finally say, "I believe you."

"Really?" she mumbles, averting her gaze like she's afraid I'm about to take it back.

Moving my hand to her chin, I lift it up until she has to look at me. "Really," I confirm.

She opens her mouth to speak, but I cut her off with my mouth. I claim her lips in a hard kiss. Our teeth clash, our tongues fight, and I swallow the sobs wracking through her. Each and every one goes from her mouth and into mine, where I absorb them.

"I thought I'd lost you," she whispers when we come up for air. "I couldn't... it was... please don't leave me."

"Never," I vow. "I'll never fucking leave you, and I won't let anyone take you away. I don't care if you're Lucia Carter or Lucia Russo. All that matters is that you're *mine*."

She smiles through her tears. "I think..." pausing briefly, she shudders. "Is it okay if I'm Lucia Perry?"

Those words... words I thought I never wanted to hear wrap around my heart, stirring something dark and untamed inside me. "Say that again," I rasp, grinding against her.

"Lucia Perry has a nice ring to it," she smirks.

After letting go of her wrists, I pick her up, and she immediately wraps her legs around me while I squeeze the soft globes of her ass. "LP has a nice ring to it."

"LP?"

Now it's my turn to smirk. "Limited Partner. Lovely Pussy—"

She cuts me off. "Licking Pussy?"

I'm about to laugh when I notice how wide her eyes are, and the fire in them. "Are you saying..." I trail off, wanting her to confirm what I'm suspecting.

"Yes, Sawyer. I want you to put me down on the bed and feast between my legs." She shudders, but doesn't back down.

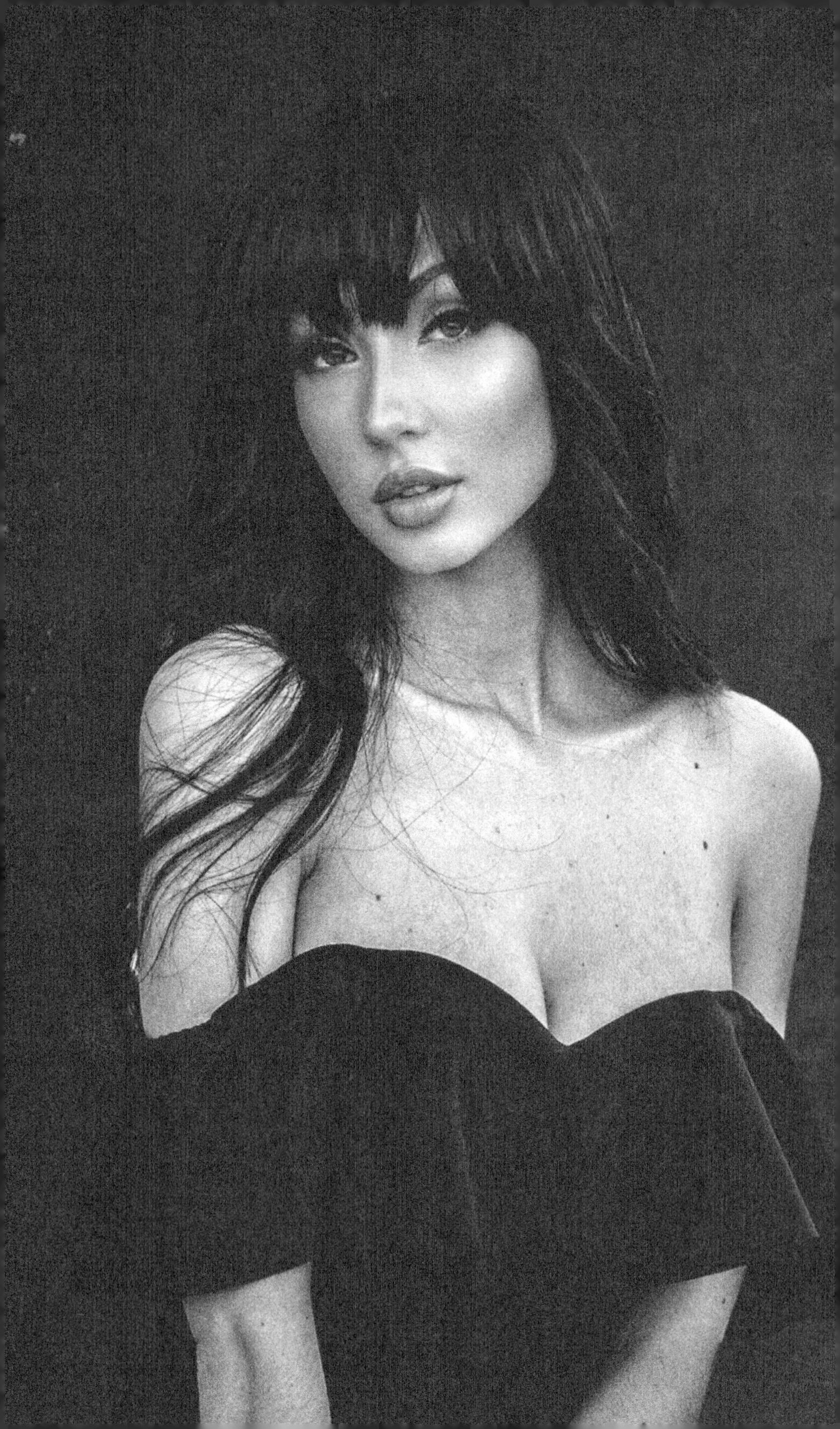

CHAPTER 26

Lucia

Panic claws at me the second my back hits the mattress, and it takes everything in me not to scurry away from Sy's probing gaze.

"Look at me," he commands.

I do; I watch him slowly undress and as long as I can see his eyes, I'm okay. But even for the brief moment his face is obscured when he bends to push his pants down, is enough to send my panic skyrocketing again.

"Sawyer," I plead.

"Yes, sweet bunny?" he rasps.

I don't know what I'm asking for, so I don't continue talking. Instead, I greedily run my eyes all over his gloriously naked body. From the top of his head, his intense eyes, chiseled jaw, and the way the ends of his hair caress his shoulders. Then I shamelessly ogle his broad chest, his dark, peaked nipples, the grooves and hard lines on his torso. The dark line of hair leading from his navel and down to the enticing V that's pointing to his hard cock. Precum glistens on the purple tip, making it all shiny and tasty looking.

Without meaning to, I lick my lips. "Like what you see?" he asks, amusement dancing in his eyes.

"Yes," I croak.

"Mhmm, me too, wife. Me fucking too." He moves closer, slowly sitting down beside me rather than between my legs. "I love the way you shudder when I kiss you here." His lips graze the column of my neck.

Slowly, he licks his way down to my tit. "Sawyer," I moan as he sucks my nipple into his hot, wet mouth.

"I love the way you moan my name when I lick your nipple," he rasps, moving over to the other one. My back bows off the bed as he closes his teeth around it. "And when I bite it."

He continues to lick a fiery trail down my body until he reaches my mound. Rubbing his nose against it, he inhales sharply. "I can smell your arousal. Are you ready for me to eat you out?"

Each caress, lick, kiss, and nip, has made my fear dissipate, and as I lie there, panting beneath him, I want nothing more than his mouth on my pussy. "Y-yes."

The way he made his way down my body has him almost lying upside-down, his ass is near my tits, so he isn't between my legs. I want to tell him to crawl between my parted legs, but I don't. I want to see where this is going.

Running my hand along his muscular back, I close it around the nape of his neck. "Do it," I hiss, squeezing slightly.

Not needing to be told twice, Sy rubs my clit with his nose, making me moan loudly. When I buck, using my body to beg for more, he places his hands on my thighs, firmly holding them wide. Then he licks across the seam of my swollen pussy lips.

"Don't tease me," I whine, too horny to care how desperate I sound.

"Don't rush me, sweet bunny. I want to savor your delicious cunt."

Oh, fuck. Those words and the gravel in his tone make my inner walls clench, and I'm panting harder. "P-please..." I lose the ability to speak when he hardens his tongue and thrusts it into me. I reach for his hair, tangling my fingers into the mess while pressing him harder to me.

It doesn't take long before I'm crying out his name, begging for his cock. "Please, Sy. Fill me. I need... fuck! I need your cock." He doesn't relent, licking my opening until I scream out his name, shuddering underneath him.

"I'm gonna lick your cum from your cunt, wife. Then I'll fuck you until you can't walk for days." The deep timbre of his tone amps up my pleasure, and I'm on the cusp of asking him to stay down there when he greedily licks at my opening.

"Wait," I pant. "Do it properly, Sy. I want you to eat me out with your head buried between my thighs."

"My head is between your legs," he replies before swiping his tongue over my clit.

I pull at his hair and use my arm to nudge him in the side at the same time. "You know what I mean," I huff. "Please? I want to know what it's like with you."

He lets go of me and sits up, moving so he's hovering above me with his legs around me rather than between mine. Making it look like he's caging me in. He rests his weight on his arms and lowers himself until our bodies touch. "Are you certain?" When I nod, he growls, "Use your words, baby."

"I-I'm certain." I hate how unsure I sound when I'm in fact not. Sure, I'm scared, but that has everything to do with my past and nothing to do with my present. "Do it."

Before I can verbalize my need again, he leans in to capture my lips with his. His tongue is merciless and persistent as it's seeking mine, parting my lips, and granting him access immediately. I moan as I taste myself on his tongue.

Shifting, he places his hand on my side, slowly trailing up toward my chest. I arch my back, pushing my tits forward, causing a delicious friction when his chest meets them. Eagerly anticipating his touch, I'm getting frustrated when he keeps moving so slowly.

"Please," I beg into his mouth.

Before I can ask again, he kisses his way across my jaw and down my neck. I squeeze my thighs together, trying to create some friction to satisfy the need for him.

"None of that," he commands as he forces one of his legs in between mine. I whimper in protest, but it doesn't do me any good. Lowering his head to my tit, he licks the areola, making me writhe beneath him. Moving my hands to his head, I let my fingers play with his hair. He starts moving down my body toward my pubic bone, and I'm practically trembling with anticipation of what I know is to come.

One of his hands cups my pussy, and I can hear his sharp intake of breath when he finds me soaking. "You're even wetter now, sweet bunny," he grits out before tracing a single finger through my wet folds. I lean up on my elbows so I can see the top of his head, which is now between my legs. He gently kisses the inside of both my thighs before running his face across my mound. "Mhmm, you're so brave, baby." The words make everything in me clench, both in fear and excitement, but before I can prepare myself fully, I feel his warm tongue licking between my folds all the way to my clit.

"Oh fuck," I moan out loud and throw my head back. His dark and sexy chuckle reaches my ears.

With soft kisses, Sy slowly kisses up my left leg, making his way back to my needy core. When he starts licking slowly around my clit, I can barely keep myself upright. I still wanna see him, but the sensations each flick of his tongue sends through my body make it too difficult. I finally give up and sink back into the mattress with a loud moan, just as he pushes a finger into me.

"How are you feeling, bunny?"

Feeling? Oh, right. I realize that his words help me relax, assuring me it's him between my thighs while reminding me I want this. "I-I'm good," I rasp.

"Good?" he mocks. "I'm doing a piss poor job if you're only good."

Without meaning to, I burst out laughing. "I'm perfectly fine, Sy. It helps that you're talking to me."

Every time it feels like the orgasm is just within reach, he blows on my sex and it retreats once again. I'm a panting mess switching between cursing him out and begging for more. The smug fucker just keeps promising me it'll be worth the wait.

"S-stop. No more. I have to… I want to…" I curse him out when he once again robs me of the pleasure I'm so desperate for. His dark chuckle lets me know that he knows exactly what he's doing and that he's entirely too pleased with himself.

"Baby, you're so wet for me. Your pretty cunt is all glistening and swollen." His husky voice sends shivers through me, and I instinctively want to squeeze my legs together. But with him mercilessly eating me out, I can't.

"Yes," I moan. I don't know if I'm agreeing with him or reacting to the way his tongue works my clit. When Sy inserts a second finger into my dripping heat, my hips lift of their own accord, but he puts his other hand on my pubic bone to keep me down. "Fu-fuck, more, I need more, Sy."

"What do you need more of, sweet bunny?"

His hoarse voice sends shivers through my body, and I try to answer him, but I'm unable to do anything but pant and writhe as he continues his slow assault on my needy nub. As he once again steals my orgasm from me, I cry out in frustration.

"I need you," I scream, desperate and so fucking horny.

It feels like my arousal is seeping from my pussy, and I wouldn't be surprised if his face is drenched in my juices, especially not with how long he's spent down there. I have no idea what time it is, but I know it feels like he's spent hours tormenting me.

Curving the fingers deep inside me while sucking my swollen nub into his mouth, I'm unable to hold back anymore. "Sy!" I cry out as the most intense orgasm I've ever had crashes through me, and I feel his tongue inside my pussy as I spasm around him. I don't know when he replaced his fingers with his tongue, only that it feels fucking amazing.

My entire body feels like mush. I'm entirely too spent to move so I still can't see him, but I feel him giving my pussy one more lick from top to bottom, before he kisses his way back up my body, making sure that almost no area of my hypersensitive flesh is left without his lips grazing it. When he reaches my lips, I can taste myself on him.

"We're definitely doing that again," I say, grinning lazily.

"I'm so proud of you, baby," he rasps. "And you've never looked more beautiful than when you came all over my face just now."

Pride shines in his eyes, and I think I fall even more in love with my amazing husband. He's everything I never knew I needed, but that I now know I can't live without. When I'm weak, he doesn't overpower me. He lends me some of his strength, helping me stand on my own. And the fact that he just helped me… I don't know what to call it. We didn't rewrite history, and we didn't erase the past. But together, we created something beautiful.

"I love you so fucking much," I murmur.

"Now and always," he replies, grinning down at me.

Pushing myself up, I gently bite his bottom lip. "Now get your perfect cock inside me, Sy. Fill my pussy up."

I reach down, cupping his rock hard dick. Then I wrap my hand around the base of his smooth shaft. "Sweet bunny." He squeezes his eyes closed as I cradle his balls with my other hand.

"Fuck me hard, husband," I demand in a sultry tone.

Sy doesn't speak, just leans down and kisses me again. It's a toe-curling kiss that says more than he ever could with words. It makes me feel... I don't even know how to describe how he makes me feel. All I know is that I wish I could freeze this moment between us. He looks at me as if I am his entire world, which is exactly how I feel about him.

The freedom I've craved for so long means nothing if I don't get to share it with him. I still need to tell him more about the Senate. I didn't get to it earlier as we got a bit... distracted.

Home is wherever he is, and I want this with him. I want to love him with my body.

Sy pulls me out of my head as he removes both my hands from his crotch and lets out a shuddering breath. When I look at him, he must sense my confusion because he hurries to explain himself. "I won't make it inside you if you keep touching my dick. Seeing you come like that almost made me nut without being inside your sweet cunt."

I do as he says and lie back down. Unable to keep the satisfied grin off of my face. Sy lowers himself to rest on his elbows. His lips are so close I could reach out to lick them, with his breath tickling me on every exhale. Feeling the head of his cock at my entrance, I lift my hips and spread my legs wider.

Claiming my lips once more, I almost don't notice he is moving his hips ever so slowly, inching himself into me. I gasp at the welcome intrusion, and I lock my ankles behind his ass to give him better access.

Sy's hands are trailing through my hair, his lips on mine as our tongues wrap around each other, locked in a heated dance. I feel my pussy stretch, making room for his dick to slide further into me.

"More," I moan, high on the feeling.

Whispering heated words to me about how good I feel around him, Sy's rough hands make their way to my heavy tits, and he begins kneading them. I feel the rush of lust taking over my body again.

"You still with me, sweet bunny?" I'm about to answer him when he rolls his hips, making me lose my words in a moan.

The way he feels inside me now is so fucking good. He starts thrusting into me more eager, and I tilt my hips up, taking him in even deeper, as I'm moaning out his name in sheer pleasure.

Taking a shuddering breath, Sy stops moving his hips, lowering his face to my tit, and softly licks and nibbles on my peaked bud. Tangling my hands in his long hair, I hold him as close to me as possible, moaning unashamedly.

When he reaches between us and finds my sensitive nerve bundle, my back arches off the bed, and my core squeezes him again, my legs tighter around him. I use my feet to try and get him even deeper, but since he's already balls deep, that's not really a possibility. Sy continues to play with my clit, and I feel the pleasure building within me.

"I'm gonna come," I pant. My hands are on his back and I'm digging my nails into his flesh, fully focused on all the sensations I'm feeling.

As my orgasm crests, I pull his face back to mine, wasting no time in claiming his lips with my own. Our tongues tangle, and I'm panting hard into his mouth.

Once my core is no longer squeezing him as tight, he pumps his hips again. Still keeping a finger on my clit, I'm feeling so sore I can no longer tell the pleasure from the pain. "Don't... it's too sore, I need..." I don't know what the fuck I need or what I'm even asking for. "Fuck me harder, Sy."

Immediately answering my demand, he picks up the pace. Pulling almost all the way out of me, before slamming back inside. The burn he leaves in his wake is delicious, and I crave it as much as my next breath.

"I'm not going to last much longer, wife, you feel too amazing wrapped around me."

His gravelly voice shoots straight to my center, and I involuntarily clench around him again. The deep and heavy groans falling from his mouth cause me to shiver while I fuse my mouth to his, wanting to taste the ecstasy on his lips.

Sy flicks my clit twice before I'm coming on his dick again. My pussy clenches around his hardness as I'm riding my pleasure. "Sweet bunny!" The way he groans my nickname, like a breathy plea, makes my inner walls flutter again. I feel him pump into me twice more before his cock jerks, and I feel the hot evidence of his release deep inside me.

"I love you so much." I'm almost afraid to speak above a whisper, not wanting to ruin this perfect moment between us. Instead of giving him time to answer, I slant my lips to his, slowly stroking his tongue with mine and basking in the afterglow of what we just did. To say it felt right would be an understatement.

Sy breaks the kiss and collapses next to me on the bed. "The bed looks like a fucking crime scene," he chuckles breathlessly.

I push myself up on my elbows and look around. He's right. There is blood all over the sheets, and both our bodies. "Oops," I laugh, running my fingers up and down the cut on my arm. "Guess we got carried away."

Instead of laughing, Sy cups my cheek and turns my head so I have to look at him. "You'd tell me if you weren't alright, right, bunny?"

"Don't," I hiss in warning. When he furrows his brows in confusion, I keep on talking. "Don't ruin this by second-guessing me. Not when… not when I'm high on what we did. Not when I, for the first time ever, feel like my past isn't defining me."

I don't know if my words make sense to him, but I can't explain it any differently. That's how I feel, and I don't want him to put a damper on it even if he means well.

His eyes darken and he runs a hand through his unruly hair. Some of it still gathered in a messy semblance of a bun slash ponytail, but most of it has escaped. "I'll never stop worrying about you, my sweet bunny. Never."

"I guess I can live with that," I say, doing my best to sound put out. Though the smile splitting my mouth in two ruins it.

Chuckling, Sy gets up and walks toward the bathroom. "Let's get cleaned up," he suggests. "And then we'll get something to eat."

I follow him to the bathroom, and while the shower runs, I shoot him a playful smile. "How can you be hungry when you just ate?"

Thank God Sy's shower has multiple showerheads so we don't have to wait for each other. It's totally handy when we're as dirty as we are. While wetting my hair, I watch as our blood mixes with the water and disappears into the drain. It feels symbolic, somehow. Like we're washing away the past.

"What can I say, I need my food to keep up with you," he laughs. It takes me a second to remember he's answering my question from before we got under the water spray.

Even though I'm tempted to initiate another round of amazing orgasms, I focus on washing my hair and body. When we're both done, we towel dry before seeing to our cuts. Neither of them are deep enough to need anything but some antibacterial ointment and bandages, which he keeps under the sink.

Afterward, I get dressed in one of his team t-shirts, but don't put on any underwear. He puts on underwear but nothing else. Together we almost make one somewhat dressed person. Then we order Chinese food and lounge in the living room while we wait for it to be delivered.

The delivery guy does a double-take when Sy opens the door and even asks for his autograph. While Sy grumbles about privacy and just wanting to eat, I laugh loudly.

"Come feed me," I call when the delivery guy keeps going on and on about Sy's games.

I almost regret interrupting, because I like how awed the guy sounds. But I'm hungry, dammit. Besides, tonight isn't just any other night; it's special, magical almost. Getting up,

I return to the bedroom, throwing drawers open while I look for things with the Sabertooths logo on it.

"Here," I say, holding out a jersey and a cap for the young guy. "Take these."

The guy's eyes widen. "Really?" he asks, excitement making his voice high pitched.

"Really," I smile. Then I hand Sy the pen I found and gesture toward the items. "Come find me once you've signed those."

It doesn't take Sy long to get rid of the guy, and when he does, he finds me waiting in the kitchen. "I should spank you for letting him see you like that." He points at my bare legs before swatting my ass.

I squeal playfully. "If you're good, I might let you do it later," I laugh, waggling my eyebrows.

This behavior is so unlike me, but I can't stop. Knowing that Sy doesn't just know everything, but is still here, is making me giddy.

After dishing up the food we snuggle up in the living room. There's no TV or music on, we're alone with our thoughts, and I like it. It's not awkward or forced. It's comfortable and really nice.

I've just claimed the last egg roll when Sy says, "You never told me about the scars on your thighs, baby."

The bite I've just taken gets lodged in my throat, making me choke violently. My eyes water and I reach for the wine I poured while waiting for him to join me. "W-what?" I croak, swiping the tears from my eyes.

Sy leans back, and I take the opportunity to stretch my legs across his. "I can wait if you're not ready to tell me," he clarifies.

I shake my head. "No, it's fine. I wasn't *not* going to tell you. It just didn't feel right earlier." Taking a deep breath, I ready myself for telling him. "Fabian liked to mix his punishments and rewards together. He said it was his way to balance the scales, to even things out so we didn't linger on the past too long."

Sy's eyes stay on mine, and though I want to look away, I can't. His dark orbs are like magnets keeping mine in place. "Twice, he said I deserved his mouth on my... on me. But he also wanted to punish me for displeasing him. I don't even know what I had done wrong and right, all I remember is the pain. There was never any pleasure. He didn't... umm... lick my clit. He bit it, used it to keep me still while he sliced into my skin."

I startle as the glass table suddenly breaks, sharp shards of glass spraying everywhere. Blinking, I look up at Sy, who's standing in the middle of the carnage. It feels like my thoughts are moving in slow motion, and it takes me several moments to remember I was talking to him, not reliving the horrible memories by myself.

"I'll fucking kill him."

Red, hot fury rolls off Sawyer in potent waves that threaten to pull me under. No, that's not right. Sy would never do that to me, so if anything, his anger is bringing me closer to him and further from my family.

I get up, careful not to step on any glass. Then I reach for Sy and he uses his bare feet to kick some shards away before coming to my side. "You can't kill Fabian—"

"The fuck I can't," he spits. "He's fucking nothing. It wouldn't even be much of a fight." His harsh words are a stark contrast to the way he gently rubs my skin.

Shaking my head, I clarify, "It's not a matter of whether or not you're physically able to. His life belongs to the Senate."

"Fuck them, and fuck their rules."

I pull Sy back down on the couch, and then I straddle him, placing my hands on his broad shoulders. "If we do anything rash, it's our lives on the line. Don't give him that power," I plead.

"Fine," he grinds out. "Tell me about the Senate."

"I don't know a lot about them myself. Until Remus came here, I didn't even know they were real. All I know is that the rumors state they're made up of the heads from the most prominent families in our... well, family." I sigh when I realize how hard it is to explain.

"Go on," Sy urges me, squeezing my hips.

"I suppose they're Remus' council, and on certain things he requires their votes. Like giving me my freedom."

Sy's quiet for so long I don't know if he's going to say anything else. But then he rolls his eyes and scoffs. "Fabian is part of the Senate, isn't he?"

"Yeah," I admit in a small voice. "But Remus assured me that their vote doesn't have to be unanimous."

Of course, Sy has more questions, but I'm not able to answer any of them. In the end, I promise we'll call Remus tomorrow and demand answers.

"How long do we have to stay in Rome?" Sy asks.

Not liking the look in his eyes, I shrug. "I don't know."

"When you call Remus tomorrow, tell him we'll go right away."

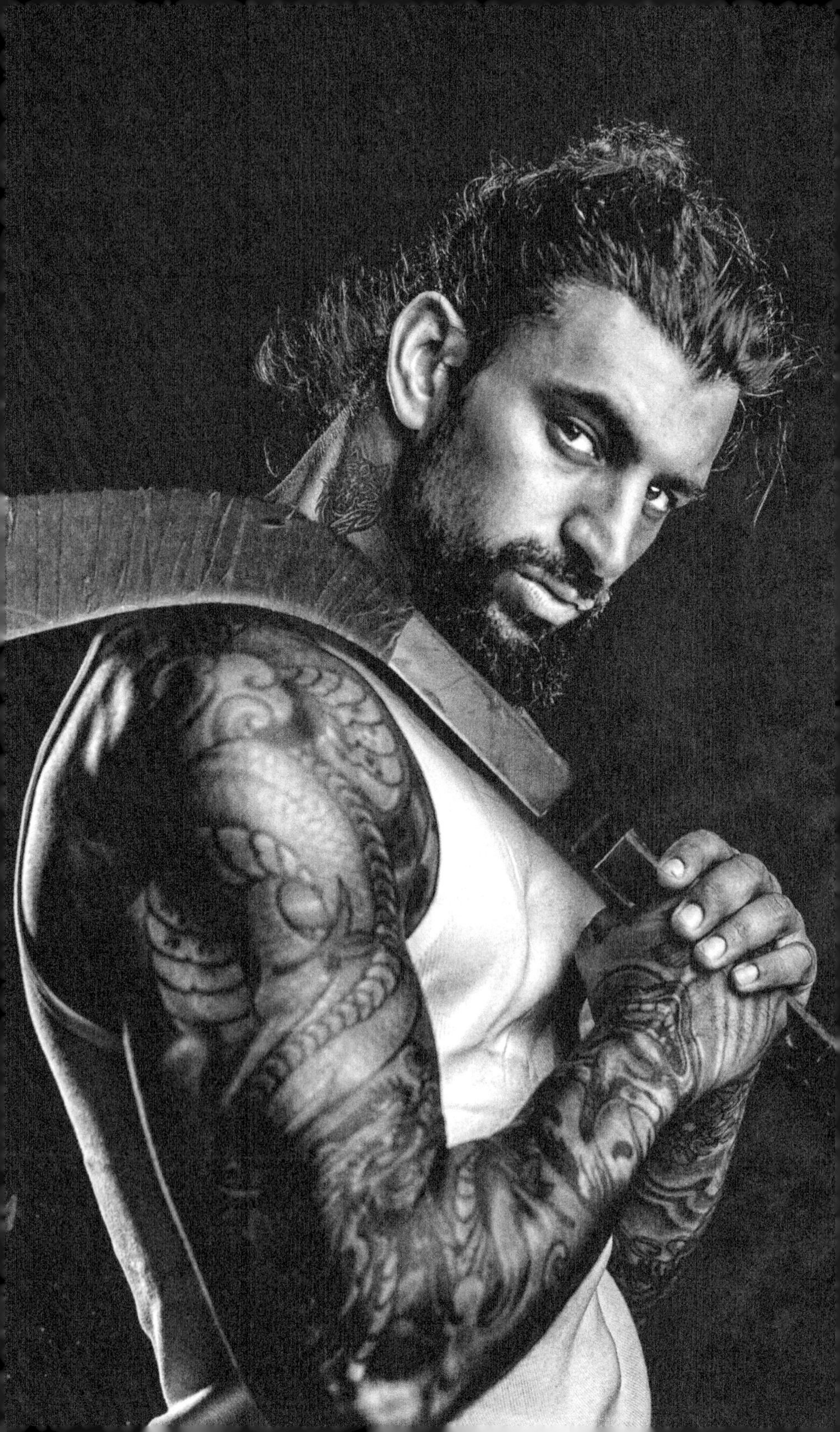

CHAPTER 27

Sawyer

We rise early the next morning, the weight of everything she told me last night hanging heavy in the air. It's as if neither of us truly slept, our minds preoccupied with the looming uncertainties that lie ahead. I may not fully grasp the intricacies of Lucia's Mafia family or the Senate, but I've gleaned enough to know danger is ahead.

This is so fucking outside anything I've had to deal with before that I feel like a fish out of water. Give me a stick and a pair of skates, and I can do no wrong. But family politics and... Mafia shit, and I have no clue what to do or say. It doesn't matter though. Making sure my sweet bunny is safe is all that matters and to hell with everything else.

Lucia wastes no time, reaching out to Remus to arrange a meeting. Despite my apprehensions, I can't deny the sense of relief that washes over me knowing that he's on his way. Not that I particularly want to see him, because I don't. It's not that I trust him. But having him coming here means things are moving ahead, and that has to be better than standing still.

As we wait for Remus to arrive, Lucia moves about the apartment with a sense of urgency. First, she systematically got rid of the glass in the living room, refusing any help. Then she moved on to tossing items into a suitcase as if preparing for our imminent departure. The atmosphere is tense, our silence punctuated only by the occasional rustle of fabric or clatter of objects hitting the floor. Lucia's actions speak volumes, her implicit expectation that we'll soon be bound for Rome hanging heavy in the air.

When Lucia reaches for my third suit, I gently wrap my hand around her wrist. "Stop," I say softly. "I don't need any more suits."

Tossing her hair over her shoulder, she rips her wrist away and places her hands on her hips. "How do you know? What if it's an insult to the Senate to only have two suits?" She abruptly stops talking and walks into the bathroom. "Do you need a razor? What about any... what products do you use for your beard?"

Yeah, she's definitely losing it. "Breathe, baby," I say, coming up behind her. I slide my arms around her middle and rest my head on her shoulder. "No amount of clothes or grooming products are going to make a damn difference."

"They might," she argues stubbornly.

"Really?" I ask, finding her eyes in the mirror. "Or are you projecting?"

"I don't know anymore," she admits softly. "It's just... I keep feeling like if I do this right, we might stand a better chance."

As much as I want to assure her that everything will be okay, I don't give her any empty platitudes or insult her by lying. If everything she's told me is true, it might not be okay, and this could be our one and only trip together.

I'm saved by having to come up with anything to say when someone, probably Remus, rings the doorbell.

"Showtime," I murmur, kissing her cheek. Then I take her hand, and together we go to let her cousin into our home.

Remus stands outside the door, a self-satisfied smirk playing on his lips as he gazes at us. My sweet bunny greets him with a respectful bow and a smile, but I can't muster anything more than a scowl for the man who isn't protecting my wife as much as he fucking should.

"Don," Lucia addresses him, her tone laced with respect.

"Remus," I mutter through gritted teeth, my disdain barely concealed.

Remus seems unfazed by my obvious displeasure, his amusement evident as he saunters into the apartment uninvited. With a casual gesture, he dismisses the two hulking bodyguards flanking him, leaving them to wait outside as he strides confidently into our midst.

"I think this is the first time I've been summoned," he grins. "To what do I owe the pleasure?"

I clench my fists, hating his nonchalant behavior and careless words. "First off," I growl, moving closer to him. "Show some fucking respect in our home."

"Sy," Lucia pleads, but I ignore her.

"Secondly, how fucking dare you treat Lucia like that? She's your family and you're not even protecting her. If you're so powerful, why the hell aren't you reining in Fabian?"

"Watch it," Remus warns me, cocking his eyebrow. "We all have rules to follow and parts to play. Just because she's told you what's going on doesn't mean you understand it."

I throw my head back and laugh loudly. "I don't need to understand it, you bastard. All I need to know is that you're no better than her abusive ex husband."

Remus takes a step toward me, but before he can act or speak, I slam my fist into his jaw. His head snaps to the side at the same time as Lucia lets out a scream. But instead of going to her cousin, she steps in front of me, holding up her hands.

"Don't even think of retaliating, Remus," she hisses. When I try to move around her, she shifts with me, keeping herself in front of me. "You had that coming and you're in his house—"

"Our house," I correct like that's the important part.

To my surprise, Remus guffaws while rubbing his jaw. "You've got a mean right hook," he laughs. "Glad to know you're looking after Luce."

Well, I can't say I was expecting this to be his reaction. I expected him to fight back, maybe even to... I don't know. Threaten my life or some bullshit like that.

"Now that we got that out of the way, can we talk like civilized people?" he asks, gesturing toward the sitting area like it's his home and not ours.

"If we must," I grumble.

At the same time, Lucia says, "Of course. Please sit down, Remus."

I sit down in the chair, pulling my sweet bunny with me so she's perched on my lap. When she tries to argue she can sit by herself, I just shrug. "But I like you right here," I say playfully, holding her in place.

Plus, if she's sitting on me I'm less likely to attack Remus again, and since I'm not sure a second punch would go unpunished, this is for the best.

"So," Remus says, looking around. "Judging by your call and by the suitcase waiting by the door, can I assume you're ready to stand in front of the Senate?"

"Yes." My sweet bunny wrings her hands together nervously. "How quickly can we leave?"

Remus pulls his phone out of his pocket and looks at it for a brief moment. Then he frowns. "Now. We should leave right fucking now."

"Why?" I bark. "What's happening?"

"Fabian has requested use of my jet. He wants to return to Rome," Remus says thoughtfully.

"That makes no sense, unless..." Lucia trails off. Then she jumps out of my lap, and I quickly stand with her, sensing she's about to say something bad. "He's going to return and claim I've done something."

"Like what?" I ask, hating that I don't know enough about her world to figure it out for myself.

Instead of answering me, Lucia retrieves her phone and holds it up to her ear. When I open my mouth to repeat the question, she shakes her head, telling me not to speak.

"Jo," she rushes out. "Look, I'm sorry to call you like this. I know you're probably going to tell me you can't tell me, but I have to ask anyway."

Not able to hear Jo's answer, I move to Lucia's side. Taking the phone out of her hand, I press the speaker.

"What do you need, Lucia?" Jo asks, sounding worried.

"Do you know for how long Fabian and Tom discussed the terms of Fabian becoming a sponsor for the Sabertooths?"

Jo sighs. "For a year or so. But Tom wouldn't bend on a few things that Fabian was adamant about."

"So what changed?"

"What's this about, Lucia?"

Unable to stay quiet, I say, "Fabian is blackmailing Lucia."

"Sawyer?"

"Yeah, hi Jo, it's me. Look, I know we have no right to ask you anything. But we think Fabian is trying to ruin the Sabertooths from the inside."

Jo swears under her breath. "I knew something was off about him." There's a pause where all we can hear is her heels click-clacking against the floor. "I can't tell you much. Only that the second he found out the two of you were dating, he asked Tom how he could be sure it would last and not damage the reputation of the team."

I look over at Remus just as he looks up from his phone. He indicates with his hand to keep Jo talking. At least that's what I think he means. Giving him a nod of confirmation, I say, "Go on, Jo."

"Tom showed Fabian the contract you two signed, and that's when Fabian agreed to Tom's terms and retracted his own. All he asked for was a copy of the deal for his own records."

Lucia takes a shuddering breath. "And do you know if Tom gave him that?"

"He did," Jo confirms. "I'm sorry, Lucia, but I can't really say more than that."

Even though Jo can't see her, my sweet bunny nods. "Thank you, Jo. And I'm sorry, I know I have no right to ask."

Looking over at Remus again, he gives me a thumbs up and points at something on his phone. Reaching him, I angle the device so I can look down at it. It takes me a second to understand what I'm seeing.

"Motherfucker," I growl when it clicks into place.

It's Fabian moving through the Saint Paul International Airport. He's clearly in a rush, and every now and then he looks around like he's expecting to be followed. Considering what I now know about my bunny's family, I can't really blame him for that.

"Shouldn't we go?" I whisper to Remus. "Catch him or something?"

Shaking his head, Remus explains. "He's already in the air. There's no stopping him."

Fuck. Fuck. Fuuuuck.

Remus locks his phone and puts it back in his pocket, then he walks over to the door and opens it. Although I hear him saying something to the bodyguards, I can't make out the words. So I refocus my attention back on my wife and the call she's still on.

Jo lowers her voice. "There's something up with that guy, isn't there? I've caught him asking around about you, and now you call and Sawyer says Fabian's blackmailing you… do you really think he's trying to ruin the Sabertooths?"

"Hopefully it's nothing," I interject. Since we can't risk Jo alerting Tom, I do my best to sound like it isn't a big deal. "Thanks Jo."

"Oh, the meeting tomorrow? Yep, I have that under control. Talk to you later." Jo ends the call, and I know it's because someone else is around. Or at least I assume that's the reason for her subject change.

"He knows," my sweet bunny breathes. "He's going to use it against me. It's proof, and I... we have nothing to dispute it."

"Hey," I rasp. Placing my hands on her hips I pull her flush against me. "We'll come up with something. Since he's already on a flight—"

I'm interrupted by Remus. "We have to go. Now. The Senate has summoned all of us, and we have twelve hours to appear in front of them."

"Even you?" Lucia gasps, fear making her eyes wide.

"Even me," Remus growls angrily.

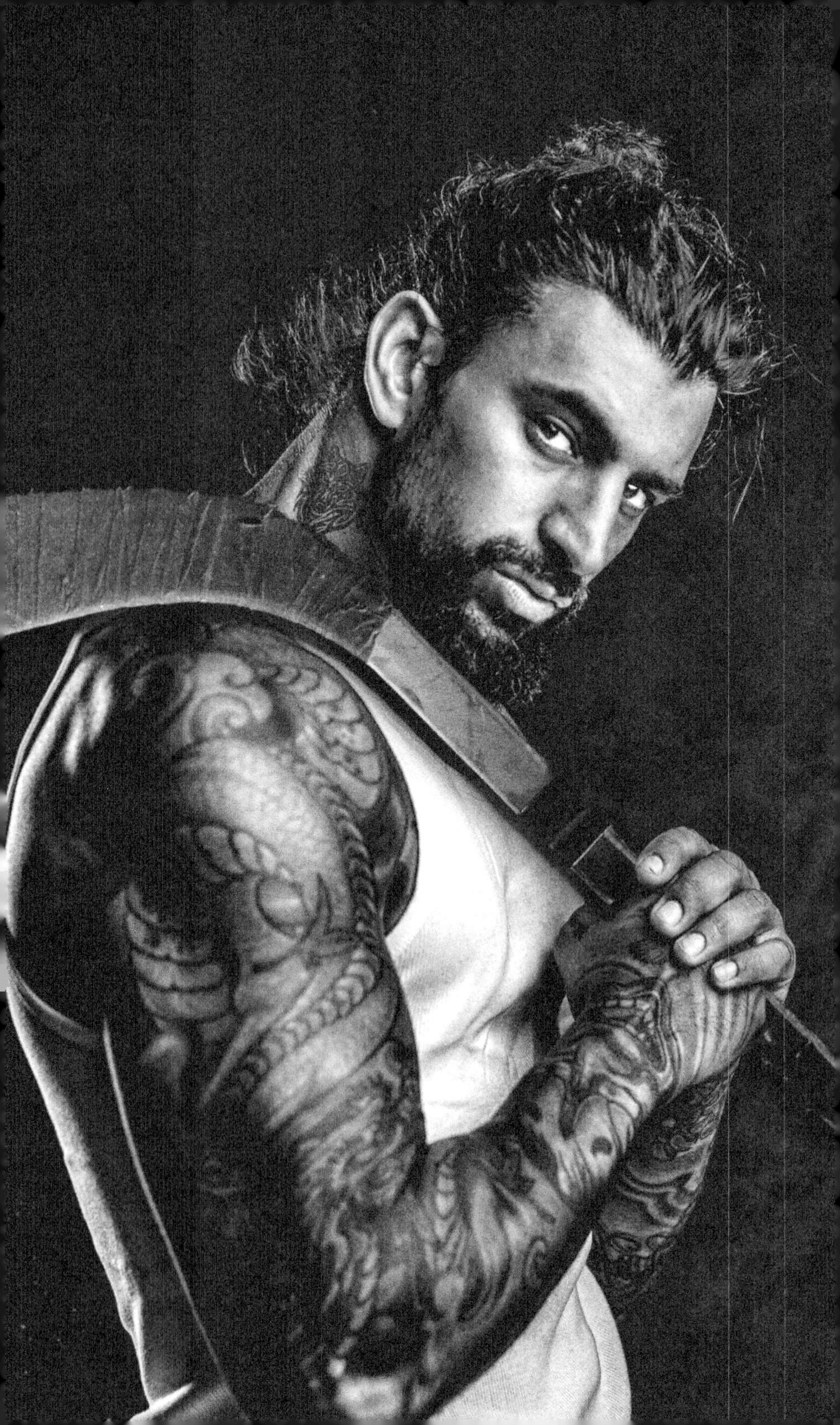

CHAPTER 28

Sawyer

As we touch down in Rome early next morning after a surprisingly short flight on Remus' private jet—just seven hours, a blink of an eye in the grand scheme of things—I'm struck once again by the sheer scale of Remus' influence. Leading a Mafia empire that few even know exists, he commands a level of secrecy and power that is both intimidating and awe-inspiring.

During the flight, Remus and Lucia took the time to educate me on the intricacies of dealing with the Senate and navigating the customs of the Russo family. Remus delved into details about the Senate that even Lucia seemed unfamiliar with, unsurprising given what she told me about them, emphasizing the importance of our upcoming meeting. And with the requirement to appear before the Senate dressed in togas, Remus sent my bunny to the back to get changed.

When she argued she didn't want to leave me, he scoffed and promised not to harm me. It wasn't until he was sure Lucia was out of ear shot, he told me the exact details of our meeting with the Senate. Before Lucia came back, he made me promise I wouldn't tell my wife. It was the easiest promise I've ever made because all that matters is getting her out of all of this.

I know I should feel angry about the depth of her lies, but I can't. Not when I know how much hinged on her relationship with me. It's flattering, actually—in a fucked up way.

Although this is probably the entirely wrong thing to focus on, I can't stop looking at how amazing my wife looks in the white toga. Instead of being loose, it's form fitting and very revealing. It's so long it hides her feet, but with a slit on the side that goes all the way up to her pussy. Luckily, it isn't on display, or I'd have to punch Remus again.

It's sleeveless, and adorned with gold jewelry near the neckline and shoulders. On the clasps are wolf heads that make it look like the wolf is biting into the fabric. No detail is accidental, and it shows. Lucia's long, red hair hangs loose down her back, making it look like the toga is backless. And fuck me, now I'm hard. I'm hard while wearing a toga.

Unlike the one my sweet bunny is wearing, mine is short. Reaching just above my knees. It's not as form fitting, but still tight enough it shows my muscles. Since I'm not a Russo, mine doesn't have any gold or wolves on it, which I like.

Stepping off the jet, we are greeted by an impressive line of guards, each bowing respectfully to Remus and Lucia as they pass, a clear indication of the reverence and authority that Remus commands in this city.

"Why does Remus get to wear purple if we're wearing white?" I ask when we're inside the car taking us to the Senate.

"It's tradition," she says like that's an explanation. When she notices my quizzical expression, she continues. "It's the imperial color worn by the Head, or the Don, if you will. So, yeah, it shows his status."

I suppose that makes sense, but since there's nothing else to talk about, I ask, "Why does he need the color to show his importance? Don't people know who he is?"

My sweet bunny gives me a wry smile. "The best place to hide is in plain sight. Many think they know Remus, but have only seen decoys. As far as I'm aware, only few here know what he actually looks like."

As if on cue, Remus pulls a box out from under his seat. When he opens it, it reveals a white theater looking mask. A mask of deception, I think it's called. Placing it on his face, he says, "The sheep don't deserve to see the real face of the wolf. It just makes them complacent."

Scoffing, I growl, "But you're fine painting a target on Lucia by letting them see her?"

"It's too late to hide her now. People have seen her for years before she made the deal with my dad."

Taking my hand, my sweet bunny whispers, "He's right, Sy. Besides, it's to our advantage to keep them scared of Remus."

I hear all too clear what she's not saying; she's expecting her cousin to save the day. But unlike her, I don't have unwavering faith in him. I'll admit, the more they told me on the plane, the more I understood how hard it is for Remus to navigate the Mafia empire. Upholding the laws and rules for all, without being able to favor those he actually cares about.

But just because I understand it doesn't mean I forgive or condone it. He should make protecting Lucia a priority, and not use her to make an example.

As if sensing the change in my mood, my sweet bunny unbuckles her seat belt and crawls into my lap. I immediately wrap my arms around her, and turn her so her head is resting on my chest. No words are needed, we both know that this might be our last time together.

"If something happens, I want you to run away," I murmur into her ear. "I texted Mickey on the flight, and he has... connections. He can help you, baby."

She shakes her head. "I'm not going anywhere without you, Sy. You're mine, my life. Now and always."

A lump forms in my throat. "Now and always," I promise. "But still—"

"No," she hisses. "Stop that bullshit right now. We're making it out alive. And if... if something happens to me, you need to take this." She discreetly presses something into my hand. "Don't look at it now. But it's your safe passage. Having that means Remus himself owes you a favor and you can use it to bargain for your freedom."

Her words piss me off, and I fail at keeping my voice low. "Are you fucking kidding me right now? I'm not leaving you, baby. We face this together."

"Yeah, but—"

"No!" I roar. "Either we make it out together or we don't make it out at all."

Remus chuckles. "How very touching," he observes. "Shame this is Rome and not Verona, otherwise it would be like a modern day Romeo and Juliet."

I tighten my hold on my wife, reminding myself I can't punch Remus when he has guards in here with us. One look at them, and I know they'd kill me before I could even reach him.

The thought of dying for Lucia, for my wife, doesn't scare me. What scares me is her dying for me. I fucking refuse to live in a world where she doesn't. Because life without her wouldn't be living, it would be existing. Something I've already been doing all the years before I met her, and I know it's something I can never go back to again.

My thoughts are interrupted by the car slowing down and coming to a stop. The guards file out, forming a protective circle. Then Remus gets out, and lastly, Lucia and I step out. "Damn," I whistle, impressed when I realize where we are.

Not just Vatican City, but the very heart of it all, with the ancient buildings I've only seen on TV surrounding us. As I look around, I'm hit for the first time with the sheer magnitude of everything.

The things Lucia explained about her family seem more real, more dangerous now that we're here. It's no longer a far out possibility or story. As we walk down the paved path, it all becomes much more tangible.

My sweet bunny takes my hand, dragging me along as a guard opens a door at the side of one of the buildings. We're outside of the tourist areas, so no one sees us descend into the darkness. With each step it becomes darker, but it doesn't smell old or damp.

Lucia startles as light suddenly illuminates us, from one of the guards holding a burning torch. "This way, please," he says.

When I look around I don't spot Remus anywhere. I bet the fucker used the darkness to slip away undetected. Is it any fucking wonder I don't trust him? Pulling shit like this just makes him seem more shady than Lucia tells me he is.

"Where are we going?" I finally ask when it feels like we've walked for an eternity.

"The Vatican Necropolis," she explains softly. "It's a place hidden beneath the Basilica of St. Peter and it's said to be where he's buried."

It's clear from her tone that she's awed, which, okay, it's pretty cool. Maybe if we weren't walking toward our potential deaths, I might be able to appreciate it.

"It's an ancient city of death. There are mausoleums and tombs. At least that's how the story goes. I've never been here before, but it makes sense the Senate wants to meet here."

As we are led into a brightly lit area by the guards, I can feel the tension in the air thickening with each step. The room we enter is grand, with ten figures seated on pedestals, their identities concealed behind elaborate gold masks. Only one person stands unmasked, and as my gaze settles on him, I feel a surge of anger coursing through me.

Lucia

Fabian smiles cruelly as he looks at me, and it sends a shiver down my spine as he utters those words that cut like a knife. "Welcome home, wife." Every fiber of my being screams with fury at the sight of him, but I force myself to maintain composure, to keep myself in check.

Next to me, Sawyer lets out a menacing growl. "I think you mean ex wife."

Even though he's breaking protocol, I can't bring myself to care. If they execute us for it, I'll die fucking happy. Knowing we stood tall and didn't cower to a bunch of cowards hiding their faces.

"Enough!" Since the Senate's gold masks cover their mouths I don't know who spoke. "We're not here to trade insults. We're here to determine the fate of Lucia Alexandria Russo."

"Noted," another says.

I assume they're speaking English for Sawyer's sake, and maybe mine. Language is like a muscle, even your native language gets rusty after hardly using it for ten years. So I appreciate it no matter the reason.

Fabian looks behind us. "Where's the third accused?" he asks in a sharp tone. "We demanded three to appear but I only count two."

Sy takes my hand, squeezing it, as I shift my weight from one foot to another. I mentally curse at myself and stop fidgeting. I shouldn't show them my nerves.

Just as I'm about to say… something, anything, Remus' voice rings out for all to hear. "You don't command me, sheep." The sneer in his tone is all too clear. It even makes some of the people on the Senate flinch. "I'm here. But you don't deserve to see me unless you're ready to bow and swear your loyalty to me again."

Two people stand, taking a knee simultaneously. "Please, Don," one of them pleads. "We didn't know you would be summoned and we know we have no right to do so."

"Mercy," the other cries.

Remus' laugh reverberates around the room. Then there's a wind blowing out the torches, and when they're finally relit, the guys kneeling on the floor are gone.

"What's the meaning of this?" Fabian roars, slamming his fist into the marble wall. "Show yourself."

Again, Remus laughs, but doesn't say anything else.

Someone stands, pointing at Fabian. "This is your meeting and your summoning. The Senate will not favor you for playing games. Get to why we're here."

Fabian sneers. "This is Lucia Russo's trial, and—"

The man shakes his head. "It was meant to be her trial, yes. But you summoned the Don as well. That changed the rules of the game. As the accuser you must state your case in front of the Senate."

"I am on the Senate you dumb fuck," Fabian spits angrily.

Another stands. "You cannot both be the accuser and judge, jury, and executioner."

I try to hide my smile, but it's hard. This is exactly what Remus foresaw would happen, and so far it's turning out in our favor. So far...

Instead of looking bothered, Fabian grins. "I was going to recuse myself, anyway. I chose to be the accuser, as is my right." He runs his hand through his hair as he walks to where Sawyer and I stand. "You all know Lucia Russo was given to me and married me upon her sixteenth birthday."

A chorus of agreement sounds.

"But then the bitch betrayed me and struck a deal with our old Don. And that deal is coming to an end."

Someone clears their throat. "The loophole for her freedom to become permanent was marriage. Is she not married to Sawyer Perry?"

Sy stiffens, and I squeeze his hand, trying to wordlessly tell him to remain calm. "She is," Sy confirms. Then he lifts our joined hands to his lips and presses a kiss to the back of my hand.

Fabian scoffs. "A fake marriage. One created just for publicity. The fact that the Don allowed it is an insult to all of us."

Even though I know I should keep my mouth shut, I can't. "If you have an issue with forced marriages you don't have much of a claim," I accuse.

"Noted," one of the masked men says.

"For fuck's sake," Fabian shouts, completely forgetting his manners and the importance of protocol.

Okay, I know I don't have a leg to stand on since both Sy and I have done the same, but we're not in the Senate. Fabian is, and he should act like it. Right now, he's just showing everyone how personal this is.

"And me?" Remus asks. I discreetly look around, but I can't see him anywhere. "Why am I summoned by a sheep? And why is my own council permitting this atrocity?"

Fabian's satisfied smirk sends another shiver down my spine. "Glad you asked." He pulls his phone out and plays something on it.

"Oh God," I whimper as I realize what it is we're listening to. It's the conversation from mine and Remus' dinner.

I want to snatch the phone from Fabian's hand and smash it to pieces as I'm forced to listen to me and Remus casually discussing the fact I needed to get married. I look at Sy, trying to gauge how he feels about it, especially now that he knows I was willing to do anything to get my freedom. But he doesn't give anything away as he looks straight ahead, his jaw clenched.

The recording continues being played.

"How long do I have to be married? I mean, what if my new husband dies or wants a divorce? What's the time frame for my marriage, Remus?"

"I'd say at least a year. But I'd also caution you that exactly three hundred and sixty-five days would look odd if that's when your husband mysteriously dies or divorces you."

Oh no, I'd completely forgotten about the specifics of our conversation. It seems like it happened in another lifetime. But it wasn't. Fuck, it wasn't even that long ago I considered hiring someone to become my husband, and even considered killing them after I'd gotten what I wanted.

Knowing in your heart what you're capable of is very different from hearing it said out loud. The implications of my questions and Remus' answer are heavy. And Sy... my heart contracts at the thought of what must be going through his head while listening to the terrible things I said.

"Stop it," I cry out.

"But there are still so many things to play for the Senate," Fabian laughs. "Like the way you told your friend that you were making Sawyer your unsuspecting victim."

"What?" I gasp. "I never..." Shit, I did do that. With Gail when we met up at O'Jackie's after my dinner with Remus.

"If Sawyer is innocent, why is he here?" a man asks as he stands. "You told us he was part of the plan to cheat the Senate. But now you say he's innocent. Which is it?"

The others murmur their agreement, also demanding Fabian answer the question.

"He's here because Lucia married him," Fabian defends. "How do we know he isn't part of it?"

"You said he was innocent," the man says. "He can't both be innocent and part of deceiving the Senate. Choose. One or the other, but not both."

Fabian's eyes flash with anger. "Fuck. Fine. Then he's innocent."

"Sawyer Perry is excused."

A guard comes toward us, and I sigh in relief, but it's short-lived. "I'm staying," Sy growls. "Unlike this asshole, I'm not leaving my wife."

The guard doesn't slow down, instead he rushes to us. As soon as he reaches for Sy, my husband moves to the side. Then he retaliates by slamming his shoulder into the guard's stomach. He doubles over with a string of Italian curses leaving him.

"He just attacked a guard in this holy place," one of the men shouts. "Get him. Get him."

As more chime in, I realize this is where we get to see who's backing Fabian. And the real reason they haven't openly shown their support until now is because they've been biding their time. Fucking cowards.

"Stop!" Remus shouts. I want to cheer as he strides into the room. "If you touch him, I'll have you executed for treason. Sawyer is here as my guest and is under my protection."

One of the men clears his throat. "Forgive me, Don. But it sounds like you're saying we, the Senate, can't touch him even though we summoned him?"

"I won't forgive you, Aldo. But you are right, that's exactly what I said," Remus retorts.

While Remus debates with the Senate, I whisper, "Are you okay?" hoping Sy hears me. But he doesn't react at all, still refusing to even look at me.

I know in my heart that once we're out of here, my marriage is over. Sy will want a divorce, and I can't even say I blame him. The things I've said and done are horrible. He deserves so much better than me.

"As for my conversation with Lucia, I'm not going to defend myself," Remus says, gaining my attention. "The terms of her deal with Romulus Russo were that she could gain her freedom completely by getting married. It never specified it had to be a love match or any length of time. Does anyone here dispute those facts?"

Some say no, and others don't answer at all.

I'm surprised when Remus reaches for his white mask and in one fell swoop removes it, exposing his face. But the biggest surprise is that all the members of the Senate follow his example. One by one, they take off their gold masks.

"What the fuck is going on?" Fabian shouts, echoing my own thoughts.

These aren't the Senate, it can't be. I recognize at least half as guards, and the other half... well I don't know them. But it definitely isn't the Senate.

"So good of you to show up, Fabian," Remus smiles. "Tracking you down has been harder than I'd like to admit. But I knew you couldn't resist the chance to summon me like you had the right."

"But I..." Fabian stumbles over his words, looking around with a wild, unhinged look in his eyes.

"I what?" Remus asks casually like they're discussing the weather. "That sentence can end in many different ways. If you meant to say I'm the one who organized all of this, you're right. I'm also the one who leaked Lucia's whereabouts last year, knowing you would follow the breadcrumbs I planted for you."

"You what?" I interject, looking between my cousin and husband. "You're the one who told Fabian where I was?"

Remus doesn't spare me a glance. "I know you were behind the attack on someone I love dearly, and I couldn't let that go unpunished. So I'm the one who sowed the seeds about bringing Lucia home."

"You infiltrated the Senate?" Fabian roars.

My cousin shrugs. "The Senate is mine and I can do with it what I goddamn please. That includes using whispers to remind everyone about the deal Lucia made with my dad all those years ago."

"You made a mockery of everything," Fabian spits, pointing an accusatory finger at our Don.

Shaking his head, Remus takes a step toward him. "No. I'm the one who eradicated the Senate. I knew it was corrupt when I took over, so I cleaned my house. I just never saw the need to explain any of that to you."

Fabian backs away from Remus. His eyes are wild, reminding me of a cornered animal. Knowing just how unpredictable he is, I don't dare take my eyes off of him. Not even for a second. I track his every movement; from the way he weirdly shakes his arm to the way he moves closer to Sy.

I narrow my eyes, wondering what he's up to. But the second I realize it, it's too late. The knife is already in Fabian's hand as he whirls around, holding the weapon high and bringing it down in a stabbing motion.

A scream is torn from me as I realize what's going to happen, and then I lunge. Using all my strength, I push Sy out of the way. Then a pain unlike any other makes my vision waver as black spots dance at the edge of my...

Thoughts become hard. I open my mouth to speak, but no words come out. Only a sickening gurgle. I think I hear a roar, but I'm quickly losing my grip on reality, so maybe it's only in my head.

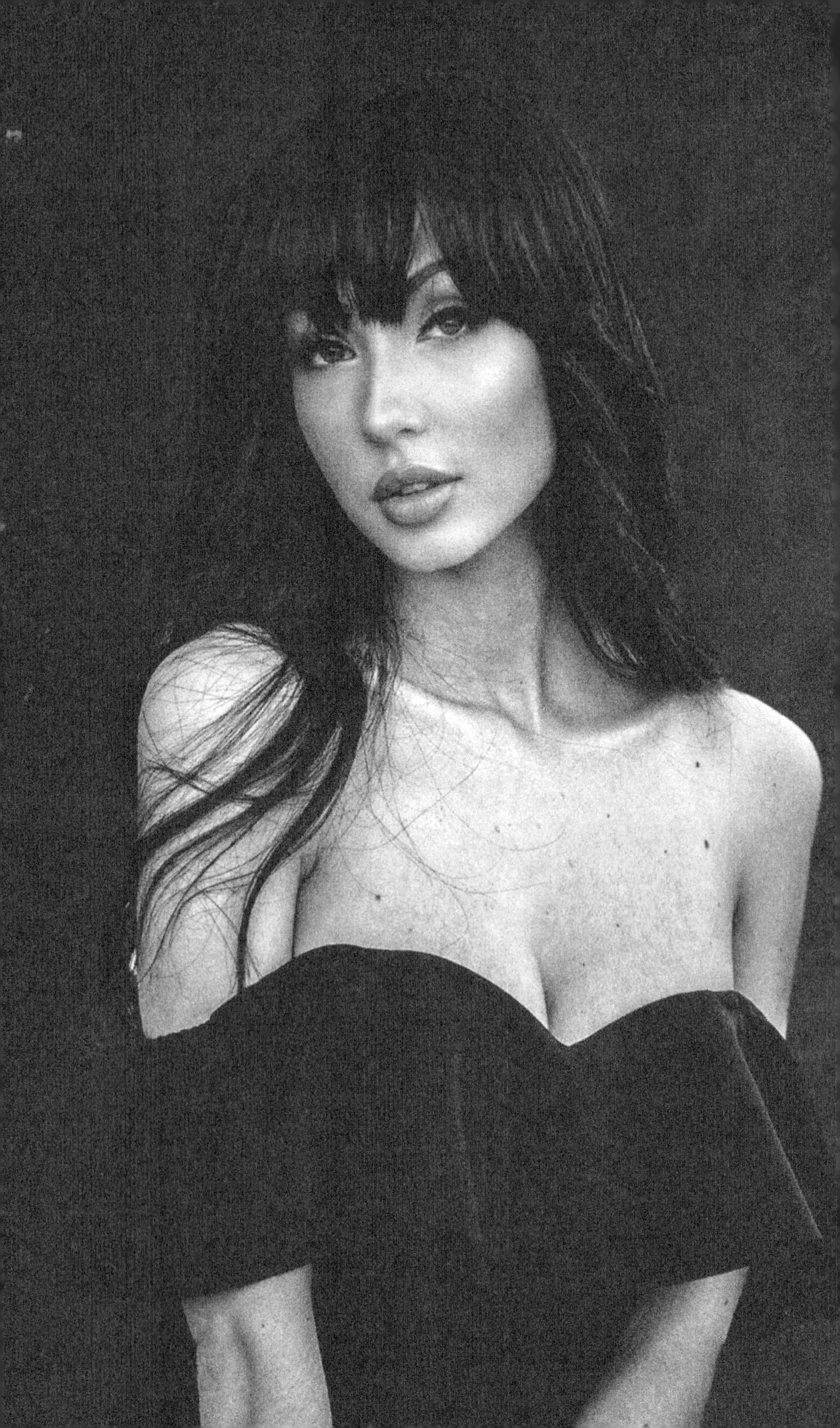

CHAPTER 29

Lucia

As I slowly drift back to consciousness, the world around me feels hazy and surreal. I blink a few times, trying to clear the fog from my mind, and find myself surrounded by bright, swirling colors that dance and twirl in the air. It's mesmerizing, and I can't help but giggle softly at the sight.

"My sweet bunny."

That voice... I know it... I think. Yes. It's deep red. Wait, how can a voice have a color? Frowning, I try to put the two together, but I can't. I know it doesn't fit, but that's what it is.

"What are you mumbling about?" he asks. "Don't you know who I am, baby?"

Of course I know who he is. He's red. The... why am I thinking about blood? Blood and something good, something safe. Is red safe? No, red means danger. Yet I don't feel scared, I feel very much at peace.

I scrunch up my nose, hating how impersonal and sterile it smells around me. The burn annoys my nostrils, and I feel like I'm going to sneeze. But I can't do that. The colors will disappear if I do, and I feel like I need them.

"Lucia, baby, try to focus."

What's he talking about? I am focusing… oh, look at the blue, it's totally mixing with the orange. Since I don't want to see that, I try to lift my hand to swat it away. But my body isn't obeying my command. I'm being betrayed by… myself.

"Fuck's sake. I'm going to call someone."

Yes. Call someone to tell them blue and orange should never mix.

There's a swooshing sound, and then a woman speaks. "How can I help?"

Is she the color police? Oh no, now the green is out of control. Why are all the colors acting up like this? And why do I care?

"Oh dear," the woman says. "Maybe her dose is too high."

I notice a pressure on my hand, and when I look down, it quickly becomes clear why. The man, the red one, is holding it—squeezing it.

"You can call me anything you want, baby. Just please tell me you remember me," he says.

Looking up at his handsome face, I'm filled with a sense of relief. He's so pretty, and his beard looks fun to play with. I wonder if he'd let me twirl it around my fingers.

"There's not a thing I wouldn't let you do to me, sweet bunny."

Huh, how can he read my thoughts?

"You're speaking out loud, Lucia," the woman giggles.

Moving closer, she bends over the man, her tits grazing his arm. I hiss and bare my teeth at her. She's gray and orange. Two colors I don't like or trust right now.

"Sorry," she rushes out as she readjusts her position. "I was just trying to reach your drip. I promise that's all."

I huff and try to give her a benevolent look but I don't think I succeed. I like that she corrected herself, so for now,

I'll give her the benefit of the doubt. Especially since her gray is tinged with green, and I like green. It's so pretty, and it's... wait, what was I just thinking about?

The longer I lie there, the colors seem to become duller. Some of them are impossible to tell apart, and the more I blink, the fainter they become. A lump forms in my throat and I want to cry as I'm slowly losing all the pretty colors.

"Don't cry, baby. It's all going to be okay."

I look over at... "Sy?" I murmur, my voice sounding distant and dreamlike.

He's there, sitting beside me, his hand gently clasping mine, his eyes filled with a mixture of worry and relief. "Hey, bunny," he says softly, his voice cutting through the fog in my mind.

I manage a weak smile, my thoughts still scattered and disjointed. "What... happened?" I ask, my words slurring together as if underwater.

Sawyer's expression darkens slightly, and he takes a deep breath before speaking. "Fabian happened," he explains, his voice heavy with sadness and anger. "He tried to stab me, but you jumped in front of me." Instead of sounding grateful, he sounds angry.

"A simple thank you will suffice," I smart, trying to lighten his mood.

He squeezes my hand harder. "You're lucky you're in a hospital bed right now, or I'd make you pay. You're not meant to risk your life for me, baby. Never that."

"But I—"

Shaking his head, he talks over me. "What do you think would happen to me if you died?"

Blinking, I remember the flight to Rome, and the drive to the Vatican that followed. "I-I gave you what you needed to get out," I croak. My throat feels raw, and it hurts to speak. "Can I have some water?"

Sy's quick to reach for a bottle, even uncapping it before handing it to me. Once again, I try to lift my arm, but every movement is slow. He chuckles before placing his arm under my head, gently pushing me upward. Then he places the bottle between my lips, slowly pouring water directly into my mouth.

"Thank you," I whisper once I've had enough.

When he goes to remove his arm I complain, and he pushes the remote so the headrest moves me into a half-seated position. Much better.

"It's not about my safety," Sy says firmly, picking the conversation back up. "I already told you I didn't want to live without you. We're a team, baby. You don't just get to pick and choose when that suits."

"And you don't get to tell me off for saving your life," I wheeze. The words don't come out as firm or bad ass as I wanted them to. Not when I'm constantly feeling like I don't have enough air in my lungs.

"Shh, don't worry about any of that now." Sy strokes my cheek gently. "Just focus on getting better, bunny."

Looking up at him, I try to recall what happened. Like, the events themselves. But it's... all a blur. "Where's Fabian?" I ask, suddenly feeling panicked.

"He's... not here," Sy assures me. "He's gone and he can never hurt you again, baby."

I try to nod, but drowsiness settles in. "Why are we in the hospital?" I ask, even though I feel like he's already told me, or like I should have figured it out myself.

"You had surgery." Sy's tone is clipped, but when I look at him I know it's not from anger at me. "You had a collapsed lung and a few other things. But it's all fixed now, and they said you'll recover completely. You just need to rest. Nothing else matters."

The words sink in slowly, like pebbles dropped into a pond, sending ripples of confusion and fear through my mind. But just as my eyes are about to close, I remember something else. Sy was going to leave me. He wouldn't even look at me, that's how angry he was.

"You were going to leave me," I accuse, or try to. "... wouldn't even look... and you..."

"Sleep, baby," he murmurs. "We'll talk more when you feel better."

The first three days after I was attacked, they wanted to keep me for observation. Something to do with the chest tube, residual air, pleural something, and whatnot. Honestly, I gave up listening. All I heard was that I needed to stay, and Sy was completely useless, refusing to support me in getting out of there.

I don't remember much from the time I woke up, high on the morphine after the surgery. But ever the dick, my husband made sure to record some of the shit I said. Though I bitch about that, I secretly like it. I love Sy more than I thought I could ever love someone, and having him do little things like that makes my day. I like the more playful side of him, and I'm so excited to see what our lives will be like now that there isn't a deadline ruining our lives.

"Have you had enough air?" Sy asks, kissing the top of my head.

We're in one of the lavish gardens outside Remus' home. We've been out here for hours because I want to soak it all in one last time. "Not yet," I murmur, loving the way the sun kisses my face and the wind plays with my hair. "Isn't it beautiful?"

Sy shrugs. "I mean, yeah. But it's like a museum where you can't touch anything."

"You want to touch the naked statues?" I giggle playfully, poking him in the side. He huffs in reply. "You can touch them if you want to. There's actually one just a bit further ahead that has a crack in its leg because Remus threw something at it when he was a kid."

This is the first time I've ever told anyone that. Back when it happened, I was terrified someone would find out. I was supposed to be watching over him, and took my eyes off him for just a few minutes. Guess that's all it takes to break a piece of history.

"I have to ask, what's with all the wolves?" Sy asks, scrunching up his nose.

Laughing, I point at the statue of a wolf with two small boys suckling on her teats. "That's the original Remus and Romulus," I say.

"The who?"

I begin to weave the tale, my voice soft yet filled with passion. "Remus and Romulus were twin brothers," I explain, my words taking on a rhythmic cadence as I recount the ancient legend. "They were abandoned as infants and left to die, but fate had other plans for them. They were rescued by a she-wolf called Lupa, who nurtured them as her own, and they grew to become fierce warriors."

Sy listens intently, his eyes locked on mine as I continue to speak.

"Eventually, Remus and Romulus founded the city of Rome together," I say, a sense of wonder coloring my tone. "But their bond was tested when they disagreed over where to build the city's walls. In the end, Romulus became the first king of Rome."

I pause, allowing the weight of the story to settle between us. "It's a tale of brotherhood, loyalty, and the enduring spirit of perseverance," I conclude, a wistful smile gracing my lips.

"Hmm, so the wolf-crest is like a tribute to them?"

Taking a moment, I consider his question. No one has ever asked me that before, so I'm not sure how to answer. To me, it just is, always has been and always will be. But putting that into words is harder than I thought.

"It's more who we... *they* are. Whether you want to claim the Russo family is Mafia or a secret society. Maybe both? Or neither? But the family is linked to Rome in ways that stood the test of time."

"I like it," Sy says, pulling me closer. "But to me, you'll always be my bunny."

Smiling up at him, I let the words wash over me. Hearing him say he loved me the day after my surgery is one of those memories I'll always treasure. During the trial, or whatever you want to call it, I was so sure things were over between us. So learning Sy wants me around forever makes everything worth it. All the heartache, pain, and suffering I've ever felt led me into the arms of Sawyer Perry, the single best place in the world.

"Am I interrupting?"

I look up as Remus makes his presence known. Before I can say anything, Sy growls, "Yes."

"What's up?" I ask, looking straight at Remus.

He looks good. It's hard to describe it, but it's almost like he's aged backward. The lines under his eyes have vanished entirely, giving him an almost boy-ish look.

"I came to give you this."

He holds out a scroll of paper that I'm quick to take from him. "Oh!" I exclaim. It's my freedom—literally. He's severing our familial ties, irrevocably setting me free. "Thank you." My voice is hoarse as I choke back a sob.

"I'm sorry for playing you, Luce," Remus says, his tone sincere. "But I didn't know any other way. Taking over from my dad has been harder than I thought."

Pressing my lips together, I swallow back the words on my tongue. I categorically refuse to say it's okay because it's unquestionably not. Do I understand it? Sure. I'm not even holding a grudge, I just refuse to tell him it's fine. Though I should be angry about it, I'm not. Weirdly, I'm relieved that Remus was behind it all rather than Fabian being clever enough to pull it all off by himself.

"You fucking should be," Sy retorts. "You used my wife to save your empire. What kind of man does that?"

Remus chuckles. "You got a wife out of it. If it wasn't for me, you'd still be fucking your way through... what do you call them? Puck bunnies?"

Sy clenches his fists, but now it's my turn to speak before him. "Y-you're the one who made the sponsors complain?"

"I don't know what you're talking about," Remus grins. "But yeah, it sounds like something I'd do, doesn't it? One could even imagine I'm behind your GM picking Lucia. But of course, that's just speculation. No one knows who did or didn't do anything." Then he turns to Sy. "By the way, that woman wasn't married."

My jaw drops. I know exactly what Remus just alluded to, and by the way Sy shoots to his feet, he does as well. "You fucking what?" he roars.

Even though my husband is towering over my cousin, the latter doesn't back down or even look apologetic. He just shrugs. "It all worked out, didn't it? You two are together for real, so what does any of it matter?"

I slowly push to my feet, panting like I've run a marathon. "Remus," I say, intending to make it sound like a warning. Sadly, it comes out more like a wheeze, making it very anticlimactic. "We get it. You're behind everything. You had your reasons, but don't for one second think we're going to thank you."

My cousin dips his head. "I respect that, Luce." His eyes lock on Sy who still looks like he wants to throttle him. "I've already put word out and made things right with your team. The official story is that Fabian was blackmailing Lucia, and that he was so obsessed he kidnapped her."

He already told us he was going to do this, so I just nod.

"Oh, come on now. I deserve at least a thank you for making Sy the hero who protected his wife."

In fairness to Remus, he has been very thorough. When the police ransacked Fabian's home in Minneapolis, they found a room littered with pictures of me. Even some of Sy with his eyes scratched out. The security tapes showing Fabian at the airport show me at his side, and everyone on the plane has testified I flew with Fabian and that I looked scared.

The public loves Sy more than ever now that they know he dropped everything to charter a private jet and set after me as soon as he learned where I was. How did he find out, you might ask. Well, apparently, a brave stewardess recognized me and contacted Sy directly to let him know I was headed to Rome.

While the story isn't perfect and has plenty of holes, I know no one will ever poke at them. Remus' reach and power is enough that he could kill the American President without much clean up. So this is just one of those things people will talk about, and come the next juicy gossip, it'll be forgotten. The only people who truly know what happened are standing here, and I'm satisfied with that.

"I'll never fucking thank you for using my wife as a pawn, you dick," Sy growls. His words bring me back to the two men who look like they're only seconds from throwing down. "But I will thank you for sending Lucia into my life."

Shock reverberates through me as my husband holds out his hand to my cousin, and I feel like rubbing my eyes when they shake to make sure I'm really seeing it.

"There's a few things to go over before you leave," Remus says, turning to me. "As you know, anyone leaving the family in disgrace isn't allowed to keep their brand—"

"The fuck?" Sy spits, moving so he's standing protectively in front of me. "If you lay as much as a single finger on her, I'll—"

Remus waves him off. "Yeah, yeah. You'll punch me again. Spare me the theatrics. I was going to say that since she's not leaving in disgrace, she's allowed to keep the brand."

I flinch at the reminder of seeing the skin being cut from my dad's body before he was executed all those years ago. "O-okay," I stammer, blinking furiously to get rid of the unwelcome memory. Squaring my shoulders, I step around Sy so we're standing next to each other. "I want to see Fabian's body."

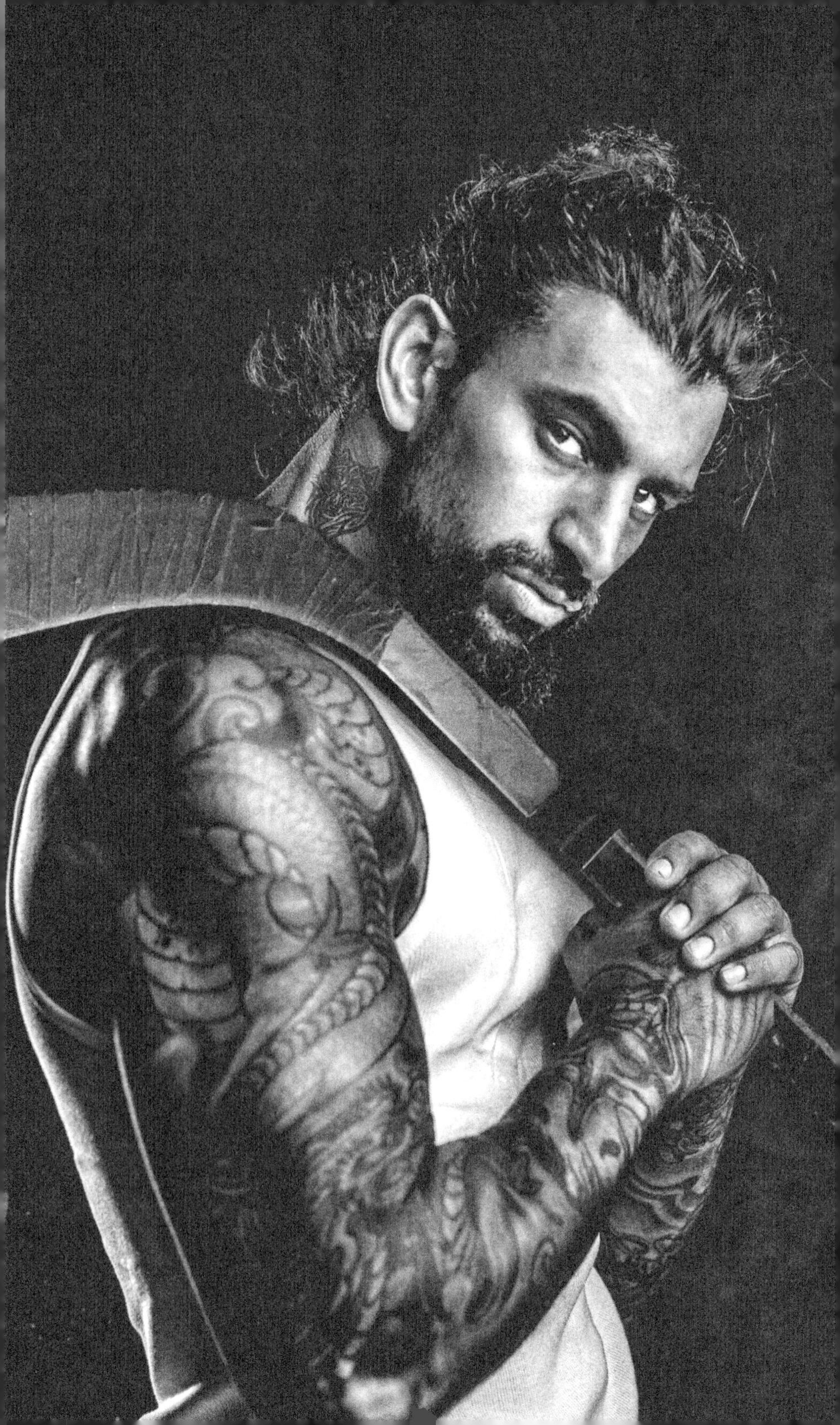

EPILOGUE

1

Sawyer

A few weeks later.

"I'm not doing it."

Laughing, my sweet... no, fuck that. My naughty bunny laughs and shakes her head. "Okay."

Cocking an eyebrow, I reach for her, but she moves out of my reach. "Okay?" I grunt, knowing there's no way it's that easy.

"Mhmm," she confirms. "You can stay home then. But I'm going."

I groan and look up at her. "Tell me why," I demand, not at all amused by this ambush she's orchestrated.

She cocks her head to the side and slowly moves closer to the bed where I'm lying. "Do you want to discuss it now?" Her eyes trail down my naked body. "Why waste time talking when I could be sucking you off?"

My cock twitches and hardens on my leg. "You're not being fair," I accuse. Of course, I'd prefer having my wife choking on my cock, but that doesn't mean we can ignore what she has in store for tomorrow.

Lucia scoffs. "What can I say, Sy? You deprived me of having your big dick in my mouth for almost a month. So you can't fault me for creating the opportunities I need." Winking, she strips out of her tank top and thong.

Instead of coming to me, she crooks her finger and beckons me over to her. I don't hesitate; I get off the bed and walk over to where she's waiting for me on her knees. "Naughty bunny," I rasp. Then I tangle my fingers in her hair, pulling until she willingly shuffles to where I want her. Leaning against the wall, I cradle the back of her head. "Take my dick in your mouth, wife."

Since we got back from Rome, my bunny has been insatiable. Not that she wasn't before, but there's an almost feralness and possessiveness to the way she wants me in her mouth at every opportunity. I can't say I mind it since her blowjobs are to fucking die for.

"Oh, fuck," I groan. She swirls her tongue around the crown, allowing her teeth to graze the sensitive head. It feels so fucking good I moan my approval. My bunny's tongue darts around the rim, caressing every part of me inside her hot, wet mouth. "You love having my cock in your mouth, don't you?"

She hums low in her throat, taking me further into her mouth. Her nails dig into my thighs as I move my hand to the nape of her neck, squeezing. "Yes," she whines. It's easy enough to hear, even if it's somewhat muffled. "I love having your cock in my mouth. I love using my mouth to make you come."

I let my head fall back against the wall, closing my eyes as I focus on how amazing it feels to have her worship me.

"Fuuuuck!" I can barely stop myself from thrusting into her mouth when she creates suction, taking me in further.

My bunny hums again, the vibrations feeling amazing around my cock. Unable to stay still, I flex my hips. She pulls back, my cock slipping out of her mouth. There's a single strand of saliva spanning from her lips to my dick as she looks up at me through her dark lashes. "Fuck my mouth," she purrs.

Fuck. I love how greedy she is.

"Take my dick back in your mouth," I rasp.

Immediately obeying, she wraps her hand around the base and moves my cock back into her mouth. I let her take me all the way to the back of her throat, and then I cup both her cheeks. As soon as she removes her hand from my hardness, I surge forward, fucking her mouth like we both want.

She sputters around my cock, but doesn't fight me. Instead, she relaxes her throat while looking up at me with tear-filled eyes. Seeing the tears escape, running down her cheeks and leaving black streaks thanks to her mascara is so fucking hot.

I'm so focused on her mouth that it takes me several minutes to realize she's moved one hand between her thighs, eagerly fingering herself. My wife loves sucking me off, and I fucking love how much it turns her on to be my fuck toy like this.

"Is your cunt dripping?" I growl.

"Y-yes," she moans. "I'm so fucking wet for you, Sy."

I ignore the part of me that wants to continue fucking her mouth, and instead of giving into my basic urges, I grab her arm and pull her up.

"Sy... what the—"

Before she can finish speaking, I haul her over my shoulder, slapping her ass that jiggles enticingly. "You've been a bad bunny," I rasp as I carry her over to the bed. She squeals as I throw her onto the mattress, so she lands on her back.

With a wicked grin, I crawl over her, lying down so I'm on my back in the middle of our bed. "What do you want, sweet bunny?" I ask when she turns to her side and looks at me with so many unvoiced questions in her green eyes.

"You," she replies without hesitating. "Always you, Sy."

I savor the words while she straddles my hips, rocking against my hard cock. "You have me," I drawl, folding my arms behind my neck. "Now, what are you going to do with me?" The way she works her wet cunt along my shaft, is making me groan. "Goddammit bunny."

"Yes?" She places her hands on my chest, leaning forward so her long, red hair falls around her like a curtain. "Are you complaining?"

I snort. "Far fucking from it. I love feeling your cunt on my dick."

Her breath hitches and her nostrils flare. "That's what I thought," she replies slyly. A smile dances across her lips as she moves one hand between us, fisting my cock and lining it up perfectly against her entrance. Then she slams down, taking all of me in one movement.

We moan in unison as her pussy walls stretch, making room for me. As she throws her head back and cries out my name, I slide my hands up her chest, cupping her perfect tits. I roll and tug at her rosy nipples, loving the way her pussy squeezes me like it's trying to suck me further into her heat.

"Fuck me, Sy."

I rear up and claim her lips. My hands grab her hips so I can slide her up and down my hardness while our tongues snake around each other. I let out a deep, guttural groan at how amazing she feels.

Sucking her bottom lip between my teeth, I bite until she hisses in pain. Then I kiss my way across her face, down her neck until I reach her shoulder. She shudders and moans as I bite down, sucking her skin into my mouth.

Her breathing picks up, turning ragged and heavy. Her pussy tightens, letting me know she's close to the edge. "How do you want to come?" I rasp.

"From your... your cock. Fuck the orgasm out of me," she moans.

Spurred on by her demand, I spin us around so she's lying on her back underneath me. "Your wish is my command," I growl.

Her legs wrap around me, her nails digging into my abs as my hips piston against hers. My hands are on her tits, squeezing the globes. I slam into her over and over, making it harder each time. Lost in my wife and the pleasure we share, I can't think about anything but how perfectly she fits me.

"I love you," I grunt, panting hard as her inner muscles squeeze me.

"Now and al...always," she cries out. Her body tightens, her cunt holding me so tight I know I'm about to shoot my cum deep inside her.

My thrusts are manic, and I can barely see fucking straight. My balls tighten, but I refuse to come before she does. "Touch yourself," I demand, my tone husky.

She moans, quickly moving her hand between us. Without slowing down, I bring us both closer to the edge. "Fuck. Sy... Sy—" Her words become nonsensical as she thrashes and writhes beneath me. "Harder. Fuck me harder."

I fucking love the way she demands my all, never satisfied with less. Obeying, I slam my hips against her so hard the bed moves with us, and when she cries out in pleasure while her body convulses around me, I join her.

"Fuck. Bunny... Lucia. Fuck!"

I remain inside her even after I stop coming, needing to recover from one of the most intense orgasms I've ever had. Sex with my wife is like a fucking religious experience, one that always leaves me starving for more.

Just as I'm about to move, my bunny stops me. "Stay there," she says, sounding oddly serious. I look up just in time to see her hands disappear under the pillow before she pulls the small knife out. "You asked me a question earlier, and I want to answer truthfully."

"Bunny," I rasp, shaking my head. "You don't need to bleed every time you answer a question."

She pushes herself up on her elbows, looking at me with a mixture of concern and fear in her eyes. "This one requires it," she breathes. "Plus, there's something else I want you to do."

"Anything."

Pushing the knife toward me, she meets my gaze. "I want you to cut over Fabian's scars." She licks her lips. "While I answer your question."

My bunny has come a long way since our time in Rome, but this still feels like she's pushing it. "You know I don't care about your scars, right?" I ask, needing her to know I love her the way she is. "It's part of the story of you, which happens to be a story I'm very fond of. When I say I love you now and always, I mean all of you."

"Sy," she sobs.

I lean over her, claiming her lips in a salty, tear-filled kiss. "Don't do it for me, bunny."

She shakes her head, her breathing ragged. "It's not for you."

"Promise?"

"I promise," she breathes. "It's for me. I need it."

As long as I know it's not for me, I have no problem giving her what she wants. I finally accept the knife, pressing it against the soft skin on her inner thigh. I do my best to line it up perfectly against the top scar. My eyes find hers, but instead of asking if she's sure, I nod. Then I add pressure and slide the knife along the old wound.

"Do the next one," she begs, squeezing her eyes shut.

"Eyes on me," I demand.

The moment she opens her eyes, and her green eyes find my dark ones, I re-open the second scar. I don't need her to tell me to keep going, I continue until I've made eight shallow cuts on her left thigh. The only time I look away is when I need to position the knife, but other than that, we keep our gazes on each other.

"T-thank you," she stutters on a heavy exhale as she lies back down on the bed. Deciding to give her a few minutes to compose herself, I run my hand through the blood dripping down her leg, smearing it across her skin.

The sharp and metallic smell of the blood clings to my nostrils, and assaults my senses. The aroma mixes with the smell of sex and my wife, making it more appealing than it should be. To me, blood isn't just a reminder of the fragility of life, or the rawness of human existence. I'll forever associate it with my bunny, how strong and amazing she is.

"D-do the other leg," she whispers, her voice barely audible.

Since I anticipated it, I'm not surprised. But I'm not doing it unless she's with me one hundred percent. "Sit back up," I urge. "And look at me, bunny."

As soon as she's pushed herself back up, I make the cuts on top of the old ones on her right thigh. This time I do it quicker, sensing that she wants it over with rather than dragging it out.

Re-opening my wife's old wounds seems oddly right. Especially after I made sure her piece of shit ex felt every single slash he made into her skin all those years ago. Unlike the care I use now with Lucia, the cuts Fabian received were brutal and painful. I made sure the fucker felt everything before he took his last breath.

"Hey." The sound of my sweet bunny's voice brings me back to reality. "Where did you go?" she asks, reaching out so she can run her hand down my cheek.

"Nowhere," I reply, shaking my head. I don't enjoy lying to Lucia ever, but especially not when we do our moments of truth. Yet, I refuse to tell her what I was thinking about. But only because I don't want to taint what we share.

She narrows her eyes in that way that tells me she knows precisely what I'm not saying. Instead of calling me on it, she tilts her head to the side. "Ask me your question."

Palming her thighs, I meet her gaze. "Why the hell did you invite my mom to come visit us?"

Pursing her lips, she takes a minute to answer. "Because you weren't going to." Then she sighs and pushes herself all the way up so she's sitting instead of leaning. Knowing how much her skin must be burning, I grab her hips and lift her into my lap so she's sitting sideways. "I know you want to see her, Sy. But I also know you're too stubborn to do anything about it."

"But I—"

My wife carries on, paying no attention to me. "And you've been talking about her in your sleep. Plus, I've seen you wake up and go into the room with the pictures. You miss her, Sy. I knew if I asked you, you'd say no. So I decided it was better to ask for forgiveness instead of permission."

"Did you now," I growl. "And what exactly is it you imagine we'll all be doing?"

Turning her head, she presses her lips against my chest. Her warm breath tickles, causing my skin to pebble. "I don't know," she murmurs. "And if you don't want her here, I'll kick her out myself. But I think you do want her here."

My wife isn't wrong. Annoyingly, she rarely is. Ever since Mickey called me on my bullshit, my mom has been on my mind. More so since we returned from Italy. Taking Lucia's hand, the one with the wedding band my mom once wore, I bring it to my lips and gently kiss it.

"You know you're wearing her ring, right?" I ask, my tone gravelly with emotion.

"Yeah, I know. No thanks to you, though. But I saw it on her hand in some of the pictures."

I chuckle because she's right. I never did tell her. At first it was because it didn't seem like the right time. Then there was all the shit with Fabian and the Senate. And then... it just became easier not to mention it.

"You're right," I admit on a deep sigh. "I do want to see her. She wanted me to come for Thanksgiving, and I think I'd kinda decided to go. But then—"

"But then my family ruined shit," she says bitterly.

"That's one way to put it," I confirm. "Family is messy. In your case, you were born into that mess. But in mine..." Pausing, I swallow thickly. "In my case, I made a mess of it."

Lucia hums. "Are you ready to forgive your mom?"

"I don't know," I say softly. "But I'm ready to try."

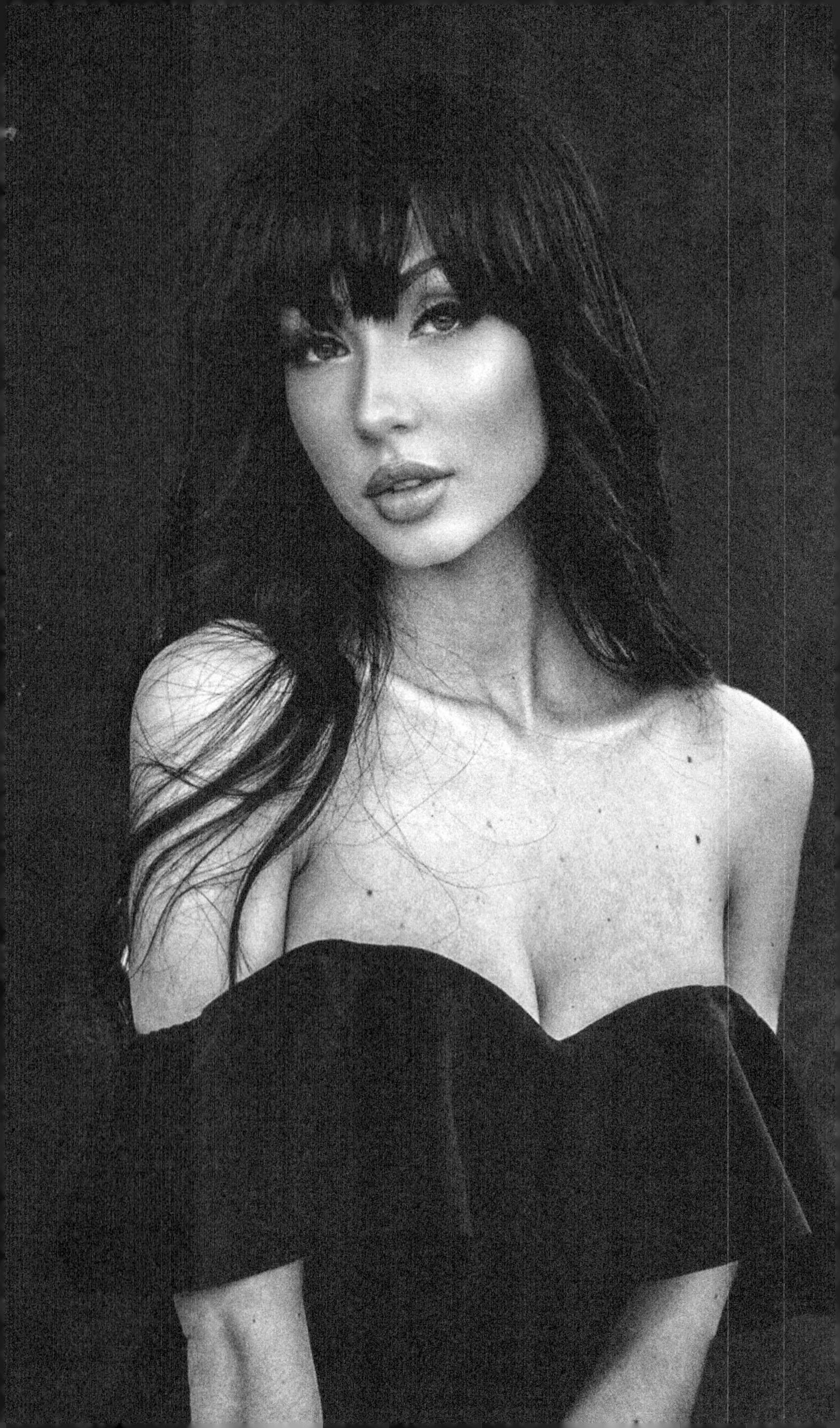

EPILOGUE 2

Lucia

My heart is swelling with pride at my husband as we stand at the arrival terminal of the airport, waiting for Sy's mom. I know my husband isn't thrilled with what I did, but he's here, ready to pick up the mom he thought he couldn't ever forgive. And maybe he never can, but the fact he's willing to try speaks volumes. So, yeah, I'm so freaking proud of him.

"It'll be okay," I murmur, squeezing his hand.

"I know," he retorts, not taking his eyes off the sliding doors in front of us.

Within minutes, people start walking through the doors. Even though I've committed the way Sy's mom looks to memory, I can't stop fidgeting. I don't want to miss her in the sea of people walking by us.

"There she is," Sy announces unhappily.

As soon as I see the woman, I want to laugh at how ridiculous I was being. With her dark hair, dark eyes, and sharp cheekbones, she looks like an older version of Sy. Well, that's just half of it. Even the way she walks is so much like her son that it would be impossible to miss her.

When she reaches us, I give her a warm smile. While she puts down her carry-on-suitcase, I wait for Sy to say something. But when he holds his hand out to her like she's a stranger rather than the woman who gave him life, I'm over it.

"Welcome to Minneapolis, Clarissa. I'm so excited to finally meet you," I gush. Letting go of Sy's hand, I step around him and hug the woman that had started to look a little lost.

"Lucia," she beams, hugging me back. "Thank you so much for inviting me."

Once we let go of each other, I look pointedly at Sy, but he still just stands there. By now, people have started pointing and staring, and it's clear the cap he's wearing is doing a shit job at hiding who he is.

"We should get going," I suggest. When she reaches for her small suitcase, I grin at Sy. "Why don't you take that?"

With an eye roll he takes the suitcase, not bothering to roll it. Because taking the two seconds to pull the handle up would obviously delay us gravely, he lifts it all the way to the car. During the short walk, I make small talk with Clarissa, and she tells me all about the flight.

"I'm not much of a flier. But it wasn't that bad," she explains, and I nod sympathetically.

"It can be rough this time of the year due to the weather, so I'm glad it was smooth," I offer.

Though I act like I don't notice it, I see the way she keeps looking in Sy's direction. Her eyes are so sad I can barely stand it, and I'm starting to wonder if I made a mistake by inviting her here. Not just because my husband is being a dick, but because he's clearly breaking her heart.

Without another word, we get into the car. Clarissa automatically climbs into the back while I slide into the front passenger seat. After about twenty minutes on the road, Sy finally joins the conversation.

"Where are you staying?" he asks gruffly.

"At a motel near—"

He scoffs. "A motel? Why the fuck are you staying in a motel?"

I slap his arm before turning in my seat. The forlorn look on Clarissa's face makes my heart contract. I'm starting to feel really bad for her. This isn't how I thought it would go. I mean, sure, I suspected Sy would be closed off—expected it even. Just not to this level where he's being incredibly rude.

Almost every single night around 4am he tosses and turns, then after a few minutes he says something about his mom. That has to mean something, right?

"Maybe there wasn't any vacancy anywhere else," I suggest. "Most establishments are booked out this time of year."

"But not all," Sy grumbles. I turn just in time to see him look at his mom in the rearview mirror. "I figured you wouldn't want to pay for a decent place, so I made a reservation for you."

My head snaps to the side. "You did?" I ask incredulously. "Where?"

"Of course I did. She's my mom," he deadpans.

I frown, not liking the way he speaks about her in the third person. Lowering my voice, I say, "If this is too hard for you I can go to lunch with her myself. I really don't mind."

My husband looks at me out of the corner of his eye. "It's fine," he says curtly.

Well, okay then.

We're all quiet for the rest of the drive, and when we reach the fancy hotel, Sy tells her we'll wait in the car while she checks in. As soon as she's gone, I turn sideways so I can look at him fully.

"Is this too hard?" I ask. "Because if it is, I really don't mind if you leave. We can say something came up, or—"

He runs his hand down his face and exhales loudly. "No, it's better I stay." He shifts and looks out the window, staying quiet for so long I don't think he's going to say anything else. "I meant what I said, bunny. I want to forgive her. But seeing her... it just brings everything back. And I'm still so fucking angry with her."

Nodding, I bite down on my bottom lip. I hate how much this is upsetting him, and it hurts me to know he's still hurting. "Why are you so angry with her?" I ask softly. "I mean, I get she cheated, and I'm not going to defend that. But she really cares about you, Sy."

"How do you know?" he retorts.

Taking a deep, shuddering breath, I pull my phone out and show him my message thread with her. "See," I point at the date stamp for the first text I got. "This was the day the public found out Fabian had been stalking me, and that you flew to another continent to save me."

"How did she get your number?" he asks.

Rolling my eyes, I admit, "I don't know. Maybe from Tom? Does it really matter? Just read the texts."

I stop talking, giving him time to read the texts. Every single one is about him. Clarissa was so desperate for news about her son that she asked me what was going on, probably knowing he wouldn't answer her if she asked him.

"She was really worried about you. All she wanted was to know that you were okay." I take his hand, holding it between both of mine. "I don't know what kind of woman she was, Sy. But I think the woman she is today really cares about you."

"Maybe," he allows. I can hear the doubt in his voice. "But how can I know for sure?"

"Have you ever asked her what happened? Why she cheated on your dad?"

He scoffs. "I know why. It's because she was a selfish—"

"Do you really know or do you just think you do?" I ask, interrupting him. "Because there was a time where you thought I'd cheated on Fabian with you."

"Don't bring up that bastard," Sy growls, his nostrils flaring with anger.

Refusing to back down no matter how uncomfortable it is to bring up my dead ex husband whom we both hate, I carry on. "Then stop making the same assumptions and ask the fucking questions, Sy. Only two people can tell you what really went down, and as far as I know, only one of them is eager to be in your life. So either cut her off for good, or listen to what she has to say." By the end of my tirade, I'm almost shouting.

It's not that I don't understand how hard this must be for my husband, and I hate that for him. But he's not going to do himself any favors by being pigheaded. Sometimes we have to ask the hard questions, and stick around long enough to hear the answers.

"Sorry," I say, softening my voice. "But look at us. If you'd never been willing to hear my side of the story, we wouldn't be where we are. Maybe she deserves the same opportunity?"

Before he can answer me, Clarissa returns to the car. Her cheeks are flushed like she's been rushing around, which seems likely since we haven't waited that long at all.

"All set?" Sy asks, finding his mom's eyes in the rearview mirror.

"Yes, thank you," she replies hesitantly.

Letting go of my husband's hand, I move it to his thigh, my thumb running up and down his leg while he drives away from the hotel. "What are you in the mood for?" I ask Clarissa, doing my best to look at her over my shoulder.

"Oh, I'm not fussy. Wherever you want to go is fine."

Her eagerness not to be a bother makes it hard to make any suggestions. If Sy wasn't so closed off, I'd have suggested O'Jackie's since he feels comfortable there. But no, that doesn't seem like a good idea. Since we're all dressed casually we could go to… hmm.

I look to Sy for help because it's his mom and I'm unsure of what suggestions to offer. "How about the steakhouse?" he says, and I nod.

PrimeCuts is a steakhouse close to our apartment that we've been to a few times. The food there is outstanding, the dress code is informal, and all the employees are incredibly friendly. They always let us eat in peace, even if the women eye Sy more than I'd like. Can't blame them, though. My husband is super fucking handsome.

As we step into PrimeCuts Grill & Steakhouse, I can feel the tension thickening with every silent moment. Sawyer, Clarissa, and I are ushered to our table, and the weight of unspoken words hangs heavily in the air. I try to break the ice by suggesting some of the restaurant's specialties to Clarissa, but the conversation fizzles out quickly.

Once the server takes our orders and brings our drinks, the silence settles over us once more, like a heavy blanket. I notice Clarissa's gaze lingering on my hand, where the glint of her old wedding band catches her eye.

"Sy gave it to me," I say, holding my hand up to show her. "It used to be yours, right?"

Clarissa nods slowly. "Yes, it did. May I?" When I nod, she takes my hand and moves it closer so she can better see the ring. "I hope the ring brings you better luck than it did me," she says almost wistfully as she lets go of my hand.

Sy scoffs. "Yeah, luck." He throws his arm around my shoulder and pulls me closer to his side. "Lucia doesn't need luck, Mom. She's not the unfaithful kind, unlike certain others at this table."

Ouch, that was harsh—too damn harsh. "Sy," I admonish.

"No, it's fine," Clarissa says. "Don't hold back, son. I've been waiting for you to let it all out for years. So let me have it." Her tone is hard, and she holds his gaze without wavering.

We're briefly interrupted when the server brings our food over, which feels like a breath of fresh air. Sy and I ordered the porterhouse, and Clarissa went for the filet mignon. All three of us chose the salads and roasted potatoes as well.

"This is delicious," I say around a bite. "How's yours?" I know I should shut up and let them continue their stand-off until one of them cracks. But my skin is crawling with how uncomfortable this is, and since it's my fault, I feel responsible for the lack of conversation.

"It's fine, bunny," Sy replies. His tone is softer now that he's speaking to me.

"Yes, thank you for suggesting it," Clarissa says, daintily wiping her mouth with her cloth napkin after taking a few bites.

Now that everyone has answered my question, the silence ensues again. This time I focus on my food instead of forcing meaningless conversation. I make it halfway through my plate before Sy clears his throat.

"You ruined our family, Mom," he says, his words laced with pain and anger. "You cheated on Dad repeatedly, and then you asked me to keep your secret."

Clarissa's expression tightens, her eyes flickering with hurt and regret. She opens her mouth to respond, but then closes it again, allowing Sy's words to hang over the table. I shift uncomfortably in my seat, feeling like an intruder in this intimate moment between mother and son. It's clear that there are wounds here that have yet to heal, wounds that have shaped Sy in ways I'm only beginning to understand.

My heart contracts again, and feeling at a loss for what to do, I rest my head on my husband's shoulder, silently letting him know I'm here.

Clarissa's voice trembles slightly as she responds, her words heavy with remorse and sadness. "I know, Sawyer. I made mistakes, and I've regretted them every day since." She shakes her head and mutters something under her breath. "Actually, that's not true. I don't regret what I did. The only thing I regret and am so sorry for is how it affected you. As your mom, I should have shielded you, and I didn't. That I regret."

Sawyer's jaw tightens, his eyes reflecting a mix of anger and frustration. "Saying you're sorry isn't enough, Mom," he says, his voice strained. "You tore our family apart, and you expect us to just move on like nothing happened."

The crushing weight of Sy's accusation makes it hard to breathe. It's a raw and vulnerable moment, one that lays bare the deep-seated emotions and unresolved issues that have plagued their relationship for years.

"If I may," I say, speaking up. If I keep quiet, they're just going to continue in the same loop of her ruining what Sy thought was a happy family, which I very much doubt was the case. "Why did you cheat on your husband, Clarissa?" God, I sound like such a rambling idiot, but I don't know of a better way to ask.

Clarissa takes a deep breath, her eyes glistening with unshed tears. "I wasn't happy," she admits, her voice trembling. She reaches her hand toward Sy, but when he doesn't take it, she just lets it fall to the table. "Your father and I, we should have divorced long before we did. But I was scared, and I made mistakes."

Sawyer's expression softens slightly, but there's still a guardedness in his eyes. "That doesn't excuse what you did, Mom," he says, his voice softer now but still tinged with hurt. "Wait a fucking second. What do you mean scared? Did Dad hurt you?"

"He never raised a hand to me if that's what you're asking," she hurriedly replies. "But he was the breadwinner. Everything we owned was bought and paid for by him. I didn't have anything of my own, so I was scared he'd be able to take you away from me." She laughs bitterly. "Ironic that my own actions drove you away, huh."

Tears gather in my eyes as I look at the woman. Her shoulders slumping with the weight of her guilt as she looks down at her trembling hands.

"Why did you never tell me any of this?" Sy asks, sounding more curious than angry. I decide to take that as a good sign.

"When should I have told you, Sawyer? You've been angry with me since you were just a boy, and the second you could, you left my house. You rarely answer my calls, texts, and emails. I can't even get you to spend any time with me."

Sy slams his fist into the table. "Don't you dare make this my fault—"

She exhales audibly and pinches the bridge of her nose. "I'm not. I've spent years trying to make amends, trying to rebuild what I've broken. But I can't change the past. All I can do is try to be better, to do better."

There's a moment of silence as Sawyer absorbs his mother's words, his gaze flickering between her and me. I can sense the conflict raging within him, torn between the pain of the past and the desire for forgiveness and reconciliation.

Finally, he lets out a heavy sigh, his features softening as he reaches across the table to grasp his mother's hand. "I'm not ready to let it go, Mom," he says quietly. "But I'm willing to try."

"Thank you, son," Clarissa sobs. Tears stream down her cheeks as she gets up and excuses herself to the bathroom. Luckily, we're seated in a quiet area so she doesn't have to walk by anyone but the servers on her way.

My heart is about ready to burst with pride for my husband. I know it might not seem like a big step, but I know a little about what it takes to heal, and him allowing himself to try is a big deal.

Turning, I cup his cheeks and look into his dark eyes. "I'm so proud of you," I say.

"Yeah?"

"Yeah," I confirm, nodding my head.

"How proud are you, bunny?" A grin tugs up the corners of his mouth. "Enough to give me your panties?"

I roll my eyes. "You perv," I say as I lightly slap his shoulder.

He just shrugs. "That's not an answer."

Tilting my head to the side, I study him, trying to work out if he's okay or not. Sy internalizes most of his shit, and that's okay. That's his way and I respect that. Ah, fuck it. If he wants my panties, he can have them.

"Fine," I agree. "But I'm not going out there until your mom comes back."

There are many things I'll do for my husband. But as it turns out, stripping out of my thong with his mom in the next stall isn't one of them.

"Deal," he rasps, his eyes hooded with the same desire that's making his voice gravelly.

"I love you so much," I whisper.

Sy fuses our lips together. His hands tangle in my hair, pulling back so he can deepen the kiss. I moan into his mouth, momentarily forgetting we're in public. "And I love making you moan," Sy rasps into my mouth. "Something I'll do a lot tonight. You owe me, wife."

Getting lost in the kiss, I decide not to point out it's the other way around. If it wasn't for me and my meddling, Sy and his mom still wouldn't have talked. This is one of those moments in life where we all know it, but no one—myself included—will say it out loud. Rightfully so. This isn't about me, even if I'm feeling smug as all hell.

When Clarissa returns to the table, I leave them alone and head to the bathroom. It doesn't take me long to hoist my skirt up and push my thong down my legs. Then, since I'm already here, I check on the bandages covering my inner thighs. They're still fine, and thanks to the painkillers I had earlier, I can't really feel the cuts.

I take my time walking back to the table since Sy and Clarissa look deep in conversation. Rather than heading straight to them, I go to take care of the bill, and only then do I return.

"There you are," Sy grins wickedly. "Are you ready to leave?"

"Yeah," I confirm.

Sy takes my hand and pulls me to him. "Do you have something for me, sweet bunny?" he asks.

As discreetly as possible, I pull the rolled up thong from my pocket and hand it to him. He immediately closes his hand around the fabric. To my horror he doesn't hide them straight away. Not before bringing them to his face and sniffing loudly.

"Sy!" I hiss, looking around to make sure no one is paying attention to us. Clarissa's several paces in front of us, and everyone is caught up in their own stuff. "Put them away right now." I both love and hate the smirk he shoots me as he tucks my used thong into his jeans pocket.

When we're back in the car, Clarissa eagerly tells me that Sy's going to show her around the arena. Her tone is filled with so much hope and happiness, I feel like I should excuse myself and let them have the time together alone.

"Why don't you drop me off at home?" I suggest casually. "Gail wants to go over a few things, so I need to call her."

"Oh, no. You should come with us," Clarissa insists. "I want to spend more time with you, as well."

One glance at my husband convinces me I've made the right decision. "Why don't we all have breakfast together tomorrow?" I offer as a compromise. "That way I get to see you again before you leave."

Clarissa doesn't answer until we reach mine and Sy's apartment. After kissing my husband, I get out of the car, and to my surprise, she gets out with me. "Thank you," she says warmly as she pulls me into a hug. "Thank you for forcing him to see me."

Feeling awkward about accepting the gratitude, I pull back. "It was all him," I say with a smile. "If Sy didn't want to see you there was nothing I could do. But he wanted it as much as you did."

She nods. "You're good for him, Lucia. I'm glad he's found you."

My eyes dart to Sy who's watching us. "Me too," I say truthfully. "I'd be lost without him."

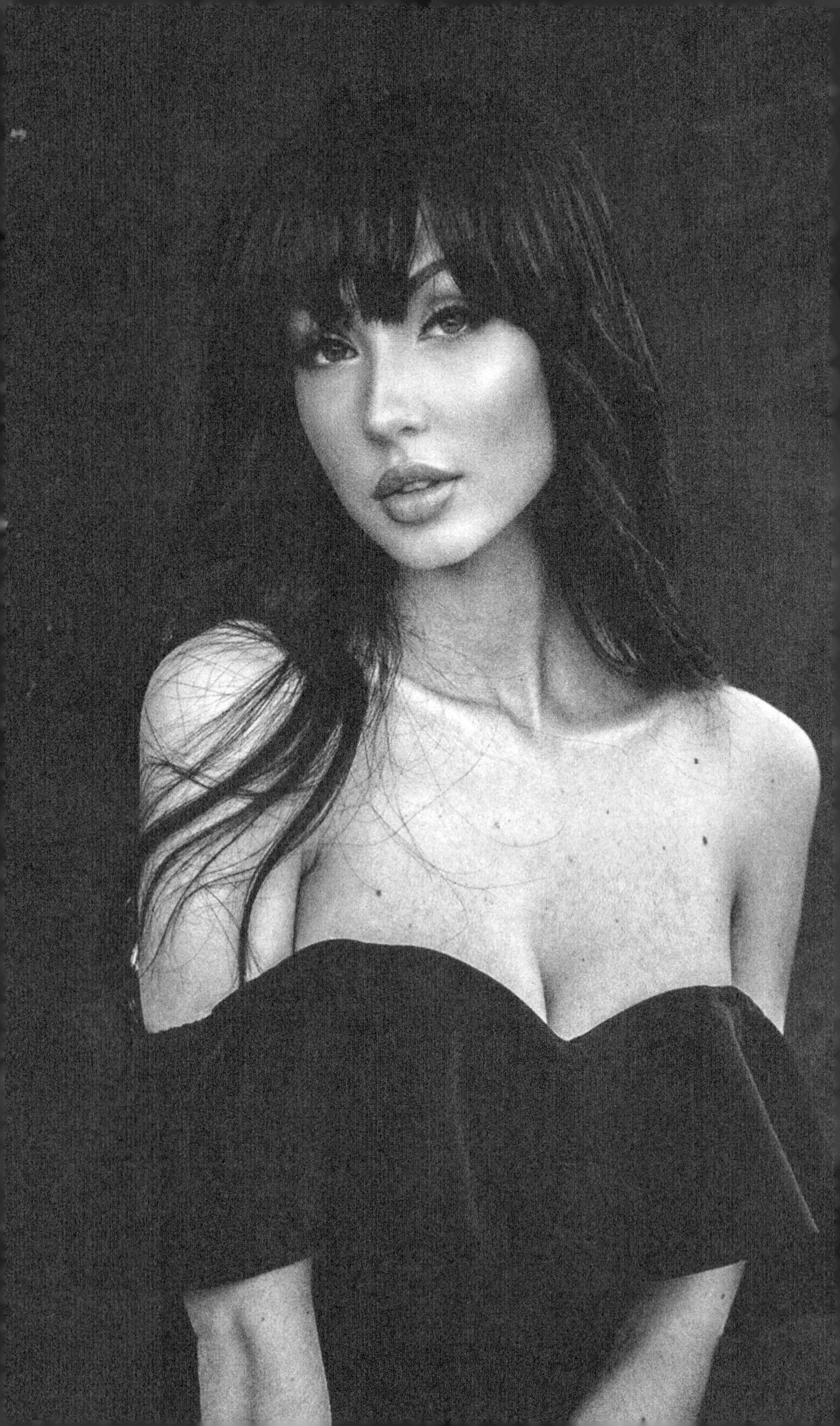

EPILOGUE

3

Lucia

A week later.

As the days pass, I notice a subtle shift in Sy's demeanor. Gone are the restless nights that plagued him before Clarissa's visit. It's as if the weight has been lifted from his shoulders, and he's used all the extra energy to throw himself harder into his training and practice sessions this past week.

It's been one week since his mom left, and it feels like I've hardly seen him since. Of course, that's not true. Two days ago, I traveled to San Fran with the other wives and girlfriends to watch the Sabertooths' last game before the break. The game was legendary, and the night I spent with Sy was even more unforgettable. Seriously, that man is like a fucking machine after a game... literally.

Since I had a date to keep with Gail tonight, I left yesterday. Sadly, Sy couldn't come with me as he and the team had commitments and stayed an extra day—until today. I look down at my phone, noticing that only a few minutes have passed since I last looked.

"I'm going to take that thing away from you if you don't stop looking at it every ten seconds," Gail threatens.

"You wouldn't," I retort, knowing full well that she would in a heartbeat.

"Try me, and see what happens, Luce."

With a dramatic sigh, I put my phone away. I know I'm being a shitty friend, acting like a lovesick teenager that can't stand not to text with her guy every minute of every day. But dammit, we're newlyweds. Aren't we supposed to act this way?

"Fine," I relent. "The phone's gone and I'm all yours. So what do you want to talk about?"

Gail cackles. "Well let's see. So far we've discussed how you just manipulated your husband into making up with his mom—"

"Hey!" I exclaim. "I didn't manipulate anyone."

"Didn't you?" Gail challenges. "You controlled their reunion without being completely honest and upfront about it. Sounds like manipulation to me."

Stunned, I bite on the inside of my cheek. "It wasn't like that," I argue weakly. Despite having plenty more to say, the impact of her words compels me to restrain myself.

She's correct, I completely manipulated the situation. Wait, no. I didn't do it for my gain. I did it to help both of them. Shit, I'm so confused right now I can't decide if what I did was good or bad. A small part of me did it because I know what it's like not to have any family, something I don't wish for my husband.

"Luce!"

Shit, I must have completely zoned out because the way Gail almost shouts my name sounds like it isn't the first time she's calling me.

"What?" I snap, immediately regretting it.

"I was just messing with you," she clarifies. Her brows are pinched together. "You know I don't think of you as a manipulator."

And that's the problem in a nutshell; I'm the one thinking it. "I really was only trying to help," I try to explain. "They both seemed like they needed it."

"I believe you," Gail says, smiling at me. "Look, I'm sorry, okay? I was only joking around."

"Whatever," I say. "Let's get more to drink."

Gail fist bumps the air and immediately offers to go get more shots from the bar. As soon as she has her back turned to me, I fish my phone back out and check if there's an update from Sy. Of course there isn't. I text him again, letting him know I'm still at O'Jackie's with Gail.

"Jesus," I mutter when Gail returns with a tray filled with so many shot glasses I can already feel the hangover I'll suffer through tomorrow.

"Cheers," she whoops once she's seated and is double-fisting shots.

I laugh and take two myself. "Cheers."

More people file in while we sit at the same table we occupied the night I ran into Sy here. It feels like another lifetime, and not at all like it was only about a month and a half ago. I'm enjoying myself much more this time around. Knowing I'm free to live my life as I want has given me a newfound appetite, and I'm hellbent on wanting to live every minute to the fullest.

"Have you figured out what you want to do about a job?" Gail asks.

A smile pulls at my lips. "I think I'm going to create some online courses." This is something I've thought a lot about for the last week. "It'll give me the flexibility to travel with Sy if I want to, and just... do whatever I want."

"What will you tea... teachsss?" Gail slurs.

I burst out laughing at how drunk she is. "You're ssso... sso drunks," I accuse. When my speech isn't much better, we fall into hysterical laughter.

"Do we need more drinks?" Gail asks, making an effort to speak normally.

I point at the tray that still has some untouched shots left on it. "I think we're covered," I observe dryly.

"I want to teach social media. If I do it right, I should be able to make a course that's... umm..." I trail off as my thoughts keep eluding me. I know I was in the middle of explaining my business idea. But fuck, the alcohol is making it harder and harder to think. "Multiple markets," I blurt out as soon as I remember what I was talking about.

Damn, I need to switch to water. I do not want to fall asleep in the car again when Sy picks me up. Telling Gail this, I struggle to get up, and the trip to the bar takes longer than it should with all the zig-zagging I'm doing. But in the end, I manage, and I actually feel steadier as I head back to our table with two bottles of water and some nuts.

Gail eyes the water like it's public enemy number one, but she eagerly throws herself at the nuts. We continue to talk about my business idea, and it surprises me how interested she is. I mean, she's always been interested in my life, so there's that. Maybe I'm reading too much into it.

"Is there a reason you're asking all these questions?" I ask teasingly. But before Gail can answer, my phone rings. I drunkenly fumble to slide the bar to accept the call, but I keep missing. "Damn it," I curse frustrated when I miss Sy's call.

Just as I'm about to call him back, I feel a presence at my back. It's silly considering the amount of people here, but I know without a shadow of a doubt that my husband is here. My body is heating and every hair stands at attention. I turn around, immediately spotting him a few feet away. He's flanked by both Mickey and Soren, all of them looking tired.

"I guess you're leaving now," Gail pouts.

Feeling bad for ditching her, I offer, "We can stay for one more drink if you want."

Her eyes trail over both of Sy's friends. "Nah, go. I'll be fine." She playfully waggles her eyebrows.

It takes me a few attempts to get up, and I don't succeed until Sy's at my side, helping me. "How much have you had to drink, wife?"

"Enough," I giggle. Noticing that Mickey and Soren are both sitting down, I shake my finger at them. "Be nice to Gail." Then I hug her goodbye and let Sy take me home.

This time I'm awake for the ride, and I listen as Sy tells me all about the interviews they had to do. It doesn't sound different from the normal stuff they do, so I mostly let him do the talking while we drive through the quiet streets to our home.

We barely make it in the door before I pull Sy to me and climb him like a tree. "I want you," I purr.

He places his hands on my ass, squeezing the globes tight. "You have me, sweet bunny," he rasps.

"Then take me to bed," I demand, loving how tightly he holds me.

I'm still drunk enough that I can feel each step more than normal, but I'm not slurring my words—at least I don't think I am—and the room isn't spinning, so I'm good to go.

When we reach the bedroom, Sy puts me down on my feet, and I sit down on the bed, not taking my eyes off him as he tugs off his tie, tossing it on the floor. I watch as he starts working on his shirt, undoing the cuffs first before working the buttons down the front. Arousal thrums in my veins; it's hot watching my husband undress.

"Like what you're seeing?" he rasps, and I nod as he peels off his shirt. "Why are you still dressed?"

I can't take my eyes off him, and it isn't until he undoes his belt, sliding it through the loops on his pants and swings it in the air that I realize I still haven't answered him. "Umm..." Having no words, I stand up and kick my ankle boots off. The next thing to go is my black cashmere sweater.

I come to a halt, unable to continue undressing as I notice Sy's pants are now pooling around his feet. As he steps out of them, my eyes are drawn to the huge bulge in his boxer briefs. More specifically, the wet patch where precum has seeped through the fabric.

Licking my lips, I step closer to him, forcing myself to look into his dark eyes. Then I undo the button on my pants, quickly shoving them down my legs so I'm standing in front of him only wearing my black lace lingerie.

"So beautiful," he rasps, cupping my hips and spinning me around so my back is to his front.

Sy quickly unclasps my bra and gets rid of my panties. I lean back against his bare chest, goosebumps spreading across my skin as the cool air in our bedroom hits me.

"I want to spend the rest of my life worshiping you," Sy rasps, making me whimper as he sucks my earlobe into his hot mouth. "I want to fucking drown in you, Lucia. My bunny, my wife. My everything."

As his hands come up to cup my tits, I turn my head, and his lips meet mine in a searing kiss filled with more passion, more need, more love, more everything than I've ever experienced.

He rolls my nipples, and I awkwardly reach back, grabbing his ass to pull him closer to me. His dick is rock hard, nestled into the crevice of my ass cheeks. I grip his long hair with one hand, never wanting him to stop kissing me, I think I even moan that into his mouth. Then I move my other hand from his firm ass to between our bodies so I can grip the outline of his cock.

Sy growls into my mouth, his tongue dominating mine as he continues to palm my tits, gliding his fingers over their peaks. I keep my grip firm on his cock, feeling it grow impossibly harder, and one of Sy's hands slides down my front, grazing a searing trail over my slit before he cups my sex, pulling me further back against him.

Breaking the kiss, Sy uses his foot to nudge mine, telling me he wants me to spread my legs further. I do. Then he spreads his fingers still cupping my weeping cunt. "This right here, that's my heaven," he rasps.

"Sy," I moan, arousal making my tone low and sultry while heat ignites deep in my core. "I want you inside me."

"Not yet. Tonight I want to savor you." He releases my folds and then circles his fingers over my clit. "To devour you." He presses his digits into the heat of my entrance, making me cry out as need slams into me like a freight train going at full speed.

"Fuck, bunny. You're so wet for me." He slides his fingers back out to smear my wetness across my clit before he growls. "Legs wider."

I quickly follow the demand, widening my legs even more, and the second I do, he slides his fingers through my pussy lips before slowly pushing three digits inside me. My legs begin to shake as I push against his hand, working his fingers deeper.

"Sy!" I cry, as he fucks me with his fingers. I'm already close to coming, and I swirl my hips, desperate to fall over the edge.

I palm my tits, pinching my nipples and tip my head back against his shoulder, my eyes falling shut. The way he's working my pussy, his fingers delving deep inside me while the heel of his palm presses against my clit sends me into a frenzy, and I ride his hand until I come hard.

My moans and cries are loud, even to my own ears, and so much fluid rushes out between my legs that it feels like I just peed myself.

"Ohmygoshdeargod... I can't... donotstop," I ramble, so far beyond anything but what my body craves as Sy keeps fingering my pussy. I look down as the waves keep coming, and clear liquid rushes from me.

"Fuck, yes." Sy groans, "Give me more. Give me all of it."

He doesn't let up, and I explode in another orgasm that has me absolutely gushing. As it pours, or sprays, from me, Sy moves to my front. I don't know how he manages to keep his fingers inside me, but I feel them as he curls the digits.

My lips part in an O as he drops to his knees, catching some of my wetness with his mouth. "So fucking delicious," he rasps, scissoring his fingers, which makes even more liquid spray from my pussy.

I'm so spent I can barely stand up. Sy uses one hand to help steady me, and when I'm no longer gushing, he pulls his fingers out of me and places both hands on my hips just before my knees give out. His mouth is still on me, and the pressure from his tongue is almost too much.

"Sy," I moan, unsure if I'm wanting him to stop or to do more.

"I got you," he reassures me, and when I look down to see his heated stare, I don't fight it. How can I when he's looking at me like a man starving? "I'm not done with you yet, bunny. Mhmm, the things I want to do to you. *With you.*"

"Yes," I whisper. Before I can say anything else, Sy gets up and carries me over to the bed, gently sitting me down on the edge. Then I spread my legs so he can stand between them.

He fists his cock with one hand while moving the other one to the back of my neck, squeezing until I look up at him. "You're mine, aren't you?" I don't know what's prompting him to ask, but his tone is serious so I know he's expecting me to answer.

"Now and always," I vow. "I'll always be yours, Sy, and you're mine."

"Yes I fucking am," he growls. "Now and always, bunny."

Looking up at Sy's dark eyes, I lick my lips. Now's the time to tell him. "I'm no longer on the pill," I admit, the uncertainty of his reaction makes my tone low, barely audible. "I haven't been since we went to the Vatican, and—"

Sy silences me by pushing me back and crawling on top of me, slanting his lips to mine in an all-consuming kiss I can feel in every inch of my body. "I know. Well, figured since you didn't have them with you in Rome," he pants. "And it makes me so fucking hard to know my baby could already be in your belly."

I gasp in surprise at his words, but it morphs into a moan as he kisses and licks his way down my body, not stopping until he reaches my belly button. His tongue delves into the orifice, sending electricity through my body.

"You want us to make a kid?" I ask, surprised and yet not.

"A kid? No, wife. I want to make enough we need a fucking minivan when we go anywhere. I want our house to be filled with the family we'd create together."

Tears distort my vision as I hear the longing in his words. The way he describes our future perfectly matches what I want, and I'm suddenly impatient for it to happen. "I want that too," I confirm. Reaching between us, I fist his hard cock. "So get this in my pussy and put a baby in me, Sy."

Grabbing my hips, Sy turns me around so I'm face down on the bed. He kisses a burning trail down my spine, biting into the soft flesh of my ass cheek. "Fuck, wife," he rasps. "Get on all fours. Now."

I quickly push myself up, and as soon as I'm in position, I feel the tip of his hard dick against my entrance. I push back, panting hard as he thrusts all the way to the hilt. Despite all the times I've had his cock in my pussy, I'm still not used to his size, especially at this angle where he's so deep inside me, and it takes a few moments before I'm ready for him to move.

"My beautiful wife," Sy rasps almost reverently. "You're so fucking perfect. Your body, your mind… everything about you. I'm the luckiest man alive." I look at him over my shoulder in time to see him bite his lip for a moment before he starts moving.

The stretch of his cock sends heat rushing over my skin, and a whimper escapes me. "Sy," I plead. "Fuck me. Put your baby in my belly."

"Oh, fuck yeah," he growls. "I'm going to fill you up with my cum."

"Fill me." I breathe, my voice needy and husky.

Sy groans as I tighten my inner muscles around him. "Oh, I will. But first…" Without warning, he flips me to my back so we're looking at each other, and he looms over me like the wicked sex god he is. "I want to see your face when I knock you up."

"Oh, God. Sy... I..." My words turn to nonsensical sounds as he slams into me so hard I slide up the mattress. He follows me, making sure his cock never leaves my warm, wet hole.

"Rub your clit, wife," he commands huskily. "Come all over my cock."

With a whimper, I slide my hand down my front. My eyes stay on his as I rub my sensitive bundle of nerves, and it doesn't take long before my legs shake, everything in me tightening as my pleasure builds.

"Sy!" I cry out his name, squeezing my eyes shut as my back arches off the bed.

My lips part as he fucks me at a brutal pace that has my tits bouncing. It's so perfect I can't do anything but surrender to the wild ride that is being loved by Sy. We move in tandem, both our bodies covered in a light sheen of sweat.

"Fuck. Bunny. I'm going to—" He cuts himself off with a groan, and I moan in response.

"Me too. Just a bit more. Sy, I... I need... I'm... fuck!"

As Sy picks up the pace, he steals my senses with each piston of his hips. I lose the ability to hear, and all I can see is Sy's face, but even that becomes blurry as my vision begins to wane. His dick in my pussy and my fingers on my clit is too much, and my orgasm hits me hard.

"Sy!" I scream.

He's relentless as he thrusts into me with wild abandon, dragging out my orgasm. Or maybe it's another one that hits, I can't tell. I'm boneless, barely able to catch my breath before he slams his lips to mine, immediately sliding his tongue into my mouth.

I feel the moment he finds his own release, shooting his hot cum deep inside me. "Fuck. Lucia. Fuuuuuck."

A satisfied smile spreads across my lips. Sy doesn't use my name often, making it all the more special when he does.

Instead of pulling out, he keeps his dick inside me even after it's grown soft. He's once again looming over me, but this time his attention is solely between my thighs. "What are you doing?" I ask around a yawn, feeling thoroughly spent.

Making sure none of my cum leaks out of your sweet pussy," he rasps like it's the most natural thing in the world. And maybe it is since he's said something similar to me in the past.

I hum, loving how seriously he's taking this. Closing my eyes, I smile as he moves a pillow under my hips, and I imagine feeling one of his swimmers making its way to the right place for us to create life. I don't know if I'm ovulating, or if the contraceptive pills are even out of my system yet. But it's nice to dream about the future; our future.

Printed in Great Britain
by Amazon

COPYRIGHT

The Worst Pucking Deal Copyright © 2024 by B. Lybaek
Cover Designer: Cady @ Cruel Ink Design
Photographer: Emma Jane Photos
Cover model: Jay Lam

No part of this book may be reproduced in any form or by any electronic or mechanical means, including information storage and retrieval systems, without written permission from the author, except for the use of brief quotations in a book review.

Any unauthorized distribution, circulation or use of this text may be a direct infringement of the author's rights, and those responsible may be liable in law accordingly.

All names, characters, events, and places found in this book are either from the author's imagination or used fictitiously. Any similarity to actual events, locations, organizations, or persons, live or dead, is entirely coincidental and not intended by the author.

All rights reserved.